Tuscaloosa Moon

Carolyn Breckinridge

hehehehehehe

Tuscaloosa Moon

A Murder Mystery

Carolyn Breckinridge

authorHOUSE®

AuthorHouse™
1663 Liberty Drive
Bloomington, IN 47403
www.authorhouse.com
Phone: 1-800-839-8640

Cover design by Jim Ezell, 2012

Tuscaloosa Moon is a fictional work. All characters were born in the author's imagination and have lived solely in the minds of author and reader. Perceived similarities, including similarities in name to any person, living or dead, are coincidental and unintended. The lone exception is the inclusion of an eccentric female who raised a pet starling. She has unequivocally and enthusiastically given full permission to be captured in the printed word as found within these pages. All places, behaviors, and incidents are likewise products of the author's imagination or are used fictionally throughout.

Published by AuthorHouse   04/15/2013

ISBN: 978-1-4817-1893-6 (sc)
ISBN: 978-1-4817-1892-9 (e)

Library of Congress Control Number: 2013903181

This book is printed on acid-free paper.

To

Life's unsung heroes,

Sandra,

Jon, Laura

And especially,

Jim

With additional thanks to Dolores for gracious loan of writing implements,

Ruth for her discerning eye,

Jack,

And Carralyn and Claude for opportunities unique

The author also expresses gratitude to The University of Alabama for granting permission to use the text of the football cheer, "Rammer Jammer."

Restless. Antsy. Nerves pinging inside her skin as rapidly, as randomly as the popcorn she microwaved for the boys before bed. She actually halfway burned the kernels, white corn a beigy-brown, some of the kernels black. Joey'd accepted the bag anyway, eaten around the overcooked parts, but Andrew had wailed and bitched and fussed. Apples never fall far from the tree, her grandmother used to say. And Andrew she felt sure, was Red's child. Hot tempered, egocentric, intelligent. Andrew and Red, two peas in a pod. She'd popped another bag to shut him up.

Coral colored fingernails tapped against her textbook. Test on Friday, her mind much too unruly to concentrate. The class wasn't all that tough, elementary school administrative practices. She'd crack the books tomorrow. Have her Ph.D. by December. Land a school principal position by forty-five. She picked up a pen. *Roll Tide Roll* it said on its plastic cartridge in crimson letters. A scrap envelope left from the power bill sat beside the elephant salt shaker. The elephant was crimson and had a white blanket on its back with a red A. A for Alabama. A for football season. A for the Crimson Tide. She pulled the envelope closer with her fingertips. Dr. Priscilla Q. Beaty, she scrawled across the paper. Too school-girlish. She made the D narrower. Dr. Priscilla Q. Beaty. The D needed more flair. Dr. Priscilla Q. Beaty. The loops looked right. The signature looked good. Professional. She crumpled the envelope.

The moon. It lured her outside onto the front porch, past the cedar rocking chair and the rusty chained porch swing. She yawned, sighed, slapped at a mosquito buzzing around her neck. The moon in the night sky was nearly full and it threw soft light onto the front lawn of their rental house with its prolific weeds and patchy grass. But it was not this moon that sucked at her gut, baring a deep black hole in her belly. It was a smiling crescent moon across town with fluorescent yellow tubing and red lips and a winking blue eye. Held in the night sky by a nondescript green sign. Moon Winx Lodge the sign read. Restaurant. Air Conditioned. Telephones.

She pulled her hair into a ponytail with her left hand and held it while her neck sweat evaporated. She tipped her head back and stared at the moon, studied it, tried to see faces in it, but all the while she knew the distraction would never work. There was no way to avoid it. She would wake up the boys, load them into the car, go for a drive.

Her image crossed in front of her as she moved past the living room mirror. Great butt and legs. High cheekbones, strong chin. She sucked in her stomach. Stuck out her boobs, *Crimson Tide Pride* printed across them in white block letters. The University of Alabama tee-shirt flirted with the hem of her white shorts. She looked good. Just in case he was there. Red. Just in case he happened to see her. Her jaw tightened. Her heart quickened. If she saw his car, she knew she'd never stop.

She slipped into the boys' room. Joey was sleeping on his back, Alabama football pj's uncovered. Little brown footballs on the shorts, a crimson A on the shirt. Softness in his face, in his breath.

"Joey, honey," she whispered. His foot moved to the right. Long toes. His feet were dirty on the bottoms. Gray almost. The floors needed cleaning. She'd get to it next weekend. "Joey?"

Movement in the other bed. "Mama?" Andrew said, sitting up. Some box-chinned cartoon superhero stared at her from Andrew's chest. Its eyes and lips hinted a faint glow in the dark. "Mama, not another stupid ride!"

She'd laid out University of Alabama pj's for him to wear. Just like him to ditch them. "It'll be fun," she said, wiggling Joey's foot.

Andrew picked up the pillow, covered his face, flopped back against his mattress.

"Come on, Andrew," she pleaded. "Don't be difficult. Not tonight."

Her hand on Joey's foot stopped moving. He was holding his ankle firm. He was awake.

"Joey," she said. "Get up. Let's go riding."

Joey stretched, sat forward, swung his legs out of bed. He yawned. "Again?" he asked.

Their company reassured her. Helped to fill the night. "It's pretty outside," she said. "We'll have fun."

Joey shook his head. Stood.

"Honey, help get 'Drew up."

Joey leaned toward Andrew's pillow. Tugged it off his face. "Come on, Andy," he said. "Ride time."

Andrew opened one eye and stared at his brother. He shrugged, sighed. Rolled off the mattress onto the floor. Stood and followed Joey who followed their mother out of the bedroom, down the hall and out into the moonlight.

July. Sweaty. She rolled down the windows as they traveled along University Boulevard toward Alberta City. The air movement provided little relief. Past the University's Quadrangle and the obelisk Denny Chimes. Past Druid City Hospital where the boys were born. "Look up at the stars, boys. Such a glorious night! Just listen to those frogs and crickets!" Past the Jaycee Park fairgrounds where amusement rides and 4-H animals appeared each year with cotton candy and corn dogs and goldfish swimming in little bowls of colored water. Joey'd thrown a ping pong ball right into a bowl one year. Won a fish that didn't live until morning. Sometimes she drove on past the motel, making a grand loop along the old, old Birmingham highway onto the old Birmingham highway, gradually meandering back toward home. Sometimes she pulled into the motel parking lot and drove slowly past the cottage units, each with a metal crescent moon on its chimney. She had no idea what she'd do if she ever found his car parked there. Anticipation. Dread. There would be drama.

The Habanera from Carmen played loud in the CD player as they rode. She left it in the player always. She began to sing.

"Stop! Stop singing, Mama! We hate that song! Turn it off or I'll jump!" It was Andrew. She slowed and glanced around. He had his fingers on the door handle.

"Andrew Beaty, get your hand off that door right now!"

"Turn it off."

Joey nudged his bare foot against Andrew's. "Come on, Andy. Don't show out," he said. "Mama, please turn it off. It sounds like sick cats."

Andrew took his hand away from the door. She pushed eject.

They were there. She slowed, pulled into the parking lot. "Look, boys. The moon's winking its eye at you both."

Joey stared at the fluorescent sign. "I don't get why it winks, anyway."

She smiled. "It winks because of secrets it keeps, things it sees, things it knows. Not everybody has such a fine winking sign! We might be the only city in the country with a winking moon sign." She pulled slowly past the office cabin toward the cottages up the hill. Cautiously.

"Why do we always come here?" It was Andrew.

"Just to turn around," she said. "That's all." But she felt sorry. Sorry that his father refused to acknowledge him. Refused to know him. She felt sure Red was his father. There were one or two other possibilities but Red was almost certainly the one. One day she'd explain it all, but right now Andrew was too young. Thank God Joey's father, Thomas, took time with him, included him, treated him like a son.

The dachshund puppy, probably six or seven weeks old, eyes silver discs in the car's headlights, stood alone in the parking lot.

"Look, Mama!" Joey exclaimed. "Stop!"

"Stop!" chimed in Andrew, leaning out the window to get a better look.

The fur on top of the dog's head was slicked down with oil drips or worse. "No. No dog in our house."

"Stop the car! Stop! We can't leave it!" Joey, her quiet child. Her child, unlike Andrew, who never demanded in that tone of voice. She put on the brakes and before she had time to reconsider, Joey's door flung open and garish light filled the inside of the cab. He jumped out, scooped up the dog like he scooped up his basketball, jumped back in. The car door slammed. Darkness returned. She pushed in the CD. The Habanera played.

"We have a dog!" said Andrew.

"No," she said, scanning the cars parked at the front doors of the cottages. Red wasn't there. Relief. Regret. Eerie feelings of something else, too. She didn't know what. "No, the dog will find a new home tomorrow. Ask around your friends."

"Winx," Joey said decisively. "His name is Winx. Just like the sign. W-I-N-X."

"Don't name him," she said. "You can't keep him." The dog smelled. "Don't let him pee."

"He's in my lap, Mama," said Joey.

Andrew laughed. "Winx," he said. "That's crazy, Joe."

Joey held the puppy up in the air as they passed the winking moon. The yellow fluorescent light made the puppy look sort of greeny-gray. Four short legs wriggled. The blue eye blinked off and on. The red lips smiled. The puppy's tongue stretched out to lick.

She pulled out onto University Boulevard. "Joseph Chalot, don't you dare let that nasty animal lick you!"

Joey laughed. He rubbed his cheek with the back of his hand where the dog's tongue had gotten him. "You're my puppy now," he said, "cute little Winx Beaty Chalot."

1

"Rammer Jammer Yellow Hammer! Give 'em HELL, Alabama!" the alarm blared in a tinny voice. Dr. Priscilla Q. Beaty, fifty-three, principal of Tuskaloosa Gardens Elementary School, placed her hands under her hips and raised her legs upward. Her mattress was hard and it gave only slightly as she bicycled. *"Rammer Jammer Yellow Hammer!"* she cheered. *"Give 'em HELL, Alabama!"* Even before she opened her eyes, through the tender skin of her eyelids, she could see shadows of pulsating crimson light emanating from the clock's plastic football. And she knew a plastic University of Alabama football player was cradling the blinking ball, his legs running in cadence with the cheer. She pedaled faster to match the figure's movements. "Rolllllllllll Tide! Roll!" A little click and the lights stopped blinking. The cheer stopped cheering. She turned her head sideways, her legs still cutting circles through the air.

The clock was a gift from Bob the Tree Surgeon. One thing about Bob, she thought as she kicked, he sure as hell knew how to have a good time. He'd given over a thousand a piece that weekend to a sidewalk ticket scalper to get them into the game, and he'd shelled out more than two hundred bucks to claim his little piece of motor home heaven. Then there was the clock. It was identical to one Andrew'd smashed during a particularly lengthy tantrum. She'd told Bob about the tantrum and how the football player's arm broke off with the football attached to it and about how it didn't cheer the Rammer Jammer cheer anymore, and Bob listened thoughtfully and found one somewhere to replace it. It was remarkable, she thought, that he'd found a duplicate. And so she'd playfully performed a strip act for him in the Winnebago, tossing her thong onto his head where it landed like a gift-wrap bow above a face chameleoned as crimson as the underwear itself.

She'd first found Bob's name in the Yellow Pages under tree care and removal. The trunk of one of her backyard pines had a hollow in it oozing honey colored sap. The sap crystallized on the bark in golden droplets, but there was gooier sap, too, that caught bugs like quicksand and glued them to the tree. Within minutes they were talking Alabama football and he told her about his den decorated in Alabama memorabilia and about how he never missed a game. He wasn't the most handsome man she'd ever met but she liked that he never missed a game, and she admired the way his hands moved up and down the pine's trunk, exploring, caressing, experienced, and she told him she oozed honey, too, if his hands wanted to explore her hollows. He looked at her sort of dazed at first but then he smiled a cockeyed kind of smile and let out a strange whooping noise like he'd hit jackpot on the slot machines over at the Native American casinos in Philadelphia, Mississippi.

Bob owned a wood frame home in Coker, a quiet town about twenty minutes from the city. But even when they were seeing each other hot and heavy, he rarely invited her there. Everybody'd get in their business, he told her. Old Mrs. Blakney across the road watched through her living room window, hiding behind her curtains. And she didn't miss a thing. She didn't have much else to do since her husband died after his tractor rolled on him last November. So no way could he sneak her out of the house in the morning unseen. No way. She definitely didn't want scandal she'd answered. She couldn't afford it as a principal. It's like Mayberry, he said. A town nice to come home to every night. Frogs. Stars. Sweet potato pies.

The weekend Bob gave her the clock he'd sandwiched his Winnebago as close as possible to the Black Warrior River in one of myriad makeshift villages that sprang up in Tuscaloosa before all home games. Motor homes with Crimson Tide flags and canvas awnings, Crimson Tide paint jobs, barbeque grills and TV satellite dishes, lined up side by side. They wandered among them, the smell of barbeque intoxicating at first and nauseating as the night wore on. Tailgaters welcomed them as they passed, inviting them to eat or just sit and talk a spell, but they said no thanks and Roll Tide, and strolled on hand in hand counting the different state license plates. In the end they counted forty-one and a plate from Nova Scotia. She found the Canadian plate and said it trumped his Alaska. Nova Scotia, he argued, wasn't a state at all.

They wandered off the lot then and onto the asphalt path of Riverwalk, stopping when they reached the white wooden paddlewheel boat offering short excursions up and down the Black Warrior. Jazz and laughter and the sloshing of water bumping against the sides of the Bama Belle. He said he wanted to take the dinner cruise with her, maybe even before the next home game, and he put his arm around her and told her how much he loved her, how glad he was she'd come into his life.

She didn't reciprocate, the word *love* hanging rigid and obtrusive like a billboard in the humid air, and they stood in silence watching the river flow and the bats dart low zigzags over the darkening water. There was eagerness to please in the way he handed her the shoe box sized package wrapped in white paper with a crimson bow that had a pipe cleaner white 'A' tacked to its center. And she was truly pleased with his gift even though she knew their relationship, like football season, was coming to an end. And so she graciously accepted the clock. She could never turn down anything crimson and white. That was her primary self-descriptor when she searched for relationships on the Internet.

Her legs were tiring. So were her fingers holding up her hips. She glanced at the clock. Three minutes to go. She kept cycling.

It's been a grand season, Bob, she eventually told him. But how could it not be? Alabama football was an Experience, a Happening, a subculture all of its own. Tide fans dressed in crimson and white slacks and dresses, shorts and jackets, socks and shoes, tee-shirts and hats. And money changing hands faster than at a high stakes table in Vegas. Plenty of it. Sixteen million plus pouring into the metro area for each home game. Season stadium boxes going for half a million give or take, game weekend condos purchased for about the same, while the sleepy Tuscaloosa municipal airport swarmed like a disturbed fire ant bed with corporate jets. The atmosphere was positively electric. Other people could have their conquests of Everest, their African safaris, their vacations to the Taj. There was nothing anywhere in the world as thrilling, as intoxicating, at times as heartbreaking, as Crimson Tide football was to Dr. Priscilla Q. Beaty. Any avid fan of Alabama football understood. Joey and Andrew, on the other hand, didn't even try to stifle their yawns.

*   *   *

Her left baby toenail's pink polish was chipping off, as was the polish on her right big toe, and she made a mental note of it. She'd phone Leah from Heavenly Feet to schedule a pedicure between school meetings. Leah made house and office calls. She wished she could schedule the appointment before her lunch date with Harry but her morning was already full. Harry had a thing about sucking her toes. She was sort of adjusting to this aspect of his foreplay. At least she hadn't reflexively kicked him in the nose this past month. He'd been a pretty good sport about all the nosebleeds, and once, the cut lip, even though blood got all over his sheets. He always said not to worry, he'd tell his office staff he'd had a run-in with a horse or a cow or one of Benny Stuart's emus on his way back to the office.

She glanced toward the clock. Six forty-seven. She stopped cycling, lowered her legs, sat up. "Lord help me make it through this day," she said out loud to the plastic football player. The football player's lips, red and straight and thin like thread, didn't seem sympathetic. It was a strange group of feelings she had. The same sorts of feelings that came every year when she took down Christmas. An emptiness, maybe even regret, dread of the job itself, yet, immense relief it was all over. Life would be simpler without Andrew in the house, she was sure of that. After work she was taking him to a preplacement interview at Metamorphosis, a local residential treatment center for adolescents. Well, she wasn't really taking him at all. She was meeting him there. She'd played the trump card this time, circumventing all the drama by asking Joey to drive home from Auburn University to help. Andrew behaved for him. It wasn't that long a drive for Joey, only about three hours. As long as he could get back in time to make the study group for his microbiology class at eight, he'd said. It was, Joey reminded her even though she didn't need reminding, April, and it wasn't long until finals.

Maybe Joey'd make it back in time for his study group, maybe he wouldn't, she thought as she pinched the sides of the black plastic cap of her mouthwash bottle and twisted. "It'll serve him right if he has to study alone," she said to her reflection. Her reflection nodded curtly. If he were enrolled at the University of Alabama there'd be no sweat getting back in time. But, Auburn University! The Auburn Tigers! Orange and blue were such hideous colors together. When she'd argued this point, a maddening smile flashed across his face and he quietly answered that he was going to college to become a veterinarian, not a football player, and Auburn University was the State's home for veterinary medicine.

*   *   *

Her phone vibrated, its face glowing soft yellow light. She stared as it vibrated off the bedside table and hit the rug. She knew it was Harry. She told him repeatedly he called too much. That he was ridiculously insecure. She knew that by not answering, he'd call again and again and again, filling up cyberspace with increasingly agitated messages. They'd had the same conversation at least three hundred times. Him yelling at her for not answering. Her refusing to pander to his insecurities. Muffled vibrations came from the rug beside her bed. It was a rug she'd found at an estate sale years ago when Joey and Andrew still liked to run errands with her on Saturday mornings. Hand woven in Pakistan with lots of dark reds and yellows in it. There was a pronounced stain in the right hand corner, she guessed from ink or black fingernail polish. She'd placed an overstuffed chair on top of the stain. Back then, the boys chose to go with her. She missed those times. The vibrations stopped.

She walked toward her closet, lifting her legs high marching style to help maintain toning. Ever since she was a majorette at old Tuscaloosa High she'd made it a point to keep her muscles toned. And to this day every man she dated commented on her great legs and tight abs. It upset her a little bit that most of them had never heard of Tuscaloosa High. Her alma mater was replaced by Old Central High in the late 70's, which was replaced by the modern Central High standing on 15th Street now. Without exception, though, they became aroused, clearly very aroused, during the marching and strutting routines she performed for them. Routines drilled to perfection, although back in high school she didn't perform them wearing Victoria Secret underwear with ballpoint pens clutched horizontally in the muscles between her gluts and hamstrings. Their pens, plucked from their pockets as she marched past. There wasn't a man alive who wasn't impressed that she could keep their pens in place. They always stuck them back into their shirt pockets with attitudes of reverence.

A muffled thud. Her bent knee straightened sharply and she cocked her ear toward the second floor of her house. "Not Andrew," she pleaded. He'd gotten himself kicked out of school for the day, and she wanted him to sleep through the morning. She definitely didn't want a scene before breakfast, before work. She held her breath, chest puffed out with household air, listened. Somewhere nearby she heard Winx's red heart-shaped rabies tag jingling against his blue bone-shaped ID tag, and she guessed he was scratching. Next year Joey planned to get an apartment and take the dog with him to Auburn. She argued Winx would look ugly in an Auburn doggie sweater and he looked so cute in his white one with the crimson A in the middle of his back, just down from where the leash hole was. As much as she hated to admit it, the dog was good company on lonely nights when she was between relationships. Better company than Andrew, who stayed gone from the house or holed up in his room. She rolled her neck around in a circle, her head going from front, to right, backwards, to left, around and around, releasing tension that sneaked into her body unaware. Having Andrew away from home at Metamorphosis would be like a long, relaxing trip to the spa.

"What to wear?" she said out loud. She opened her closet. It was already hot. Tuscaloosa had somehow skipped Spring. One day it was forty six degrees and the next it was near ninety. Spring in Alabama was predictably unpredictable. One year it even snowed in May. She shifted her attention between two lightweight suits, one pale green, the other sky blue. Suits gave the message she was in control, efficient, confident, successful. She looked down toward the shoes. She had new shoes to wear with her green one. The green one, then. She pulled it out and hung it near the shower. She reconsidered wearing a suit at all. Harry liked slinky, silky, sexy clothes. She liked slinky, silky, sexy clothes. Maybe she could put her red dress in the car. Change before lunch. That dress was slinky, silky and she knew it was sexy. No. She wouldn't have clothes on at Harry's, anyway. Except for the surprise she'd made for his eyes only. She chuckled softly. Like most murder victims, had Dr. Priscilla Beaty known it was her last day on Earth, she might have re-evaluated her day's priorities. She almost certainly would have worn a less provocative bra.

2

Her breast fit snugly into his cupped hand. He massaged its smooth skin and ran his thumb and index finger around her hardened nipple. Although he wanted so badly to appear sophisticated in her presence, air caught in his throat and he gasped, nearly choked. He kissed her eyelids and the bridge of her nose, anticipated running his tongue around her breast, kissing her nipple. With his kisses, she moved her body even tighter against his. She was naked and smelled clean and like lemon. Lemon was her favorite body wash and shampoo, and whenever he smelled lemons anywhere now, her presence lingered beside him. He crumpled some of her long brown hair in his hands and breathed deeply. "I love you, Bethy," he murmured. "I swear to God, you are so beautiful."

"*Rammer Jammer Yellow Hammer . . .*" He awakened with a hard-on. He opened his eyes and stared at the poster taped to his bedroom wall. It was a poster from last year's Earthfest celebration held at the University. A blue and green world with animals in various stages of running, eating, and raising babies printed across its surface. It was an all day event crammed full of local bands, independently produced CD's and silk screened tee-shirts. He'd had a good time. Three girls who all giggled a lot and who wore tight shorts and tank tops zeroed in on him and he spent the day hanging out with them. They said they went to school at Holt and all three were a year younger than he. One of them had a dragonfly tattoo in the middle of her back at waist level and when she bent forward, he could see it in entirety. He told her he thought it was hot. At the end of the day they'd exchanged e-mails and phone numbers, but except for a couple of texts he'd never heard from any of them again. All that was pre-Bethy.

"*Give 'em HELL Alabama!*"

"Shut up!" He heaved a pillow against the wall and put another over his head. He'd smashed her first clock, little plastic football player decapitated, arm and the football amputated, but some dumb ass bought her a new one. "I'll smash it, too," he said, lips moving slowly, sticking to the pillow case.

He moved his long arm toward the bedside table and picked up his phone. The pillow slid off his face. Two messages. He opened the first. *Andrew, let's have lunch and hang out before the meeting. We'll make it through this, bro'. Please don't try anything funny.* It was from Joey. He hit Reply. *Other plans 4 lunch. Meet you @ 2 here?* He pressed Send. He smiled and rolled onto his back as he read the second text. *Good morning! I luv u! Drop by school at break. Look 4 u at 10:30. Same place.* He paused before he answered, wondering if he could get everything done by then. *B there,* he answered. Somehow he'd make it work. Tuscaloosa Magnet School was a long way to go for the ten minutes they'd have together. Not really even ten minutes. She'd have to get to class before the bell. Mr. Victor Abernathy made that clear every semester the first day of math class. No tardiness, no phones, no gum, no food, no drinks, no talking, no passing notes, no cutting, and of course, no cheating. Such behaviors would not be tolerated.

Mr. Abernathy was old. He wore silver colored wire rim glasses over reptilian eyes, and his skin was wrinkled and hung from his neck, a lot like the iguana, D-Tail. Andrew bought D-Tail with his first paycheck from Spotless Shine Carwash where he worked last summer earning cash under the table detailing cars and trucks. It was a good job but the business closed in October for selling drugs out the back door. Andrew kept D-Tail in an aquarium in his room until his mother commandeered his pet for her elementary school at the beginning of this school year. He always worried about Iguana Man catching Bethy with her phone even though she assured him it was hidden in her bra. The old man'd throw it in the trash for sure if he knew they were texting. Into the trash, covered with wads of gum, food wrappers, dirty tissues, and crumpled papers, love and sex notes passed back and forth whenever Mr. Abernathy was suitably distracted. A year ago when Mr. Abernathy was his teacher, Andrew spent half his class time in the hall or in the office. The worst time was when he sketched Mr. Abernathy's iguana face and bald head, improved by reptilian ridges, and the man intercepted the drawing. "Next year," Andrew thought, "she'll be at Northridge with me. Unless, I never go back." There was a lot to talk about when he saw her this morning.

3

1. **Feed Winx and let him out to pee.**
2. **Take out the trash.**
3. **Put your dirty clothes in the laundry and fold the towels.**
4. **Bag up the recycling.**
5. **Don't make a scene this afternoon at your meeting.**

Her hand paused with the pen poised above this last sentence. Red ink. She couldn't scratch it out. She crumpled the paper and began again, uncomfortable with the control and power she was handing to him by her phrasing. **Don't make today harder for any of us, especially for you or Joey.** Joey. It was always helpful with Andrew to include Joey.

She picked up her purse, threw the crumpled paper in the trash and headed toward the door, but as she wrapped her fingers around the knob uncertainty flooded her. Maybe he'd already run away, sneaking out while she slept. It was so quiet upstairs. He might be in Birmingham already if he'd hitched a ride or called a friend, or maybe even out of Alabama if he left early morning. She held her breath and listened intently. Nothing. Despite the carpet and her intentionally quiet steps, the wood of the stairs creaked ever so slightly as she climbed. Her phone vibrated, this time muffled by the leather of her purse. Harry, she was sure of it. She walked down the hall and gently tried the door to his room. She anticipated it would be locked, and her eyes widened in surprise when the door cracked open with the knob's turning. She saw one foot sticking out from under the covers and felt a wave of relief. He hadn't run, at least not yet.

Despite her better judgment she opened the door wider and stepped in. His room smelled like dirty shirts and stale cigarette smoke. There was a half drunk cola in a paper cup on his dresser and two crumpled potato chip bags, jalapeno flavor, beside it. Her eyes scanned the room. The cigarette pack was hidden somewhere. No ashes. No butts. Even though she'd searched his room frequently during confrontations, she'd never been successful discovering his hiding places.

His toe wiggled a little, apparently part of a dream, but instead of backing out of the room she found herself staring at the huge foot with body hair growing out of the top near his ankle. What size shoe did he wear now? Twelve? He was already tall, one of the tallest barely-sixteen year olds in his class, and she guessed he might eventually outgrow his father who was six feet, two. Six two but less than a foot tall in character.

Who is he, Mom? Who is he? Why the hell won't you tell me?

So help me God, Priscilla, if you tell him I'll look him square in the eye and tell him he's a mistake. And the support will stop. See what you get if you try taking me to court. You think he'll be able to afford those class trips to DC and New York? Think about it before you do something stupid and screw up his life.

So, it had come to today. Placement out of their home. Andrew's breathing was deep and steady. His eyelids fluttered. Pursing her lips, hardly breathing herself, she reached out slowly and let her fingers skim his cheek. "I love you. I'm so sorry, baby." The words flowed easily through her mind, evaporated before reaching her lips. His pale cheeks, the way his lips slipped downward along the edges, deep sadness unmasked. For the first time in her angry son's life it dawned on her. Being bullied into silence about Red's paternity was a monumental miscalculation on her part. It was time for Andrew to learn the truth. Turning abruptly she hurried from his room. There was really nothing more to lose. She'd call Red this morning.

4

He heard her climbing the stairs, soft footsteps and little creaks in the wood. Damn, he'd forgotten to lock his door. He threw his phone under the covers and rolled onto his side to hide his woody. He closed his eyes and slowed his breathing to a peaceful rhythm. The door opened. The smell of astringent roses. Never a subtle garden scent, but roses mixed with some kind of alcohol or paint thinner and concentrated until the smell was enough to gag him. Her trademark, perfume splashed on the nape of her neck and the inside of her right elbow. It repulsed him, and especially when blended with the smell of beer on her breath and sounds of flirty giggling. Usually he held his breath as long as he could when she was so close. This morning, though, he allowed the scent to waft up his nostrils, concentrating on maintaining a slow, even breathing pace and rolling his eyes beneath his eyelids to simulate sleep. "Get out of my room," he thought fiercely. "Get the hell out of my room." Deep breaths, slow breaths. He twitched his big toe slightly. People twitched in their sleep.

Suddenly, inexplicably, soft fingertips, long fingernails brushed across his cheek. They fluttered against his skin like a mosquito or a moth. An odd, unwelcome feeling rose inside him, twisting through his body like a python, wrenching and strangling his gut before writhing out toward her. It was a hated feeling all through childhood. To grab her hand and press it hard against his face, to sit up in bed, bury his head in her stomach and cry. Like a baby. Deep breaths. Slow breaths. Closed flickering eyes.

Her hand jerked away as though her fingers had been bitten. He didn't move until he heard the front door close and the Lexus' motor turn over. "Bitch!" he yelled, slamming his knuckles into the dark blue wall, punching again at the resultant sheetrock crater. His knuckles burned and he sucked on them. His other palm searched his cheek for the trail of her fingers and he pressed hard. The blue wall was crumpled gray and white where he'd punched the hole. He pulled his Earthfest poster down. A thumb tack fell on his forehead, another got lost in his sheets. He ran his hand across his pillow and down across his bed. He found one of tacks and used it to stick the poster back on the wall to

11

cover the damage. If she saw the hole before he ran away all hell would break loose. He made a mental note to be careful. There was still a thumb tack hiding somewhere in his bed.

He fished for his phone. It was wedged in a little sheet crevice near his knee. No messages. He hit Create Message. *Will have shit to sell 2day. Meet at 1? Park behind house?* He searched his addresses until he found the name, Tony, and pressed Send. He and Tony had done business before. Tony was a gangbanger and fenced almost anything. Cash upfront. No questions asked.

He got out of bed and pulled on jeans lying crumpled on his rug. He was hungry. A list of chores, in neatly measured printing and red ink, greeted him from the kitchen counter as he made his way to the refrigerator.

1. **Feed Winx and let him out to pee.**
2. **Take out the trash.**
3. **Put your dirty clothes in the laundry and fold the towels.**
4. **Bag up the recycling.**
5. **Don't make today harder for any of us, especially for you or Joey.**

"Six," he thought, picking up the list, ripping it into confetti. "Screw you." He threw the paper into the air, and opened the refrigerator as bits fell onto his arm, onto the floor, into Winx's purple water bowl. He had a long list of his own that would take all of his day to accomplish. He pulled milk and cheese from the refrigerator, grabbed the bread, and sat down at the table. Wheat bread with seeds on top. Skim milk. His phone vibrated. It was Tony. *Hope the shit's good.*

5

Detective Adelaide Bramson, Addie to family, co-workers and friends, lifted the lid off the Volkswagen cookie jar and reached in. The VW was blue, the same general color as her automobile, except the jar was darker, closer to navy. With the lid off, the jar was a convertible like the car she'd wanted. There was a cute lime green one with a white canvas top on the lot back then, but Luke, her husband, suggested a convertible didn't offer the level of security required. Not for her job. She reluctantly agreed.

She wrapped her fingers around a lump of cookies, pulled them out, spread them on the counter. A lion. A monkey. A horse. A camel. She culled the four from the group and popped them into her mouth. They were crunchy and tasted remotely like shortbread. A lion for courage. A monkey for agility. A horse for speed, and a camel for endurance and plain orneriness. Four animals every morning. It was a big part of her pre-work ritual. She'd add other animals throughout the day. She reached into the cabinet above her head, pulled out a zipping sandwich bag and scooped the remaining cookies in. Thus corralled, she dropped them into her purse before hanging it back on the kitchen doorknob.

She got a bowl from the cabinet and dumped a brown envelope's premeasured oatmeal, cinnamon raisin, and a cup of water into it. She set the microwave for three minutes. Luke was already gone. An early morning he'd told her. He was trying to figure out where one of the boys was going in the afternoons when he ran off. He was taking other kids with him, like an expedition leader. Never stayed away long. And obviously stayed on campus. But wherever the boy was going, he ran off a lot. The other kids wouldn't talk, looked at each other shiftily and giggled and snickered when they were asked. Not even the reliable tattlers were talking. They weren't called tattlers anymore, anyway, he'd corrected himself. They were snitches.

She considered the term snitches as she ate her oatmeal. In her office they were called informants. She was looking for a good informant.

Someone who could finger the person calling in bomb threats with some regularity to the Department of Human Resources.

Music was already playing in the den. Luke had left it on for her. Happy plucky harp notes arranged in Oriental melody. She was still barefoot and in her pajamas. Soft red velour pants and a top she liked to slip on after her shower. The den carpet rose up between her toes and she wiggled them as she raised her hands over her head and inhaled deeply. There was a circular furry lump juxtaposed on the corduroy couch cushions.

"Good morning, Miss Agatha Kitty," Addie said.

Miss Agatha opened one eye halfway. The tip of her tail flicked like an independent entity. It was in Miss Agatha's contract. No socializing, absolutely no expectations of her, until at least ten. Some mornings, eleven. Her eye closed.

Addie closed her own eyes and let her mind dance through space and time with the perky, staccato music, inhaling and exhaling, rolling her shoulders back and down, lowering her arms until they met in a half circle, palms facing her body, pulling positive energy back toward herself. Collecting the Chi, her instructor called it. This morning she mixed T'ai Chi with yoga, moving her body into Warrior One, Warrior Two and Reverse Warrior positions, feeling the stretch of the muscles in her thighs, back and hips. She liked to start with the warrior positions, even on days when she didn't have tough crimes on her caseload. Today was starting light. There were the bomb threats at DHR and she and her colleague, R.J., were still trying to figure out what the gangster, Tony, was doing these days. Illegal stuff, that much they knew, he was dangerous and slick. He was the kind of kid her husband Luke could have probably helped if he'd gotten a hold of him at age five or six. She liked to think there was still hope for Tony even though statistics weren't in his favor. Addie felt sorry for his grandmother. The woman certainly appeared to be doing her best.

The music smoothed, notes running slower, more peacefully. There was time for the short form of T'ai Chi before getting dressed and heading to the station. "Wu Chi," she said softly, standing at relaxed attention. "T'ai Chi," as she moved her left foot sideways and raised her arms to waist level. She moved her left foot against her right heel, toe on the floor, knee bent, T-stance, and her left hand to her waist, palm up. Her right hand came to heart level, palm down. As if she were holding the moon. Glowing imaginary light balanced like a lantern at her belly. *Part the Wild Horse Mane.* She let the moon slip from her hands, brushing her fingertips close to one another like slow motion ballet. Luke called it turtle aerobics. Done correctly he wasn't far from the truth.

6

Shelby McDonald put down the stack of papers and opened the refrigerator. "Ohhhh!" she exclaimed. "What a cute cake!" A chocolate dog stared out at her, complete with a yellow icing collar decorated with M&M's, a long, red icing tongue, a jelly bean nose and two large blue icing eyes. "Who's it for?"

"It's Benjamin's birthday," said Luke. "He claims he's never had a birthday party, a cake, or a dog. So," he laughed, "apparently today's his lucky day."

She laughed too. "Apparently so," she said. His eyes were sky blue, startlingly so, and friendly-warm, and when his gaze locked with hers she always felt no words were necessary. When she was a sophomore in college, before she moved out into an apartment of her own, she was assigned a roommate, a neo-hippie. Levonna was her name and she wore long cotton skirts that flowed behind her when she walked and she had a butterfly navel ring. Levonna's world was divided into old souls and new souls. Old souls, she explained to Shelby, had wisdom in their eyes gleaned from past lives' lessons. New souls basically demonstrated little insight into the life process at all. In Levonna's world, Luke was an old soul. He had a short brownish beard, darker brown hair pulled back and gathered neatly on his neck, and freckles. He wore sort of punk style black framed glasses. When Shelby talked to her friends outside of work she always described Luke as her best work friend.

"When's the party?" she asked, wedging her own yogurt and small container of low sodium tomato juice in between a left-over Chinese food container and a paper lunch bag. The dog took up most of the middle shelf.

"How about right after school?"

Shelby's forehead wrinkled. "Don't we still have pre-placement for the Beaty case?" she asked.

"Oops, yep we do. I guess the party's right after dinner then."

Shelby didn't like it. It was the way it was but she still didn't like it. She made a mental note to phone the babysitter to say she'd be late again. "Seems like these days, Molly eats with the babysitter more than with me," she said, imagining her three-year-old daughter, strawberry blond hair tied in pigtails, sitting in her high chair with food all over her mouth and clothes. She missed Molly. She wanted to eat dinner with her.

"Know what you mean," Luke said. "Addie says she saw more of me before we got married, when she was still living in New York."

"Maybe I'll slip home at lunch after our Records meeting and spend some QT with her," Shelby said. QT was a Metamorphosis' abbreviation used in intra-agency notes. QT. Quality Time. "Would that work with your schedule?"

"Sure, Addie's picking up lunch from one of the Mexican places and we're picnicking on the grounds. I'll be around." He covered a yawn with his hand. Large fingers with a gold wedding band on his left hand and a dragon ring of some sort on his right. "Been here a while already this morning," he said. "Came in early to try to figure out where Benjamin and the others are running off to all the time. No luck though."

Shelby picked up her stack of papers and shuffled through them, skimming the secretaries' notes. Phone calls to return. Other calls with messages. A memo about upcoming changes in the cottages' dinner schedules. A subpoena to court. Three envelopes from other agencies. She sat down in one of the chairs across from him.

He immediately identified that her stay was temporary, the way she was perched on the seat's edge. Perched and looking so damned cute. He leaned forward anticipating her question. Right before she asked questions, her head tilted very slightly to the right and her eyebrows lowered almost imperceptibly. So imperceptibly he doubted anyone else ever noticed, and he felt certain she was also unaware. Although he'd gone to graduate school at Cornell, he'd seen lots of photos of her as a University of Alabama gymnast. Her team went to the national championships all four years she was an undergrad, placed in the Super Six three of those, and came home with the championship the other. Blonde hair pulled back tight into a pony tail, a pixie nose, feet long and narrow for her size, wearing a spangled crimson and white leotard. High cut on her thighs. On the balance beam with her arms poised high in the air, her muscled left leg held out at a ninety degree angle, bare toes pointed. She was still petite and full of spunk and had proven herself skilled at keeping her balance in clinical social work, weaving in and out of their teenagers' behaviors and feelings, a feat he felt sure was tougher than performing at any gymnastics meet. He admired her willingness to take huge leaps of faith with the kids, free falling into their worlds, landing squarely, frequently leading them toward firmer emotional ground.

"So, Benjamin turns fifteen today?" Shelby asked. "What did we get him in way of presents?"

"Three video games, one of them's an NFL game, and I think there's a wrestling game and a NASCAR one. That's apparently what he's wanting the most."

"And a doggie cake any self-respecting three-year-old like Molly would love," Shelby laughed. It was just the way it was, one of the most endearing, frustrating and confusing aspects of working with emotionally disturbed youth. Large pockets of personal development arrested at the ages when traumas occurred. Adolescent behaviors and interests, toddler behaviors and interests, and at times, wisdom, compassion, and knowledge light years beyond their ages. "Well," she said, "I'm off to return phone calls." She stooped to touch the ground, threw her head back comically, then jogged dramatically from the room.

Luke chuckled. It was a joke between them. Hit the ground running. A reality at Metamorphosis, Inc. There was never enough time, no matter how much time there was. His phone vibrated as he stood. He pulled it off his belt. It was a text from Dr. Lydia P. Hutchinson. *Luke, please meet me in the Blue Room as soon as possible.* Pivoting on the heels of his faux alligator skin boots, he headed down the hall.

7

Metamorphosis, Inc. was a one hundred and sixty bed residential treatment facility located on two hundred and twenty acres outside the Tuscaloosa city limits but still in Tuscaloosa County. It was comprised of sixteen cottages, each with ten bedrooms, a common room, a dining room, ten small bathrooms, a laundry room, a kitchen, four 'cool down rooms,' and a small staff office. Ten resident bathrooms per building set Metamorphosis apart from probably every other treatment center in the state, but the founder and owner of the agency insisted that every person in the world had the right to one little corner of personal privacy and that by demonstrating such respect, the children would feel safer and more inclined to accept treatment. The cottages were nestled among pines, mimosas, redbuds, dogwoods, and oaks and all of them were within hiking distance of Lake Tuscaloosa, as the property included a large peninsula that jutted out into the water.

It was known as the Cadillac of treatment centers. It boasted of a therapy pet house with dogs, cats, rabbits, guinea pigs, snakes, lizards, mice, hamsters and an ornery green parrot named Shishka Bob, horse and llama stables, a climbing tower, canoes and kayaks, a religious center, as well as a technical skills building where residents learned basic car repair, carpentry, cosmetology, financial management, first aid, and other valuable life skills. The Center treated both females and males which created daily challenges for staff, even the most experienced, energetic, and adolescent-savvy among them. Although it was known as an adolescent treatment facility, preteens as young as nine had been accepted, as had youth aged twenty, and even once, twenty-one, all based on the needs of those requiring treatment.

In the middle of the campus was the Rec building filled with pool tables, a ping pong table, a large screen television with multiple smaller screens set up for video games, a piano, a large room used for dances and other such activities, two conference rooms, a library, a kitchenette, and two group rooms. There were four 'cool down' rooms in the corners of the building. The school building and the dining hall were attached to the Rec building in different directions, with professional offices scattered throughout in an effort to help insure quality care. The entire complex was known formally as Hutchinson Square, named after Dr. Lydia P. Hutchinson, founder of Metamorphosis, Inc. No one at the Center really knew how to pronounce or spell her middle name, it was a long, foreign one, spelled wrong so often that most thought it was spelled wrong when it was spelled right. But that was of little consequence. Almost everyone, staff and kids alike, referred to her simply as Dr. Lydia.

Dr. Lydia was in her eighties. It wasn't uncommon to find her all hours of the day and night, on weekends and even at two in the morning, checking on the general running of her sole birth child. She'd never married. She'd graduated in psychiatry before women were generally accepted into medical school. She was a pioneer. A character.

She sat in one of the twelve navy blue swivel chairs in the Blue Room and watched Dr. Luke Bramson with crow-like eyes as he entered. Piercing eyes, intelligent. She sought his advice often and was still somewhat irritated with him for turning down her request that he become clinical director for the entire facility. That was three months ago. In her opinion Dr. Bramson was the best clinical psychologist and diagnostician in the state of Alabama.

He looked straight into her eyes. "Good morning, Lydia," he said. He liked crows. He was the only one at the Center who called her only by her first name, not Dr. Lydia, like the rest of the professional staff. She insisted on it.

She ran her tongue across her lips. He saw her front teeth. Straight and white. He remembered the difficulties she had getting used to dentures. "You know, I'm almost eighty-four." There was wistfulness attached to her words.

He sat down across from her. "I hope I have your magic when I'm eighty-four, Lydia. You still outsmart and out-wrangle even the most deviant of our rapscallions, and you can out-swim us all."

Thin, broad shouldered and sturdy. She had a swimmer's build. She was there every morning as he parked his car in the lot to the left of the main building, swimming laps in the Metamorphosis pool. She claimed to swim thirty a morning, another twenty at day's end. Long arms, almost no splash as her cupped hands cut through the water. Rapscallion was her word, not his, but the way it described their residents, the way it rolled off the tongue, the way it inferred mischievousness, naughtiness, made it one of Luke's favorite descriptors. He studied her face, skin wrinkled like tissue paper pulled out of a gift bag. Soft creases, lines crisscrossing, folds. The quiet, the intensity of her demeanor told him there was something important, very important, on her mind.

She folded her hands together on the table. Big knuckles. Pronounced blue veins on the backs of her hands that traveled from her fingers up to her wrists and then tunneled into her skin until they popped back to the surface on the insides of her elbows. "There's something I've wanted to propose to you, Luke. For you and your wife to consider."

She hesitated and he waited. It was her way to put thoughts together carefully, lining them up like dominoes.

"I've been talking to my lawyer." Another hesitation. He waited. He could smell bacon cooking in the kitchen. He'd had oatmeal for breakfast but the bacon smelled better. "Four years ago when I was turning eighty, I placed Metamorphosis into a trust. So fiscally the Center will smoothly survive my demise. But, here's the question, Luke. How do I insure continuity of my vision, the best stewardship for Metamorphosis when I'm no longer here?"

She hesitated. He waited. But he jiggled his leg, his right leg, underneath the table.

"My lawyer advises me to name someone in my will. Someone I explicitly trust, someone in whom I can entrust the well-being of the Center. She thinks, as do I, this person will need to commit to at least ten years of oversight, and then will be responsible for helping choose a successor if the need arises."

His heart was pounding in his throat. It jetted him back in time. He was trying to spell M-Y-O-P-I-C during Mrs. Leary's spelling bee. He'd never sweated so much at school before. Big wet islands under his armpits on his red knit shirt. The whole auditorium full of people. He'd pressed his elbows into his ribcage and didn't move his arms when he walked across the stage to get the ribbon pinned to his collar. It was a green ribbon with Second Place printed in a stiff gold paint. Mrs. Leary pinned it on with a straight pin that jabbed his thumb later. He went home that night, sneaked into his parents' bathroom and lathered on deodorant. He never went without it again.

"As I'm sure you've surmised, you're that person, Luke. The salary would be exceptional and for the most part, the responsibilities could be fulfilled however you best saw fit."

21

He reached across the table past some rolled up architectural plans and put one hand on top of hers. Her hands were almost the size of his. Good piano hands. He was stunned. But his heart was calming, no longer pounding.

"The Board of Directors will continue to help with vital issues but I'm sure you understand the role you'd play."

"Lydia, thank you."

"I don't want an answer now. It's quite a commitment. For both you and Addie. Preliminary exploration, you understand." She chuckled. "And not to fear, young man, I plan to be around for quite some time. At least until I'm too decrepit to dive into the pool."

She could still do a mean swan dive. Arms curved out and back, scapulas close to touching, back arched in a half moon curve. He squeezed her fingers gently. Her ring was rough against his palm. Eighteen blood red rubies set in yellow gold with at least a half carat ruby in the middle. She was eighty when she boarded the plane to begin a twenty-three hour journey to Bangkok to attend a world conference on at-risk children. Children with no homes. Children with no attending families. Female children sent by well-meaning parents out of the northern hills of Thailand to find better lives in the city. Children who ended up selling their bodies. She brought the ring back with her.

"You're right, Lydia," he said. "Addie and I will have a lot to consider, but I'm so grateful for your trust."

"Please keep this confidential," she said. She stood.

"Of course."

"If God had seen fit to give me a son, I would have wanted him to be you."

"Lydia . . ."

"See you at the Records meeting shortly." She squeezed his left shoulder as she passed. She didn't intend it, but her fingers had the grip of a C-clamp. "The Beaty case," she said stopping briefly. "He'll be one of yours. Lots of opinions in the community about Dr. Beaty, the boy's mother, and almost no middle ground. Seems like she could try some other options first, but when I spoke with her by phone and suggested that, she refused to consider my recommendations."

"Hmm. Well, at least from the referral information I've read he should fit right in."

The scent of jasmine and chlorine lingered as she closed the door.

He pulled out his phone and made a note to remind the others about her birthday. It was next month. Never in his wildest dreams while slogging through tedious years of doctoral study, running rats through mazes, collecting data on children's empathy and pet ownership in at-risk urban youth, editing and re-editing and re-editing his document to meet American Psychological Association standards, had he ever imagined working for a lady like Dr. Lydia P. Hutchinson. She rarely talked about it, being abandoned as a baby inside a circus tent not far from the exit flap. There were little bits and pieces she'd gleaned from diligent informational searches and every once in a while when her mood turned melancholy, she'd recount them to him and sometimes to Shelby, too, in an organized, repetitive manner, as though by doing so she'd uncover the clues she was missing.

Her parents were from somewhere near present day Romania she said. They traveled with small circus troops as acrobats and sometimes also helped with the elephants. Her father had a way with the elephants. Her mother was beautiful, daring, the way she flew from the trapeze with abandon, the trust of youthful love that her father would never miss catching her. Lydia was their reason for coming to America. To give her a better, richer life. But then the circus take went missing. Her father was seen nearby. There were accusations. Denials. Threats. Her parents disappeared in the night. Some suspected foul play. Some said they'd fled. The police searched other traveling troops and came up with no leads. Lydia searched all of her young adulthood both in the U.S. and abroad, seeking out people like Theo the Tortoise Man and Caleb the Canine because they'd been there, they'd known them. To Luke, the circus people Lydia met were at least as fascinating as the rest of her story. Theo with his hardened shell of a back, curved and calcified, and Caleb with his fang-like teeth and hirsute face and body. An extraordinarily wealthy couple from Texas, Erma Livingston and Jakestonian William Hutchinson, adopted her when she was almost three. She was their only child. Once grown, Dr. Lydia devoted her professional and personal life, as well as the immense fortune she inherited, to the mental health treatment and overall well-being of children and adolescents, as well as the treatment of their families. She poured her money and life blood into it, bringing in state of the art techniques and providing opportunities for the residents of Metamorphosis that many would never have otherwise.

And she was choosing to entrust him with it all. The mother lode. The million dollar sweepstakes of career opportunities. But it was a jigsaw puzzle piece that belonged to a different picture. He and Addie were talking about moving to Oregon in two or three years. And Addie wanted to spend part of next summer backpacking across Europe and part of the next in Alaska. She was a total travel junkie. And they wanted children, probably three, and they weren't getting any younger. Without question Metamorphosis could devour his life, their lives, as voraciously as the caterpillars that were painted all over the Center's signs and murals munched big holes in the painted, veined leaves. Metamorphosis certainly consumed Lydia. She even lived on campus, moving from cottage to cottage residing among the residents depending on where she sensed weaknesses or needs in the program at any particular moment.

"There's not one behavior taking place inside the walls of this Center that I didn't try or fantasize trying at one time or another when I was growing up," she'd told staff on more than one occasion. "And, if you're honest with yourself, you'll admit to at least fantasizing about such behaviors yourselves. Each of you will make a difference in the lives of some of these children. And, it's rarely the big things you do that make the greatest impact." How true that last statement was. It never ceased to amaze him how the most mundane interactions sometimes had the most positive impacts of all.

8

"Your staff deserves hazardous duty pay today," chuckled Reverend Jeremiah Lincoln to the others sitting around the conference room table in the Green Room as Luke joined them.

"Every day," interjected Luke.

"I mean," said Reverend Lincoln, "Esmeralda had a *real* snake in her purse when she came in from outside. Staff was pouring juice for snack when several of the girls screamed at the top of their lungs. I thought someone'd been murdered. I opened my eyes, I was praying with one of the girls at the time, and there was Esmeralda pulling this snake out of her purse and letting it crawl up her arm. And she kept yelling that it was a garter snake and wasn't poisonous. So, two of the girls got real interested and wanted to hold it, too, but the others were shrieking and running around the cottage and picking up shoes and books and trying to kill it. So, then she started cursing because they were clobbering her arm with everything they could get their hands on. And staff kept giving the direction to stand back and be calm, over and over again. And, I kept thinking, 'How do they psyche themselves up to come to work everyday?' Snakes have never been my favorite creatures. Satan used them to tempt Adam and Eve in the Garden of Eden, you know."

Dr. Lydia Hutchinson smiled. "So what happened?"

"Finally, *finally*, your staff Jennifer convinced Esmeralda to let it go free outside, but she certainly didn't want to. I can tell you that. She wanted to add it to your pet center. She announced to everyone she wants to study herpetology in college and work in a zoo. That she used to have twenty-five to thirty pet snakes at a time when she lived with her dad. Said she used to go with him every year to the rattlesnake rodeo in Opp. A million dollars wouldn't be enough to get me to that rodeo."

Luke laughed. "Addie and I went once. It was actually pretty amazing. And, they let the snakes go after the round-up."

"Except the ones they eat," said Shelby.

"Tastes like chicken." He laughed and winked. She wrinkled up her cute pixie nose. He laughed again.

"It's a bad idea for her to be picking up snakes in the wild," said Shelby.

"That's what I told her," said Reverend Lincoln. "But she rolled her eyes and got a real disgusted look on her face and said *anyone* who knows anything about snakes can tell a garter snake from a poisonous one. Like I didn't have any sense at all."

Ms. Moffiti, one of Metamorphosis' special education teachers, cleared her throat. "That's interesting," she said. "Maybe I'll ask her to help me present the upcoming science chapter on reptiles."

"Brilliant," said Shelby. Esmeralda needed a confidence boost. She was sort of a gawky kid. The others didn't cut her much slack.

"Well, it makes sense," said Rico. He was tall and lean with narrow shoulders but healthy biceps. "Her father being one of those religious snake handlers from Sand Mountain. The minister of his church, if I remember right. Kept poisonous snakes right in their living room and dining room."

"Oh my gosh!" said Reverend Lincoln. "In their house?"

Luke and Shelby and Dr. Lydia bounced information among themselves with their eyes. It was confidential information that Esmeralda's father was the minister of his church, that he was a snake handler, that he was from Sand Mountain. It was because of the snakes that Esmeralda was removed from her home. Freedom of religion, her father argued vehemently. Danger to a child argued the Department of Human Resources. Luke made meaningful eye contact with Rico. It was obvious from the man's face he realized his mistake. There was an awkward silence. Reverend Lincoln glanced from Rico to Luke then back again. He coughed and looked at his watch.

*   *   *

There were seven of them around the table in the Green Room. Interestingly to Luke, and almost certainly perplexing to observant persons from outside Metamorphosis, there was no green in the room at all, the chairs having been recovered in orange fabric approximately a year earlier. Luke sat next to Dr. Lydia and across from Shelby. Rico, a residential mentoring staff who even-temperedly tolerated the children's mocking of his accent and their pride in showing off expletives they'd learned in Spanish on the streets, worked in the male Luna cottage. Ms.

Moffiti from the special education classroom, Reverend Jeremiah Lincoln and Miss Zenah Elenrude rounded out the group. All Records meetings included a rotating religious leader from the community and a Tuscaloosa citizen who understood the needs of emotionally and behaviorally disturbed adolescents. Generally, this last citizen was someone retired from the Department of Human Resources, especially retirees familiar with the principles behind the R.C. federal lawsuit brought against the State of Alabama's foster care system decades earlier. The philosophy of the R.C. lawsuit was straightforward. Whenever safety permits do not disrupt the integrity of the family. Build safety nets around them. Enhance their strengths. Shore up their needs with services. Try to find relatives if parental care is not possible. Locate community resources if relative care is not available. Residential treatment should be a last resort.

Luke saw the Reverend look at his watch again. The man's wrist was puffy and the watch circumnavigated it too close to his hand, like a tight collar. Reverend Lincoln had been a heavy-set man ever since Luke met him around three years ago but he'd added at least another thirty pounds recently. His face was fleshy and he had a very distracting blue vein that popped out of his skin on his forehead above his nose and disappeared again near his scalp. When he got excited or overheated the vein grew more pronounced and it throbbed, pulsed might be more accurate, like it was going to burst. The man's nose was not remarkable, he was probably of British ancestry, but there was a little hump in the nasal bridge, a remnant from all the years he'd worn glasses. He'd had his eyes lasered last year to correct his vision but in Luke's opinion he'd looked better in glasses because the nasal hump did distract from his profile. He wore a short graying beard that was trimmed neatly. His hair was thin, combed over toward the right and totally gray. "Do you have a pressing schedule today?" Luke asked, glancing toward the Reverend's watch.

"Spring's a busy time of year in the ministry," Reverend Lincoln said. "We're coming up on May. Wedding season, you know. In fact, I have a funeral and a wedding rehearsal on docket for this afternoon. And this weekend I have the wedding itself and I'm on rotation over here."

There was a group of ministers from various faiths who volunteered their time, offering non-denominational services to Metamorphosis residents. There was also always a minister on-call should anyone request pastoral counseling. Reverend Lincoln was a Southern Baptist.

"My ex and I got married in May," said Miss Zenah Elenrude. She had very, very short hair, blue eyes as pale as Luke's were startling, and dangly earrings. She always wore dangly earrings. Today they were cloisonné hummingbirds. Luke liked her hair. It was artificial sunshine yellow. Arty. "We walked down the aisle thirty-three years ago next month. And we divorced thirty three years ago this August." She smiled an ironic smile.

Luke had heard her say this before. He'd always wondered about it. "Still enjoying retirement, Zenah?" he asked.

"You'd better believe it," hummingbirds flying little circles beneath her earlobes as she answered. "I just got back from Yellowstone and Vegas. I was out there three weeks and could have easily stayed another month but as you know I'm only half-retired now. I call myself re-treaded."

Retired. Re-treaded. Luke found himself again drawn to her smile. It spread across her lips and up into her eyes like a brush fire. It was happening a lot these days due to spending cutbacks. Retired DHR workers returning part time, recruited to work hourly or on contract.

"Well," said Dr. Lydia Hutchinson, pulling a sheet of paper out of her turquoise notebook. It was a confidentiality agreement. "If everyone will please sign this we'll get started. What's said in this room stays in this room." She handed it to Shelby McDonald to sign and pass on. "We're thrilled you're back, Zenah. And we all know DHR's better off with the old-timers around. But we'd better press forward since Reverend Lincoln has afternoon commitments elsewhere."

Luke nodded. A routine psychological nod. Addie pointed out even before they got married that therapists nod excessively. She first noticed it when she attended a psychological conference with him. The whole audience looks like dippy birds, she'd said. He started audience watching at psychology meetings. It was true.

"Okay," said Dr. Lydia. "First up today is a sixteen year old Caucasian male local to Tuscaloosa named Andrew Beaty. Andrew is the son of Dr. Priscilla Beaty, whom some of you might know as the principal of Tuskaloosa Gardens Elementary School."

Miss Zenah Elenrude nodded enthusiastically. Hummingbirds flitting around and around. Luke smiled inwardly. If nothing else, Zenah was perpetually enthusiastic. Reverend Lincoln squinted and coughed. Luke viewed this as also predictable. Over time he'd observed that Reverend Jeremiah Lincoln liked to be the center of every group's attention. Probably one reason the man found his way into the ministry. Luke and Addie attended his church once out of Luke's curiosity. Jerry Lincoln had a booming, riveting voice from the pulpit. Ernest. Inspiring. Theatrical.

"Actually," said Miss Elenrude, "Dr. Beaty and I go way back. We had lots of meetings together, not all of them so friendly, either. She's a remarkable principal for gifted and advantaged children, but at times I found her to be somewhat," she paused, obviously trying to sanitize her adjectives, "um, somewhat harsh with our children who have special needs."

Reverend Lincoln shifted in his chair. "Beaty . . . did she have a son named Joey?"

"Did and does. Joey's her elder child. Apparently he's at Auburn," said Dr. Lydia. "But, he's supposed to come home today to help his mother get Andrew to our Center. Apparently, Andrew respects Joey tremendously and will listen to him better than to his mother. Dr. Beaty says Joey's sort of been like a father figure to him."

"I thought I remembered the name," said Reverend Lincoln, "but it's been years. She attended our church when Joey was young. In fact as I recall, she may have been pregnant when she stopped coming. She was known among the matrons of our church, if you will forgive my being blunt, as a very sexually active woman."

"Yes," said Dr. Lydia Hutchinson. "I think that reputation still stands."

"So," said Luke, "we're probably looking at adolescent anger focused on mother related to her promiscuity?"

Dr. Lydia nodded toward a hand painted sign hanging above the dry erase board. It was decorated with caterpillars, moths and butterflies and said in big letters, ASSUME NOTHING. It was her favorite, most repetitive statement and similar signs hung in nooks and crannies throughout the Center. Shelby and Luke often talked about how important this advice was. Assumption was a major foe of good therapeutic assessment and treatment. Over time with so many adolescents and families coming and going from treatment, behavioral histories and life stories as unusual and unique as they might seem, grew uncannily similar. It was easy to generalize, to assume.

"Actually, Dr. Beaty reports her son's anger stems from not knowing the identity of his biological father," said Dr. Lydia. "His half-brother, Joey, apparently has a strong relationship with his father. Dr. Beaty reports knowing the identity of Andrew's birth father but she says she's never revealed it. She claims it's for Andrew's sake. She says his father has threatened public rejection and private humiliation of Andrew if she breaks her silence. Apparently, though, he's provided financially for them in ways regular child support might not."

"I didn't get a chance to read all his referral information before today's meeting," said Ms. Moffiti. "We had an emotional melt-down with Benjamin this morning in class. No behavioral problems to speak of, but he's spent most of the day in the cool-down room crying."

"Really?" asked Shelby. "Today's his birthday."

"I think that's at the root of his upset."

Miss Elenrude leaned forward and flipped to a back page in her legal pad. "This is my Benjamin we're talking about?"

"And mine?" asked Reverend Lincoln leaning back in his chair.

"Yes," said Luke. Benjamin's case had been transferred to Miss Elenrude about a month ago when one of the younger DHR workers left on maternity leave. And the current plan was for Benjamin to soon phase into one of Reverend Lincoln's church managed foster homes.

Rico frowned. "It's not like Benjamin to cry in public," he said. "But you know, he's been talking a lot this week about his mom in prison."

Reverend Jeremiah Lincoln stared quietly at clasped hands, as though trying to recall something. He looked at Luke, eyes puzzled. "Has Benjamin been informed he may eventually move into one of our foster homes?"

"Yes. I talked to him about it last week, in fact."

"And I explored it with him before I left for the West," said Zenah Elenrude. "He, um, didn't appear too thrilled about it at the time."

"No," said Luke.

"He expressed a preference for moving to the Metamorphosis independent living cottages and remaining there until he's grown," said Zenah.

"Yes," said Luke.

"Perhaps I could stop by and see him on the way out," said Jerry Lincoln. "I project we'll have two open homes by the end of May."

Dr. Lydia rested her right arm on the table. Her bracelets clinked against the wood. "Good idea, Jerry. Just keep it vague. You know, no names or specific foster family information in case anything falls through."

"Or in case he's not ready to be discharged by the end of next month," said Luke.

"Of course," said Reverend Lincoln.

*　*　*

"Back to Andrew," said Dr. Lydia Hutchinson. She glanced down at her notes. "The record indicates numerous conduct disordered behaviors including lying, stealing, selling stolen items, smoking tobacco, suspected but not confirmed alcohol and drug experimentation, runaway behaviors, verbal aggression and aggression against objects, as well as school refusal and school ambivalence. On a positive note, there's no history of arrest and reportedly he has several friends, although Dr. Beaty reports not knowing them. He apparently never invites them home. She says he has a girlfriend, but she has no idea if he's sexually active. His mother, incidentally, is the one who reports all of the above. She describes their relationship as very strained and his behaviors toward her as oppositional. She says his recent suspension from school is the last straw for her. He apparently got caught with cigarettes and a lighter. From her reports, he's out of control."

"His IQ scores indicate above average intelligence and no apparent learning disorder," said Ms. Moffiti. "He attended the Magnet School last year but he apparently exhibits periodic academic ambivalence."

"What better way to get back at your principal mom than to act out at school?" asked Luke.

"His ambivalence might be a sign of depression," said Shelby.

"True," said Luke.

"His mother thinks he might run away before placement," said Dr. Lydia.

"Well," said Shelby, "From your description he sounds like a good candidate for placement in the Luna cottage."

Zenah Elenrude frowned. "Can Andrew and his mother receive individual and family counseling in the community? Try to work out their issues without residential placement? In some ways, residential placement seems premature to me."

"I suggested that," said Dr. Hutchinson. "But Dr. Beaty made it very clear the problem is totally her son's and she's not willing to participate in therapy. I also suggested that she consider filing a CHINS petition through juvenile court so she'd have the back-up authority of a probation officer. But to be frank I think she's reached the point where she just wants him gone."

Reverend Lincoln glanced up at the wall clock, it was a plain clock about the size of a dinner plate with a white face and black numbers and it had a chrome frame around it, and he pushed his chair backward. "So," he said, "to summarize. We have an angry adolescent male who is reportedly out of control at home, and probably in the community, most likely as a result of his relationship with his mother. Because Dr. Beaty is known to be unsympathetic to those with special needs," he said, nodding his head toward Zenah Elenrude as a way of crediting her with this observation, "and because she has an apparent long standing and widely recognized reputation of promiscuity, there is no telling what this boy has seen and experienced due to her behaviors. His lack of an identified father may or may not have anything to do with his problems despite Dr. Beaty's opinion. We all know that lots of children grow up quite successfully in single parent homes. However, he apparently has lost a significant male figure with the move of his older half-brother to Auburn, and this also may be influencing his overall mood."

Dr. Lydia Hutchinson closed her notebook. "That's it in a nutshell," she said. "So do we think Andrew is appropriate for admission, assuming today's meeting with him indicates this as well?"

"Sounds like he'll fit right in with our boys," said Rico.

"Maybe I'm off-base," said Miss Elenrude, "but I'd like for us to talk with Dr. Beaty one more time about other options."

Dr. Hutchinson smiled at her. "That's not off-base at all, Zenah." She reached for the phone. It was sitting on a table that had been spray painted a chocolate brown. There were several long dried paint drips, ending at different lengths, trailing down the legs. She handed the phone and the phone book to Luke. "I've already had this conversation with her," she said. "Maybe you'll have better luck. If we can reach her we'll put her on speaker."

Luke laughed and pulled his phone out of his pocket. "I can find the number a lot faster this way," he said. He picked up the office phone and dialed. The spelling was peculiar but historical. Tuskaloosa, Tuscaloosa, several other ways, too. All were attempts to capture the name of the famous chief, the war lord who ruled over Native Americans living in the region nearly five hundred years earlier. The name meant "Black Warrior." There was a history professor Luke got to talking to at a coffee shop along the University's strip. She'd told him Tuscaloosa was one of the oldest written place names in North America, having first been written down in some phonetic sort of way by a Portuguese explorer with the DeSoto expedition to define the region the chief ruled. She said that was back around 1540.

*   *   *

"Good morning. Tuskaloosa Gardens Elementary School?"

"Dr. Beaty, please."

"May I say who's calling?" Efficient. Polite.

"Dr. Luke Bramson."

Jerry Lincoln tilted to his left and pulled his phone from his back pocket. He looked at the screen. "I've been waiting for this call," he whispered. "I'll try to make it quick. Good morning, this is Reverend Jeremiah Lincoln," he said, standing, walking around the table and toward the door. "Yes! Yes, thanks for returning my call." The door shut behind him.

"He's got a darn quiet phone," said Luke, resting the phone's mouthpiece against his neck.

"Hello? Dr. Bramson?" said Dr. Priscilla Beaty.

He moved the mouthpiece back to his face. "Yes. Good morning, Dr. Beaty. We haven't had the opportunity to meet yet, but I'm calling from Metamorphosis. I'm the clinical psychologist assigned to your son's age group."

"Oh, yes?"

"Is this a convenient time to talk?"

She paused. "I have about ten minutes."

"That should do it. I'm calling because we're holding a records meeting, reviewing possible admissions, and there're one or two points we hoped to clarify before this afternoon."

"Yes?"

"I'm putting you on speaker phone if that's okay. I'll ask everyone around the table to introduce themselves to you."

"That's okay. Don't bother. What do you need?"

"Dr. Beaty, this is Miss Zenah Elenrude. I'm a retired part-time DHR worker who sometimes serves as a community member on this committee. Actually, we've met several times at your school when I was working full-time. Meetings for different children on my caseload."

"Oh, yes?"

"And actually, I'm the one who asked to clarify several points with you."

"Yes?"

"I'm wondering if you've already tried individual and family therapies to work through issues that are causing problems for Andrew and you at home? And if not, would you be willing to let us set that up for you? To try to avoid his having to enter residential treatment?"

There was a long pause.

"Dr. Beaty?" said Luke. "Are you still there?"

Several more seconds of silence. "Yes, I'm here." There was significant irritation, in fact, restrained anger, a tremble in her voice.

Luke looked at Shelby and raised his eyebrows. Shelby smiled at him. Zenah looked toward Dr. Lydia with widened eyes. Dr. Lydia Hutchinson nodded.

"I've already explained to Dr. Hutchinson that Andrew has deep-seated problems because he doesn't know his father's identity. It's been a source of anger, rage really, for years. He takes it out on me because I'm the easy target. His behaviors are getting worse and harder to handle. He needs intense treatment before it's too late to help him. I don't have any of these problems with his older brother. This is about Andrew, not the family."

"Whenever a child's in trouble, I'm sure being a principal you know, it's always about the whole family," said Miss Elenrude. "It affects everyone."

"Has he told you why he's angry?" asked Luke. "That it's about his father?"

Silence.

"Dr. Beaty?"

"Yes, I'm here. But I won't be the bad guy in this. Do you have *any* idea what it's like to wake up every morning and sneak around your own house because you don't want to listen to your son's cursing and yelling? Before you've even had a shower and coffee? Or to be principal of a school and get a call from another principal saying your son's **suspended** for carrying cigarettes and a lighter? He lies, he's disrespectful, he steals, he runs away. He's got to go. Either to Metamorphosis or somewhere else if you won't take him."

Dr. Lydia leaned toward the phone. "Dr. Beaty, this is Dr. Hutchinson. Please recognize these questions are always part of our admissions decision-making process. We just want to be certain residential placement is the best option for everyone in your family, so bear with us. I know we talked earlier about your filing a Child In Need of Supervision petition."

"A what?"

"I think I called it a CHINS petition."

"Oh, yes. I remember. Through the juvenile court."

"That would give you the back-up authority of a probation officer if he misbehaved," said Miss Elenrude.

"If you think I'm going before a judge in Tuscaloosa County with my son and jeopardize my reputation as principal because he chooses to act up, you clearly don't know a thing about me. That's all I need is for word to get out among the parents that I can't take care of my own son's behaviors. How do you think that would sit with them?"

Shelby stared at the phone solemnly. "There are boundaries between parents and their children," she said gently. "Parents have influence over their children's behaviors but they don't behave for them."

"Well, words sound good, but it still doesn't fly for me. The bottom line is Andrew needs help and he can't stay home until he gets it. Something new, Dr. Hutchinson. I've made the decision to tell Andrew the truth about his father. I'm going to do it while he's in treatment with you. I hope your agency can help him with it."

"That's certainly an interesting option for you to explore with Dr. Luke Bramson and Ms. Shelby McDonald once Andrew is settled in here," said Dr. Lydia. "Dr. Beaty, we know you're on a busy schedule. We'll talk about these things later today in our meeting. Thank you for taking time to clarify your family's needs for us."

"Yes," said Miss Elenrude. "Thank you, Dr. Beaty. You've cleared up my questions."

"Fine," said Dr. Beaty. "I'll be there at 3:45. Andrew's coming separately with his brother."

"Okay," said Luke. "See you then." The phone clicked to a dial tone. He picked up the handset from the table and returned it to the base.

*　　*　　*

"Well," he said, glancing impishly toward Miss Elenrude, "I think she made that clear enough for us."

Miss Elenrude looked at Dr. Hutchinson. "It appears admission is his best option."

"I hope she'll work with us," said Shelby.

"Hmmm," said Luke. "Fix my child." All in the room knew what he meant. Fix my child but don't ask me to change my behaviors or routines. Don't ask me to come to therapy. It's not me at all. Just fix my child.

"We don't know that for sure," said Shelby. "She may be feeling helpless and vulnerable and isolated."

Luke nodded. One never knew.

Miss Elenrude leaned back and straightened her leg out under the table. She reached into her slack's pocket and pulled out her phone. "My turn," she said, standing up and heading toward the door. Just as she reached it, the door opened and Reverend Lincoln walked in.

"Sorry," he said. "That call was one that couldn't wait but I was hoping the timing would be better. So, what was the outcome of your call?"

"Admission appears to be the most viable option for Andrew and his family right now," said Luke.

"I'd tend to agree given the family's referral information," Reverend Lincoln said. "There're skeletons in every family's closet, I've come to believe. Even our best families. In fact in all my years as a minister it never ceases to amaze me how disturbed some families are beneath the surface." He watched Shelby McDonald's face because curiously it was reddening. He was sure he wasn't imagining it. He'd hit a nerve. Definitely some sort of skeleton there. He pulled his chair back, sat, and thought about it.

"No one's perfect," said Shelby making eye contact with him. Direct. Defiant.

The door opened and Miss Elenrude walked back to her chair. Her face appeared flushed as well. "That was my secretary telling me to take my time," she said. "There's been another bomb threat at DHR this morning. Addie's over there now along with the canine teams. And I had so much work to do today."

"Addie's working hard on it," said Luke. "And once she sinks her teeth into something she doesn't quit until the case is solved."

"We're lucky to have her," said Miss Elenrude. "And I know she'll get it figured out. You know, the folks at DHR are giving me a lot of grief, though. They didn't have a bomb threat the entire time I was gone out West."

Reverend Lincoln chuckled. "Coincidence," he said. "I wouldn't take it personally, Zenah."

Miss Elenrude returned his chuckle. "Social workers can't afford to take things personally, Jerry. Not with the names our profession's called."

"So," said Dr. Lydia. "Are we all in agreement that Andrew Beaty's appropriate for our Center, barring any unforeseen problems during this afternoon's meeting?"

"Yes," said Luke.

"I agree," said Shelby.

"Me, too," said Rico.

"Yes," said Ms. Moffiti.

Miss Elenrude nodded.

"I'll go with the group's decision," said Reverend Lincoln, "since I missed the salient phone call."

Luke pushed on the arms of the chair to stand. "That's it for us, isn't it?" he asked, knowing through experience another group of treatment staff was already gathered in the hallway waiting to discuss referrals related to their cottages.

"Beaty meeting, 3:45," said Dr. Lydia.

Luke nodded toward Reverend Lincoln. "See you again soon, Jerry."

"Too soon, I suspect. Since I'm on rotation for the ministers all this week and weekend."

"We'll hope for no crises," Luke said.

He nodded toward Miss Elenrude. "Great seeing you, Zenah."

"Bye," added Shelby standing to leave. Rico followed and Ms. Moffiti trailed behind. As the group walked from the Green Room, the treatment team for the twelve and thirteen year old cottages entered.

Luke paused in the hallway. He touched Shelby's arm and she stopped and looked toward him. "Ms. Moffiti," he said. "Thanks for the information on Benjamin. You, too, Rico." There was a penny on the floor. Tails up. He bent down, flipped it heads side up before palming it. He hoped nobody noticed. It was silly and superstitious and he didn't believe in luck but why tempt fate, that's what he always asked, and Addie always laughed.

"No problem," said Ms. Moffiti.

Luke studied her face. She had teeth that jutted out slightly too far and a long, thin jaw that created a sort of horsey-look. Her nose was also long and too sharp. But every adult male on campus forgave her these imperfections, he was sure of it. Silently, of course. It would be sexist to say anything outright. She was a serious runner and when she jogged around campus after school in her running shorts and sports top he, for one, gave thanks to the architect who had the foresight to include panoramic windows in all the offices.

9

Her feet hurt and it was just the beginning of the day. Particularly, it seemed to Dr. Beaty her right shoe was too tight and was rubbing a blister across the top of her foot. The shoes felt fine when she'd tried them on at the store, even after she'd walked around on the carpet and turned her feet this way and that in front of the little floor mirror. She pried them off now using the toe of one foot against the heel of the other. She let her stockinged feet rest on the cool linoleum floor behind her desk. "That's better," she said holding her right foot out to inspect the damage. There was a spot, angry red despite the nylon mesh. An irritated blister. She picked up her desk receiver and dialed the number for Leah at Heavenly Feet. She knew it by heart. *"Heavenly Feet. Heavenly Feet. Keep your little toe-seys happy and neat. We'll make them forever grateful they're on the ends of your feet. Help us pamper and spoil your heavenly feet,"* sang a couple of girls on a recording as she waited to confirm a time. She frowned as the jingle began again.

"Dr. Beaty?"

"Yes?"

"Leah can fit you in at 1:45. She knows you have bus line responsibilities at 2:20."

"Perfect," she said. She opened her bottom left hand desk drawer and pulled out a pair of elephant slipper socks. Gray feet with little elephant heads that permanently smiled at whatever she was approaching. Their trunks were raised, trumpeting, and little white tusks were attached on either side of their mouths. The socks themselves were houndstooth, small black and white checks, symbolic of all things football at the University ever since Coach Paul Bear Bryant immortalized houndstooth by wearing his signature hat. "Tell Leah I'll see her then."

"Dr. Beaty?"

"Yes?"

"Actually I think she's dropping by to see you any minute now. She was in the neighborhood and had some new polish samples she wanted to show you."

"Really?" New samples. "Excellent. I'll keep an eye out for her. And, thanks."

"Have a nice day, Dr. Beaty."

Dial tone. She returned the receiver and pulled her toes carefully into the houndstooth, down into the elephants' heads. She was careful because if she put too much pressure on her heels, sound chips sewn into the socks made elephant trumpeting noises. It was a good gag and Harry apparently saw the humor even though he was an Auburn graduate. Or maybe, because he'd graduated from Auburn. Either way, the elephants represented Big Al, the mascot of the University of Alabama. She frowned. Actually, football season might be a mess this year, what with Harry rooting for Auburn and their relationship being on the sly in any case.

Her thoughts morphed from Harry to Auburn to her son, Joey. She dialed his number. Her own phone was ringing again from inside her purse. She confirmed it was Harry. "Damn," she said, slamming the phone back into her purse and her purse back into the drawer. The drawer caught on her bracelet. "Damn!" she said again. One of the silver links had twisted open. She unfastened the clasp and the bracelet fell into two pieces. "Damn! Damn! Damn!" It was a special gift from long ago. A charm bracelet from Joey's father, Thomas. A little silver Mardi Gras mask from their trip to New Orleans, a sterling silver dachshund, a Six Flags charm from Atlanta, a silver baby boy. Joey. And two little silver discs with nondescript boys' profiles on them. Both engraved on the backs. Joey. Andrew. Their birthdates. She scooped up both pieces of the bracelet, reopened the drawer, reopened her purse, and dropped them in.

"Hallo?"

"Hey, it's me. Have you talked to your brother this morning?"

"No, but we've texted."

"Oh . . . Look, just make sure he doesn't run away, okay? That he gets to the meeting."

"I'll do my best, Mom."

"Why don't you go over to the house now? Keep an eye on him?"

"He has plans and I'm running errands. We're meeting after lunch."

"What plans can he possibly have? Go on over anyway."

An irritated sigh. When did Joey start getting irritated with her? It was something new. Uncomfortable. A little threatening. "Can't. Like I said, I'm running errands. Some things I need to do. And, anyway, I'm meeting Thomas in a while. I'll do my best to get him there, Mom. Don't worry. See you later, okay?"

"You're meeting your dad?"

"Yeah, for coffee." Joey didn't fill the pregnant silence with more information.

"Are Holly and the kids going to be there?" Holly was Joey's stepmother. A real Plain Jane. Boring dresser, boring hair, boring nails, boring shoes, boring conversationalist, boring life. In fact, never even did her nails and probably bought her shoes at discount stores. She had no idea what Thomas saw in her and why Joey was crazy about her too. Joey went on and on about her cooking, how neat she kept the house, how much she loved their two dogs and one cat, and about special things she did with her children. Holly's and Thomas' children. Three little girls. What a wonderful mom she was to them. Thomas married Holly nearly five years after their relationship ended. It took him that long to commit to another woman. Now when he called he was all business, all about Joey. Sometimes about Andrew, too. Before Holly, she knew Thomas still loved her. Did she ever really love him? She wasn't sure. But she knew, had always known, he was the only real keeper out of all the men she'd dated. She'd always fantasized they'd get back together. Somehow he'd overlook the affairs she had while they were together. His face was flushed pink and his eyes darted back and forth like a madman's the night he explained why he could never commit to a relationship with her again, even though he forgave her, even though he still loved her. She'd cried, begged, even admitted she had a problem, she knew she had a problem, that the other men were just that. Just men.

"Mom, I don't know. I don't think so. I think it's just gonna be Dad and me."

She was young then, but she did her best explaining to him that sometimes when she met a guy she went to autopilot. Autopilot and the guy really meant nothing. "Have you ever had an itch on your back and it keeps moving when you try to scratch it, and you never really get relief, even when you know you've nailed it?" she asked him. "That's sort of what it's like. Even when I know it's going to wreck up things. Even if I don't want to do it, I still do."

"You need help," Thomas had said, voice heavy with concern.

"I'll get it if you'll come back. I promise. I'll call tomorrow."

41

"I can't, Priscilla. I just can't. But, please. For yourself and even more for our baby boy, get help anyway." And he'd walked out the door and she'd hugged an embroidered couch pillow to her chest and buried her face in it and cried until it was gooey with snot before she picked up the phone and called a man she'd met in the grocery store check out line earlier that day. She was buying strained vegetables for Joey and a bottle of wine for herself. He was behind her holding peanut butter, salami and dog food. He had a mermaid tattoo on a very pronounced bicep. He'd made a joke about serving wine, should it be red or white with strained vegetables, and before she left the store they'd traded phone numbers.

"Mom, I've gotta go. Bye."

"I'm counting on you," she said. "Take care of your brother." The telephone clicked dead.

Her heart beat faster, harder against the constraints of her bra. The bra designed especially for Harry. She knew the number by heart even though nowadays she rarely phoned him. Red. She hoped he was there. That he'd pick up. She hoped he wasn't there. That he wouldn't. She braced herself for abusive language but they both knew it didn't really intimidate her. One ring, two. Her intercom buzzed. She hit the button with her left hand. Three rings. "Yes?"

"Dr. Beaty, there's a Dr. Luke Bramson on line one and a Dr. Harry Greene on line two."

"Dr. Bramson?"

"Yes, Ma'am."

Her forehead wrinkled. Four rings. She knew Red's answering machine would pick up after the fifth. "Did he say who he's with?"

"No, Ma'am."

"Okay. Tell Dr. Greene I still plan to take my dog to see him during lunch. Take a message if he needs to change the appointment." She tapped her index finger against the smooth wood of her desk. She'd given Harry strict instructions to never, ever call her on the school's line. And he continually ignored her. It was becoming increasingly apparent she needed to break off their relationship. They agreed from the outset, sex with no strings. His insecurity was insatiable. But so was his sexual appetite. Breaking up would mean losing that. Red's canned answering machine message, some recorded woman's voice, monotone and nondescript, droned.

"Yes, Ma'am. And, both Ms. Leah Mosselliana from Heavenly Feet and Mr. Larry Ryan are here to see you. Mr. Ryan says he has a meeting about Sammy's suspension."

She glanced at her wall clock and hung up the phone just before Red's answering machine beeped. She never left him messages. Too risky. The clock said ten-thirty on the dot. Mr. Ryan was always punctual despite his other failings. She'd see Leah first. Just for a minute. She toyed with whether to take off her slipper socks. Her toes wiggled protest. She'd keep her feet hidden underneath her oak desk. "Okay, I'll take Dr. Bramson's call first," she said, visually identifying the blinking line. "Then I'll see Ms. Mosselliana briefly before my meeting with Mr. Ryan." She punched line one with her index finger. Her pink nails looked embarrassingly worn. She was anxious to see Leah's samples.

"Hello? Dr. Bramson?" said Dr. Priscilla Beaty.

"Yes. Good morning, Dr. Beaty, we haven't had the opportunity to meet yet, but I'm calling from Metamorphosis. I'm the clinical psychologist assigned to your son's age group." The voice was that of a young man. A deep, friendly voice. Energetic.

"Oh, yes?"

"Is this a convenient time to talk?"

She thought about Leah. And Mr. Ryan having to wait in the front office in one of the stiff-backed, metal armed chairs lining the wall. Waiting was good for him. "I have about ten minutes."

"That should do it. I'm calling because we're holding a records meeting, reviewing possible admissions, and there're one or two points we hoped to clarify before this afternoon."

She frowned and picked up her pen. "Yes?"

"I'm putting you on speaker phone if that's okay. I'll ask everyone around the table to introduce themselves to you."

She jabbed her pen at the faux leather framing her desk calendar. "That's okay. Don't bother. What do you need?"

"Dr. Beaty, this is Miss Zenah Elenrude."

Dr. Beaty's pen stopped jabbing. Blah, blah, blah. Blah, blah, blah. She rolled her eyes. Miss Elenrude, bleeding heart Miss Elenrude. She thought she'd gotten rid of her. Hadn't she retired? "Oh, yes?"

"And actually, I'm the one who asked to clarify several points with you."

That figured. "Yes?"

"I'm wondering," blah, blah, blah. Blah, blah, blah, "to avoid his having to enter residential treatment?"

Dr. Beaty's eyes narrowed. From the first day Miss Elenrude set foot in her school she'd been an apologist for children's bad behaviors. What was she doing out at Metamorphosis anyway? But there she was, talking on speaker phone. She imagined an entire room of people glancing back and forth, listening.

"Dr. Beaty?" said the man Bramson. "Are you still there?"

She jabbed her pen into the faux leather again. "Yes, I'm here. I've already explained to Dr. Hutchinson that Andrew has deep-seated problems because he doesn't know his father's identity. It's been a source of anger, rage really, for years. He takes it out on me because I'm the easy target. His behaviors are getting worse and harder to handle. He needs intense treatment before it's too late to help him. I don't have any of these problems with his older brother. This is about Andrew, not the family."

"Whenever a child's" yadda, yadda, yadda, "it's always about the whole family," said Miss Elenrude. "It affects everyone."

Dr. Beaty ran her fingers through her hair. The whole family is *responsible.* She knew that's what the woman meant.

"Has he told you why he's angry?" asked the Bramson man. "That it's about his father?"

Her back stiffened. Subtle inferences couched in a therapeutic tone. She considered hanging up.

"Dr. Beaty?"

She wasn't going to like Dr. Bramson any more than she liked Miss Elenrude. She recognized a thinning higher pitch and a trembling in her voice when she spoke. "Yes, I'm here. But I won't be the bad guy in this. Do you have *any* idea what it's like to wake up every morning and sneak around your own house because you don't want to listen to your son's cursing and yelling? Before you've even had a shower and coffee? Or to be principal of a school and get a call from another principal saying your son's **suspended** for carrying cigarettes and a lighter? He lies, he's disrespectful, he steals, he runs away. He's got to go. Either to Metamorphosis or somewhere else if you won't take him."

"Dr. Beaty, this is Dr. Hutchinson. Please recognize . . ." She stared at the carat diamond on her right ring finger and the emerald solitaire on her index finger. She turned her chair slightly to allow the rings to catch sunlight coming in from behind and she wiggled them. Sparkling. She liked sparkling. ". . . a Child In Need of Supervision petition."

"A what?"

"I think I called it a CHINS petition."

"Oh, yes. I remember. Through the juvenile court."

"That would give you the back-up authority of a probation officer if he misbehaved." It was Miss Bleeding Heart again.

Her fingers curled into a tight ball. Rings hidden from the sunlight. Stupid woman. Stupid, stupid social work woman. "If you think I'm going before a judge in Tuscaloosa County with my son and jeopardize my reputation as principal because he chooses to act up, you clearly don't know a thing about me. That's all I need is for word to get out among the parents that I can't take care of my own son's behaviors. How do you think that would sit with them?"

"There are boundaries between parents and their children," said a new female voice. It sounded therapeutic too. Soft, slow, like melting butter. "Parents have influence over their children's behaviors but they don't behave for them."

Talk normal. Like you're talking to a car mechanic or a store salesman or a grocery clerk. That's what she wanted to say. "Well," she said, "words sound good, but it still doesn't fly for me. The bottom line is Andrew needs help and he can't stay home until he gets it. Something new, Dr. Hutchinson. I've made the decision to tell Andrew the truth about his father. I'm going to do it while he's in treatment with you. I hope your agency can help him with it." She prepared for disagreement.

"That's certainly an interesting option for you to explore with Dr. Luke Bramson and Ms. Shelby McDonald once Andrew is settled in here," said Dr. Lydia. "Dr. Beaty, we know you're on a busy schedule. We'll talk about these things later today in our meeting. Thank you for taking time to clarify your family's needs for us."

Thank God. It was over.

"Yes." Miss Elenrude again. No surprise. The woman always tried to get in the last word. "Thank you, Dr. Beaty. You've cleared up my questions."

"Fine," said Dr. Beaty. "I'll be there at 3:45. Andrew's coming separately with his brother." She swallowed, deciding not to add, "I hope."

"Okay," said the man named Dr. Bramson. "See you then."

45

She didn't need a second invitation to hang up. She covered her face with both hands. "Damn you, Red." She rolled her neck in a slow circle and did eight shoulder lifts and drops, and felt goose bumps on the back of her neck as some of the tension dissipated. She thought about Harry, his nimble tongue hungry against her neck and the curve of her shoulders. His body, toned and disciplined on top of hers. He'd laugh like hell at her bra. She'd gone to one of the big hobby stores in town and bought fabric paint and animal stencils. She fancied herself a fairly good artist. She'd taken a lot of art electives in college. She glanced at the clock. Two hours and fifteen minutes and two meetings before lunch. And a few extra minutes to see Leah's samples. She pressed the intercom.

"Yes, Ma'am?"

"Send Ms. Leah Mosselliana in please."

"Yes, Ma'am."

There was a quick knock on her door but before she could say 'come in,' Leah was in the room and headed toward her desk. That's the way Leah was, always in energetic motion, but never annoyingly so.

She was dark and petite, maybe of Greek or Lebanese or Italian ancestry, and had a quick wit and very steady hands. Dr. Beaty liked that she was a pragmatic conversationalist, asking pertinent but non-invasive questions and making observations without small talk. She could talk to Leah and know it would stay in the room. That's just the way she was.

"Good morning, Priscilla," Leah said laying a cosmetic briefcase on top of the desk, unzipping it, pulling out one bottle of polish and a color sample board. "We've just gotten in a new line of polishes and I wanted to show them to you. There's one in particular I think you'll like. It's called Crimson Chameleon. The color's a little deeper and fuller than most crimsons, I think. But its real magic's in the way it changes hues depending on what you're wearing. It has to do with light reflection." She held out the bottle and Dr. Beaty took it.

The color was astoundingly deep. She unscrewed the crimson top and breathed deeply. She loved the smell of polish, the shine of polish, the sophistication of polish. She dabbed a little paint on her pink thumbnail, held it at arm's length, tilted it to the left, to the right, and smiled. "Perfect," she said.

Leah handed her a tissue and she wiped it off before it hardened. "There're some other nice colors on the board, too," Leah said. "I particularly like this peach and this blue and the pink pearl. This red as well."

"Yes," said Dr. Beaty. "Yes. Absolutely."

"The whole line is exciting."

"You're right about the crimson. That's what we'll use today."

"Okay, I'll leave it here." Leah reached out and reclaimed the sample board.

"Wait. I haven't looked at the other colors yet. What's your rush?"

Leah ignored her. Zipped the sample board into the briefcase.

"Hang on. I want to see the other colors."

Leah swung the briefcase off the desk. "Can't," she said. "I have an appointment across town in about twenty minutes, and I'm holding you up. There's a gentleman waiting to see you. He looks impatient."

Dr. Beaty smiled. "The man's no gentleman," she said, "and he can wait. He's always impatient. Annoying, really. Always complaining about my treatment of his kids."

"This afternoon," Leah said. "I muscled in on his time."

"You can muscle in on him anytime, anywhere, Leah, I promise you. No problem."

Leah shook her head in a scolding sort of way. Her hair was curly and as black and shiny as crow feathers. Iridescent almost. Blue black in certain light. Dr. Beaty still didn't believe it was a natural color. "You should work on being kinder, Priscilla," Leah said. "He looks like a nice man. A concerned father. Behave yourself."

Dr. Beaty laughed. She never took Leah seriously. Not when she said things like that. "I love your sandals," she said as the door opened. They had thin heels and gold straps curled artfully around Leah's toes accentuating light orange polish.

"Thanks. See you this afternoon." The door closed quietly, quickly, efficiently.

10

She'd kept Mr. Ryan waiting a full twenty-one minutes. She imagined him sitting uncomfortably in the uncomfortable waiting room chairs. The image was delightful. She hit the intercom button with her index finger. Her nail cracked. "Damn!" she said. She held it up to study the damage. Not too bad. Regrettable but fixable with Leah's help.

"Yes, Ma'am?"

"Send Mr. Ryan in. And I'd like coffee."

"And Mr. Ryan?"

She hesitated. But how else could she answer the question? "Okay. Yes. Offer him some, too."

The pair walked in together, Mr. Larry Ryan clad in a brownish-gray shirt and brown pants that resembled a uniform even though she was almost certain DHR security personnel didn't wear uniforms, and her secretary, Doris, who was holding only one cup of coffee. The girl was in her early twenties and was too thin and too pale and her hair was cut extraordinarily short. She almost always dressed in black. She was jumpy, uncomfortably subservient, and irritatingly high strung, as though a raised voice might send the coffee cup smashing to the floor. She rarely made eye contact and today was no exception. She placed the coffee on the desk near Dr. Beaty's right hand, sloshing it right up to the rim as she did so, smiled fleetingly in Mr. Ryan's direction and backed away. The door shut quietly behind her.

Dr. Beaty stared at him briefly before motioning toward a chair across from her. "Sit down," she said.

Mr. Larry Ryan stared also, ignoring her invitation. "I'm getting damn tired of our meetings," he said. He pulled the chair backward before sitting.

"Shall we cancel it then?" she asked. "This meeting is to help clear the air between us, Mr. Ryan, so we can both work toward the well-being of your son, or rather sons, but in this case, Sammy."

"We're not canceling anything after I took off work to be here," said Mr. Ryan. "And like I've said repeatedly, my sons do fine except when you're involved. They don't have problems anywhere else in town."

She started to stand, but remembered her slippers and her subsequent inability to walk toward the door. "It appears, Mr. Ryan, you may have nothing productive to say."

"Oh, I have plenty to say," he said leaning forward in his chair, "And, I don't plan to leave until we've come to some kind of agreement. It's damn absurd for my six year old son to be suspended for two school days for getting scared when Coach started yelling at his class. For God's sake, all he did was hide beneath the bleachers."

"According to Coach, Sammy refused to come out for the remainder of PE and as I understand it, didn't move until his kindergarten teacher came to pick up the class."

"He feels safe with her," he said.

"What values are you trying to instill in your child, Mr. Ryan? As his principal I see no value in rewarding cowardice or lack of respect for authority." She watched. His hands were tightening into muscled, red balls. There was a sickly yellow color around his knuckles. She'd been trained to watch for signs of impending violence at education workshops. But even at the workshops she'd thought it was a no-brainer. Who wouldn't interpret clenched fists as threatening? She nodded toward his right hand. "You apparently have a significant anger problem, Mr. Ryan. It presents itself in all of our meetings, and I will warn you now I will not tolerate angry outbursts in my school." She moved her hand, poising it over the intercom as back up.

He stared, a piercing look that stabbed into her pupils, made her want to close her eyes. Look away. She stared back. "I don't presume to know what goes on inside your home," she continued, "but I'm sure you're aware that all three of your school aged boys have problems with fear. With your first, it's fear of failure and consequent shutting down in the face of perceived challenges. The second, complaints of peers bullying him when others don't see the bullying take place at all, and subsequent attempts to hide in the nurse's office with somatic complaints. And now Sammy, refusing to come out from under the bleachers, even though no other child in his class had problems with Coach's tone of voice."

"You don't know that," Mr. Ryan said. "None of the others hid, that's all you know." His chin jutted forward significantly but he made a clear effort to unclench his fists. "And what goes on in my children's lives outside of this school is none of your damned business. But let me make this as clear as I can for you, I want Sammy back in class today by noon."

"I don't appreciate your language or your tone, Mr. Ryan. I've wondered. Perhaps problems with anger caused you to leave the force?"

The movement was liquid but defined. He lurched forward, checked himself, leaned back and sat stiffly upright in the chair, every muscle tensed, prepared to leap. She knew he wouldn't dare. "I repeat," he said too quietly. "I want Sammy back in class before noon."

"No." She shook her head adamantly. The movement jarred loose a sharp pain in her temple, her right temple immediately above her jaw. She blinked hard. It helped only momentarily. "Sammy will serve his full suspension, just like any other child. Hopefully he'll learn that hiding from problems is nonproductive. And that he must follow rules and the directions of authority. You're an ex-policeman, of all things. You certainly must recognize the importance of that."

Mr. Ryan's forehead visibly tightened, his eyes narrowed as he stood. "What *I* recognize is an insensitive, unqualified, control freak **bitch.**"

"Our meeting is over," she asserted, standing to punctuate her statement.

He loomed forward across the desk, blocked her view of the door with his body mass. He was in superb physical condition. She was sure he could bench press three hundred, easy. Years of experience taught her to puff up. Birds puffed their feathers, puffer fish morphed into spiked balls, cats, dogs, lizards. They all puffed. It was the sure way to answer threats. She squared her shoulders, filled her chest full of air, planted her slippered feet firmly against the linoleum and dug in with her heels.

"Damn!" She rocked quickly forward onto her toes.

"What the hell is that?" he asked, and she watched confusion move like thunderheads through his eyes. "Sounds like some kind of damn elephant tent in here."

She sat down like she'd been stabbed, but stared determinedly into his angry eyes. "My security alarm," she lied. It was feeble and she regretted saying it as soon as it came out of her mouth.

"Not hardly," he said. "Some weird dial tone you've downloaded most likely." Still she saw him glance toward the door, check for security. "I'd move my children if I could," he said icily, eyes still darting. "I've considered it. Just move them the hell out of your damn school zone. But, with five children and one salary, moving's out of the question. So since we can't move, you've got to go. And, you will, believe me."

"I would remind you, Mr. Ryan. Threats will result in my calling the police. And I can, you know, obtain an order against your coming onto school property in the future."

His eyes flickered. She thought she read uncertainty in them before he turned and stalked toward the door. "Don't **even** try to intimidate me," he responded forcefully. "You're a cream puff compared to what I've dealt with in my life. You'll see." The door slammed hard enough to shake the clock on the wall.

She leaned forward to pull off her slipper socks, careful as she pulled the houndstooth over her blister. It was sticking to the yarns, and it burned like a lit match was pressed to her skin. She laid her head on the desk, letting her cheek rest against the smooth, cool surface. Her eyes closed and she breathed deeply. Her right temple was filled with little jabbing pains. She frowned. The desk's smoothness was actually irritatingly disrupted by little nits of something, probably pencil eraser, and they distracted from her overall comfort. She lifted her head abruptly and brushed off her check. Only briefly did she allow herself images of Mr. Larry Ryan lurking in the dark outside her home, or outside her school, or worst of all, inside her house. With his law enforcement experience, he'd know ways to leave no trail. And he'd be an excellent shot. He was definitely the type to own a cache of guns. He'd be smart. He'd be patient. He'd be an exceptional stalker. "You'll see," his voice thundered across her brain. "You'll see."

She clenched her molars and chided herself for being so easily intimidated. She knew she hid her emotional cave-ins well. Even when she was a little girl and her mother fussed at her and fussed at her for things that all these years later still seemed inconsequential, she hid her feelings like a pro. And always her dad rode in on a white horse to protect her, treating her good, spoiling her unabashedly. That's the way she saw it then. Daddy's little girl. His precious little girl. She didn't know it was wrong. Not then. Their special secret, he always told her. Mama'd get so mad at her if she ever found out. 'I won't tell Daddy. Don't you tell either, okay?' And she didn't and he didn't and she never did until the night she told Thomas after her mother died of lung cancer and her dad of heart failure. Thomas cuddled her and stroked her hair that night and thanked her for telling him and said he'd always suspected something like that. And there were therapists who could help with such things. It was all a long time ago, another life ago. She swallowed hard.

But Larry Ryan should thank her. It was important to stand up to life. Not hide from it under gymnasium bleachers.

She held the grinning elephant socks, suspended them in front of her face, opened her drawer and pulled out the scissors. "Surgery time," she announced. She poked the blades into a heel. "Damn sound chips," she said. The elephants kept on smiling. Eleven-ten. She had twenty minutes before the Individualized Educational Plan meeting, IEP for short. Special planning for one of the school's numerous children diagnosed with psychopathology. In this case, she thought, probably correctly. She eased her feet into her shoes, tossed the computer chips in the trash, stuffed the slippers into her bottom drawer. The raw skin on top of her foot burned the second her shoe slid across it. But in some strange way, the blister pain stilled the pain in her head. Eleven-eleven. Nineteen minutes gave her ample time to try to contact Red.

11

Larry Ryan jerked open the door to his Escort and heaved his body into the driver's seat. He slammed the door, then slammed his palms down on the steering wheel. His anger scared him. This kind of anger. Despite anger management groups, despite learning all the cool-down techniques therapists could offer, despite all the successes he'd had over the years, he knew he could still lose control. In group therapy he'd called it "blacking out," and told about once finding his teenage pal's blood smeared all over his hands and seeing his friend's two jagged front teeth on the store's floor, all because the guy zapped him at the mall with a laser pointer. Lewis Pallinski, Jr. Just an idiot kid doing an idiot thing like kids have done for eons for a laugh. He'd paid impressively to fix Lewis' mouth. He could easily have gone to jail. Instead he lucked up, got Youthful Offender Status since he had good advocates and because he hadn't been in legal trouble before. Nineteen years old. Probation. Community service at the Salvation Army. And the incident, sealed in a juvenile court record, didn't prevent him from pursuing a career in law enforcement shortly thereafter. He had been a little less than candid about this aspect of his history during interviews, and to this day no one had any clue how close he sometimes came to the edge.

Deep breaths. Slow breaths. He turned the ignition key toward him and picked up in the middle of Sonata in G. He tried to distract himself by watching the older boys play basketball on the playground, presumably they were in PE class. The coach who'd caused Sammy such problems was nowhere to be seen. He'd asked Dr. Beaty to have Coach in their meeting but he didn't expect she'd accommodate his request. She'd try she'd said, but Coach was a busy man and someone had to supervise the children. He praised himself for leaving the meeting before bashing Dr. Beaty's head against her office wall. The impulse was there. Pick her up, smash her down with only one arm. He'd go to jail, he knew that, but watching horror flood into her eyes when she realized her perfect face was forever altered almost felt worth it. Except for his children. Saying their names over and over and over in his head was how he'd kept his cool. He leaned forward in his seat until his stomach wedged against the steering wheel, careful to avoid blowing the horn. His wallet was in his back pocket. In it, stuck between his Visa debit card and his car insurance verification card was the most recent formal photograph of his four sons and one daughter. Ten hopeful, perhaps even somewhat carefree now, eyes stared back at him. Looking at their photograph was the best way he knew to trust himself to act rationally, carefully. "But I'll still get her," he pledged to them. "I promise all of you, she'll regret screwing with our family."

He pulled his phone out of the glove compartment.

"Hello?"

"Hey."

"Hi, Larry. How'd the meeting go?"

"Bad. Sammy'll be with the other two for the rest of today and tomorrow. Okay?"

"Sure. We're up to our elbows in Play-Doh right now."

He imagined piles of red, blue, and yellow Play-Doh globbed all over the kitchen table. He'd always liked the smell of that stuff. "Good, see you around 5:30, then."

"Okay, I'll have all five of them bathed and fed for you."

"Thanks. You're the best." He flipped his phone closed and laid it on the seat beside his wallet. He started the car's engine and tried to psych himself up for sitting in the Department of Human Resource's lobby the remainder of the day. The office seemed dingy and germy to him, with poor lighting, nondescript furnishings, dreary walls and scuffed floors. The chairs were as inhospitable as those at the elementary school and were lined up in just the same way, side by side against the walls like those in a hospital emergency room. His task was to help provide a violence-free environment for the adults and children who came and went from meetings with their social workers throughout the day. His presence was usually enough to discourage real problems, but he dealt with his fair share of cursing, threatening and shouting.

It was a depressing job almost every day, but some days were better than others. Child abuse, child neglect, drug abuse, domestic violence, parental abandonment, plain-out poverty, "deadbeat dads," children and parents struggling to make sense out of having to live separated from one another, relatives and foster parents struggling to help children understand the same, these same guardians trying their best to cope with the behavioral problems that often resulted, and children bouncing from foster home to foster home, institution to institution in their determined efforts to return to sometimes deplorable conditions, their parents, their homes. And the social workers themselves, almost always overworked, some looking as exhausted and depressed and trapped and angry as their clients, propelled forward by idealistic, internal callings to help. Or by their own power bills. To change the world one child, one adult, one family at a time. It was one hell of an impressive concept. But it seemed a hell of a job.

And addictive. Because there were successes. He counted on them to remain positively focused. He knew everyone at DHR did. There were families who worked hard to solve problems so they could reunite, children without families who found adoptive ones, foster parents who could work magic, young parents who found support in overcoming domestic violence, drug addiction, and poverty. There were parenting skills classes, anger management classes, help with health care, help with mental health care, help with hunger and bills, help for teens in job skills and college and independent living. And there were some social workers who radiated hope, nonjudgmental effort, and boundless energy.

It was a harder job for him than police work had ever been. Ironic that the worst parts of police work turned out to be the voluminous paper work and all the days wasted testifying at court. They never showed that part accurately on television. TV cops were too busy with high speed chases and climbing chain link fences in hot pursuit to sit for hours filling out reports and forms and preparing for court. At least he thought as he pulled into a parking space in the DHR lot, his security job didn't require that.

12

Dr. Priscilla Beaty held the phone to her ear and again counted the rings. When she got to four the machine clicked to voice mail. She hung up and tried again. No luck. She imagined Red sitting at his desk staring at caller ID. He'd do that. She dialed one last time. When the generic computerized woman's voice message began, she tapped her fingers on her desk impatiently and sat up straighter. She was glad she was at work. When she was behind her office desk she felt more confident. She'd noticed that years ago. What the hell? She was going to leave him a message.

"Red, it's me. Check your e-mail."

She accessed the Internet and typed in her home password. Her screen popped up and she clicked on her address book and then, his name.

It's time for Andrew to know, Red. We need to meet. Civilly.

It was early October when he pulled her aside in a room full of people and told her he could no longer keep his hands, his mind, his tongue off her. She followed him to the Moon Winx where he paid for a full night even though they were there less than an hour. They met all fall, all winter, all spring at the Lodge, stealing time at night and on lazy weekend days, pumped by the adrenaline of secrecy. During the summer their meetings became more frequent, more comfortable, more regular, until her period was not.

She read through the message several times, pausing each time she came to the word, "Red." It was the name they adopted as lovers. Red for satin sheets he supplied to the maids when they made up the room. Red for rose petals he sometimes scattered across the traveler-weary floors. Red for the dozens of roses sitting weekend after weekend on the rooms' scratched veneer nightstands. Red for the edible underwear they both nibbled, giggling like teenagers. It tasted like strawberry licorice. And red for the color of his face the day she told him she was pregnant with his child. She clicked Send. He had a wife, he said, a career, a reputation to uphold. He'd pay to get rid of it. They could keep meeting if she did. No way she'd said. No matter what. No way. There'd been trysts since, whenever they bumped into one another and got carried away by the moment. But always afterward he vowed to her, he swore to God, it would never happen again.

Even now the scent of mimosas, the crescendo of cicadas shrill in the air, the way the night air wrapped around her, steamy and stifling, carried her back to red sheets in the worn room with red petals on the floor and red roses on the nightstand. On just such a night Andrew was conceived. And she'd find herself driving down University Boulevard deep into the belly of Alberta City. Past tattoo parlors, cash and title loan businesses, Mexican tiendas, and on past the shop Andrew and his buddies called the "A-rab Store." Then the police substation and the elementary school. Past Mexicans and others walking home after long days at work. Past persons she assumed were drug dealers, drug users, street walkers. Past children and their parents carrying brown paper bags and lumpy plastic bags of food and dollar store treasures. Past people picking up Chinese take out and driving through drive throughs. Past teenagers walking just to walk. Lovers meandering hand in hand.

'Restaurant,' the motel's faded sign still read although the adjoining Lamplighter Restaurant had burned to the ground decades earlier. 'Telephone. Air conditioned.' And the fluorescent yellow moon smiled as a reminder of a time no longer, a time before interstate travel bypassed its parking lot. And the fluorescent blue eye winked. A reminder of a time when Red was hers. When she was certain she'd met the love of her life.

The intercom jarred her. She blinked, took a shallow breath. "Yes?"

"Everyone's here for your eleven-thirty IEP meeting, Dr. Beaty."

She smoothed her hair's mirrored reflection with her hand. Another tiresome meeting. But at least she was somewhat fond of the child they'd be discussing. He was odd, like a dwarf robot in a sci fi made for T.V. movie. He had trouble making friends and interpreting the teachers' directions. But his math and science scores were off the top of the scales. He was a tremendous help in boosting the school's averages on national SATs. She studied her mirrored reflection, sucked in her stomach, glanced toward the bra hidden under her blouse and tailored suit. After the IEP it was time for Harry. She watched her lips curl. What did her mother always say about that smile? Priscilla! Priscilla, dear. Young lady, you're smiling like a Cheshire cat.

"Dr. Beaty?"

"Send them to the conference room," she directed. "I'll be there in a minute."

"Yes, Ma'am. Oh, and Dr. Greene said there are no changes in his schedule. He plans to see your dog during lunch."

"Thank you, Doris." She punched off the intercom button and shifted her weight irritably. Her right green shoe still hurt.

13

The boy named Benjamin Ball sat across from him, eyeing him, sizing him up. Reverend Jeremiah Lincoln was accustomed to that from kids. It seemed the boy was a good candidate for therapeutic foster care. He'd been watching Benjamin ever since he arrived at Metamorphosis. To some extent Jerry Lincoln kept his eye on all the adolescents at Metamorphosis, searching for ones he thought were good matches for his foster parents. A good match wasn't the whole secret for success but it was a start. This Benjamin fellow was quiet. Polite, well, as polite as adolescent boys usually were, anyway. He had discerning, intelligent eyes. And he was a damn fast runner. Be great in track.

The boy was still watching him. His long fingers with man-sized knuckles rested on the leather armrests of the chair. There was a hole that almost looked like a cigarette burn in the left armrest and a puff of dirty white stuffing showed through. Benjamin's thumb and index finger played with it, tugging it out a little further. They'd stopped at the snack machines on the way to the room. A chocolate and coconut candy bar and an unopened orange drink were propped in Benjamin's lap. He'd open them later, he'd said. He'd turn them in to cottage staff until he was ready to eat them. He promised.

"Benjamin," Reverend Lincoln began. "I understand from Dr. Bramson that he's spoken to you about moving into one of our foster homes sometime soon. Maybe this summer. That'd give you a clean start in school next year."

The boy's eyes narrowed. Green eyes. Really green, like a cat's. "Yes, sir."

"And perhaps you're aware that our church, not just my church here in town but our church statewide, trains families to be foster parents so that boys and girls can grow up in homes and do the things they might have always dreamed of doing, like going on vacations and playing sports and having a real bedroom of their own."

Benjamin's eyes narrowed further. Horizontal slits. "We do those things here, sir. And I have a bedroom already."

Jerry Lincoln smiled kindly. He was accustomed to nervousness when he talked about foster care. "Yes. I guess you do." He shifted positions. From the moment he sat down he recognized the chair as exceedingly uncomfortable. It was a mate to the one Benjamin occupied. The humped leather seats weren't shaped for human backsides. It was probably why the chairs were in this small visiting room. It wasn't one of the larger family rooms. More like an extra place to put people when there was an abundance of visitors. Even the pictures on the walls looked more thrift store than those in the rest of the building. One of a log cabin in a field of corn. The other of a catfish or bass pond. Across from them was an observation window, mirrored to prevent people in the room from seeing anyone who might be monitoring the visit from the other side of the window. It was a necessary supervisory precaution in a lot of family situations.

"I like it here," said Benjamin. "I don't want to leave."

Reverend Lincoln nodded slowly. "Yes," he said. "I can understand your reluctance to move. You haven't even been here very long. Less than a year, right?"

"About eleven months."

"And today's your birthday, I hear."

Benjamin's face brightened. "Yep."

"And you're having a party tonight."

"Yeah, you can come if you want."

Reverend Lincoln paused, smiled, leaned back trying to look comfortable. "Thank you," he said. "I'm, um, unfortunately, I've got obligations. But look. I'm not here to force you to go anywhere. But I feel good about you, Benjamin. I've had my eye on you. I think you'd be real happy, fit right in, to one of our homes."

Benjamin sat forward. "Which one?"

"Oh, I wasn't referring to one specifically. I mean I think you'd be happy in our program." He paused, framing his words carefully. "You'd have opportunities to grow up in a nice family who wanted to raise you. Who'd treat you like their son."

Benjamin smirked.

The boy was smirking. He hadn't expected it. "You look like you disagree."

"No, sir." Shrugging shoulders belied his words.

"What is it then? There's something. I can tell."

Benjamin leaned back against the leather. He cracked the knuckles of his left hand and started on his right before he stopped at his index finger and stared at Reverend Lincoln intensely. "Last year, I think it was summer, they had this stuff in the paper about foster care month."

"That's right. It's in May."

'Yeah, well, good happy foster parents doing good things for the world, taking in kids whose parents are on drugs, who abandoned their kids, whatever."

"Yes?"

"Yeah, well this one lady, she said her husband and her call their foster kids their children and don't think of them any different even though they've been thrown away by their parents. Thrown away, her words. Thrown away kids. Kids who don't have parents, the article said. A second chance at life."

"I see."

"It's bullshit. All of us kids here have parents. They might be screwed up. But we have parents."

Reverend Lincoln nodded. The boy was sharp. "I hope you wrote a letter to the editor to express your opinion."

Benjamin looked at the floor. He shrugged.

It was hard, Jerry Lincoln thought. So hard for them. "Look," he said gently. "Think about it for what it really is. Foster means to care for, to promote, to help, to nurture. So, foster parents take care of children until they can return to their birth parents. If they can. That's all. Simple as that."

Benjamin rolled his eyes. "You have kids?"

Jerry Lincoln hesitated. It was awkward. He didn't like sharing personal information, blurring the boundaries. "Yes, yes I do."

"Would you let a foster kid baby-sit them? Date them?"

The questions caught him off guard. Second class citizens, that was the point. Products of broken families. Damaged themselves. It was true. Some people thought like that. "Of course I would," said Reverend Lincoln but he heard his voice, hollow, unconvincing. "They'd be held to the same standards as everybody else. A person's character is the only measure of importance, Benjamin."

Benjamin shook his head, wrapped his hands around the orange drink and candy and stood up. "Yeah, sure. Thanks, Reverend Lincoln," he said. "Some of the other kids here want families bad."

Reverend Lincoln stood as well. "Take your time," he said. "Think about it. We'll talk again soon."

Benjamin opened the door. "May I go back to class now?" He smiled disarmingly. "Ms. Moffiti doesn't like us kids missing too much class."

14

Andrew unzipped his backpack and dumped his school stuff on his unmade bed. His crumpled black sheets swallowed paper clips and pencils in their folds. "Won't be needing any of this crap," he said aloud. He moved toward his dresser and pulled out his Game Boy, paused, then threw it into the backpack. Dunk shot. It was part of last year's Christmas, something he really wanted at the time and still enjoyed when he was bored. He rifled through his underwear drawer and pulled out eight games, all sports related, some with pretty fair graphics. Beneath the underwear he found an extra I-Pod never used, and an old cell phone with no sim. He dumped them in with the Game Boy. He moved toward his CD rack, yanked out hip hop, emo, heavy metal, r & b, punk. Out of date but still decent enough.

Hanging from the side of the rack was a key chain he'd gotten at Graceland in Memphis when he'd gone to see Elvis' home with Joey, his mother and one of his mother's boyfriends two summers ago. It was a clear plastic tube with a little Cadillac sealed inside that drove forward and backward, floated in some kind of water really, back and forth in its tiny world. Shag carpet on the ceiling and walls, the jungle room, glittery costumes behind glass, and later that night, swimming in the motel pool together until it closed at midnight, then going for an early breakfast of waffles and sausage at the truck stop next door. A few weeks later Joey headed off into the world of orange and blue, leaving him behind with their mother and Andrew couldn't imagine how he would survive. He unhooked the key chain and held it up, tilted it back and forth several times, tried to decide if it were worth selling. He threw it in the pack, stared at the little car as it drove toward his Game Boy, then fished it back out. He stuffed it in his pocket instead. He scanned his room for other things but there was nothing else he was willing to sell. He hurried toward his mother's room, the pack bumping his left shin as he walked.

Her Alabama clock. He studied the plastic figure in his crimson helmet, football tucked under his arm, a straight line lip painted on his face. The thought of selling it flickered across his mind. No, he'd smash it later. She'd notice immediately if it were missing. No drama today. He moved past her bed, his jeans brushing against the gold quilt embroidered in flowers and smothered in pillows embroidered the same. Probably made in a sweat shop in China or Mexico or India, but if it made her bed look good he knew she didn't care. At least they're earning money, she'd say when he accused her of supporting such enterprises. Lots of people in third world countries have no money, no jobs, nothing, *nada*. She always said it in her know-it-all voice. He stopped in front of her jewelry cabinet.

Was it fourth grade or was it third when he took a handful of bracelets to school and sold them for snack money? A pack of peanut butter cups, a bag of plain potato chips, and a pack of orange square crackers sandwiching paper thin peanut butter layers. And then the damn crackers were stale. He remembered the snacks exactly because he had to stare at them a long time, displayed as evidence on the principal's desk. Third, it was third, because Mrs. what was her name? Spalding. Mrs. Spalding. It scared him because Mrs. Spalding's soft and kind eyes at first registered confusion when she met with him and his mother in the office, but then turned piercing, daggers right through his skin, into his soul, or brain, or heart, but in any case, into his insides, and he remembered wanting to jump up and run like hell. Something about that stare. He hadn't touched her jewelry since.

He'd left the jewelry alone but had been grounded countless times for taking money, knick knacks, silver he didn't think his mother would miss, and once, last year, he took the car for a few hours to go to the mall. His skill at finding money she hid around the house was, how did she describe it to the new guy Harry not long ago on the phone? Uncanny. Uncanny to her but a no-brainer for him. A sign of higher intelligence, the way he stayed one or two steps ahead of her. Yesterday he pulled $250 from behind a framed picture of a loon floating peacefully across blue green water down their hallway toward their kitchen. It struck him as funny that after she realized the money was gone, she never thought to go back to see if he might stash contraband in the same hiding spot. She never found his cigarettes, nor anything else she was searching for, despite yelling and threatening and otherwise diligent efforts.

Her jewelry cabinet was an independent piece of furniture and had nine drawers and a top that opened upward where she kept more commonly worn pieces. If he were careful in what he chose she wouldn't know he'd taken anything, maybe for months, and even then she might think the piece was somewhere in the house. He opened one of the drawers toward the bottom, searching for jewelry that looked unfamiliar, pieces rarely worn. Eleven or twelve watches sprawled across purple velvet drawer lining. He recognized the purple velvet. Cut from a scrap of an emperor's robe she'd sewn when he was in an elementary school play. She'd always been a watch-a-maniac. He pulled out one with a shiny band and inspected it closely. Cubic zirconium probably. He draped it across his arm and grabbed one with a blue ceramic band and a moving moon face. Like a little grandfather clock. He stuck both in his pack and opened the next drawer up. Rings. She had six rings made with turquoise and silver. He picked two and moved upward. Bracelets. He pulled out three silver-looking bangles, thin ones, and searched on the inside of one. Sterling. He threw them in the pack. There was a thicker bracelet, maybe it was real gold, toward the back of the drawer lodged underneath four or five others. He pulled it out and searched for the hallmark. "Oh my God," he said, staring at the bracelet's inside markings, backing away from the cabinet toward her bed.

He sat on the corner of the gold quilt and read the inscription again. "*To my beautiful Prissy with everlasting love. Red.*" He threw it onto the carpet and picked up his heel to smash it, but his foot hung in the air. It was the only thing he had ever seen in the house from his father. The metal felt cool as he retrieved it. He stared at the inscription, wondering how long their affair had lasted, what else in the house might have come from him. He put the bracelet up to his face and cupped his hands around it, inhaling with closed eyes. His nostrils filled with a subtle metal smell. Nothing else. His mother refused to talk about his father except to say he lived in Tuscaloosa County and had a respectable job. He knew his father helped pay for the extras in his life, guitar lessons, summer camps, his school trip to Washington DC in eighth grade. *Prissy.* Would his mother ever allow anyone to call her Prissy? He couldn't imagine it. "*To my beautiful Prissy with everlasting love, Red.*" Was it? *Everlasting.* He knew his mother, how she was. Everlasting until she lost interest, hooked up with a new man. He slipped the bracelet into his pocket with the Graceland key chain, stood and carefully smoothed out the quilt.

He moved back to the jewelry. His hands scanned quickly, skillfully across the metals, stones and crystals as he went drawer to drawer, hungry for more pieces of his father. Nothing else obvious. There was a man's bulky college ring from the University of Washington and a silver locket about the size of a quarter that had a photo of a tall, broad shouldered man with brown hair, glasses, a full beard and a dusting of a mustache. The man was smiling at the camera and it was probably Spring somewhere because there were pink azaleas in the background. Just a few azalea blossoms, the rest were cut off when the picture was stuck into the pendant. The pendant didn't have a cover and Andrew wondered how many years the man had stared out into the dark drawer, abandoned and geeky. It couldn't be Red, he felt pretty sure. The guy's hair was brown and he looked too nerdy. But still. And the college ring. He had no idea who'd gone to the University of Washington. There was a florist's card stuck underneath the pendant and it had a small bluebird with a red heart in its mouth printed up in the corner. It was signed "Thomas." The script was awkward, with varying slant to the letters and different amounts of space between them. "*Priscilla,*" it said, "*please reconsider. Marry me.*"

"Oh my God!" he exclaimed, wondering if Joey knew his dad actually tried to marry her. Thomas! Why didn't she? Thomas was a good guy. But maybe this was a different Thomas. No. It looked like Thomas' writing. Clumsy with the two L's of Priscilla different heights and almost colliding with one another. He closed the drawers and dropped the college ring and the florist's card into his pocket with his other treasures. He stared at the pendant and photo again. They had the same broad shoulders. Their hair was sort of the same color. They were both tall. He heard his breath coming faster, almost synchronized with the clock's ticking as he worked to flick the photograph out of the pendant with his baby fingernail. The right side of the photo bent a little, dog eared with the prying. It buckled in the middle like a deflating ball before it gave way to the pressure. He turned it over and slanted it toward the morning light. The writing was precise, tiny rounded letters, a firm hand, almost old fashioned. It was written in pencil. **ve, Re.** "Oh, my God," whispered Andrew staring at the four letters and the comma, filling in what was missing. The writing was hardly slanted at all, straight up and down almost. The **e** was written almost as a printed letter but with more flair. The leg of the **R** had a long tail that extended below the others. He flipped the photo back over. The cheeks, the nose, the eyes, the chin. He couldn't see a resemblance. Weird. He didn't look at all like his mother either. But maybe he looked more like her than he looked like this guy. He looked at the man's hair again. The photograph might have faded some. He still couldn't make out any red in the picture at all. He used his pinky finger to shove the picture back into the pendant, smoothed the photo with his index finger and looked toward his mother's dresser. Tissues. He pulled one from the cardboard box with yellow and white daisies printed all over it. He wrapped the pendant then pushed it into his pocket with the rest of his collection before picking up his backpack. The room felt eerie. There was a presence hanging in the air, above his head, beside his arm, in the eyes of the plastic football player, in the pit of his stomach. He felt confused, a little giddy. *Always.* **Everlasting.** Everlasting. The words answered a question he had feared ever since he was old enough to understand such things. Even maybe before. Emotions flooded through him, a strangled sob erupted past his Adam's apple to meet tears streaming down his cheeks. Now he knew. Thank God he knew. He was not the product of a sperm meeting an egg after a one-night stand.

15

She was standing on the fringe of school property, her gaze searching the access road leading toward the school, and when she saw him approaching on his bike she waved with her trademark abandon. A laid-back kind of freedom like she was free falling or hang gliding or something. He'd never been able to adequately define it, and it drove him crazy at night when he couldn't sleep for thinking about her. He watched her smile grow broader as he approached, and then suddenly her eyes looked shyly toward the asphalt before returning to his face. "Don't look at my chin," she said. "I've got a zit."

He studied the pimple, a red, angry little mountain slightly below her bottom lip. "You're still the most beautiful girl I've ever seen," he said taking her hand. Her skin was warm, smooth, and without even looking he could tell she was still biting her fingernails. Short. Jagged. She was trying to stop she said. Even putting vinegar on them sometimes to remind herself not to chew. He told her he didn't give a care about her nails but he didn't want to kiss a vinegar mouth. They'd both laughed. He held her hand up toward his lips. She was wearing the friendship ring he gave her three weeks ago to celebrate their four month anniversary, a silver band with cut out hearts punched all around it. Size five. She had little fingers. "Wish I could kiss you," he said. He settled for kissing her hand.

She turned her body in a little circle, all 360 degrees. "Nobody's looking."

He smiled as she moved, watching her brown hair shimmer the way it did in shampoo commercials. The sun brought out subtle blond highlights. Lemon juice, she said. It made her hair blonder. He wanted to tell her about the bracelet, about how it felt to know his mother and father had been in a real relationship, but he knew he wouldn't. Maybe someday.

"No," he said. "No kissing." He smiled cynically. "My old pal Mr. Abernathy's probably squatting behind those bushes spying, just waiting to give you detention."

Her eyes widened. "I see him," she said nodding toward the evergreens. "Squatting down like you said. He's got something with him. Looks like binoculars."

He stared harder. "Where?"

She pulled their hands up to his chest and shoved him playfully. She laughed and he laughed but he felt stupid for believing her.

"Psych," she said. "But he did do something weird today. Tripped us all out for real."

He was afraid to take the bait. He waited.

"He had a slide show. Slides of himself and his friends. Pictures when they were our age. Older, too. He said something like when he was our age he didn't believe he'd really get old and have responsibilities and stuff and we all needed to take our schoolwork seriously and start thinking about what we're gonna do because before we know it we'll be old like him."

"He called himself old?"

"No. But he is. He looked like a geekazoid then, too. He had thick black glasses and sideburns and curly red hair."

Andrew's stomach churned. "Red?"

"Yeah. Totally freaked us out."

He swallowed hard. The cheese sandwich he'd had for breakfast. All of a sudden it felt stuck in his windpipe. He could feel his mother's gold bracelet in his front pocket as it pushed ever so lightly against his thigh. Red hair? He tried to remember how his mother acted at PTSO meetings when she and Mr. Abernathy were together. He couldn't remember. He'd never paid any attention. In a way, that was reassuring. When his mother was flirting it was like he had some kind of antennae equipped with radar. He hated it but he could be on the other side of the house or a quarter of a mile away in a park and sense when his mother was on the prowl. It was in her movements, in her laugh, in the way she used her eyes. But it might explain why old Iguana Man zeroed in on him the whole year in class. *Prissy. Everlasting love. Red.* Daddy Iguana Man. Oh God.

"And he looked so gay."

The lump of cheese toast in his throat seemed to melt. Of course! There'd been rumors around school forever. "Gay? He looked gay even then?"

"For real."

"But he had black glasses?"

"Yeah. You know, those thick plastic kind." She took a step closer. "Anyway, now I'm with you and not watching dumb slides of him."

She opened her purse and pulled out a bag of jalapeno potato chips. She unfolded the top. "I saved these," she said. She held the open end toward him and wiggled it playfully. "Your *favorite.*" He reached into the bag and came up with three. Salty. And the jalapeno burned his tongue and the insides of his cheeks in an oddly pleasant way.

She handed him the bag and he stuffed it in his shirt pocket. "Thanks," he said. She ate jalapeno potato chips all the time. It was the only snack she ever bought and now he was hooked too. Sometimes they gave him stomachaches.

*   *   *

In January when there was frost on the ground and mist on the river she'd quietly slipped up beside him on the grass right past the red roofed pavilion at Riverwalk and held out a bag of half eaten jalapeno chips. He'd actually stopped his bike there because of her, because he wanted to meet her but didn't know how. So he'd stopped at an historical marker near where she was standing with her dog and he pretended to read it. At first he was pretending but then he got sort of interested and so he didn't see her when she approached. You look hungry she'd said, and he told her he was but he didn't think he could eat jalapeno chips before breakfast. He'd seen her at the river in the morning once before and wondered about her. Both times she was alone except for a large silver gray dog on a navy blue leash. The dog's collar was navy, too. Although he'd never tell her regardless of how long they dated, it was the dog he'd noticed first. He'd never seen a silver dog before.

She was bundled up both mornings in a white down jacket with a hood and she was wearing camouflage patterned gloves. Her nose and cheeks were pink from the cold. Strands of brown hair poked from under her hood near her ears. He took his hand off his bicycle handlebars and removed his leather glove and took a chip from the bag just to keep her there. Well, maybe one, he'd said, or something like that. He didn't even like jalapeno chips back then but he ate it and mumbled something like thanks and he looked up the river because that's where she was looking.

It was the University of Alabama's female crew team, their long boat cutting a nearly rippleless path about half a mile upstream.

"I want to do that," she'd said. "When I go to the University, I'm going to do that." Her dog sat down and scratched a floppy ear with a hind foot. "It's so beautiful. Like poetry, or something."

He watched the boat and the oars rowing in unison and the mist rising around it and to him it looked more like a gargantuan water spider, the kind that walks on top of water using surface tension. "Hard work," he said, taking another chip to keep her talking. He liked her camo gloves.

"Yeah? Well, I'm a hard worker." She moved closer to the historical marker, closer to him. The dog moved forward with her and sniffed at the metal post. "I saw you out here the other day," she said. "You stopped your bike by that other marker up the hill. You were reading it."

He felt embarrassed. "Sort of nerdy," he said.

"I read them too," she said. "I've read them all. But I forget some of the stuff." She brushed a strand of hair out of her field of vision and squinted at the words. Her nose was getting pinker. The wind had picked up considerably. He re-read it because she was.

The Black Warrior River

Plied for thousands of years by Indians, then by early explorers and American settlers, this river extends 169 miles from the Sipsey and Mulberry Forks near Birmingham to its confluence with the Tombigbee at Demopolis. It drains 6228 square miles of one of the world's most ancient watersheds and has 130 species of fish and many rare plants and animals. Part of a navigable waterway system, this point is 339 river miles above Mobile. About 5 billion gallons of water flow past here each day. In the past it was designated as two rivers, the "Black Warrior" upstream and the "Warrior" downstream since Federal funds were appropriated on a per river basis. In the Choctaw language "Tuscaloosa" means Black Warrior.

"No way can five billion gallons of water flow past each day," she said. "Hardly looks like the river's moving. What's that bottle you have on your bike? A quart?"

He'd filled it up with orange juice before leaving home. "Yeah. Want some juice?"

She frowned. "No thanks. I can't wrap my brain around five billion anything."

"I bet it'll feel like five billion gallons when you get out there with an oar and try to row against the current," he said. God, she was sexy. Her body, even all wrapped up in the jacket like it was, was turning him on. Or was it her eyes? Or her way of just talking flat out about things? It wasn't something he readily admitted but intelligence turned him on. He'd had more than his share of boring phone conversations that went on and on for hours. *So what 'cha doing? Nothin'. What're you doin'? Nothin' much. My cat's tail's flopping all over my pillow. (Giggle). It keeps slapping me in the face. It's sleeping but its tail's flopping. Yeah, my dog's paws move sometimes when he sleeps. Probably dreaming. Chasin' a squirrel or something. Yeah, weird that animals dream. Yeah. Maybe my cat's dreaming. Yeah. So, what else ya' doin'?*

"I've never seen a silver dog before."

She ran her glove along the short fur. The dog stared up at her with intensity, and he felt startled. Greenish yellow eyes. Cats' eyes. He'd never seen a dog with cats' eyes before. It was wagging its short tail. The tail was clipped at about an inch or inch and a half.

"She has cat eyes," he said.

"She has Weimaraner eyes because that's what she is," she said. "Her name's Sterling. My dad bought her before he walked out on me and my mom."

He had no idea what to say. "Oh."

"For a younger woman, how predictable is that? A just out of grad school colleague. He's a professor at the University. Religious Studies."

He still had no idea what to say. "Oh."

"I'm Bethy."

"I'm Andrew."

"I'm fourteen. Well, almost fifteen. I come down here sometimes with my mom before school. She's jogging. Sometimes I run with her but it's not really my thing."

"I'm sixteen, just barely."

"Andrew or Andy?"

He shrugged. "Either, I guess. I like Andrew. Everybody calls me Andrew."

"I've never known an Andrew before. Sounds preppy."

"I'm not."

"Me either."

He took another chip and she did, too, and he knew right then, with the steady sound of traffic moving behind them along Jack Warner Parkway and with the crew team moving close enough to hear the punctuated directions of the coxswain pushing the boat forward like a well-oiled machine, with jalapeno pepper burning his esophagus and making his stomach queasy, and with his ungloved fingers growing redder and already numb from the cold, he was falling in love.

*   *   *

Bethy tugged on his arm, jerking him back to the edge of the Magnet school campus. "Hey, you okay? I didn't even sleep last night worrying about your meeting today at that place."

"Bethy, you can't tell anyone this. No one . . ."

Her face got a strange kind of color, like she'd been in a tanning bed. "You're running, aren't you? That's why I couldn't sleep. I was gonna text you but my battery was dead and the charger was in the kitchen and I knew Mom would have a fit if she caught me walking around the house in the middle of the night messing around with my phone."

"No way I'm going to any f'n treatment center." He stopped himself. "Oh, sorry." He was careful of his language around her. "Not to stay, I mean. I'll go today. I'll be with Joey. But, I'm leaving after that. Probably this afternoon after the meeting. Mom'll be at her boyfriend's. She's always there. She's the one with the f'n problem. Oh, sorry."

She shrugged at his apology. He didn't think it was his imagination. She was close to crying. "Where are you going?"

"I don't know for real. But, I do have a plan about hiding and I have money."

Her lips curled in on themselves. Tight. She stayed that way a long time or at least it seemed like it, her nose turning from pink to red and her eyes brimming. When she blinked, they'd drip. He was sure of it. "How will I see you?" she asked. Thank God she hadn't blinked.

"You will. I promise. And, I'll still have my phone. Mom won't cut it off. She never does. In case I need to call her. A real emergency or something."

She blinked. Tears made little water paths along each side of her nose, other paths near her ears. She wiped them away with the back of her hand. Her eyes. He'd written a song about her eyes. Gray. Astonishingly soft. Sometimes when she wore blue or there was lots of blue around, they looked more blue than gray. He still was working out the melody on his guitar. And he needed to think of two more words that rhymed with gray that didn't sound too contrived. It was going to be part of her birthday present next month.

"Don't run away," she said. "I have a plan. I'll act up and get sent to that Metamorphosis place, too. We'll do it together."

He took a step backward. "Not hardly. You stay in school and do good."

"But what about you? What about school?"

"I'll be truant, I guess."

Her jaw lifted. Tightened. "I just don't get it. Why is your mom doing this to you?"

He'd never really told her about his mother. About her craziness. He'd wanted to. And about his dad, too. He'd hinted about things but it was all too embarrassing. "Don't worry," he said. "I've got some pretty big surprises for her, too."

"Like what?"

"I don't know." He shrugged. "Surprises, that's all."

"The police'll be looking for you."

He shrugged again. "They've looked before. Never found me. I just show back up after mom's had time to think about how she's screwed up." Anger always came first, he was sure of it. And it morphed into worry, then guilt and actual fear he'd never come home. That he was sitting hungry in a gutter somewhere, or he'd been forced into prostitution by a bus station pimp, or he was lying naked and dead with multiple stab or gunshot wounds somewhere in the woods. That's when he usually returned. When she was truly scared. And for a night or two she wouldn't leave him alone in the house. A night or two and then it started all over again.

The first break bell rang. Two minutes until class. Andrew looked toward the red brick building.

"I can be late," she said. "It's okay."

He ran his hand along her arm. "No," he said. He fished around in his jeans pocket. The bracelet, the locket, the ring, he wrapped his fingers around the key chain and pulled it out. He closed her hand around it.

74

"Here. Keep this," he said. "It's from Graceland. You know, Elvis Presley's home. I got it on the last real trip I took with Joey."

Her hand unfolded slowly. She watched the little car move back and forth down the clear plastic tube. "I wish we were in there. Just you and me in that Cadillac. Going to the beach." The second school bell rang.

"We'll go one day, I promise. You and me. In a Cadillac."

She leaned forward, giggled. "You're crazy." Her lips were smooth and she pressed them hard against his and her warm, soft tongue pried gently through his lips and into his mouth. She tasted like cherry vanilla. He knew it was her lip gloss. The taste was odd, cherry vanilla and left-over jalapeno flavoring and salt. And he could feel her zit rubbing against his chin. He cut the kiss off. He had a bad feeling that Old Iguana Man was watching from his classroom window.

"You'll get detention," he said.

"Nobody's watching," she said.

"How much you wanna bet Mr. Abernathy is?" It was hard for him. The words were there, but they were stuck inside his head like they were Velcroed. "I love you so much," he said. There, he'd said it. He didn't say it often enough, he knew that. He turned and walked toward his bike without looking back. The kickstand snapped up, a metallic clicking sound. "Keep your phone charged," he said. "I'll come to see you but don't blow my cover."

"What cover?"

He laughed. "You'll see."

"I love you, Andrew."

He still had that weird taste in his mouth as he pedaled back toward Fifteenth.

16

Mr. Victor Abernathy squinted through the smudgy school window toward his student, Bethy Smithson. What was she doing? Who was she with? A tall boy with a bike. Obviously not from the school. Buying drugs? She was almost off school property. No, not drugs. Her body language gave it away. Flirting. A boyfriend of some sort, he was sure of it. It almost looked like Andrew Beaty but Andrew would be in class over at the high school. Unless he was cutting. Cutting would fit. Priscilla needed to keep a firmer hand on the boy. He'd told her that during a PTSO meeting last year. It offended her, he could tell, but it was the truth. He watched the boy reach out and take Bethy's hand. It had to be Andrew. It looked just like him. So that's who Bethy's heart doodles in the margins of her notebook were all about. She certainly drew a lot of them. Well, they were well matched in brains even if Andrew underachieved a preponderance of the time. He'd ridden the boy hard, sent him to the principal and out into the hall more times than he could count. Andrew'd been a smart ass, but the potential was there. Definitely college scholarship material if he'd just apply himself. That's what he'd told Priscilla. And always the impression the boy had a decent heart hidden under a heap of attitude.

Nobody would have guessed it. The boy was actually one of his favorites last year. It was no secret the Beatys had family problems. Anyone who'd grown up in Tuscaloosa with Dr. Priscilla Beaty could surmise that. Who'd have ever imagined she'd wind up principal of an elementary school? A little unnerving, really. Prickscilla was her name in the high school locker room. She was part of their coming of age. He'd had her, too. Twice. Looking back now he felt regret. Kids that age, at least kids back then, didn't have any idea. She needed help. Rumor in the community was that she still did. He remembered her as emotionally needy. Hungry for touch, attention, validation.

They made sort of a cute couple, Bethy and Andrew. Puppy love sorts of body language. He smiled. The boy was a pretty good artist, too. Drew a hellava picture of him as Iguana Man. He'd acted outraged in order to maintain propriety, set the limits, but it didn't really bother him a bit. He'd gotten over having a double chin. He'd gotten over being called gay. Lord knows you couldn't work with adolescents and not grow a skin at least as thick and tough as an iguana's. It went with the territory. The warning bell. He didn't have to turn around to know that students were filtering into his classroom. Noisy. Giggly. Whispery drama. Forget learning. It was all about their social lives. Tough years for even the most popular. He watched Bethy lean forward and kiss Andrew on the mouth. It almost looked like Andrew was discouraging her. He clearly wasn't encouraging her. Curious. A school infraction for Miss Bethy Smithson. Kissing on school grounds. And she was going to be late to class, too. Mr. Victor Abernathy smiled a second time. As far as he was concerned he hadn't seen a thing. She was a sweet girl. An eager student. Anyway, she'd surely turn out to be a good influence on the fellow. He might make it to college yet.

17

They lived on Dearing Place right off Queen City Avenue in the Dearing Municipal Historic District of Tuscaloosa. There was a little brown sign about a block from his house saying so. When he was younger most everybody he wanted to know lived in upscale subdivisions "across the river." He was probably still a kindergartener when he figured out that "across the river" was a euphemism for having what it took to be accepted. As he turned his key in the front door and took the stairs to his room two at a time, he reflected that his mother's choice of locations actually turned out to be good. He liked the history of the old neighborhood and he could bike almost anywhere in half an hour or less. He glanced at his bed, sheets crumpled, stuff scattered everywhere including that lost thumb tack. He flopped onto the floor and wiped the sweat off his face with his tee-shirt. Winx appeared at his door and wagged half-heartedly.

"Hey, boy," said Andrew. "I'm gonna miss you, believe it or not." Winx stretched out on a dirty green tee-shirt. Before his mother whisked the iguana, D-Tail, off to her school in the name of science education, Andrew rarely acknowledged the dog except to give him food and water. He took care of Winx mainly out of loyalty to Joey. He rolled onto his side, stretched his arm out to pet the dog's head, then pried his wallet out of his back jeans pocket. He pulled out the money, counting it again. Two hundred and seventy-three dollars. With the stuff he'd sell to Tony he'd probably top three forty, maybe three fifty. Not great but enough to get by until he figured out what to do next. He shoved the wallet back into his jeans.

The walnut-cased grandfather clock that had been such a bitch to help move into the house chimed, sounding full and lazy. He counted the bongs. Eleven . . . twelve. His mother reveled in finding special deals. It was a hobby of hers, and when he was younger he actually enjoyed getting up early and hitting garage sales and estate sales with her. He'd found some decent video games and almost all of his action figures that way. When Joey was around sometimes he'd go too, lugging home golf balls, tennis racquets, almost anything that had to do with sports.

Joey's dad, Thomas, was majorly into sports, and almost always included Andrew in planned activities with Joey. Most of the time Andrew declined. Sports never really did it for him. He wasn't very good at them for one thing. And it somehow felt wrong to be with his brother and his brother's dad and have no dad of his own.

Andrew groaned to a stand then moved around his bedroom quickly, throwing items into a pile on his bed. Black hair dye he bought yesterday at the drug store and temporarily stashed in his top drawer. Wire rimmed glasses he'd found at a local novelty store. A plain dark tie. Three button down, short sleeve white shirts from his closet. Two pairs of black dress pants. Three pairs of socks. Two undershirts. Three pairs of underwear. A pair of shorts. Dress shoes. He pulled a book from under his mattress and thumbed through it quickly. A sharp laugh erupted as he threw it on top of his shirts. Winx lifted his head, looked Andrew in the eye, put his head back down and closed his lids. His toothbrush and the other toiletry stuff were hidden beneath the sink. He'd collected them last night. He stood at the bedroom door and studied the collection. If he needed anything else he'd come back and get it while his mom was at work. He'd done that before. He picked up his backpack and made his way down to the kitchen to eat.

He remembered the first time he and Joey made freezer bag omelets. It was one of those pajama-lazy Saturdays and Joey's father dropped by. 'Hungry guys?' Thomas asked. They watched him fill three freezer bags with egg and milk mixture, add salt, pepper, cooked ham and cheese. They sealed up the bags and threw them into boiling water until the eggs were done. His mother walked into the kitchen just as Thomas was pulling the bags out of the water with tongs. Thomas offered half his eggs to her, and for a split second, their eyes met and she smiled. It always felt weird to Andrew to watch his mother and Thomas together, looking at each other's faces but never into each other's eyes. Walking past each other in tight spaces being very careful their bodies never touched. Polite words, formal sentences, arranging dates and times related to Joey without hint of emotion between them. Did they really have sex? Conceive Joey? Was his mother as careful not to make eye contact, not to allow physical contact, with his own father? Maybe the man had been in his life all along.

Andrew moved quickly around the kitchen throwing together an omelet in a quart sized storage bag. He turned a pot of water on to boil.

Salt. Pepper. Chili powder. Garlic. Butter. Thomas was a businessman who'd done well in the local real estate market, especially renting houses to University students. He was a tall, slender man with piercing brown eyes and a slight receding hairline. His hair was reddish brown, his mother joked that it was auburn, and until he was eight or nine Andrew regularly prayed that Thomas was the man his mother called Red. But then Thomas married the choir director of one of the local Methodist churches, Holly was her name, and they had three girls who adored their older half-brother. Joey often spent weekend nights with them growing up, and when he was gone Andrew usually sneaked outside into the park behind the house and sat beneath a massive pine, wondering if he had half-brothers, half-sisters, maybe even a stepmother of his own. The loblolly pine was taller and thicker now, an old friend, his confidant. Joey was the one who told him it was a loblolly. He said if he didn't grow up to be a veterinarian, he'd be a forester. Andrew said he didn't have any idea what he wanted to be. A rock star maybe. Even as he said it he knew it sounded lame. The egg steamed as he dumped it onto his plate, potholder in hand. A wisp of steam licked his baby finger and he dropped the potholder and put his finger in his mouth. Damn! Winx looked optimistically at the falling potholder, sniffed it and lost interest. He moved strategically toward Andrew's feet, positioning himself barely to the right of Andrew's chair just underneath the table.

18

His backpack sat crumpled, hidden sort of, against the pine's trunk behind him. In the center of the park far from the loblolly, several young children played in the splash pad fountain, squealing, laughing as they ran through vertical spray. Two vigilant females sat on benches nearby. Annette Shelby Park, its perimeter framed by a black metal fence that had taken Andrew about two weeks to learn to scale from his back yard without bruises or cuts, was a relatively new addition to the neighborhood. For most of his life the land had been the playground for Stafford Elementary School, a one story, ramshackle red brick building. He'd grown up swinging on its rusty-chained swings and climbing on the sliding board, its shiny metal chute worn by years of children's bottoms and dented by shoes and rough play. Joey, and sometimes Thomas, too, would stop there to let him play before racing him along a children's footpath to the back of the school where there were basketball courts in need of repainting and rims without netting. Joey was agile like his father and good at the game. Andrew tried to emulate them, tried to listen to their constructive comments, but after a while he generally drifted away from the court to play on the square balance beams and a couple of other obstacle course stations that were nestled among weeds and fire ant hills. The school and its playground were gone now, as were Andrew's dreams that he would ever be good at basketball.

He'd brought his basketball with him though and as he watched Tony approach, he rolled it back and forth on the ground between his propped up knees. The ball was part of their cover, an alibi in case the eyes of Neighborhood Watch or other concerned citizens witnessed their meeting. Even though the loblolly was a fair distance from the splash pad and a safe distance from the street, Queen City Avenue was one of the major routes into downtown, well traveled by police. Andrew knew it was crazy but he imagined curious, beady eyes peering from the windows of the seven homes facing the park, the houses on the other side of the Avenue. His mother once told him they were bungalow style homes built in the 1920's and 30's. She said their own house was built around the same time. When he was younger he sat in the park against the loblolly for hours, imagining ghosts dressed in historic clothing floating in and out of the bungalows' walls, walking ghost dogs down the sidewalk, and once, he could have sworn he saw a man in a dapper cap driving a Model T Ford. The man took his cap off and waved it in the air as he passed two old ladies floating down the sidewalk dressed like they were coming from church.

But this time the ghost was real. Tony was a gangbanger, called a "ghost" by some of the kids at school because he was white. Andrew didn't know a lot about him. Just whispers, innuendos. Everyone understood. Keep out of Tony's business. If you hear anything keep your mouth shut. But he'd heard some stuff. That he'd dropped out of school almost two years ago, then got arrested for fencing stuff. That he'd been sent to Mt. Meigs, Alabama's 'juvie prison' somewhere down near Montgomery, and while he was there he finished his GED. Andrew knew this last part because Tony was all the time bragging that getting his GED earned him a faster ticket out. Tony had an eyebrow ring and always wore muscle shirts so his tattooed arms showed. Except he called the shirts 'wife beaters' the way tougher kids did. He had the arms and chest of a lifter, and his chest, what Andrew could see of it, was hairy and decorated with a thick gold chain. A heavy metal cross hung from the chain, which piqued Andrew's curiosity. But he never asked questions and he never told Tony anything, either. Friends of friends said Tony ran a fencing operation again, much bigger than before he went to Meigs. That he had stuff stashed all over town. That his cousin in Chicago got rid of it for him. Different homeboys drove the stuff north to keep the cops clueless. He'd also heard rumors that Tony was the one who knifed a convenience store clerk a year earlier in Northport, the city next to Tuscaloosa, leaving her for dead inside the store's beer cooler.

Tony swung his foot out and around and kicked the basketball. It flew about ten feet into the air and came down for its first bounce around four feet away. "What's with the B-ball?" he asked.

Andrew was glad he'd moved his legs fast. Tony's foot almost clipped his kneecap. The ball slowed, hopped little grass humps. The whole thing pissed him off but he shrugged, careful to display no emotion. "Makes us look legit," he said. "If anyone's watching, I mean." He leaned forward and pulled the backpack out from behind him.

"Yeah. Whatever." Tony stooped and unzipped it. He dumped the contents onto the ground and picked through the items with his left hand. Andrew saw a long pinkish scar that ran from Tony's thumb up his wrist halfway to his elbow. "Just the two rings?"

"Yeah, man."

"Well, the turquoise's good, anyway. I'll take the watches and bracelets, too. No gold?"

"Nothin' that's not here," Andrew said, fighting the urge to reach into his pocket to reassure himself the *Everlasting* bracelet was still there. Safe.

"So, you running?"

Andrew looked toward Tony's face but not into it, his stomach churning. Tony was still studying the stuff in the dirt. Andrew forced a casual glance toward the basketball. It had stopped about nine feet from them. "Not sure," he said. He shrugged one shoulder for emphasis.

"Yeah, well, Metamorphosis's no Meigs."

Andrew sucked in air, choked on phlegm. Damn. He hocked a loogie, tried to clear his throat. How the hell did Tony know? "What d'ya mean?"

Tony chuckled, more to himself. "I mean it's like summer camp. A place for pussies. Got little painted caterpillars all over the walls." He ran his hand through the pile of stuff and stood. Andrew concentrated on staring at the toe of the black boot facing him. The leather was scuffed so there was an uneven patch of brown and beige on top. He could feel Tony leering down at him, heavy like having the boot pressing down his shoulder. "You gotta know I have homeboys there and at the group home and at Brewer-Porch, too," he said. "I got people all over this town." Andrew was familiar with Brewer-Porch Children's Center. When he was younger his mother drove him down the curvy, hilly blacktop road that wound through the woods to Tuscaloosa's other residential treatment center. Three, maybe even four times. It was, the white sign with crimson writing announced, part of the University of Alabama. It was next to the grounds of the V.A. Hospital and behind the old University of Alabama golf course and arboretum. *"I swear to God, Andrew,"* she shrieked like a badly cast cartoon witch, *"I swear to God. I'll drop you off on their doorstep if you don't straighten up NOW."* Go ahead, he told her. Because he knew she wouldn't.

"I'll take everything except the B-ball," Tony said, unzipping his own backpack, dropping it to the ground. Andrew shoveled in the CDs and jewelry and video games. Out of the corner of his eye he saw Tony reach down and pick up something and stick it in his back pocket. He had no idea what. A fifty dollar bill fluttered from above and landed beside Andrew's foot.

"'K," said Andrew. Ripped off. All that stuff. He palmed the money, slung his empty backpack over his shoulder and stood. He stared at the basketball.

"Hey man, about your mom. A thousand . . . she's gone. Off your back. Permanently."

For the first time in the two and a half years since they'd met, Andrew looked squarely, boldly, into the emotionless brown eyes of the gangbanger.

19

Finally. Lunch time. Molly time. Shelby watched Luke and Addie greet each other at the picnic table across from the gymnasium. He picked her up playfully, kissed her forehead, swung her back down. Addie threw her head back, laughed and swatted his bicep. Their hands fell toward one another and entwined. It appeared reflexive, no more complicated than breathing. Addie said something to him. He said something back. Addie had lots of personality and she was Mensa smart. But when Shelby first met her she was surprised because Adelaide, call me Addie she always said with a sparkling smile, was almost unattractive. Shelby wasn't sure why she expected Luke to have married a beauty, and even though she knew this wasn't reasonable or relevant, she still found it curious. Sexist, she called herself whenever these thoughts came to mind. Superficial. Small-minded. She watched Luke open a white paper bag and remove what looked like a cardboard container as she pushed her remote unlock. The driver door button popped up. A wave of envy washed through her.

The tears that followed surprised her. She got into the car quickly so no one would see. The whole meeting about Andrew had shaken her. Even though Shelby didn't know Dr. Beaty she felt empathy for her. Sometimes there just wasn't any clear way to make things okay for children. What could she ever tell Molly about Steve that would make any sense? Somehow despite all of her therapeutic skills, despite all of her training, she'd made a terrible mistake choosing a father for her little girl. It was a mistake even more blaring than the poor choices most of Shelby's adolescent clients made choosing boyfriends. She had believed in Steve, believed in love, let him sweep her right off her feet into the bedroom, blind to his major character flaws. Somehow. This still awakened her at three-thirty too many mornings, her mind lying as tangled on her pillow as her hair. And always there remained the same basic question although the packaging of it differed. How could she ever justify thinking she could help others if she couldn't even identify a sociopath sharing her bed?

It was hot in the car. She started the engine. The digital clock nagged her, reminded her she had only fifty minutes before lunch break ended. She rubbed her palms across her cheeks and tasted salt at the corner of her mouth on the left side, then backed out of the parking space. When she passed Addie and Luke she smiled and waved. Out of her rear view mirror she saw Addie waving back before Luke regained his wife's attention, crumpling up the white bag, tossing it playfully into her lap.

*   *   *

He looked forward to days when Addie had time to pick up lunch and picnic with him on the grounds. Her sense of humor was infectious and almost as warped as his.

"So, how's the detective business this morning?" he asked after settling on the bench. He pulled the paper away from a fish taco, medium heat, extra lettuce and tomatoes with banana peppers on the side. She was young to be a detective, especially being a woman, and he had no idea how she'd done it. For all practical purposes law enforcement was still a man's world. But there she was, Detective Adelaide Joanna Bramson, Addie for short, and he was convinced she met more weirdoes, psychopaths, personality disordered and manic people in a month than he'd meet in a lifetime of psychology.

"Great!" she said climbing on top of the table, hugging her knees to her chest. She'd ordered a grilled chicken taco salad and had opened the clear plastic top already. Extra hot salsa, a little grated cheese, hold the sour cream, add jalapenos. A container of banana peppers sat beside it. "Want my peppers?"

"You don't?"

"Maybe just a few."

He picked up the container, removed the top, dumped several on her salad and the rest on his pepper pile. A yellow jacket honed in on his taco. He swatted it away unsuccessfully. He swatted again. "Gosh!" he said. "What is it with the yellow jackets this year?"

"Got me," she said. "It's early for them but they're everywhere. Maybe because of the honeybee shortage." She pulled the paper away from a square pack labeled extra hot sauce, licked its aluminum backing and dumped the contents onto her salad. "It's actually been frenetic this morning," she said. "There was another bomb threat at the Department of Human Resources. We brought in the dogs, another false alarm. That's the fifth one in two months. I thought maybe we were done with them. Hadn't had one in a while. It's so frustrating . . . the prime suspects just aren't panning out."

"Kids here pull the fire alarm to get out of class. One of my college roommates did it just to see girls pour out of their dorms in nightgowns and underwear, or lack thereof. Maybe you're looking at a disgruntled employee who wants a longer coffee break or something."

"A DHR worker willing to risk the charge of making a terrorist threat? Maybe, but I have my doubts. I'm still looking for a pattern. I'm missing something."

"Well thank goodness there're no real bombs so far."

"No lie," she said balancing a cherry tomato and a clump of lettuce on her plastic fork and steering it toward her mouth. "And then I've got that Tony kid. The one who's worn out the State's entire juvenile justice system. We've had him under surveillance for almost three months and undercover's still trying to figure out where he's fencing his stuff. Word on the street is he's got a major business venture going. In the past he unloaded merchandise locally but he's not biting at our offers to buy or sell. He was observed this morning at a park with some unidentified juvenile." She waved a fly away from her salad. "But that's not even the tip of the iceberg with him. In the last two weeks we've gotten three anonymous calls through Crime Stoppers that he's trying to set up some kind of murder for hire service around here. Using gang neophytes, I'm sure."

Luke put down his taco and stared at his wife. "That's getting a little freaky, Addie." Tuscaloosa had some gangs and gang violence. Anyone who worked with adolescents knew that. These days anywhere and everywhere did. But homicide was almost always attributed to crimes of passion and still took front page lead in the Tuscaloosa News. It didn't happen every day. Not even every week. Sometimes not even every month.

"You betcha," she said. "The theft ring's small potatoes in comparison. I suspect one day soon he'll feel right at home in Holman."

"Prison does sound likely. But I'm serious, honey, watch your back."

"You can be sure I prefer my back without bullets in it." She laughed softly. "And then there was a wreck down on Jack Warner Parkway this morning. Rubberneckers trying to watch a pretty bizarre wedding ran into each other. The story'll be on the local news tonight, I'm sure. I saw the WVUA cameras there."

"They asked you to cover a wreck?"

Addie laughed. "No, not really. But I got curious. Apparently the couple met through the kayaking club. So there they were, the bride in a white bathing suit with pearls sewn all over it, a veil and a garter, and the groom wearing a black bathing suit with a bow tie around his neck and a top hat. Wedding party dressed pretty much the same way except for the minister. All the kayaks decorated with mums and roses. Handel's water music playing from that pavilion with the red roof. Afterwards they all paddled off toward the reception at one of the riverfront restaurants, I think."

Luke laughed. "That's pretty wild," he said. "Bad wreck?"

"Four car pile-up, fender-bender stuff."

They both laughed. "I went into psychology because obviously it'll never be boring," he said. "But it pisses me off your job's a hell of a lot more exciting than mine." He leaned forward and up since she was still sitting on the table and kissed the tip of her nose. He loved her nose. It was a long, aquiline, sophisticated nose. He knew it was too weird to admit many places but he'd always had a thing for noses. They were such unique appendages. He first started noticing them, studying them, when he was about eight or nine. He kept trying to draw them on his cartoon characters. It wasn't easy to draw a good nose. "I love your nose," he said, like it was the very first time he'd said that when it was really closer to the four hundredth.

"You're crazy," she laughed. "Been in the business too long. You know that, don't you?"

He tickled her leg with pine straw. Her salad, balanced on her lap, tilted toward the right. She almost dumped the remaining lettuce. He laid a hand on her knee and left it there. "Addie, speaking of jobs and business. I had an intriguing meeting with Dr. Lydia today, but this is totally confidential."

Her plastic fork and a jalapeno pepper poised in midair. "What about?"

"Basically she wants to name me in her will as the clinical guardian of the Center upon her death or departure, I guess. She said her lawyers have suggested she name someone who'll commit to ten years at the helm at least."

"You're joking."

"That's what I thought. From the way I understand it, the Center's assets will be placed in a trust."

"Interesting," she said, guiding the pepper slowly toward her mouth. "How do you feel about it?"

"I don't know. A ten year commitment might be a real burden on us. But she suggested the salary'll be exceptional. And it might be a great step up the ladder. We'll need more details. In some ways it could be really good, in some ways, not so good."

She reached her free hand toward his and squeezed his big fingers. "That's an amazing offer regardless of what you decide to do with it."

"What we decide."

She laughed her infectious laugh and tossed a pine cone in his direction. It had been dropped on the table by a squirrel no doubt, gnawed like a half eaten ear of corn. "Where your kayak goes, I will paddle." It was not a submissive thing. It was the part of their wedding vows she valued most. Unwavering support for each other's life goals and dreams and accomplishments.

"Missed," he said.

"I must be slipping." She dug into her purse and pulled out the bag of Animal Crackers. "Want one?"

"Sure." He picked out a monkey and danced it in the air in front of her face. "Let's split this joint and go monkey around," he said wiggling his eyebrows up and down.

"Damn, you're corny."

"You almost got the consonant right."

She rolled her eyes and consumed three or four animals before he glanced at his watch. "What time do you think you'll be home?" he asked.

She stretched her arms behind her, arching her back, poking out her chest, face soaking up the sun. He felt certain there were children watching somewhere. He practiced restraint. "Probably on into the evening," she said. "It's almost a full moon, you know. Crazy things happen in the world of crime and psychology when the moon is pulling on cerebral fluids."

He laughed. "I don't think the full moon theory has been supported definitively by research." He covered her hand with his, squeezed it affectionately. "Well, I'd better get inside. We have a pre-placement this afternoon and a birthday party after the kids eat dinner. Then hopefully I'll be home."

"How's Shelby?"

"Good, I think. Well, I say good, but today's meeting seemed to upset her for some reason. I don't really know. She keeps her personal life extremely private."

"Well, tell her and Dr. Lydia hi."

He kissed the tip of her nose again.

"Dr. Bramson, your nose fixation is diagnosable."

"Only for your sexy nose," he said, watching her swing her body around and hop off the table. "Love you, baby. Be safe. Take the bomb threats seriously and be careful of that Tony kid. Thanks for lunch."

She squeezed his waist. "Don't eat too much birthday cake. We're having microwave meatloaf for dinner."

"Yum." He picked up their trash and headed for the rusting metal can mounted on an unpainted wood post. One thing for certain. It was a good thing her nose was deliciously sexy because her cooking skills definitely were not.

20

He didn't recognize the number. It came up Private on his caller ID. Usually he avoided calls he couldn't identify but today he impulsively hit the talk button.

"This is Reverend Jeremiah Lincoln," he said squinting toward the convenience store, in through the darkened window plastered with advertisements. He'd stopped to buy something to drink. Caffeine. His body was screaming for it after the three Metamorphosis meetings. Stressful as hell. Sad, too. He didn't know how the Metamorphosis staff did it everyday. Thank God he had four months before his next pre-admission records rotation.

"Reverend Lincoln?"

"Yes?"

"This is Irma Myloh from the Probation Office." Had to be her mobile phone. The ID would have caught the Probation Office. Irma. They'd talked before. She sent him young lawbreakers. Part of a church project, really a multi-church, multi-denomination project. CHANGE it was called, but he couldn't remember exactly what the letters stood for. Something like Children Have Answers: Need Guiding Education. Bored bureaucrats and passionate do-gooders were always coming up with cutesy anagrams like that. The program was born out of a brainstorming session of concerned citizens about four years earlier. It offered juvenile criminals a chance to make money legitimately. He hired them for yard work around the church grounds. Hard work, decent pay, experiences to teach young offenders how to be successful walking the straight and narrow. "Yes, hello Irma." He paused expectantly.

"I have one for you if you can take him. A hard core kid, nineteen, gang affiliated. Slick, so you need to keep your eyes open. Previously been involved in serious theft, fencing rings, that kind of thing. He's been through all the major Department of Youth Services programs. Can be aggressive and he's a charmer around girls, but mainly I'd lock the church doors if he's helping you around the grounds." There was a noticeable pause. "I'd keep him outside at all times."

Jerry Lincoln scrunched up his face. He wished he hadn't answered the phone. Some kids honestly didn't want to be rehabilitated. Thought they were smarter than their PO's and their therapists. Thumbed their noses behind their 'yes, ma'ams' and 'yes, sirs' and played the systems to their advantage. It didn't take a sociology doctorate to figure it out. Anyway, the money they earned in honest endeavors was pigeon droppings compared to one good night on the streets. "All right, Irma. I'll put him to work cutting grass if nothing else."

"Good deal. He's in the waiting room now with his grandmother, a Mrs. Rebeka Arrington. I get the impression she works hard trying to keep him straight. Seems like he's kept his nose cleaner for the past several months and he was successful in getting his GED while at Mt. Meigs. So there is some promise there. I'm eager for him to get started, Reverend Lincoln. When can I send him by?"

Jerry Lincoln shrugged even though there was no one around. "I don't know . . . Um, give me an hour. Tell him to meet me out in front of the chapel. I'll be watching for him."

"Okay, let me bring them back in here and make sure that'll work for them." He heard the receiver meet the wood of her desk. He heard the door open, muffled talking in the background. A crinkly muffled voice, female. A louder voice, male. Irma's voice, assertive but muffled as well. He imagined her hand over the mouthpiece. He'd never seen her hand and he wondered what it looked like. He imagined Irma was dumpy-looking. He had no idea why. Maybe it was the name. Discussion back and forth. "Okay, he says he can be there, one forty-five sharp. His grandmother will drop him off on her way back to work. She's on her lunch hour. And thanks, Reverend Lincoln, for your participation in our program."

"Sure thing." He ended the call and leaned back in the tan seat. He had his hand on the door handle but his seat belt still on. To be honest he'd always found excellent uses for the CHANGE kids despite what he saw as major flaws in the program. And he had a way with the kids. Their probation officers didn't ever know the half of it. It didn't take long for them to get to bragging around him about their exploits. He was blessed with the skills to help people open up quickly, bare their hearts so to speak. That, and probably his assurance he'd hold what they said in the strictest confidence, regardless of what they told him. He was a man of the cloth, gathering lost sheep no matter how far they'd strayed, after all.

*   *   *

He unbuckled and unfolded his body from his Prius. A little green Chevy, paint faded around the front bumper and door dented on the right side, pulled in across from him. Missing a back hub cap, too. Shelby. Shelby McDonald, pert and efficient. The parking lot was stained with car fluids. He stepped over a rainbow of oil near the gas pump.

"Shelby, hello again."

"Oh, hi, Reverend Lincoln." She didn't feel comfortable calling him that, it seemed too formal, but she didn't like calling him Jerry, either. Reverend Jerry, maybe. She smiled at the thought. "So you've finished the records meetings?"

"Just a short while ago actually. Stopped by to grab some caffeine." He chuckled. "Get my blood moving again."

He was standing in her space. Personal space that she taught all her kids at Metamorphosis to recognize and respect. Stick your arm out straight. Always stand the length of your outstretched arm away from other people.

"I think the Beaty referral was the most complicated of the group that we looked at this morning," he said. "The mother'll be the issue, I think. I remember her as pretty hard-headed and egocentric when she attended our church, God forgive my sounding judgmental."

Shelby swatted at a skinny yellow and black wasp that was exploring the area around her head. It had apparently taken the wrong flight pattern from the nearby garbage can. The can was blue and had a white plastic liner and was filled with cola bottles, cigarette butts, and snack papers. It smelled like there was a diaper in there, too. She moved back a step and looked around. No one else was in the parking lot to overhear their conversation. "Hopefully she'll feel comfortable with Luke and me. A lot of our parents seem to settle in pretty well with the program."

He matched her step backward with a step forward. "Pardon my observational skills and I trust you won't think this out of line, but you seemed somewhat discombobulated today." He looked down at her with a fatherly, inquisitive smile.

Damn, where was her poker face? And he looked so pleased, so prideful of his perception. It was written in his laser corrected eyes, he always talked about the miracles of modern ophthalmology, and in the little smirky upturn of his lips and even in the blue blood pulsing a little harder through the vein in his forehead. She felt seriously irritated with him. With herself. "Not really," she said. "I've got some things on my mind, but don't we all?"

He moved forward again, this time covering a little less distance, and his gaze traveled, she felt certain she wasn't imagining it, traveled from her face to her breasts to her thighs and back up again. Slowly. And still the smirky lips. "Well," he said. "If you ever need an ear, I'm happy to listen. We helpers sometimes need listeners, too. You know my church is right down the road."

Coming on to her? Was he? Probably older than her dad and married and a minister too. "Thanks but I just stopped to get orange juice to take home for Molly tonight. I should already be back at work." Mommy, bring orange juice home please. Mommy, don't go back to work. Mommy, I love you. Bye bye, Mommy. The fresh smell of no tears shampoo lingered even after she gave her child a final bear hug, a kiss on her cheek, and put her down on the floor beside her plastic zoo train.

"Okay, well, the offer stands." The smirky grin seemed even more pronounced. "As ministers we're sensitive to the issues of damsels in distress."

Damsels in distress. What a chauvinist. "Yeah," she said. "I'll keep that in mind when I'm reading to Molly. Damsels in distress and rescuing princes. Fairy tales, they're called."

It was like she'd slapped him across the face. She could see it in his eyes. Confusion about how to respond. "I didn't mean to intrude," he said, spider veins on his cheeks reddening, blue vein in his forehead pulsing, back straightening. "Nor to insult. I merely was offering the hand of a friend. I admire you. You're a single mom, I believe?" He was blocking her way into the store.

"Yes."

"And surrogate mom to the kids in both Luna cottages."

"No, therapist to them."

"That's a heavy load."

He was fishing. So damned obvious. Prickly warmth climbed her neck into her cheeks. "I do need to get back to my office," she said. "And I remember you have a wedding rehearsal and a funeral today so I'm sure you do as well."

"Oh, sure," he said. He stepped slowly out of her way. "You know, my mom raised me and my brother by herself. It was tough but we made it. Lots of folks make it, even when life's grueling. For example, that Beaty boy today. He'll be okay if he can settle down and not look for excuses for his behaviors. Like I said in the meeting, lots of kids grow up without one parent or the other. Especially these days. I'm not sure I've ever told you but my dad died of a heart attack when I was two. And I think I grew up to be an okay dad, even without his role model. I've got five kids. The oldest one's finishing high school this year. Youngest one's graduating from elementary."

She found odd comfort in his words. It was fruitless. Silly. Irrational. She knew it, but she was always, always searching for reassurance that Molly would be okay without Steve. Better off never knowing him. But still. Still it felt good to be offered reassurance. "Everyone experiences events differently," she said quietly, "as you know. And, I'd think a father's death, as difficult as that surely was, might feel different from knowing your father never claimed you and promises to reject you, as in the Beaty case."

He swatted at a yellow jacket circling his head. Maybe the same one she'd chased away earlier. She watched it crawl near his neck just along his shirt line. "These yellow jackets are damned annoying," he said, deciding not to follow her into the store, to forego the caffeine. "They're everywhere this year. There's a nest of them somewhere behind the church, saw them coming out of a hole in the ground just yesterday. Got to get the exterminator out before Sunday."

She thought about agreeing, saying that in fact all the bugs were worse this year. There were fire ants and mosquitoes and ticks everywhere. She'd put fire ant bait in her garden just yesterday. It made no sense. Winter had been colder than usual. She shifted her weight and he read her body language. Impatient. Irritated.

"Well, I'm heading on to the church before one of us gets stung," he said. He nodded toward the dented can. It was rusty toward the bottom. "Looks like a whole swarm of the critters in that trash there."

"They're always attracted to sugar," she said.

"You're right about my busy afternoon, and it just got busier because of a CHANGE referral. Just wanted to check on you. I was concerned." He winked. "If you change your mind, just remember I can loan you an ear."

She started to say she had two of her own but censored herself. In any case his ears were big, red, misshapen, with hairs growing out of the lobes. She sure as heck would never borrow one. She laughed loudly as she walked toward the store.

Mommy, don't go. Molly's hair draped across her cheek and she'd closed her eyes as they hugged. I don't want to, Mol. All I want is to sit on the floor and watch you push your red train around on its track and help you color that bear purple and yellow and watch you grow. What a big girl you are, coloring inside the lines so well. And, only you would color a bear purple and yellow. What a good imagination you have! Steve was artistic. She was athletic. Steve was whimsical. She was logical, down to earth. Steve was impulsive. She made lists. Between them they'd had a daughter who colored the bear purple and yellow but stayed neatly, cautiously inside the lines. See you tonight, Molly. And I'll bring orange juice. I promise.

*　　*　　*

"You're one of the most perceptive women I know," said Luke just a few minutes later when she stopped by his office. He was composing a psychological assessment on his computer but rolled away from his desk, leaned back in his chair and motioned for her to close the door. "I doubt you imagined it."

"Maybe I did, who knows? It was just this feeling."

So the Reverend tried to come on to her. It didn't really surprise him. Shelby was sexy in a cute kind of way. And there was some kind of alluring vulnerability about her. But it pissed him off. There were lines one didn't cross, as clear as roads blocked with orange traffic cones. Random thoughts, even secret undisciplined emotions, were one thing. Behaviors were something entirely different.

"He has a nice wife," Luke said. "Sort of low key but throws her energy into worthwhile projects. I've run into her at various charity benefits. And a bunch of kids, I think."

"He told me five."

"Seems like that blue vein of his is getting bigger," said Luke. "Looks like the Colorado River pounding through his forehead."

Shelby laughed. "That's mean," she said. She crossed the room to a newly framed needlepoint hanging beside his window. White water tumbled across the canvas and from her vantage point it looked like she was shooting the rapids in a rubber raft. She knew it was the Colorado

River, a scene from his honeymoon. She'd seen the original photo. "You finished it!"

"Yes," he said, smiling at the needlepoint. "I'm actually pretty pleased with the way it turned out. I'm about to start a companion piece that shows the canyon, itself. Probably as the sun sets. I was looking through our photo album last night getting ideas."

"It's so good for the kids to see that guys can do things like this," she said. Not every man would admit to doing needlepoint. Designing his own canvases no less. It's like meditation he'd told her once. Beats the heck out of reality TV.

"Shel?"

"Yeah?"

"I'm not trying to pry. But it seems like Reverend Lincoln picked up on the same thing I did at today's meeting. You seemed, well, distressed when we talked about the Beatys."

She nodded almost imperceptibly before looking him squarely in the eyes. "Thanks," she said softly. "Sometimes it just gets to me but I'm okay. Maybe one day I'll tell you about it, about Molly's dad."

Luke studied her face. Sad. A face unmasked. "Anytime," he said. "If you're ever ready."

21

He held the dark chocolate yogurt cone in such a way that his tongue could circumnavigate it and catch the drips. Slivers of almonds poked out of the chocolate and gave it a crunchy, earthy taste. The cone was part of his daily ritual but he didn't always order chocolate. Depending on his mood he sometimes ordered cheesecake, peanut butter, pistachio, peach, or just plain old vanilla. He never ordered strawberry or coffee. Even during childhood strawberry ice cream sat untouched, puddling into little pink lakes with red gooey dots in it. And it was a sacrilege for coffee to be served any way other than out of a big, steaming cup.

"How's it going today, Reverend Lincoln?" the cheerful sales girls always asked, it didn't really matter which one. They were all young, college aged probably, and somehow had well proportioned bodies despite working in a shop he imagined was surely a hint of heaven to come. He liked their cheerfulness, and their toned arms and firm breasts and narrow waists and shapely legs, and their eagerness to pile the yogurt high because he was a man of the cloth. He always responded with the most appropriate decorum. But that didn't mean he was blind to what was within arm's reach on the other side of the yogurt counter. He was after all, a man like all other mortals even if most people chose to deny it. Divinity school might heighten one's sense of morality but it certainly didn't make one a eunuch.

"Shit," he said trying to catch a piece of almond that somehow slid between his cone and his lips and landed with a big chocolate plop right in the middle of his shirt. He held the cone in his left hand and turned the wheel with his right, negotiating his way into the church parking lot. He pulled up by the side door closest to his office and looked toward the chapel. The Tony guy, it had to be him, was leaning against the red brick smoking a cigarette, standing like a flamingo on one leg, his other foot propped against the wall. He inched forward, tires scrunching pine cones, and let his window down halfway.

"I'm Reverend Jeremiah Lincoln," he said. "And you, I'm guessing, would be Tony."

The adolescent stared at him through half closed eyes, took a drag off his cigarette and let the smoke escape slowly through his nose. Reverend Lincoln didn't let adolescent angst rattle him. It was all like a game of chess, really, dealing with teenagers. A lot of posturing. Keep them guessing. Check. Checkmate. The boy allowed his head to dip minimally in acknowledgement. He took another drag.

"I'm sorry I've kept you waiting. There was a single mother I ran into unexpectedly. She required my attention." He glanced down at the chocolate on his shirt. He hated stained shirts. They were slobby, slovenly, unprofessional. His wife, Marianne, he called her Annie, was a genius in getting stains out of anything. It was one of life's little blessings. "I hate to do this but I need to run into my house for just a minute. Stay right where you are. When I get back we'll get down to business."

The adolescent blinked and one side of his mouth curled slowly upward. His eyebrow ring glinted in the sunlight. "Sure, man," he said lazily. "Go take a leak. I'll be here." He remained on one leg as Reverend Lincoln guided the car past the chapel, between it and the fellowship hall and into his driveway. He turned off the car and chomped down earnestly on the cone. It was a sugar cone with a pointed bottom and it was leaking a little, melted ice cream running down his fingers as he stuffed the pointy end into his mouth. He wiped his fingers on his shirt.

"Jerry! Hi honey," said Annie as he walked in the kitchen door. "I didn't expect you home so early."

She wiped her hands on a kitchen towel that had a printed peach on it. He walked forward and brushed his lips against hers. She smelled like fish.

"I have a kid outside from CHANGE," he said. "I'm here just long enough to change shirts. Got a chocolate stain on this one."

Her eyes followed his to a brown splotch near the base of his sternum. "Chocolate yogurt again I see," she said with her indulgent smile.

He smiled back. "'Fraid so."

She turned back toward the sink. There was an aluminum strainer full of grayish shrimp sitting in it. Grayish-white with blue and red splotches around their necks and heads. He knew she was deheading and deveining them for the ladies' Wednesday night prayer meeting. Prying off the heads, pulling out those little black lines of intestines that ran along their backs, it was a nasty business.

"I thought you had meetings all day at Metamorphosis," she said.

He studied her butt and legs. She was dressed in navy jogging pants and a short sleeve cotton top that said *Invest your soul, gain interest. Attend church* across her back. He knew their church's name was on the front. He'd never thought of jogging pants as flattering before he met her. Even after so many years and five children she still could work magic on him. He thanked God for that. His own dad hit his mid-life crisis and overnight became a womanizer and a drunk and if he hadn't collapsed on the tennis court and died of a massive coronary, his mother would have kicked him to the curb. She told him all this when he grew old enough to ask questions. He believed his mother. She was never the type to tolerate misbehavior. And he always swore he'd never, ever be like his dad when he grew up to be a man. He prayed about it. He lost sleep over it. He became a minister.

"I'm supposed to be in a meeting back at Metamorphosis in just a little while," he said. "But I borrowed a wedding rehearsal from next week and a funeral from sometime in the near future, I'm sure, and begged off. The morning meetings were enough for any mortal soul."

"You lied?" she asked.

He smiled at her chastisement. "Not really lied, like I said, just borrowed. Honestly, Annie, I don't think I could sit through one more Metamorphosis meeting this week. They're incredibly boring and depressing."

She shook her head, her hair dragging back and forth across her pale neck. There was something provocative about the movement of her hair. Her white, white neck. "Jerry, you really shouldn't stretch the truth, get out of your commitments like that."

"Well, I happen to believe God worked it out for the best. There's a guy, a real tuff waiting for me outside the chapel. The kid from CHANGE. He obviously needs some sweat equity and pastoral guidance."

"Well if anyone can help him, you can," she said popping a head off a shrimp. He watched some kind of shrimp goo ooze around her thumbnail. "You have a real way with those tough ones."

Maybe it was pride, but he knew she was right. He had the knack. He somehow was given the gift to relate. "If I had to take the heads off those things," he said, "I'd never eat another one again." It was enough to watch her do it. "Well, I'm going to change shirts and get out there with my man, Tony," he said. "He's not the kind of person I want still hanging around when the kids start getting home from school."

She nodded toward their bedroom. "Just throw the stained one in the laundry basket," she said. "Oh, speaking of the kids, I went on line and updated your calendar with their commitments. Looks like a pretty full month for us both."

"Thanks," he called from his closet. He chose a tee-shirt from the Grand Canyon. Something non-ministerial. It would help to bridge the gap. He'd shoot the shit with the kid, give him some hard work, harder work than usual, and pay him a little extra for his efforts. He always made the extra pay a conversation piece from the outset. It had an amazing way of nurturing rapport.

The Tony fellow was sitting on the gray stone ledge near the chapel. He was leaning forward, eyes closed, head bobbing, and as Reverend Lincoln approached he heard some inane song playing, a song about love. Lust and hormones, if the truth be told. "Lust," Reverend Lincoln muttered to no one at all. All those songs screwed up hormonal kids' perceptions of love, making it about impulsive sex and body parts and unhealthy attachments. But when didn't lust or the perception of lust get in the way? Hadn't Shelby McDonald looked at him like he was some kind of pervert when he offered his help? He knew that look, that series of looks, really. Confusion first, a troubled look second, a walled off emotionally colder look third. What had he said? Nothing. Nothing except he was concerned because she looked emotionally distraught at the morning's meeting. He'd bet the Sunday offering plates she ran back to Metamorphosis and told that psychologist Bramson her crazy misconceptions. Sometimes he didn't really like Bramson. There were times he acted too big for his breeches. He felt a glimmer of a smile cross his lips as he moved directly in front of the kid, Tony. Shelby's breeches, on the other hand, fit just right.

22

Joey stood beside him in front of the thigh high picket fence and stared at the magnolia. "Man, that's a magnificent tree. It's just like I remembered." He shielded his eyes with one hand and looked up more than eighty feet, probably closer to ninety, toward the top. The span of its branches across the yard was about the same distance. "A witness tree, Andy."

"No, dumb ass. A magnolia. You know that."

Joey laughed. "You're the dumb ass. That means it was living when the Declaration of Independence was signed. It's a government thing."

"Damn," said Andrew. "How'd you know that?"

Joey laughed again. "I'm older, little brother."

When they were kids and Joey said he was older, Andrew jumped on his back and wrestled him to the ground until all of their clothes were grass stained and they were crawling with red bugs but didn't know it until later that night. But Andrew was aware their upper arms were touching, just barely, sweaty where they met, and he was careful not to move at all. Closer and it would be uncomfortable and weird. Apart and he would lose contact. Joey's touch felt reassuringly good, and it felt good to be called little brother.

"Remember how we used to sneak into this yard and climb so damn high in it?"

Andrew shook his head. "You did," he said. "Not me. Scared the crap out of me how high you'd go."

Joey leaned into him, bumped him off balance. "You climbed high for your age."

Andrew studied the tree and the white plantation home behind it. When he straddled the magnolia's massive limbs as a child, with Joey thirty or forty feet above him always encouraging him upward, he usually saw Union troops marching over the grounds underneath them. He heard the crunching of thick dried up leaves giving way beneath the soldiers' feet. He heard horses snorting and men's songs about fair loves left behind. He never told anyone, not even Joey, that they were hiding from the Yankees among the dark green leaves as thick as leather, and in the Spring among dinner plate sized blossoms, but they were always skillful in evading Yankee capture. Except when the smell of the white blossoms was so overpowering that he had to climb down and surrender to the commanding officer. "I miss those times," he said.

"Yeah. Me too."

It seemed to Andrew that Joey had grown oddly quiet. He stared at the antebellum home with its columned front and sides and waited for his brother to say something. A small blue sign in the yard read "Dearing-Swaim, 1835." The troops' horses jumped the picket fence and the sign sometimes, swarming onto the property like fire ants, fanning across land now defined by the bungalow houses and Queen City Avenue and the park where he'd met Tony earlier in the day, riding their horses right into the wide halls of the mansion, looting valuables, hungry especially for gold.

"Hey, Joey, remember those Civil War tokens we found over there on the old playground the day we borrowed your dad's metal detector?" They'd found three small tokens that looked a little like pennies but they had different things written on them. He remembered one said something about preserving the federal union. And there was a penny all crusty with turquoise corrosion that covered a lot of the portrait of an Indian's head. He was wearing feathers that stuck straight up in the air and the penny was dated 1864. Dropped by some Union soldier, buried all that time until the metal detector beeped its weird low tone when it swept over it. They'd found a fragment of an old silver necklace, a dinged up silver ring and three quarters, a dime, and a nickel, too, the latter under the swing sets.

"Yeah, why?"

"What ever happened to them?"

Joey scrunched up his forehead. "Didn't we ask Thomas to put them in his safety deposit box?"

Andrew didn't know. "I guess," he said. It always seemed odd that Joey referred to his father as Thomas. He couldn't remember a time when he'd heard his brother use the word 'dad.' His voice caught in his throat but he covered it by hocking a loogie. "I've always wondered, I mean, it's no big deal or anything, but it's weird the way you call him Thomas."

Joey's lips curled ever so slightly. "It's something Thomas decided when you were little," he said. "He thought 'dad' was hurtful to you since he wasn't your father, too."

Andrew stepped back. "Really?" he asked. He wished Thomas *were* his father. He wished it all the time. "I never knew. I mean, I always wondered." It was hard to admit. He wasn't sure if Joey would think he was stupid. "You know, sometimes when I was little, Joey, I know it sounds stupid, but sometimes I'd pretend Thomas *was* my dad. Sometimes I wanted him to be." Silence. Long silence. Well, not really silence because he could hear vehicles moving behind them on the street and others traveling down Queen City Avenue.

"That's not stupid, Andy. I wished that all the time. I think Thomas did too. I heard him tell Holly about a year ago that it'd be so much better if he were your dad."

"Thomas said that?" He swallowed hard. He wanted so bad to tell Joey about the note from the jewelry box. The one from Thomas about wanting to marry their mom. He touched his front pocket. Joey wouldn't like that he'd been snooping in her stuff. Snooping and stealing.

"She's got real psychological problems, you know," Joey said.

"What? Who?"

"Mom."

"No duh," Andrew said flashing a crooked smile.

"No, I mean, I went and talked to a counselor at college. I've been having nightmares. Bad ones. She changes sex partners like most people change socks. When I was young I didn't really understand but now I'm thinking there's AIDS and hepatitis and serial killers and God knows what else out there."

Andrew's stomach churned. Just that fast. It pissed him off. "Hey, man, let's not talk about her. We both know it. She's a slut."

"Andy. I need to tell you some stuff. It's important. I mean, even though you're going into Metamorphosis, you're not screwed up. You're just pissed off. I've been pissed off my whole life. I'd never even come home if it weren't for you and Thomas and Lesa." Lesa Lavender, a sophomore at Amherst. Leggy brunette with a bubbly laugh, a very sexy ass and a sort of flat chest. She'd been Joey's girlfriend for two years. Even now Joey was holding an envelope addressed to her. Old fashioned, writing her a letter, but that's the way Joey was. The address was written in black ink in fancy cursive with lots of loops and trailing tails. There was a forever stamp in the envelope's corner. Andrew liked Lesa, and he liked that her summers at home brought his brother back from Auburn. In fact, Joey'd be home in early May to spend the whole summer. He'd gotten a job in some veterinary clinic as an assistant. "My counselor says Mom probably has a sexual addiction. He says some people think that's a real diagnosis and some don't, but either way, she's messed up. He gave me lots of information about it. I've made copies for you."

Andrew's stomach flip-flopped. "You're seeing a counselor for real?"

"Yeah, I am. I think it's helping. It really is. What I'm getting at is when you're at Metamorphosis you'll be living away from her. And they can probably help with your anger. I mean, so her problems don't fuck up your life."

There was something about his brother going to a counselor. He didn't want to think about it. "No offense to your counselor," Andrew said, "but you don't need a Ph.D. to figure out Mom's a whore or a sex addict or whatever you want to call it."

"It's a psychological problem, Andrew. The counselor, his name is Asa, he explained it's like any other addiction in a lot of ways. Like drugs or alcohol. It's all in the copies I've made. When you read them you'll be amazed. It describes her completely."

Andrew swallowed hard. There was hardly any saliva in his mouth. The little hangy-down thing in the back of his throat felt like it was stuck to his right tonsil. "I found something," he said. "From Thomas, I think. It's like a little letter he wrote to Mom asking her to marry him. A long time ago, I mean."

"Yeah, he told me. Before I went off to college he told me all about them. He said he proposed to her four times and left the offer open, especially when he found out about me. She said yes once but changed her mind. He said she kept having affairs and that was their problem. He told me she was the first girl he ever loved. He told me he had it bad."

"She was stupid not to marry him."

"Yeah, well see it all fits. Asa says when someone's addicted it's sort of like needing a bungee jump adrenalin rush or something. Always looking for new thrills."

"Yeah, well, whatever." Andrew started walking the half block toward Tuscaloosa's main post office. "She's a damn horndog, Joey. Come on, let's go mail your letter."

Joey fell into step beside him. "You remember that song she always played in the car? The opera one?"

"That screechy one? I hate it." He kicked a pebble. It bounced across the street, hit the curb, hopped up the cement, and landed on a weedy strip of grass. "I hate the way she sang along with it, and I hate the song she still sings about yellow jackets in a grave of water, too. It doesn't even make sense."

Joey laughed. "I think that's a song about the Crimson Tide drowning the Yellow Jackets, that's Georgia Tech, little brother."

They didn't have to leave the street to drop the letter into a blue drive-up box that said 'Stamped Mail.'

"Won't be long and I'll be home for the summer," said Joey. "And Lesa and I'll come visit you and take you out on day passes if you're allowed."

Andrew shook his head. "Don't want to talk about that place," he said. He stopped and picked up a handful of gravel. He threw it a piece at a time toward a Stop sign. He missed twice before he heard a plink. "I rode my bike over to the Magnet school and saw Bethy on her break today," he said.

"Yeah?"

"I want you to meet her. She's really into animals and plants and stuff, just like you. She knows the names for a lot of birds because her mom is like a big birdwatcher or something." They were back at the Queen City Avenue intersection. "Yeah, well anyways, you'll like Bethy."

"I know I will," said Joey, throwing an arm around Andrew's shoulder. Andrew elbowed him in the ribs. He missed horsing around.

"I think my last exam is May tenth," Joey said. "Then I'll be home. Well, not home, home. Thomas and I talked this morning. I'll move into their basement for the summer."

"Really?"

"Yeah. If you were home, it'd be different."

"Have you told Mom?"

"Nope. Not yet."

"She's gonna shit."

"That's her problem."

When they reached the curb they waited. A green VW beetle, a blue Ford King Cab pickup, a white Chevy pickup with a dent in its back fender, a white Prius, an open air Jeep with a roll bar and two college aged boys in the front seat, a camouflage Hummer, a red Honda Accord, another white but dirty pickup with a black lab riding in the bed, ears flapping wildly, and a Mercedes C-Class. Andrew liked the Mercedes. It was manufactured about twenty miles up the road toward Birmingham.

Maybe he'd work there after high school until he figured out what he wanted to do. He'd heard the money was good. After the C-Class they crossed Queen City and turned onto Dearing Place toward home.

Their sidewalk was made with red and brown bricks laid in sand. Antique bricks. One of them was special. His mother'd shown it to them when Andrew was about eight or nine. It was rough on the edges and chipped on one corner and it had the imprint of a finger in its middle. A slave's fingerprint almost for certain she'd told them. Left there before the brick hardened in the Alabama sun. Andrew used to lie on his stomach in the zoysia beside the brick, his nose inches from the finger signature, and conjure up images of the man who unwittingly left his mark on the world. In a walkway. Joey never seemed impressed by it. He walked across it without paying attention. Andrew always skirted it. He tried his best to never step on the man's fingerprint. He used his key to open the front door.

"Believe it or not, I miss Tuscaloosa a helluva lot," Joey said.

"No wonder when you're stuck down there in that cattle town," Andrew joked. Tuscaloosans told lots of jokes about Auburn. People from Auburn told lots of jokes about Tuscaloosa.

"Yeah, yeah, little brother. I hear ya'. But it's the only university I know that Mom would never visit. Not in a million years."

23

She got back to her office, shut the door and kicked off her shoes. God, her feet, well really just one foot, hurt. She wondered how she'd misjudged the shoes' fit so badly at the store. She'd walked around in them a little, new leather soles slippery on the stained beige carpet. Well really she hadn't walked around that much. She'd spent most of the time moving her feet to the right, to the left, to the side, to the front, to the back, and to the sides again in front of the rectangular floor mirror.

The IEP meeting had been refreshingly short and to the point. Bullies in class throw dodge balls at Scotty's head when Coach is outside with the baseball team. His parents just heard about that last night when there was something about baseball on TV. His mother couldn't say who because he wouldn't tell. He used the word snitch and said he didn't want to be one, but there had to be other kids in class who knew what was going on. Yes, she'd look into it and if true, Coach would put a stop to it and the offending parties would be punished. Yes, an anti-bullying program at school was a good idea in general, and she was already looking at putting one in place. And Scotty needs to be protected in the boys' bathroom his mother said, maybe an older trustworthy student or a teacher could stand outside the door when he needed to go. The bullies threatened to stick his head in the toilet. No, it hadn't happened yet but he's scared to use the bathroom during school. No, she didn't know who it was. Scotty wouldn't snitch. Yes, a safe escort could be provided for him. It would be arranged. Scotty's math and science test scores were astronomically high. He definitely should be challenged further in these subjects. Yes, his mother said, they take him to the McWain Center in Birmingham and to Children's Hands On Museum in Tuscaloosa as often as possible. Yes, the McWain Center does have remarkable exhibits for children and he loves to go. Scotty does have trouble with the subtleties of language and with social interactions. He's extremely literal and misunderstands a lot. Yes, the school recognizes this as one of the special needs he exhibits. Yes, accommodations are being provided. In addition, Scotty's teacher is excellent.

Dr. Beaty padded over to her computer and searched for new messages. There were seven. She scanned the addresses. Her pulse quickened and she felt a little breathless like she'd taken the stairs at home two at a time. She did that sometimes to tone her muscles. Up and down five times, if she'd gained any weight she'd do eight, maybe ten. She'd never done more than ten. She didn't understand how just seeing his address on the screen quickened her pulse but it did. She opened it. *O.k. tonight, 6, crescent moon. black lace? that'd be nice.* She read the message four times. The Moon Winx. Her black lace. Anticipation caught in her throat. Quivered. Got lost somewhere in her body. She felt light headed. Just a little. How long had it been since their last Moon Winx rendezvous? Three years, maybe four. No, less than four. There was the time they bumped into each other last minute Christmas shopping. Actually, she was only buying wrapping paper that night. Six o'clock. That didn't give her much time. She'd skip Harry's after the Metamorphosis meeting. One thing for certain. She definitely had to change her bra. Black lace. He wanted her to wear her black lace.

She scanned the other messages. One from Harry. No, two. She opened them. Blah, blah, blah, angry he couldn't reach her. The second one clearly angrier than the first. A blurb announcing a workshop in Montgomery. Working with the underachieving child: New ways to motivate. A good field trip for her assistant principal and the school counselor. Workshops were tedious. Sitting in hotel conference centers, too hot, too cold, usually on padded fold out chairs. Coffee and pastries served before eight. Water and colas stuck in ice cubes and coolers after lunch. Sometimes fruit and cookies. Making small talk with educators from around the State. There was a message from Ms. Shu, a new third grade teacher this year. The grade three teachers were planning a field trip to the bread factory. Would she please approve it? She instinctively inhaled. When she drove down 15th Street and the ovens were baking, she closed her mouth, inhaled slowly through her nose. A nasal food of the gods.

Her tongue clicked against the roof of her mouth. A message from Thomas. Thomas hardly ever sent e-mails, at least not since he married. Probably something about his lunch with Joey. *Hi Priscilla. Joey says he's in town for a pre-placement for Andrew at Metamorphosis. Before you go that route please consider letting Andrew live with us. At least for a while. Worth a try, don't you think?* She re-read the message. Sweet Thomas.

Stable, kind, good Thomas. Andrew'd be happy there. He needed a man like Thomas. It was a good suggestion, much better than residential treatment, except for Thomas' wife. No way would Holly step in as surrogate mother. No way. There was no avoiding it with Joey, but she wouldn't let the woman get her hands on Andrew. Nope. Couldn't happen.

The last message was from the Superintendent of Education. He wanted to schedule a meeting with her. She'd been expecting that. Proration and budget cuts. A preview of next year's monetary trials and tribulations. Proration was a fact in Alabama education. Tighten your belts. Do more for less. There's no money in the State budget to cover projected expenses. Some staff and teachers will have to go. And forget raises. She'd live through it. She always did. Letters to parents requesting additional tissues and crayons and toilet paper.

"I'll be damned," she said out loud. *Re: Formal complaint from parent regarding treatment of children and himself. (Mr. L. Ryan).* Her jaw tightened. Her eyes narrowed. *Priscilla, Mr. Lawrence Ryan, a father of three children enrolled in your school, expressed a number of concerns in a lengthy phone conversation with me this morning. He presented as irate. Please schedule a meeting with me asap. Our meeting is intended to clarify your positions and actions to allow rapid and satisfactory resolution of his concerns. Mr. Ryan informed me he has spoken to other parents who also have concerns about aspects of your leadership and will start a petition if he feels it necessary. I'm certain the situations he reported are misunderstandings that can be easily resolved. Thanks. (And Roll Tide!)*

She slammed her fists on her desk. Paper clips and her stapler jumped. Stupid man! Who the hell did he think he was? She hit the reply key and stared at the blinking cursor. She jiggled her foot impatiently. Thinking. Constructing an upbeat response. *Happy to meet. Parent is troublemaker. I suspect children have unsatisfactory home life. Will continue to investigate these concerns prior to our meeting. The Tide rolls! Priscilla.*

*   *   *

She glanced at the clock. Nearly fifteen minutes before she had to leave the office. The drive to Harry's home was long for lunch hour, but they both liked their meeting place. He lived in the small rural community of Fosters. She'd clocked it, twenty-one minutes by Interstate

20/59 from the outskirts of Tuscaloosa to the dirt road leading into his farm. A little longer if she took the older route down Fifteenth Street and on past the campus of Stillman College, a predominantly Black college founded by the Presbyterian Church in 1876. The campus appeared alluringly tidy to her, old red brick buildings trimmed in white, newer ones too, on a shaded walking campus defined by brick posts and a wrought iron fence that ran its perimeter along Fifteenth. With two gated entries. On past stores and house trailers in need of face lifts. Past a catfish farm and a sod farm. Past cows, horses, and goats and then the dirt road. Another three minutes beyond a gate marked by a set of deer antlers mounted on a post, past two more gates, and finally to Harry's metal one. He'd painted it red. The land originally belonged to his grandparents he'd said. Once she opened the gate she was swallowed by a world of grasses and grasshoppers, cows, horses and goats, snowy egrets and great blue herons, Bart the dog, O.T. the donkey, frogs, and one hundred twenty five acres. A curved dirt and gravel path led to his home. They could frolic naked outside. Skinny dip in the bass lake. Make love in the patch of soft mosses down by the stand of willow trees. But he always kept an eye open there, never could fully relax. Never can account for the behaviors of moccasins he told her. Wouldn't do for her to get snake bit on her fine, fine ass.

She walked toward her intercom and pushed the button.

"Yes Ma'am?"

"I need to see the two Ryan boys immediately. The two older ones." She said this even though she was certain Doris knew the youngest was suspended. Doris was a peculiar woman. But she was excellent with details.

"Dr. Beaty, their classes are at lunch right now."

"Ask their teachers to hold their trays."

An uncertain pause, short, of considered protest, rebellion. Dr. Beaty knew she wouldn't dare. "Yes, Ma'am."

War. He'd waged war. To the victor go the spoils.

Her phone vibrated in her purse. She pulled it out and frowned. Harry again. He was going to feel her wrath, too. She stared at the lighted screen with his number displayed across it until there was a timid knock on the door. Doris could be annoyingly timid. "Yes. Come in." The two boys were escorted in by Doris. They were handsome boys, really. The older one, what was he, in third grade now, had a square chin and pronounced cheekbones. His shoulders were broad for his age, like his father's. His appearance was always neat, she had to admit that. His clothes were ironed and his hair was parted on the left hand side and brushed across his head out of his face with some kind of gel that left comb marks. His eyes were sort of a muddy color, but intense. They were intense right now, looking her directly in the face, standing close to his younger brother in a protective sort of way. The younger one, the freckled one with the rounder face who had fears of bullies, was less attractive perhaps, but still appeared clean and tidy. He wasn't looking at her, but rather at her desk, as though he were memorizing everything on it.

"Sit down," she said, waving Doris away with her hand. She waited until the door closed behind her. "We just have a minute and then you can return to your lunches."

The older boy hesitated then touched his brother's arm and guided him into her brown leather chairs. They wiggled until their backs found support and their legs dangled off the cushions. Actually the younger one's legs stuck straight out. That one ran his fingers across the brass upholstery tacks outlining the chair's covered arms. Back and forth. Back and forth. Back and forth.

"So," she said to him. "I wanted to ask if you've been bullied recently. Or have the bullies stopped?"

His fingers stopped. He stared at her with trepidation. He was too worried, too serious. It wasn't normal. He shook his head.

"No one's bothering him now," said his older brother.

"Good. Good. That's what I want to hear. And what about at home? In your neighborhood? Are there bullies in your neighborhood? Maybe even in your family? Some families have bullies in them, you know."

The younger one looked toward his brother.

"There aren't any bullies in ours," said the older one. "The neighborhood's okay, too."

The younger one stared at the floor. Preoccupied. She looked down. There was a ladybug crawling toward him. The older boy hopped off his chair. He made a wall with one hand and worked to scoop the bug up with the other. It annoyed her, the way he so casually interrupted their meeting. Casually and impulsively, and the ladybug was not cooperating. There was that night, that hot and humid summer night when she heard Joey on the front porch. He was in his pajama bottoms and he was about five. His feet were bare and she noticed his toenails needed cutting and the crickets stopped chirping when she shut the front door to contain the air conditioning. He was skinny and his ribs were showing through his tanned skin but not in an unhealthy way. Crawling up his arm, leaving a trail of silver that looked like mucus dusted with mica was a gray slug about the size of a grape. "Joey, get that awful thing off you," she'd said, watching it glide toward his clavicle. The sight was both disgusting and oddly mesmerizing. "I want to keep it, Mama. Please." It took five or ten minutes, but he finally agreed to leave his new pet outside for the night. Joey loved creatures, all of them, without prejudice.

She watched the older Ryan boy ease back into his seat with his hands cupped. All three of them watched as the ladybug crawled through a small tunnel in his fingers and crossed his knuckle. He put his other hand over it. "Daddy says ladybugs are good bugs. They help farmers. We learned that in science class too," he said with an air of authority.

"That's right," she said watching the ladybug re-escape. He covered it again. Last winter an entire colony hibernated between the sheetrock and siding off her guest room. That happened sometimes in the South, probably six or seven hundred of them. She started noticing them flying around her den. She called the exterminator. "Does your Mom say that too?" she asked ever so casually.

"Our Dad says he's our Mom and our Dad," said the older boy.

So. Their mom was gone. "Really? That's a hard job. To be two people. Sometimes he must get tired and maybe he yells a lot?"

The older boy's eyebrows lowered. He hesitated, stared with those piercing eyes, moved his hands a little to keep the ladybug captive. "No."

"A lot of parents might spank a lot if they had so much responsibility."

The younger boy kept his eyes on his brother's hands. The older boy's stare was locked into hers. "Not him."

"Hmmm. Well, are your grades better now? Are you trying to answer questions even when you don't know for sure you're right?" She'd hit a nerve. His eyelids fluttered and his stare broke. He turned his attention to the ladybug, peering into his hands through a tiny hole he'd made with his palms.

"I asked you a question."

"My grades are okay," he said.

"Good. I'll be checking with your teacher, too." There had to be something. The oldest one so fearful of failing, the middle one imagining bullies, and the youngest, afraid of Coach. She'd figure it out. "Well, I guess that's all for today," she said, trying to strike a light tone. "I just want you boys to know you can come to me anytime when something's bothering you." The older one wasn't buying it. Damn his intelligent piercing stare.

"We're fine," he said.

"Good. That's what I like to hear. You can go finish your lunches now. You still have about seven minutes. Go by the front door on your way and let your little friend go. What was for lunch today anyway?"

"Hot dogs, French fries, ketchup and applesauce."

"Sounds good." Crinkly institutional potato pieces drowning in ketchup. Stale buns. Ground up animal parts. Canned applesauce.

The little one shook his head.

"What? You don't like hot dogs?"

The older one stood first. "We like them," he said. "But Dad says hot dogs aren't really healthy."

She looked at the younger one. "You know," she said. "You really need to start talking for yourself, young man. The next time you come in here I want you to answer me without your brother's help."

The younger one looked into her eyes for just a second. He was going to cry. There was something about this family. Something about the kids' insecurities and the older one's anticipation of her intentions. "Have a good day," she said cheerfully.

"Can you open the door?" the older one asked his brother. He let his little brother leave the room first. "Don't cry, it's okay," she heard him whisper.

"You can leave it open," she said. So Mr. Ryan was mom and dad to five kids. Where was their mother? Fled probably. Left the kids behind. Probably had to. If you take the kids, I'll find them. I'll find you. Kill you if I have to. The kids stay with me. It had to be something like that. Larry Ryan would live to regret declaring war on her. She didn't have enough to contact child protection authorities yet. But she'd keep digging. "Stupid man," she murmured as she stood. "*No one* ever gets the best of Dr. Priscilla Q. Beaty."

24

The interstate was never crowded from Tuscaloosa to his farm. Walls of pine trees framed both sides, thousands of them, interspersed with hardwoods and undergrowth trees like dogwood and mimosa. The dogwoods were in bloom, bursts of snowy petals, along with black eyed Susans and creamy blossomed native azaleas. "Your Land of Trees makes a Texan like me claustrophobic," some man said in a lazy sort of drawl when she stopped to get a cola at a rest stop in North Alabama several years earlier. He was wearing sunglasses and she couldn't see his eyes and she didn't fully understand the intention of his greeting. He was about her height and about her age, had good abs and short cropped black hair and a piercing in each ear. "Where I come from we can see all the wildlife from Dallas to New Mexico and cars until they're specks on the horizon. At night we can see every star in the heavens." She'd been out West when she was younger and found the naked flatness of the land unnerving. She felt exposed and unsafe there. Just as she was going to tell him that and that his piercings were hot and that she could see his eyes better if he'd take off his sunglasses, some woman who was probably his wife and three little kids approached his car and got in. He tossed his half-smoked cigarette onto the pavement, nodded in her direction, opened his car door and slid into the driver's seat. The car motor started and his car backed out of its space. She saw one of the kids hit another's arm and grab a coloring book. She watched them leave and burst out laughing. Their license plate said Maine.

It was never her intention to have sex with Dr. Harry Greene. She was simply curious and she wanted to meet him to thank him personally. He was hiring her son for the summer, after all, and Joey spoke so excitedly about the opportunity to work in his office, to study under him, to one day *be* like him. *Brilliant,* Joey raved, going on and on about Harry's reputation around Auburn as a stellar, technologically savvy young professional. Harry'd been a guest lecturer in Joey's seven P.M. class, addressing the topic of veterinary science and practice with exotic animals, both wild and captive. Dr. Greene hoped to relocate to Ngorogoro Crater in Tanzania later in his career to work with big cats, elephants, and herd animals, Joey said. But first he wanted to get a few years of dogs, cats, cows, horses, and middle class pet lovers' money under his belt. He'd need it to fund his work in Ngorogoro Crater.

She was headed home from an appointment at Heavenly Feet and from picking up her dry cleaning, a loaf of bread from the health food store, and a bag of dog food for Winx, her sole passenger. He liked to lie on the carpeted shelf at the car's back window and watch the scenery pass. His legs were so short it was the only place he could ride and see out. He was a good traveler except when they passed another dog or a cat, then he barked frenetically, high-pitched and annoying. Winx already had a vet who'd seen him since puppyhood. He was current on his rabies and other shots and his heart worm and flea pills were stored in a kitchen cabinet at home. Greene's Veterinary Hospital, the sign announced. She'd never paid attention to it before. It was one of those signs she saw but didn't see whenever she passed by. She jerked the steering wheel to the right and the bread and dog food and Winx tumbled onto the floorboard as she pulled into the parking lot. Winx waited for the car to come to a full stop and even then seemed tentative. His front paws came up over the automatic transmission, leading the way for the rest of his body to drag into her lap. She pulled his leash out of the glove compartment. "Let's go meet Joey's new boss," she said. Winx wiggled and licked her face as she snapped the leash onto his collar. "Yuck," she said, tapping his nose in disapproval. "Don't lick." She picked up the dog and placed him outside on the asphalt on a white painted line. The paint looked new. The building in front of her was covered with brown cedar shingles. There was a nondescript hummingbird feeder hanging from the small front porch. It was the type that was clear plastic with a red base and red top and the base had little yellow flowers around the sip holes. The liquid in it was clear and only about an inch deep. A parade of black ants was marching down the feeder's hanger toward the base and back up the hanger and across the porch ceiling. In back of the building there was a tall wooden fence where she assumed the kennels stood. She opened the front door and a loud meow announced her entrance. It sounded like a computer chip cat from a gag greeting card.

"Clever door chime," she said flatly to the receptionist as she balanced and corralled a trembling Winx on the reception counter. The receptionist appeared reluctant to turn her attention away from the computer. She was probably no more than eighteen. She had strawberry blond hair that was either very naturally curly or late-last-night permed. She was chewing gum. "A lot of our customers like it," she said, popping a bubble between her teeth and her tongue. "Dr. Greene finds a lot of crazy animal stuff for our office on the computer."

"I'd like a few minutes to speak with Dr. Greene if he's in. It's not about the dog."

The receptionist appeared irritated. Or perhaps bored. "I'm sorry, ma'am. All non-medical consultations are scheduled from two to three on Tuesdays and Thursdays. He's seeing patients this morning."

"I just need a few minutes . . ."

"He's very strict about his rules, ma'am. Animals only this morning."

She'd complain about her gum chewing. Gum chewing in a receptionist was crass and she would say that to Dr. Greene. The girl made a poor first impression. "Fine," she said, moving Winx to the floor. "I'd like to have my dog examined then. A healthy-dog check-up."

The girl appeared nonplussed. She reached to her left and picked up a clipboard with a blank form held firm by a large aluminum clip. "Please fill out this New Patient form and return it to me. The doctor is finishing in surgery. He'll be with you shortly."

She was taken totally aback when the interoffice door swung open and a very tall, broad shouldered, mahogany-skinned man walked into the room and behind the counter and picked up Winx's form. He smiled, displaying very white perfect teeth. "Dr. Beaty?"

She picked up Winx who was huddled in the chair beside her. "Yes?"

He extended his hand as she approached and shook hers clearly as formality. Two and a half of her hands could have fit in his. "I'm Dr. Greene. And this must be Winx. Please follow me."

He looked at least thirty nine or forty but she knew he was much younger by Joey's accounts. He was six foot five, maybe six foot seven, and muscled like a boxer. His hair was neatly braided and pulled back with a leather wrap. She was thankful she'd worn her linen capris and a cream colored blouse to run her errands. The capris were bright red and her sandals matched and were made with sexy skinny leather straps. Imports from Brazil. She knew she looked good. She knew her blouse teased casual admirers, offering subtle hints of the lacey white camisole beneath.

The examination room was turquoise and white and was decorated with thumb-tacked photographs of people with their dogs and cats and assorted other creatures, including a guinea pig with a bald spot, a ferret with a casted leg and somebody's pot bellied pig. Most of the animals had red disc eyes like demon creatures. He reached for Winx and she leaned forward. Her breasts brushed the back of his hand. Lingered, pressing. Her nipples erect, hard.

He jolted back, hand fluttering like a confused bird. Away. Toward the wall behind him. "Excuse me. I'm sorry. I was reaching for your dog."

She looked at his finely sculpted chin, his high cheekbones, into his brown eyes. "I know you were." She smiled reassuringly. "Actually, *I* apologize. It was I who bumped into you and I assure you, no harm's done." She sat down in the sole leather chair in the corner and crossed her legs, wiggling the toes on her right foot. Leah had done an even better than usual job on her nails. She liked the way the dark red polish matched her shoes. He glanced toward her leg and down toward her foot where his gaze rested on a silver ankle bracelet and her sterling toe ring. The bracelet was delicate, very small sterling links encircling, floating just above her ankle. Red had given it to her sixteen years earlier. In those days all she had to do was show him something in a catalogue, sound a little wistful, and the next thing she knew, she was wearing it.

"It's hard to believe toe rings are comfortable," said Dr. Greene. The toe ring looped around her middle toe three times. It was a copy of an Egyptian snake ring and she'd gotten it from one of those catalogues like National Geographic or Smithsonian or Audubon. She couldn't exactly remember. But she could tell he liked it. She could tell he liked her toes and her foot and her leg and her hard nipples. He seemed to be having difficulty concentrating.

"You left a lot of the form blank," he said. "But I assume Winx has a regular veterinarian."

"Yes. But I'm certain it's almost time for his rabies vaccine. Seems a shame not to get one while we're here."

"Ah, okay. A rabies inoculation. Exactly what else am I looking for today?"

She moved her foot more slowly, toes pointed, around and around. "Nothing actually," she said softly. "Well, I guess it depends who you examine. There is, Dr. Greene, quite a fascinating, very small, very elaborate tattoo located on my left scapula." She knew by the look in his eye that she would never get around to mentioning Joey.

*   *   *

A tractor trailer semi hauling a double load honked an abrupt warning as it swerved past her Lexus. She gripped the steering wheel, startled. The truck was doing at least eighty-five. She hadn't really noticed but she'd drifted out of her lane. She refocused her attention. The beaver pond was on her right, a landmark about six miles from her turn off into Fosters. She looked over at the mound of sticks piled high in the swampy water, and at the felled and gnawed trees around it. She liked the beaver pond. It changed poetically with the seasons. In the Spring it was covered in water lilies, leaves growing both horizontally and vertically, and marsh grasses, and there was always at least one blue heron standing as still as a concrete statue in the shallows. There were cypress and tupelo gum and river birch thriving in and around the water's edge, and dead decaying trees, oaks and pines primarily, whose roots couldn't tolerate the dammed up water. A large bird, almost certainly a hawk, circled lazily above her windshield, wings outstretched, tilting its body to the right then to the left then to the right again. Flapping to gain altitude, tilting again. When Joey was younger he loved to count hawks along the interstate, especially during winter migration. Most were Red Tailed, but there were Cooper's Hawks and kestrels, too, sitting high on naked branches, almost always in mated pairs, hunting areas together.

Her phone vibrated in her purse. It had to be Harry, already at home, probably already naked, impatiently awaiting her arrival. She took one hand off the wheel, found it and looked at the screen. It was another number, a puzzle, familiar but forgotten. The phone vibrated again. A voice message.

"Hi, baby," a deep cheerful Southern accent greeted her. "Long time since we talked and I'm missin' you. It's not long 'til football season, honey, and I'll be gettin' my season tickets. What the hell, Priscilla? Call your old 'Bama Bob. No strings, I promise. You've got my number."

"I'll be damned," she said out loud. The season opener was in about four months. And she sure wouldn't be going to the games with Harry. She glanced around. No Troopers, no problem texting. She divided her attention between the screen and the interstate. *We'll talk in July. Season tickets sound good.* She re-read the message. It was satisfactorily noncommittal. It was actually Bob the Tree Surgeon who first took her into the swamps and taught her the names of the trees there. He showed her how the bases of their trunks swelled up with water and how cypress grew knees, jutting little island mountains, and how alligators wallowed out plants and muddied the water. Other things wallowed around in the shallows, too, prehistoric looking grennels and gars, long fish that had heads like eels and barracuda like teeth. And one crisp December morning they explored an ancient oxbow lake near the airport and watched a bald eagle fly shyly among the tops of bare cypress. He was an okay guy. He just got too involved. But his stadium seats were exceptional. Her phone vibrated, lit up again. *July? Why wait? Let's start now.* Some messages didn't merit response.

25

She was right. He was already home. He'd left the gate open for her and his canary yellow Toyota pick-up was parked near the front porch with the driver's window down. He had a dog kennel in the truck bed and some nylon cord, also yellow, and a square bale of hay. Almost certainly for his three horses, the donkey and his five new calves. She saw them grazing in the field behind his house, separated from the yard by a chest high fence. O.T., the donkey, stood closest to her. On her first visit to the farm he'd taken her on tour. O.T.'s job was to protect the calves from coyotes he said. Donkeys won't tolerate coyotes. They'll flat kick them to death. I had no idea, she said, aware of his well-defined biceps and the mingling scents of soap and sweat and cow manure. That's why you commonly see one donkey in a field with cows, he said. I always wondered she said, really wondering if he knew she'd never given it a thought. Liar, he said. They ended up stripping, laughing hysterically, splashing water on each other on the narrow pier jutting out into the bass lake. They made love passionately but carefully, mindful of nail heads and splinters and lake water on either side.

She tapped her car horn. He wasn't outside unless he was out back, and his front door was closed which was unusual. Normally he was waiting in his underwear behind the front door screen, the front panel of cotton poking straight out in delicious greeting, if he weren't outside throwing a tennis ball for Bart. Throwing the ball without a stitch on, like a Greek Olympian. His body muscled, deeply bronzed, a work of sculpture. She glanced toward Bart's sky blue doghouse. No activity there. He had to be inside with Harry. She chuckled softly as she opened her car door and stepped onto the driveway's pea gravel. He'd love her clever bra. "You're one scorchin' hot cougar, Mama." That's what he'd say as he lunged toward her. It's always what he said. Their personal joke. She'd initiate a chase or jump into his arms and let him twirl her around waist high before he threw her onto the couch or the bed. They could never get out of their clothes fast enough. They could never make love long enough. So how would she break it off with him? Maybe she'd give him one last chance. Look, Harry, you've got to stop calling so much.

What's wrong with you, anyway? I'm a busy professional woman. I have a family and a reputation to protect. Isn't that the way Red put it to her? Her high heels sank into the gravel. "Damn," she said. Her uncomfortable green shoes would be scuffed for her afternoon meeting.

There were three uneven stairs leading onto the front porch and the middle one had a huge knothole, a hole big enough for her heel to get caught. It was outlined by darker wood and she was always mindful of it. She carefully put her hand on the wood railing. Splinters, rusty nail heads, just like the pier, and it was a little rickety. The porch was weathered a light gray and needed an oil treatment. Harry said so himself but it didn't sound like a high priority. There were two rocking chairs facing out toward the field. Sometimes in the peacefulness of sunset they rocked and watched for deer grazing in the front pasture, sometimes alongside his horses, and swatted the mosquitoes that came onto the porch seeking their blood. They'd stay outside until she couldn't tolerate losing blood any longer.

It was strange the way he wasn't around, the way he hadn't heard the car horn. She reached for the screen door's handle. It was tarnished brass plate, worn off to silvery metal in places. The hinges squeaked and she heard Bart whine from somewhere inside. She braced the screen with her hip and turned the doorknob. It was wobbly and turned a little reluctantly but she was accustomed to the door's idiosyncrasies.

"Hello!" she called stepping into the living room. It was darker than outside and a little cooler and smelled like old furniture. It was a pleasant, reassuring smell that reminded her of her own grandparents' home. "Harry! I'm here!"

She saw Bart first. He was staring into the room's front left hand corner, tail wagging, tongue hanging out of his mouth like he was about to chase a ball. Just as she looked in that direction something charged at her, a dark form hitting her full force, knocking her sideways, throwing her onto the braided rag rug. The multicolored oval rug Harry said his grandmother made by hand. The rug he said he laid on as a child when he was coloring and playing with toys. She coughed for air. There was burning pain on top of her foot where her shoe had rubbed it raw, a dull pounding in her left triceps that had taken the brunt of the hit, and she still couldn't catch her breath. His elbow had caught her under her rib cage. She looked up at his face. His eyes were intense, angry, hard. His lips were curled into a narrow snarl.

"What the hell are you doing?" she screamed.

He stepped over her sprawled legs, easily avoiding her fist that tried to pound his shin, and scooped up her purse. "Bitch!" he yelled. "Bitch, you answer me when I leave you messages. I've been chasing you all morning. You think you're better than me? You think you can treat me any which way?" He tore at the zipper, pulled out her phone and threw the purse across the room. Her green leather bag zinging over the rug, barely over her head, the movement of air lifting stray hairs that fell back onto her cheeks. It hit the couch and her wallet and keys clattered onto the wood floor. Something else, too. Something metal. Probably coins. Bart circled past her back and cautiously sniffed the leather. His tail wasn't wagging anymore. It was tucked between his legs.

She kicked off her shoes. They were too great a handicap. To hell with her stockings. She'd go without them to the Metamorphosis meeting or buy new ones if she had time. The top of her foot was bleeding through the tan nylon mesh. Not much. She scrambled to her feet, struggling against her tight skirt, holding her ribs, trying to breathe normally. Her diaphragm. He must have elbowed her diaphragm. She stood facing him with her body turned slightly to one side. *When in the room with an agitated person turn your body slightly sideways to demonstrate non-aggression.* She kept her hands open and down by her hips. *Keep your hands open, do not ball them into fists. Keep your hands down at your sides. Place them in your pockets casually unless you anticipate immediate aggression.* She made no movement toward him. She looked him square in the eyes. *Do not approach an agitated person. Attempt to position yourself near an avenue of escape. Make strong eye contact. Speak calmly but firmly. Keep verbal messages brief and direct.* "Give me my phone, Harry," she said calmly, assertively. She'd learned crisis response at an education workshop. In the event she was threatened by a violent student. In the event she was cornered by an irate parent. In case she were attacked in a grocery store parking lot. *In case.* She realized she was closer to the front door. But that was actually little help. He was strong enough to pick up a calf, to put a Labrador retriever on the examining table, to handle a bale of hay. He was stronger and faster and she knew there was no escape. She'd have to rely on her wits. "Harry, I said please give me my phone."

He ignored her, scrolling through her messages, her call log. "I've called you a damn eighteen times on this phone today. I've texted you. Called your office."

Do not argue with an agitated person. Your goal is to remove yourself unharmed. "Okay, you're right. I was insensitive, Harry. But, I'm busy. I've got a school to run."

"And, I'm not? Is that what you're saying?"

"Of course you're busy," she said in a placating tone. "But you contact me so much. I thought we agreed . . ."

"That you'd blow me off? Not hardly." He walked toward her with shoulders squared, muscled arms hanging at his sides.

Her pulse quickened. She felt oddly alive and alert. Not scared exactly. Almost titillated. Adrenalin rush she felt sure. His fists were tight. A batterer, she thought. An asshole batterer. He was going to bash her face. He was in her space, looming over her. She forced herself not to back away, to stare him straight in the eyes. *Model calm. Be assertive. Display no hostility. Show no overt fear. **No overt fear.** If he attacks, yell for help, gouge out his eyes, bite through his lip, fight for your life.* When he lunged she'd knee him in the groin. Punch him in the groin. Grab his balls and twist hard. Bite him anywhere. Yelling wouldn't help at all. Her tricep ached. She imagined the skin was already purple. She was breathing okay but the area around her ribs was tender. The top of her foot still burned. Danger. How did she miss the signs? They'd been there. She'd just ignored them. His insecurity. His perpetual need for contact. His air of authority. All the questions about her life.

He focused his attention back on the phone then looked at her menacingly. "Who the hell's this guy? What's happening in July?"

Her heart quickened. "For God's sake, Harry, you're going through my texts?"

"I said, what's happening in July?"

She rubbed her arm. It hurt to move it, especially forward. It hurt to touch it. She thought fast, tried to keep her eyes level, her voice level. "It's absolutely none of your business but I'll tell you anyway. He's a tree surgeon. He's cut down trees in my yard in the past and helped get rid of pine beetles in one of the old pines out back. There's a maple growing too close to the fence. It needs to come out. I can't afford it 'til July." *Be aware of your surroundings. Look for objects to use as weapons. A fist of sand in the eyes. Anything to deliver a blow.* There was a carving, a finely worked ebony carving of a man dancing, one foot poised in the air, both hands above his head, a toothy smile on his face, on the coffee table to her right side. It wasn't within reach. She'd wait until the right time to

124

move. She had to be cunning. She had to be clever. He put the phone on speaker.

Hi, baby. Long time since we talked and I'm missin' you. It's not long 'til football season, honey, and I'll be gettin' my season tickets. What the hell, Priscilla? Call your old 'Bama Bob. No strings, I promise. You've got my number.

"For God's sake, Harry, don't be so paranoid. I buy his football tickets. Pay a hefty price for them, too. I've been buying them for years."

"Baby?" said Harry. "'Bama Bob calls all his customers 'baby'?"

"What's the big deal?" she asked, working hard to sound believable. "Just like at the country restaurants, Harry. The waitresses call me 'hon,' you, 'sweetie.' It means nothing."

She could see the battle waging in his eyes. "You'd better not be lying. Let's just see." He pressed call.

"Harry, you're embarrassing both of us. Stop it!" She moved forward, tried to grab the phone. He held it above his head, his thumb touched the ceiling. He grabbed her arm with his other hand. Pain seared through her muscle and she froze. He dug in with his fingers. "Stop, you're hurting me."

"You stop then." He dropped his hand. "Don't move. Hear me?"

She paused, then backed up one step, two. He moved toward her. She stopped.

One ring. Two rings. Don't answer. **Don't answer**. What time was it? He was probably eating lunch at some meat and three café. He loved country cooked vegetables. Fried squash. Black eyed peas with ham hocks. Fried green tomatoes. Butter peas. Fried okra.

"Hi, darlin'. I was hopin' you'd call." She could hear the clattering of dishes in the background. Muffled voices. She held her breath and took another step backward toward the carving. Harry matched her step and shook his head, eyebrows up, eyes enlarged, daring her to move again.

"That's flattering," said Harry.

There was what seemed like a long pause. Clattering, muffling. She imagined Bob's face, trying to make sense of what was happening. A woman's voice closer to the phone. 'You need anything else, honey? No? Okay, I'll bring the check.'

"Oh, sorry," she heard Bob say. "I thought you were someone else."

"I am," said Harry. "Obviously."

"This is Bob from Bob's Tree Service. Can I help you?"

"This is Dr. Priscilla Beaty's friend. Well, perhaps friend doesn't truly capture the essence of our relationship. I'm sure you understand what I mean."

"Who the hell is this?"

"I just told you, pal."

"Where's Priscilla?"

"She's right here. Priscilla, say hello to Bob of Bob's Tree Service."

She took another step toward the carving. *Yell for help. Yell identifying information.* Too risky. It would escalate the situation. "Hello, Bob. I was telling my friend . . ."

"I'm handling this," snapped Harry, again matching her step back.

"Look, buddy," said Bob. "I don't know what's going on but I've got a business to run. Do you have a tree problem or not?" She relaxed slightly. Bob was more savvy than she thought.

"I'm calling to find out what's happening with Priscilla in July."

There was a muffled cough. A car door slammed. Another long pause. "Trees," Bob said. "That's when I'm scheduled to work on her trees."

Thank God. She smirked at Harry. "That's what I told him," she said.

"Yeah? Well, I don't think she likes being called 'baby.' And she doesn't need your tickets. Get the drift of what I'm saying?"

Another pause. Distorted country music played over the phone line. The steel guitar sounded off key, twangy. "Sorry, buddy, no harm intended. I'm just country. Anybody'll tell you that."

"No contact," said Harry. "Got that? I'll be watchin' for you."

"Works for me." Bob's tone was unemotional, unconcerned. Damn, he was good.

Harry ended the call.

"Now give me back my phone," she said.

He opened the back, flicked at the sim card with his baby finger, squinting in the low light, prying it out of its clip.

"Harry. Stop it."

Flick. Flick. Little clicking noises, fingernail on metal and plastic.

"This is insane, you know that don't you? We're both intelligent. Sophisticated. Professional. You're acting like a low life asshole." She struggled not to cry. Her body hurt. But the crisis had passed. She could feel it. He looked calmer. She'd play along. Whatever he wanted. When she got out she'd never see him again.

She backed toward the couch, eased onto the cushion. "I was so excited about today," she said, curling up against the worn brocade arm. The fabric was gold and brown, a butterfly print. She moved a throw pillow to help brace her ribs. The yarn from a brown afghan felt fuzzy, itchy, on her neck. It was one his grandmother crocheted. "I looked forward to our time together all morning," she said softly. "I'm wearing a bra I designed especially for you."

He put the sim card in his front pocket and lobbed the phone toward her. Her index finger stung as she caught it.

"You're grounded," he said. "Until you learn some manners."

Her lip quivered. She struggled not to look pissed off. "Did you hear what I said? I painted my bra . . ."

"While we're on the topic of bras, let's talk about the e-mail from that old lover of yours, what's his name? It's a color. Red, that's it. Wear black lace, that's what he said as I recall."

Her shoulders slumped. Andrew'd told her she was stupid to give Harry her password. And she'd told Andrew not to snoop in her adult conversations. At the time it seemed harmless. A trust issue of sorts. "Why the hell are you reading my e-mails?" she asked. Her voice sounded tired to her, too tired to sound angry. She tried to remember exactly what Red's message said. "You've got it all wrong," she said, working to sound emotionally disengaged and convincing. "You know that Red is Andrew's dad. And that he's been irresponsible all of his son's life. I've asked for a meeting, it's true. I'm going to force greater involvement. But do you think I'd actually wear black lace for that creep? After the way he's treated us both? Not hardly."

"It's a moot point. You're not meeting him. You'll be here with me. I'll be sitting outside Metamorphosis waiting for your meeting to end."

He still appeared calm. She sat forward and manufactured a laugh. Small, quiet, a little sarcastic. "How ironic," she said. "I had a meeting today with a parent who hates me. An ex-cop. He was so angry I was sure I'd get punched or choked or thrown across the room. Or that he'd lurk outside and shoot me on my way here. But none of that happened. He didn't even really threaten me. I had a hell of a morning before I even got here."

"Poor you," he said, sitting down in the armchair across from her. It was a wing back, brown corduroy worn almost slick on the seat and arms. "Let's see. Today I've operated on a cat with a broken back and told the owner that even after paying me $1,000 his pet may have to be put down. I've euthanized two dogs and one kitten with feline leukemia, I've had to tell the owner of a beautiful two year old mare that her horse tested positive for equine encephalitis, and I've given three boring sets of annual canine shots. I have a dog in the back that's dying of heart worms, probably the only friend of the old lady who brought it in, and I've spent God knows how much time trying to contact you."

Bart nosed the elbow of her unhurt arm, a cool damp point of contact against her skin, pushing her elbow into the air, ducking his head into the crook. He looked into her eyes with dog wisdom, it really wasn't wisdom she didn't think. But it was something she couldn't put into words. It looked like concern. Concern and maybe reassurance. Winx got that same look sometimes. She guessed what he really wanted was his neck rubbed. She obliged. "So here I am all worried about this ex-cop named Larry Ryan, and all hot and distracted thinking about getting to your place, of being with you, and what happens? You go psycho on me."

She watched for signs of increasing agitation. There were none. Instead, he appeared puzzled. "If you're talking about the Larry Ryan with five kids who's a security guard, you're the psycho. Way off base. He brings his kids' dog into my place. A basset hound. Larry's great with his children. The dog's spoiled rotten. He's got a lot on his plate. Five kids, no wife."

A positive reference from a batterer. He wasn't about to convince her, but her curiosity was more than peaked. "Where is his wife, anyway?"

"Why? You plan to screw him too?"

She jumped to standing, no longer cautious. Ready to beat the hell out of him. "That's it! Give me my sim card, Harry. It's late. Lunch hour's over. I'm going back to work."

"No sim card until you learn how to answer my calls."

She held out her hand. "I'm old enough to be your damned mother. Our relationship is what it is. We agreed on that from the start. And it can't be the way it's headed."

"Excuse me," he said. "But as I recall *you're* the one who came into my office and rubbed your boobs all over me. You're not going to be with me and go around like a cat in heat with every tom in town. I spend my life neutering cats, you know."

She stooped, ran her fingers along the floor, felt for her keys and wallet, eyes still trained on him. She put her wallet in her purse and the keys in her jacket pocket. She reached down again and ran her fingers under the couch searching for whatever made the clinking metal sound. She came up with nothing. She braced herself for burning pain, tried to slip her feet into her shoes. "I need a bandage," she said. She'd have to put it on top of her stocking. No other choice.

He nodded toward the kitchen drawer. "You know where they are. Top drawer to your right."

She walked toward the drawer and it rolled open when she pulled. Flea medicine, some sort of glue, a zipped plastic quart bag filled with flower heads, stray paper clips, a pack of new mousetraps, scotch tape, masking tape, duct tape, scissors, a box of Band-Aids. She opened the cardboard box and chose a small thin one.

"Your grandparents are rolling over in their graves right now, you know," she said. "Pushing me around. In their house no less."

"Don't bring my grandparents into this."

"You know it's true. They raised you better. Got you away from domestic violence, you told me. Gave you a real life you said."

"Get out," he said evenly. "Just get the hell out."

She balanced against the counter, pain in her arm, pain still in her ribs, and stuck the Band-Aid to the top of her foot. The nylon still rubbed against her sore. She closed the drawer and threw the crumpled wrapper into the trash. "Thanks," she said. She walked back across the room and winced as she put on her shoes. "My sim card," she said. "I've got to go."

"Yes, you do." He dug the tiny card out of his pocket and dropped it in her palm. "I don't want to ever see your face again."

Their eyes met for a microsecond. The whites of his eyes had little red threads running through them. His stare was focused. Electric. Even now he was gorgeous to her. She ignored her body's arousal. There was a fleeting fear of walking past him, of exposing her back, her skull to him. She curved her path a little to the right as she moved toward the door. She waited for a blow or a shove. She pulled on the front door knob. It stuck a little. Her arm hurt. Her ribs hurt. Her foot hurt. Bart followed her out into the daylight. She pulled her keys out of her pocket and hit unlock.

"Bye, boy," she said petting the dog's head. He wagged his tail half heartedly. She moved quickly, opening the car door, throwing her purse onto the seat beside her, putting the key in the ignition. She locked the doors and heard the tires crunch pea gravel as she backed away. She'd fasten her seat belt when she got to the main road. She watched for movement. The front door was open but he wasn't at the screen. When she got home she'd burn the bra in the fireplace. And she'd put on her black lace. Red. His breath hot and fast, uneven with passion, his tongue in her navel, traveling down. Her breath caught in her throat. God, it would feel good. He wasn't young and virile like Harry but their bodies fit together. Familiar. Comfortable. The way only old lovers could.

Three turkey vultures were eating a possum carcass in the middle of the road, blood and dirt on their beaks. The possum had been there on her way in, the vultures had not. They didn't seem impressed by her car's approach. Huge black birds with red flesh hanging down from their necks like gobblers. She was reluctant to honk. "Move!" she said urgently although her windows were rolled up. "Move!" They fluttered their wings, hopped into the air, one, then two, then three, settling back down without having significantly changed positions. She'd met a married doctor at a cocktail party once who told her a turkey vulture flew into the windshield of his car. Smashed it. Don't ever hit a turkey vulture, he advised. Never could get the smell of carrion out of my vehicle. She tapped her horn once. Twice. Wings fluttered and the birds half flew, half hopped again. They were only inches from her hubcaps as she passed. In the rearview mirror she saw them flutter-hop back to the possum. But the horn had not brought him to the door. She never, ever wanted to see or hear from Dr. Harry Greene again. Somehow she knew it wouldn't be so easy. She'd bet her first born child she'd be filing a protection order against him before the week was out.

26

The office was quiet. No parents waiting to see Dr. Beaty, no parents signing in as volunteers or signing their kids out early. The children who took noon meds were back in class. The nurse used a little room adjacent to the copy room to give prescribed medications like Ritalin, Concerta, and amoxycillin. Doris and the two other secretaries were alone. Even the high school students who worked in the office for class credit were changing shifts, so to speak, and the afternoon student was not due in for about an hour.

"Looks like Dr. Priscilla Beaty is late," said Doris.

"Maybe she got lost in Shoe And Purse Jungle," said Erin, a plump secretary who wore no make up and had not worn a dress or skirt during the five years she'd worked at the school.

"Or Nail City," said Alice, the third secretary whose job included keeping up with petty cash and keeping parents knowledgeable about school functions. "I've never known anyone so fixated on fingernails and toenails."

"I couldn't believe how rude she was to that poor Mr. Ryan this morning," said Doris. "He seems to be a pleasant enough man."

"And good looking, too. Wonder if he's dating anybody," said Erin.

"Ask him," said Doris. "But you'd better hurry. Did you see him wink at that manicurist Leah when she got up to go see Dr. Beaty?"

"I thought it was cute," said Alice. "Kind of a flirting thing."

"Yeah, maybe, but he looked like he wanted to stick a dagger in Dr. Priss this morning." That's what the three of them called her behind her back. Erin came up with the name almost two years ago. It fit like a glove.

"It's pathetic she suspended a little boy Sammy's age. In kindergarten! Poor kid. He'll have problems in school because of it. You just watch. Such a sweet boy, too."

"And then she called the other two to her office during their lunch. It really looked like the younger one was about to cry."

The phone rang. "Probably her now," said Doris punching line one. "Good afternoon, Tuskaloosa Gardens Elementary School."

"Dr. Beaty please."

"I'm sorry, she's not in."

Pause. "Oh. Um. Well, can you tell me? Is she back from lunch yet?"

Doris made a face into the receiver, forehead crinkled, mouth in a wavy line. She shrugged at her coworkers. "No sir. May I ask who's calling?"

"Please ask her to call Mr. Bob Tulane at Bob's Tree Service as soon as possible. It's very important."

Doris' eyes widened. She wiggled her eyebrows up and down several times for the benefit of Erin and Alice. "Yes, sir. Does she have your number?"

"Yes. Yes, she does. Thank you. And, please remind her to call as soon as possible."

Doris raised her eyebrows one last time, smiled at the other women. "Yes, sir. I'll give her the message as soon as she returns."

"Thank you. Goodbye."

"Well, you must have some juicy gossip," said Alice.

"That was a guy who lives in Coker. Right across the street from my aunt. Bob. Bob Tulane. He has a tree service. Pretty successful, I think."

"Yeah?" said Erin.

"Well, it sounds like he knows our Dr. Priss pretty good," said Doris.

"Like, good, good?" asked Alice with a smile.

Doris chuckled. "Sounds like it."

"Is he good looking?" asked Alice.

"Not particularly. But this guy has a *history*, for real."

Quick footsteps approached. Alice looked down at the papers in front of her. Erin got up and unplugged the coffee pot. Doris pulled out a yellow pad of While You Were Away This Is What Happened notes and wrote Mr. Bob Tulane's message on the top one. The footsteps paused in the doorway.

"Dr. Beaty in?" It was one of the fourth grade teachers, perpetually energetic and pregnant and probably going to deliver within the week.

"Not yet, June. Can I help?"

"Naw, that's okay. Just wanted to review my substitute schedule with her. Doctor says I'll be out of here by the weekend."

"A boy, right?" asked Alice.

"So says the ultrasound. Well, I'd better get back to my class. Let her know I need to see her, okay?"

"Sure," said Doris, jotting this down on a note as well. "And, just in case we don't see you again, good luck!"

"Keep us posted," added Erin. All of the women liked June.

Doris waited until the footsteps receded. "He's part of a mystery," she said. "Spent time locked up for it, arrested for murder, but eventually got off. Not enough evidence, I guess. That's what my aunt says anyway."

"Who got murdered?"

"Well, they never really proved it was murder. It was his fiancée. Some woman named Sheila. Can't remember her last name. She lived up in Lamar County. And then, poof, she just disappeared into thin air. That was eight years ago. Never heard from again."

"Maybe she just ran away, lots of people do that, you know," said Erin. "Sometimes I fantasize about it. Can you imagine? Leaving everything behind? All your responsibilities and problems? A chance to recreate yourself?"

"My aunt says there was evidence she was with him before she disappeared, but not enough to convict him. And, there were rumors around Coker, mind you, just rumors, that before he showed up in Alabama he lived out in Nevada and something similar happened to a woman he was dating out there."

"Like a serial murderer, or something?" said Alice.

"Some people say so. And it's like you always see on T.V. My aunt says he acts like a nice guy, a decent neighbor. Quiet-like. Keeps to himself but friendly if you run into him at the mailbox. When my uncle died in a tractor accident Mr. Tulane helped her out, mowed her lawn once or twice, I think." She suddenly sat up really straight in her chair. It was a gray oval backed office chair with four swivel rollers. "It all makes sense now!" Doris said. "My aunt was telling me back last Fall about some woman who was showing up at Mr. Tulane's house. She watched her comings and goings. She's not nosey, or anything, but it's a small town, you know. Left at decent hours, she said, but looked more like somebody you'd see in New York City. Tall high heels, business suits. That kind of thing."

"Oh, yeah," sang Alice. She did that sometimes. Sang her words when she heard juicy gossip. The other two were accustomed to it.

"Anyway, my aunt said some of the ladies at church said she was a principal in Tuscaloosa."

"Dr. Priss and Bob sittin' in a tree," sang Alice.

The phone rang. "She's half an hour late," said Doris watching the line blink. "Wonder where she is, for real?"

"Murrrrrrderrrrrred," said Erin, letting the r's roll off her tongue, raising her hands into the air, wiggling her fingers like she was telling a ghost story.

"I don't wish that on anybody," said Doris smiling. "But anyway, we'd never be so lucky. Good afternoon, Tuskaloosa Gardens Elementary School."

"Hi, Doris."

Doris crossed her eyes. "Dr. Beaty, hi. We were getting worried about you."

"Car trouble. Didn't have phone coverage. But, I'm on my way now. Be back in about twenty or thirty minutes."

"Yes, ma'am."

"Anything I need to take care of before then?"

"No, ma'am. Oh, except . . . A man named Mr. Bob Tulane seemed anxious to talk with you."

"Thanks, Doris."

The phone clicked dead. "She'll be back in about half an hour," Doris said. "Car trouble, she said."

"I heard from somebody who works out at that place Metamorphosis that she's putting her younger boy out there," said Erin.

"Poor kid," said Doris. "Having her for a mother."

"I thought everything about who's in places like that was confidential," said Alice.

"Supposed to be," said Erin. "But we all know Supposed to Be is a fairy kingdom."

Doris smiled.

Alice pulled out the petty cash box. "I'd better get this justified before she gets back."

"And I have two letters to type."

As if on cue three parents walked in to check their children out of school. "Can I help you?" asked Erin walking with an air of professional grace toward the counter.

* * *

134

She'd kept her attention on the rear view mirror as she drove away from his farm, a little fearful still as she drove through the open gate. She'd hit three potholes, two big ones and one smaller, and her suspension sounded a little squeaky and her Lexus looked like she'd gone mudding. But he hadn't followed. She relaxed somewhat and stopped to fasten her seat belt where the dirt road turned to pavement. There was a feed and seed store up a ways. She'd stop there and call Bob. By now he'd probably called the police. And the minute, the very minute, she got back to the office she'd follow Andrew's advice. She'd change her computer's password.

The feed and seed store looked pretty much like any country store now. The gas pumps were gone. Chain link fencing had been added. But she remembered when it was Toady Jones' Grocery and back then it embodied everything charming about the South. There was a time when "See Rock City" was painted boldly in white letters on its roof. And a United States flag hung over a wooden door, right above a sign identifying it as a U.S. Post Office. There were signs nailed all over the wooden planks of the building, one announcing that hunting and fishing licenses could be purchased inside, a rusty Dr. Pepper sign reminding thirsty passers-by to indulge at ten, two, and four. Rockers on the front porch, pickled pigs' feet in a big glass jar on the counter, pickled eggs in another, every imaginable kind of beef jerky, and candies that were hard to find in town. Like cinnamon-hot fire balls that stained her tongue dark red and took the skin off the roof of her mouth when she ate too many. Thomas used to tease her about the fireballs. When she was pregnant he said their child was bound to be hot headed. But he was wrong about that. Not Joey. Not far on up Highway 11 there used to be three silos painted to look like Schlitz beer cans, the paint long gone now, the silos themselves swallowed by kudzu.

She pulled in and around to the side of the feed and seed so Harry wouldn't see her if he headed back to work on this older route. She stopped the Lexus. Almost no coverage. One little bar. She dialed Bob's number. Static on the line. Anemic ringing.

"Hello?"

"Bob, hi. Can you hear me?"

"Thank God. I just called your office. They hadn't heard from you. What the hell happened?"

"Long story. I'm on my way back to the office now."

"Who was that asshole?"

"A mistake."

"Obviously. Are you hurt?"

It was embarrassing. "No. But thanks."

"For what?"

"Knowing what to say. It could've gotten bad I think."

"That was apparent."

"Well, just wanted to check in."

"Hope you're through with that bastard."

"No problem there."

"Hope you'll go out to dinner with me Saturday night."

She paused. "July," she said.

"You're driving me crazy here."

She laughed. "Thanks again." She hung up before he could argue. She looked at her watch. "Damn it," she said. She'd have to schedule Leah for another day. All because of a sniveling, insecure jerk. Somehow she'd finagle it so Joey worked somewhere else when he came home for the summer. She dialed Leah's number.

"It's a good day at Heavenly Feet. Can you hold please?"

"Well . . ."

"Thank you. *Heavenly Feet. Heavenly Feet. Keep your little toe-seys happy and neat. We'll make them forever grateful they're on the ends of your feet. Help us pamper and spoil your heavenly feet.*" Asinine jingle. She could sing it in her sleep. The words didn't even fit the music, the beat. She held the phone away until the canned singing stopped. The receptionist finally came on. She was much too cheerful. Annoying. Of course, Dr. Beaty. Have a blessed day. Dial tone. A blessed day. Sure, whatever. She dropped her phone in one of the car's drink holders and started the engine. She drove back to the front of the store cautiously scanning for Harry's yellow truck. The coast was clear. Her Lexus pulled out into the northbound lane of the highway.

27

Their home smelled like lemon air freshener and cooked eggs overlaid with astringent rose perfume. Andrew wiped sweat off his forehead with his wrist and plopped down in a green chair in the den. The chair had a jungle print running across it that he didn't like, but it was the softest chair in the house. He threw his legs over the arm, covering a giraffe and a zebra with his calves. He heard his brother messing around in the kitchen, ice clinking against glass. Winx walked with his rear end wagging across the hall in search of Joey.

"It's almost three," his brother said, picking up two coasters from the coffee table. He handed a coaster and a glass of water to Andrew and put the same on a walnut table beside the sofa. Winx wasn't with him. Andrew heard a faint lapping sound coming from the kitchen. "We'll have to go soon. Oh, I gave Winx some fresh water. I put ice in it."

Andrew threw his head back and closed his eyes. "This is asinine. Going to this meeting. I'm not gonna live there. I don't care what she says."

"I'm sorry," Joey said. His voice was solemn and hushed like they were talking at a funeral or something. "If Mom'd let you, you could move in with me. But she said no way."

"Of course not," Andrew said without opening his eyes. "She'd have to pay someone to cut the grass and she'd have to take out the trash herself. Or, get one of her lover boys to do it."

Joey said nothing. Andrew listened to the grandfather clock. Its ticking seemed exceptionally loud. He opened his eyes slightly to find his brother staring at him. "What?"

"I need to finish what I was saying earlier," Joey said.

"What?"

"About counseling."

"Don't wanna hear it."

"Listen, Andrew. There're things you don't know. You need to."

Andrew swallowed. There was that lump in his windpipe again. Or was it coming up from his stomach? Had to be just air. He gulped some ice water but it didn't help. "What the hell, Joey? I don't need to know your business."

"Yeah, you do. It's important."

Andrew kicked his leg in the air. "Damn!"

"The reason I went to Asa at first was because I started having dreams, sort of like nightmares in a way but they didn't scare me. They started about a year ago. They were all about Mom dying in different ways, night after night. Mostly bloody, gruesome ways, and I'd wake up my roommate, his name is Frankie, talking in my sleep. But what freaked out Frankie was that I'd feel happy when I woke up. And then I thought, what kind of person is happy about something like that, and Frankie started calling me psycho and said I needed therapy. So I started trying to stay up so I wouldn't dream, and then one night I saw this show about a guy cutting, he said to get emotional relief, he was cutting on his arm, and I tried it and bled all over the place and it stung and that scared me more and I knew that wasn't for me."

Andrew jolted up straight. He felt like throwing up. "You *cut?* You?"

"So I called for an appointment and the counselor thinks my dreams are anxiety dreams. It's not like I'm crazy or anything. He says I've had to worry about her all my life and it's even worse now because I know how dangerous her behaviors are and so I dream about her dying and stuff because of all the anxiety I've felt, and responsibility, too, because I've always wanted to stop her. And he says I'm angry and that's part of the reason I feel relieved when I think of her dead. I just hope he's right. I don't know. Honestly, it doesn't bother me at all to imagine her dying. When I was younger I used to take the big kitchen knives up to my room at night and pretend like I was going to stab her and I'd imagine blood all over the blades and blood dripping down my arms onto the floor."

He couldn't believe it. "No way!"

"When I imagined stabbing her I never felt bad about it. And everybody thought, there goes Joey, he's got it all together, it's his brother who's got problems."

"Damn bitch," said Andrew, knocking a throw pillow to the floor. "She's screwed up everybody."

"And that's my point," said Joey. "Try to go into Metamorphosis with a good attitude, Andy."

Andrew looked up in surprise and laughed. "Man, it's been years since anyone's called me that."

"Yeah, well, you'll always be my little brother."

The clock's ticking seemed to fill up the entire house. The stink of astringent roses seemed to grow stronger. Andrew still felt sick and he thought he might stick his finger down his throat before they left for the meeting. He was afraid to ask. Awkward. Uncomfortable. He worried about the answer. "So, are you okay now?"

"Yeah, I'm good. I just have to sort out my feelings, that's all. You do, too."

Winx ambled into the room and looked at them both. He walked slowly toward Joey and jumped into his lap. Andrew pondered the movement. Dachshunds did not look biologically engineered to be successful jumpers. "Never have figured out how that dog can jump onto the couch with those damn little legs."

Joey laughed and rubbed behind Winx's ears. The dachshund stretched out in an awkward way and rolled halfway onto his wiener-dog back. Joey rubbed his chest and stomach, propping him up with the side of his hand so he wouldn't fall off the couch. Andrew stared at the University of Alabama collar. Crimson elephants in a miniature parade around Winx's neck, successfully sidestepping the words Roll Tide Roll.

"Well, you'll be pleased to know Mom's got a serious conflict going on in her life right now," Andrew said.

Joey kept rubbing the dog's stomach. "Yeah?"

"Her newest victim is a serious Auburn fan."

"Ha! That's a change."

"He must be a vet 'cause I heard her telling him that some sick horse could wait until after they went out for dinner last weekend. He had the balls to tell her he was headed out to see the horse. She threw a hissy-fit, for real."

Joey kept rubbing Winx. "As long as the guy's not Harry."

Andrew knew he couldn't cover it up. His eyes had already given it away. "That's his name I think. At least, that's what she calls him."

Joey's hand balled into a fist on Winx's chest, knuckles red, fingers a sickly yellow-white. "God! Am I stupid!" he yelled, cramming his fist against his forehead and leaving it there. "She asked me all about him when I told her about working this summer. We played her game of a thousand questions. For once I didn't worry. He's almost my age, for God's sake."

"It's probably a different Harry," said Andrew although he knew it probably wasn't. How many veterinarian Harry's would there be in Tuscaloosa? It was an odd kind of name. It described chests and arm pits and groins and dogs. Anyway, she'd always gone after the men in their lives. Coach Brightlon and when that ended, the assistant baseball coach and when that ended, the Tai Kwon Do instructor whatever his name was, and when that ended, Mr. Lazeris the Boy Scout leader even though he was married, and oh God, probably even Mr. Abernathy, Old Iguana Man himself.

Winx awkwardly struggled to regain his balance. He jumped off Joey's lap.

"I've got his e-mail address," Andrew said, rolling sideways to pull out his wallet. "I heard them talking when they first got together. Can you believe she gave this guy her password? She said no at first and I heard them arguing, and then she gave in." He unfolded a ragged square of notebook paper. Her password was scribbled on the back. "Here," he said. "Is this him?"

Joey took the paper scrap. He stared at it a long time. Too long.

"Fuck!" The lamp flew off the end table. Fragments of a porcelain elephant clinked across the heart pine floor, half its gray trunk and a broken tusk almost hitting Andrew's foot. The lamp was imported from Tibet. She'd always said it was from some little hole-in-the-wall antique store in Chinatown. New York's Chinatown. It was her favorite lamp, an important part of her elephant collection. Lots of people in Tuscaloosa collected elephants but no one else had such a fine elephant lamp. At least that's what she always said. Andrew knew she'd be really, really pissed.

"That's great!" yelled Joey. "Just great! How the hell can I work with a man who's screwing my mother?"

Andrew thought it was probably the other way around, but he left it alone. "He'd never have to know," he said instead. "Your last name's different." It was all he could think of to say.

No answer.

"I broke the lamp," said Andrew. "Not you. She'll believe that."

"Who gives a shit?"

Andrew listened to the ticking of the clock, the loud ticking of the clock that not only filled the house but rained down onto the furniture, the floor, onto his body like fifty pound weights. His brother stood, stared out the window toward the splash pad fountain. His fists were balled up again and his breathing was heavy. Andrew remembered Tony's offer even though he tried not to. A thousand. Even if he wanted, how would he get it? Maybe he and Joey together. He considered telling Joey but decided against it.

"It'll be okay somehow," Andrew attempted. His words sounded lame, inept. "We've always made it okay. You said it yourself. We can't let her problems mess up our lives."

Joey was crying. Crying. "I'm sorry, Andy." He kicked lamp pieces. They scattered further across the floor. "I hate her. I swear to God I hate her."

"I know," said Andrew. Tony said she'd be gone. Out of his life, their lives. Gone for good, he'd said. Joey deserved better. He did too. The saliva in his mouth dried so that his tongue made little clicking noises when it moved.

"I can't believe I broke the lamp." Joey's face was flushed, especially his cheeks. He looked at his watch. "It was worth a thousand dollars. She told me that once."

"No sweat. I'll clean it up before she gets home." It was a lie, a white lie, and he was sure Joey knew it. He'd do anything to see her face when she walked in and saw the lamp smashed to bits. It'd be totally worth hanging around to see.

"Could you, Andy? I'll owe you one. It's late. We've gotta go."

Andrew put his hand on Joey's shoulder. There was an awful feeling in the pit of his stomach. Like he'd eaten iron filings or glass or rotten meat with maggots in it or something, and it was getting worse. He didn't have time to stick his finger down his throat. "Just remember," he said. "I broke the lamp. She's sticking me away in a mental place anyway. Why not give her another good reason to do it?"

28

"Come in, Ms. Whitesmythe. Sit wherever you want," said Miss Zenah Elenrude. Miss Elenrude was balanced in her black leather office chair that turned three hundred and sixty degrees and always felt like it could dump her over backwards regardless of which way she moved in it.

The rail-thin woman stood in the doorway, a broad, goofy grin on her face. "Welcome back, Miss Zenah," she said. She giggled. "Makes me feel funny, you calling me Ms. Whitesmythe. I like it better when you call me Dana. Did you have a good vacation?"

"Yes, Dana, thank you. But, it's good to be back." Miss Elenrude picked up a pile of papers, turned the stack sideways and tapped it three times on the desk. She ran her thumb along the edge, put it back down and motioned for Ms. Whitesmythe to sit. "Now, that looks neater," she said.

Dana Whitesmythe chose a red straight-backed vinyl chair. She perched on the edge and smiled a goofy smile again. "I bet you know why I'm back," she said.

Miss Elenrude nodded. "I have a strong suspicion. But tell me anyway, okay?"

"Number six," Dana said patting her stomach, grinning even wider. There was only a slight swelling of her abdomen, like she'd had a big lunch.

"Dana, I'm confused. Didn't you tell me you had your tubes tied after your fifth child was born?"

Ms. Whitesmythe giggled again, blushed and twirled her purse strap around in her hands. "I lied, Miss Zenah. I'm sorry." She didn't look at all sorry. She looked happy. And silly. "And I've left Rayne," she said. "The baby's not his, Miss Zenah."

It wasn't a surprise. Dana had been with the man she called Rayne for probably twelve years. They were common law married. She always called him her husband except when she left him or he left her before they worked it out and got back together. But every time she got pregnant she swore, crossed her heart and hoped to die even though Miss

Elenrude never asked her to, that the father wasn't Rayne. She was right. The DNA came back every time indicating he wasn't.

That goofy grin. It was as much a part of her as her arms and legs. Endearing in an odd sort of way. "I swear, cross my heart and hope to die, I pinky-swear, Miss Zenah, Rayne ain't the daddy of this one either. They all have the same daddy. That's good, isn't it? A daddy with a pay check." She sat up straighter and pulled her purse closer. A funny look crossed her face and she hung her head sort of shyly. "You know for a fact I've always had myself two men."

"Are you going to talk about your other man this time?" Miss Elenrude asked.

Ms. Whitesmythe shook her head back and forth like a three year old. "Nope," she grinned. "Sorry." She didn't look the least bit sorry. She leaned forward and said in a raspy voice, "He's married, remember? We meet kind of secret-like."

"Does he know you're pregnant again, Dana?"

Huge bobs of her head, chin all the way down to her chest. "Yes, ma'am." She laughed. "Threatens to kill me a lot but never has hit me yet. Says I'm always getting myself knocked up. I threaten to kill him, too. 'Specially when he won't let me have the remote. He likes to watch T.V. after we've, you know . . ." Another goofy looking grin.

Miss Elenrude picked up her pen. "So how many weeks pregnant are you?"

"Almost twelve. I went to the Health Department yesterday. They're gonna help me get set up on all my vitamins and stuff."

"Where are you staying now?"

"At my sister's."

Miss Elenrude stopped writing and looked up. "Your sister out in Holt?" Holt was a community to the northeast of Tuscaloosa. Until the seventies it had a paper mill that spewed the smell of sulfur into the Tuscaloosa night and early morning air. And it had an asphalt plant some people said dirtied up the river. But that was a long time ago and now the Black Warrior was supposedly clean enough to safely eat its fish and the paper company owned a lot of the region's land and planted it in forests. Holt had industry still, like a steel recycling plant, and part of the new Tuscaloosa bypass looped right to it.

"Yep," said Dana. "We're talking again. Her kids drive me crazy but I don't got no choice. Not really. You remember . . . It's like the other times. The daddy of this baby is telling me to get rid of it."

"An abortion?"

"Yes, ma'am. But not Dana Whitesmythe. No sir. I told him like I told him before. I'm having this baby just like all the rest." Goofy, goofy grin. Front tooth missing.

Miss Elenrude pulled out several forms. "Dana," she said. "Answer me seriously, okay? Are you scared of him?"

Another silly smile. "Sometimes," she said with a shrug. "I've called the cops on him before. Mainly he threatens to kill me when I say I'm coming to see you." She giggled and looked down at her lap again. "No offense, Miss Zenah, but he hates DHR."

"Yes, well, a lot of people say they do. It doesn't offend me. But I want you to take his threats seriously, Dana. Be careful around him. You never know about people. He could snap."

"Yep," smiled Ms. Whitesmythe. "Snap just like a pole bean."

Miss Elenrude smiled despite her concern. It was a funny saying. "Do you need anything?"

"Food would be good," said Ms. Whitesmythe. "We don't have much food and the doctor says I'm not gaining enough weight."

"Okay, I'll call Temporary Emergency Services for you."

Ms. Whitesmythe stood. "Thank you, Miss Zenah." Her smile got bigger. Wilder. Miss Elenrude smiled back. Dana held a warm spot in her heart. "When do you want me to come back?" she asked.

"How about in around a month? Unless you need something sooner. Then come back right away. But don't forget to come back, Dana. Okay?"

"I'd never forget to come see you, Miss Zenah. You're like my mama."

Miss Elenrude shook her head. "I'm not your mama, Dana. I'm your social worker."

Silly, silly smile. "I know, Miss Zenah. I know. You're my social worker."

29

"So, Larry, can you help me with today's bomb threat?"

Larry Ryan looked at his friend, Detective Adelaide Bramson, Addie everybody always called her around the police station, and shook his head. They were sitting away from the others in the DHR lobby to avoid eavesdropping, but he continued to scan the room for erupting problems. And over in the corner two of his "buddies," Juan and Julio, brothers seven and nine, were playing chess on a board he'd pulled out of his car trunk expressly for that purpose. Juan and Julio were learning to play the game at the Chess Academy downtown. Their foster mother took them religiously. A good way to help children learn logic and planning, a good way to discourage impulsivity, a good way to learn sportsmanship. And it was free. "Sorry. Afraid I'm no help, Addie," he said. "I wasn't here this morning. I had a come-to-Jesus meeting with Sammy's principal."

"Not her again."

"One and the same." Larry was still at the force when his two oldest started school. "But I've complained to the Superintendent about her. Just today. So maybe things'll get better. She needs to work at a boot camp not an elementary school, I'm tellin' ya."

Addie's mouth contorted. She was hoping for a good lead. "Well, anyways, can I pick your brain for a minute?"

Larry laughed. "If you're brave enough." When he was a cop they'd tossed plenty of theories and suppositions back and forth. She wasn't the best looking woman in the world but she was smart enough to earn detective before a lot of the old timers. That caught her some flack, too.

"I've talked to a lot of folks around here and the consensus seems to be that the person who's probably behind the bomb threats is a woman named Erma P. Wallenskowski. Several of the social workers think Ms. Wallenskowski probably has a male friend or friends call up and deliver the actual threats. Seems she's at odds with DHR because her parental rights are in the process of being terminated." She paused, opened her purse and fished out her bag of Animal Crackers. She held them in a gesture of sharing.

Larry shook his head and laughed. "I can't believe you're still hooked on those things."

"'Fraid so." She studied the cookies briefly before removing a giraffe, a bear and a bison. She let the giraffe melt on her tongue until it was gooey. She was guessing she could taste shortbread, lemon.

Larry laughed and squinted toward the front door. The glass was smudged with oily handprints. An elderly woman on a walker was slowly making her way in. It looked like probably her grandson holding the door for her. "Yeah, I can see why Erma would be at the top of a lot of folks' lists. She's quite a wild character sometimes."

"By wild, you mean . . ."

"I mean certifiably crazy when she's not on her medicine, Addie. Big woman. Breasts probably close to the size of refrigerator watermelons. You know, those seedless ones."

"Gosh, Larry . . ."

His expression looked like he was fighting indigestion. "Oh, sorry, Addie. Sometimes I forget you're not one of the guys."

"Anyway . . . ?"

"Like I said, big woman. Unkempt hair, sticks out everywhere. Clothes too tight or just not right for her body, like real short shorts, halter tops. You get the picture. Booming voice. Curses like the guys we used to lock up on Saturday nights drunk and ornery. One time came in with a red suitcase, all scraped up and dirty, pulling it on one roller, the other wheel was gone. Said it was a survival kit 'cause the world was ending that Sunday. Wanted to leave it for her children's foster parents. Didn't make trouble. Thought the Cubans were invading the U.S. I'm guessing she'd just watched something on the history channel about the Bay of Pigs. Anyway, I just said, "Yes, ma'am, I'll try to get it to them as soon as possible," and she went on her way. Then I called her mental health worker and said I didn't think Erma was taking her meds right and they got her straight pretty quick again. One thing about Erma, she does love her kids. Shame, really, the way she's so mentally ill."

"So, is she the type to pull these bomb threats? Line up her male friend or friends to call the threats in? Five in two months?"

He watched Julio move his queen toward Juan's king. Good for Julio. "Addie, I just don't think it's Erma. She's more the type to walk in and threaten to knock out her social worker's teeth. I can't see her doing all that planning. Too impulsive for that. Do you believe it's always the same caller?"

"Don't know. It's consistently been a male. But each time the call comes into a different social worker so there hasn't yet been a way to compare the voice. Still, there've been similarities in descriptions. The general voice profile is that of a coarse whisper, saying things like you'z guys, suggesting maybe a Northern connection. But two of the workers think that's a sham to throw us off the scent."

Larry watched a very skinny woman with thinning, uneven blond hair approach him with an air of uncertainty. "Just a sec, Addie," he said. He smiled encouragement toward the woman and she quickened her step. As she neared Addie could see little cratered scars on her face, maybe from chicken pox or maybe from acne, pale lips, ice blue eyes. Almost as blue as Luke's. But lackluster. No spark. No shine. Her cheekbones were much too prominent.

"Hi, Larry." She glanced toward Addie awkwardly. "I'm interrupting, aren't I?"

"No, Dana. It's okay. We can spare a minute. How's it going? Looks like you're losing weight again."

Addie watched a crooked, surprisingly endearing smile flicker across the woman's lips. A pretty face ravaged almost certainly by a hard, hard life.

"Yeah, maybe a little, but I'm okay. Miss Zenah's helping me get some food. I have somethin' to tell you in private sometime. Some news." She flashed another grin. Addie counted three missing teeth.

"I know that smile of yours, Dana," said Larry. "It's not another little one?"

"I'll see you next week, tell you then," she said, glancing nervously back toward Addie. "Unless, well, unless you're needing your house cleaned between now and then."

Larry laughed. "It's just been a few days. Nah, let's stick to our two week schedule."

Dana laughed too. "I knew you'd say that," she said. "I borrowed Flora's car. My neighbor. I've gotta get it back before her husband gets home or she's in big trouble."

"Wouldn't want that," Larry said. "Take care of yourself, hear?"

She walked back across the room and out the door. Foam flip flops slapping cracked heels.

"I've got a real soft spot for that lady right there," Larry said. "A bond, I guess you'd call it. Weird, she's got a real high-faluting last name. Whitesmythe. Like she's from some upscale London neighborhood. She's been coming in for years. Since I've known her she's had five children and all five ended up in DHR custody. But she always has that smile on her face and she'd share anything she had with anybody who said they needed it. Same with those two kids playing chess. Horrendous life stories. Gentle spirits. Like empty plastic bottles thrown into heavy surf with their caps on tight. Somehow they don't sink." He paused, refocused. Cleared his throat. "Anyway, I think I was saying, I doubt your culprit's Erma Wallenskowski. I'm leaning more toward the Neil Lamphurte type."

"Yeah, he's on the list, too."

"He's got those tattooed prison knuckles, haven't put all the letters together yet, but I'm sure whatever they spell it's no Bible verse. Had to escort him out of the building twice recently when he's gotten too rowdy. Wiry little fellow, seriously pissed off at DHR. Impulsive, but he's got those shrewd eyes like he's plotting all the time. Be like him to call in fake bomb threats. Even capable of making and planting pipe bombs, I think. Courts have ruled he can't see his kids, period. Told me one day while he was spouting off that he's more addicted to cooking meth than using it. Lost two trailers to explosions before the new manufacturing methods, or so he said. I'd talk to him if I were you."

"Thanks, Larry," said Addie. "Anybody else?"

"Lots of folks who come in here are pretty damn angry at DHR, Addie. You could be looking at somebody who's a client now or someone with a long standing grudge. Who knows how many potential suspects you have? But I put my money on Mr. Lamphurte."

Addie reopened her purse and removed her Animal Crackers again. Larry shook his head even before she offered them. She dumped three into her palm. This time she didn't even look to see what they were. "Don't guess I can talk you out of sitting here every day?" she said. "You know we miss the hell out of you. You're a damn good cop. Got brains and balls." She laughed. "That's what the guys say about me, you know."

Larry's shoulders lifted half-heartedly. Truth was, he missed the hell out of being a cop. "I'd be there in a heartbeat, but I have a gaggle of little ones to think about now. I'll be back after I get my baby girl married."

Addie's eyebrows arched. "She's what? Three?"

He chuckled. "Yeah, it'll be awhile. But I can tell you I'm not gonna be out doin' night shift when those young bucks come stomping at our door." His phone rang. Not really rang. It played the beginning of the Blue Danube. It was one of his favorite waltzes. He hadn't waltzed in what, three months, four? He glanced down at the incoming number. It was his sitter. "Just a sec, Addie," he said. "It's the lady who watches my kids. Hi, what's up?"

"Hi, Larry. Everything's okay. The kids are outside running through the sprinkler. In fact, this can wait 'til tonight if you're busy. Just wanted to catch you when the kids weren't listening."

Larry glanced at Addie who had turned her head toward the lobby in an obvious effort to give him a pretence of privacy. "Go ahead."

"Wanted to give you a heads up. When Matthew and Mikey came in from school today they told me Dr. Beaty called them into her office after you left. Apparently during their lunch time 'cause they said their hot dogs were cold when they got back."

Larry's bicep on his right arm twitched. "Called them into her office? Why?"

"I couldn't make a lot of sense of what they said. Matthew said she asked about their mother and about you and whether you hit them and about whether he was getting better about taking academic risks, I mean he didn't say it that way, of course. And he said she asked whether there were any bullies at home or in the neighborhood, and if the bullies at school were treating Mikey better. And he said she told Mikey he had to talk for himself from now on in her office. He said Mikey almost started crying but they caught a ladybug crawling across her floor and had to go let it go."

"I can't believe that woman!" He recognized immediately he'd spoken much too loudly because half the people in the lobby turned to look at him, and Addie's look was of clear concern. He lowered his voice and turned toward the wall. "What a bitch!" he said into the receiver.

"I'm sorry, I didn't want to mess up your day but I thought you'd want to know."

"Damn straight I want to know. Dr. Beaty's due a surprise visit before the afternoon's through. If this keeps up I may as well get my damn tent and camp out in her office."

"Well, the kids are fine. We'll be here whenever."

"Okay. And thanks." He hung up.

"Everything o.k.?" asked Addie. She had an incoming call. She poised the phone in mid-air, halfway to her ear, until Larry motioned for her to go ahead and answer. Caller ID told her it was police dispatch. She looked at the clock. It'd be Tameka. Intelligent, precise young woman with lots of promise. Hadn't been out of college but a year or two. Criminal justice major. The two of them hit it off from Tameka's first day on the job.

"Hey, Tami."

"Hey Addie. Just got a report of a single car accident four minutes ago. One woman dead at the scene. A Dana Whitesmythe. Twenty nine. On Northridge Road not far from Sokol Park. Ran right off that straight as an arrow road and banged into a pine. Flipped against another one, crushed the cab right at the driver's seat. Most likely fell asleep at the wheel or got distracted by something. Chief's not calling you in yet but wants you to know it's a possibility. She's called in several times recently on some sort of domestic complaint. Some guy'd been threatening to kill her. I remember her saying that. Chief's listening to the tapes now. May open it up to homicide."

Dana Whitesmythe. Addie's attention jerked toward Larry. "She was here at DHR a few minutes ago," said Addie quietly, turning away from him.

"Lots of deer cross there," said Tameka.

True. All kinds of wild life made their homes in the neat rows of pine trees planted years ago by Bryce Hospital's mentally ill patients. Back in the days when part of the State's treatment for schizophrenia and major depression was farming. Addie had seen herds of deer, and turkeys, ground hogs, raccoons, and recently even a coyote along that stretch. "Hopefully it was something like that," she said.

"Yeah, hope so."

"Got anything else, Tami?"

"Not yet. Her name's being withheld until we can notify next of kin."

"Yeah, okay, thanks for the heads up." She avoided Larry's eyes as she turned toward him. Dana Whitesmythe. Uncanny. Ms. Whitesmythe had to have a heavy foot to get all the way over to Northridge so fast. Might be as simple as loss of control, excessive speed.

"Man, you don't look so good, Addie," said Larry. "You okay?"

She wet her lips with her tongue. "Just got a report of a single car accident. Probably avoiding a deer or answering a phone or speeding, but foul play might be involved."

Larry didn't seem to be listening. She could tell by his expression he hadn't digested any of it. "Can you believe that damn principal's harassing my kids again?" he asked. "And, it sounds like she's fishing for a way to get me on some kind of maltreatment charge."

It was the wrong time. He'd find out soon enough. "Well, she's definitely out of luck there," Addie said, putting her hand on the man's shoulder. It was a stretch. She was about a foot shorter. "I can assure her of that."

"Anything else, Addie? About the bomb threats, I mean?"

She paused, looked at Larry's angry face. "Naw, nothing else today. Keep your eyes open though, Larry. I'd appreciate it."

"Sure thing," said Larry. "Let me go see if I can get off early to pay dear Dr. Beaty yet another visit. I hate to lose the time. My check'll already be docked for this morning's meeting, but she apparently didn't get my message. I thought I made it pretty damned clear."

"Good luck." She turned to leave.

"Thanks. Say hi to Luke for me."

She felt unsettled as she headed toward her car. Perhaps she should have told him anyway. He was, after all, an ex-cop.

*   *   *

The opening of the Blue Danube waltz played again as he pulled out of the parking lot. His supervisor who probably wasn't a day older than twenty-eight didn't appear thrilled by his request to leave early for another school meeting. She opened her mouth to say something but after her ruby-lipsticked mouth formed an O-shape, she checked herself, closed her lips and nodded an okay. He got the feeling he'd hear about it later. "Hello?"

"Hi honey! How's your day?"

"Sucks with a capital S. In fact, I'm on my way back over to have another showdown with our favorite person, Dr. B. That's B for Bitch."

"Really? She cancelled her appointment with me today. Sounded pissed off and sort of weird on the phone the receptionist said. Must've been something big. Nothing's more important than her nails."

"Next time jerk 'em all out with pliers. I'll help you."

Leah laughed. He loved her laugh. It started soft and tumbled down, gaining momentum as it flowed. "You *are* upset. What'd she do this time?"

Larry maneuvered through the heavy afternoon McFarland Boulevard traffic. "Long story," he said. "I'll tell you about it tonight." He hit the brakes quickly. A group of adolescents in a silver Escalade jumped into his lane from nowhere. The car was bouncing up and down. He could see four kids in the back bobbing with the music, arms weaving in the air like kelp in ocean currents, girls sitting on boys' laps. The beat was apparent. He could hear it even with the windows up. He wished he were still a cop. "We're still getting together after I get the kids in bed, right?"

"Right. I've made you chicken salad and guess what? Banana pudding from scratch."

He felt too angry to contemplate food even though she was an incredible cook. Even though banana pudding was his favorite, real banana pudding cooked on the stove, not the kind made with boxed powdered mix. And her chicken salad was gourmet. She made it with apple and celery and onion and almonds, grapes and blueberries too sometimes, all diced real small, and she threw in mysterious spices. He'd never learned the spices and what they did in foods, he just knew her chicken salad was something to anticipate. Actually, he felt too angry to even contemplate being good company but he wanted to see her. It'd been three or four years since he'd really cared whether he was with someone or not. He had no idea where their relationship was going. He had the kids to consider. But Leah was a keeper. "Thanks, babe. Thanks for doing all that. Should I pick up anything?"

"Nope. Got it all. What time's good?"

"Nine?" It took a while to get Mikey in bed. He popped up and down at least a dozen times before he finally gave in to sleep. She usually came over at nine.

"Sounds great. See you then. And, keep your cool with Dr. B." She laughed. "She's my best customer. Keeps me in business. Keeps you in banana pudding."

"I'd rather starve," he said. "Bye, baby."

She seemed okay with their dates, almost platonic except for those rare occasions he paid the sitter to stay so they could slip away for a while. Maybe tonight he'd start teaching her to waltz. She said she wanted to learn. No sex with the children around, in fact, very little touching. He never knew when one of the little rascals would appear unannounced at the doorway. Quiet home dinners. TV dates. For the longest time they tried to hide her from the children. They agreed on that in case their relationship went nowhere. His kids had experienced enough loss already.

"I need to be home most nights and weekends," he'd said straight-up. "I'm already away from them so much with my job."

"Sure," she'd said like she really understood. "I was the same way when Randolph lived with me." She had custody of Randolph when they first met. He was three, almost four, and his mom, Leah's sister, was on assignment somewhere in the Middle East, some sort of television journalist. Larry'd heard the tire store's bell clatter when Randolph and Leah entered the tiny reception office. It wasn't a fancy bell, in fact it looked like a rusty one that came from a cow's neck, but it was looped on a gold cord on the door handle. He didn't look up at first, he was reading an article in a science magazine about King Tut. In his next life he planned to be an archaeologist. An Egyptologist, actually. Randolph was singing the ABC song to himself and every once in a while he hit a learning roadblock. Larry heard a sweet sounding female voice patiently offering help. The third time he heard LNMinnowP, he glanced up and there she was. Wavy, no, curly, almost permed curly in fact, hair cascading all the way down her back. Raven colored. She'd run over a nail in her front left tire she said. Ironic because she did nails for a living and then she ran over one, she laughed. He was getting his tires rotated, he said, he had the morning off. Lots of talk about children. Toy recalls. Booster shots. Booster seats. Story time at the library. Sure, she had time for coffee as long as she could grab a snack for Randolph wherever they went. She took her coffee with just a little skim milk or liquid creamer or powdered nondairy product. She was a coffeeholic, she said. Caffeine didn't keep her awake.

They'd been seeing each other for almost three months before he asked if she wanted him to keep the sitter a few hours longer one Friday night. She offered her apartment. It was just as he'd imagined. Clean, understated. One bedroom, one bath, kitchenette. Her muscled body pressed naked against his in the shower. Purple soap. Lavender scented she said. Lavender in the water, in the steam, on their skin. Curls erased from her hair, hanging as a thick black curtain across the small of her back. Her fingers traveling up through his chest hair, down toward his groin. Hungry kisses, tongues dancing. Egyptian cotton sheets. White, soft, cool.

It was that night they realized they had an acquaintance in common. "I don't normally say anything about my clients," she said as he ranted about Dr. Beaty's treatment of his children. "But I can see how she'd drive you crazy. She's consumed with her appearance, Larry, honestly she is. Real superficial. Narcissistic beyond belief. I swear she'd postpone a school fire drill if she broke a fingernail. I'd have to come fix it before she'd go outside." Larry laughed at her non-joke joke. They both knew that as outrageous as it sounded, it wasn't far from the truth.

The silver Escalade jerked to the right and onto an exit road headed toward the lakes. No turn signal. Damn they were begging for a ticket. His fingers were tight around his car's steering wheel and he ran his right thumb across the worn gray leather. Where it was badly worn it was actually black. He slowed to twenty-five. Up ahead was the policewoman who worked as crossing guard for the walkers. The yellow buses, at least twelve of them, were lined up outside the school close to the gym. There was a long line of cars, SUV's, and pick-ups parked parade fashion, waiting for the dismissal bell so they could inch their ways toward the child pick-up area.

He spotted her immediately. Green suit, matching green heels, walky-talky in hand standing on the sidewalk with a fake smile plastered on her face as lines of children walked toward her and the buses. The bus riders were always dismissed first. Appearances. It was all about appearances. Look at efficient, involved Principal Beaty. Always outside insuring the order and safety of our children. The damn truth was he missed having his nine millimeter Glock strapped to his side. Shoot each finger off at the knuckle, that'd take care of her nails. Then one bullet between the eyes. He pulled into the parking lot, alarmed by his heavy, rapid breathing and his pounding heart. He moved his jaw back and forth to keep from clenching his teeth. He'd broken one of his molars like that once. He killed the car's engine but turned the key forward on the steering column. He fished a CD out of the arm well. Classical music. He'd close his eyes. Employ deep breathing. Look at the picture of his kids. He'd wait. He planned to demand her undivided attention.

30

Each time she bent forward to smile at a parent driving through the pick-up lane, her ribs reminded her of Dr. Harry Z. Greene. Z for Zebediah he'd told her. From the Bible. His mother had apparently gone through a period of religiosity between drug busts he'd said. And each time she took a step closer to a car window to actually speak to a mom or dad, the top of her foot felt as though it had a burning cigarette searing it. Her arm actually felt a little better, sore like she had the flu but no longer throbbing. Wave, smile, greet, wave, smile, greet. She was thankful for her years as a majorette. Smile when the Alabama sun is melting you, the Alabama mosquitoes are devouring you, the Alabama humidity is smothering you, the Alabama rain is pelting you, and when Alabama cold snaps are freezing your ass off. Smile and strut, strut and smile, the show must go on. She was so intent on not caving into her pain that she didn't even see the crimson BMW inching slowly toward her from the other side of the parking lot.

Larry Ryan didn't see it right away either. His stake-out skills were slipping, he chided himself when the car finally caught his attention. By then the car was in front of her, stopped with the passenger window down. Larry watched her bend forward and shake her head. There was a wiry-looking man with a receding hairline behind the wheel. It looked like she was arguing with him. He saw her step backward. The car didn't move. "Shit," Larry muttered. He had a bad feeling he wouldn't be telling Dr. Priscilla Beaty exactly what was on his mind. Not this afternoon. He thought about the work time he was missing.

"Get in, Kitten," Bob Tulane was saying on the other side of the lot. "We need to talk."

She'd forgotten he called her Kitten. She hated cats. "For God's sake, Bob, can't you see I'm working?"

"Me, too. We'll call this our coffee break."

"I have parents to greet."

"You've seen the bulk of them. More importantly, they've seen you. Greet the rest of them tomorrow. Right now get in the car."

"Dammit, Bob. You're causing a scene. Get lost."

"Sorry. Not 'til we've talked. Your lover boy scared me shitless today. For you, not for me of course."

She looked around reflexively. Thankfully, no one within earshot. She glanced at the cars still in the pick up line. About twelve. She shook her head in frustration, opened the car door and got in. "This kind of behavior doesn't bode well for a July reunion," she snapped.

"Yeah, well, I just want you to be around in July. We'll worry about the rest later." He looked over his shoulder and into his rear view mirror before pulling away from the curb.

"My purse is in my office and I have a meeting to attend in about an hour. And I need time to unwind. I haven't had even a second to think." It was true. She'd barely had time to drop her purse in her desk. Her computer password changes had to wait.

"A meeting? Here?"

"No. Out at the lake."

"Which lake? Tuscaloosa? Nichols? Harris? Lurleen?"

There were a lot of lakes in Tuscaloosa County. He'd named the most obvious. "Forget it," she said.

He eased into a parking space in the emptying lot and scanned the activity around them. "That's not him over there is it?" he asked, pointing toward an Escort.

"Where?" She followed his stare until she saw broad shoulders and a familiar face intently watching them. She slumped down in her seat. "Damn! Not him again! All I need this afternoon is another run-in with him."

"Is that him?" Bob asked again.

"No. No, it's not. He's just an angry parent. Probably heard I pulled his boys into the office today."

Bob rolled down the windows before turning off the motor. "I feel pretty sure your crazed Romeo will show up here. Usually they do, you know. Stalking is what it's called."

She gingerly pulled her feet out of her shoes. "That feels so damned much better. I have a terrible blister." She looked toward it. The Band-Aid still clung to the outside of her stocking. It was edged in dark brown where dirt stuck to the adhesive and the gauze was brown from dried blood. She ran her fingers across the car's white leather seats and crimson console. "When'd you get this car?"

"Like it?"

"Crimson and white BMW? What'd ya' think?"

Bob put his hand on top of hers and squeezed. He cast a sideways smile toward her but didn't take his eyes off Larry Ryan.

"I can take care of myself, you know. Did for years before I met you. Since then, too."

"Yeah, well Mr. Angry Dad's worn out his welcome. He needs to take off." He stuck his arm out the window and pointed directly at Larry Ryan.

"What're you doing? Stop it."

"Just letting him know it's time to get lost." He pointed again. Priscilla watched the Escort slowly move out of its parking space. The car turned to the right and headed toward the main road.

"Well, that's a huge relief," she said. "I want to pinch his head off, I really do."

"So, what about this lover boy of yours?" asked Bob as he watched the Escort disappear.

"He's nobody," she said. "And like I said before, we're through."

"No way you're through. Not that type. He'll be calling. Coming by. Probably today. A day or two, max."

"I'll get a peace bond if he does. He doesn't scare me."

"Yeah, well, lots of women in the morgue have said that. Gotta watch your back, honey."

"I always do. Thanks for getting rid of that parent, though. I owe you one."

Bob turned toward her, a shit-eating grin on his face. "Let's remember you said that, Kitten."

She considered telling him how much she hated cats, nasty litter box feet and sandpaper tongues, but instead looked toward her watch. It was running five minutes faster than the numbers displayed on Bob's dash. "I've got to get out of here, Bob. The meeting's about Andrew and I can't be late. Call me this weekend and we'll discuss July."

"July's too far off."

"We'll talk this weekend, Bob." She had no intention of answering her phone.

He started the car and crept toward the main school entrance. Maybe he was going three miles an hour. "You never answered me. Where's your meeting?"

He really was a nosy SOB. What the hell? She didn't care. "Metamorphosis," she said.

"What?"

"That residential treatment facility out on Lake Tuscaloosa. On past the Yacht Club." She'd always thought the name remarkably out of place. There weren't many yachts moored in Tuscaloosa County on the Black Warrior River or its dammed up lakes. There was a country club and a well-heeled neighborhood sitting on streets boasting of marine names, genuine sea anchors and anchor chains, a fountain of Neptune, and a fairly remarkable full sized cast bronze elephant commissioned from an artist in Kenya. The elephant even trumpeted although she wasn't sure how or when. She had no idea how an elephant fit into the yacht theme, either.

"What time?"

"What time, what?"

"Your meeting. What time?"

"Don't follow me around. I don't want that."

"What you want or don't want is superfluous."

She opened the car door. "What I want will never be superfluous," she said. She grabbed her shoes with her middle and index fingers, balanced them with her thumb, and stepped gingerly onto the warm concrete, trying especially hard to avoid anything that might snag her nylons. She held her shoes against her rib cage. It helped. "See you later, Bob. We'll talk."

"Sooner than you think," he called after her. "Bye, Kitten." He watched her tiptoe toward the front door and disappear inside, calves muscled, perfect. Her legs and butt were still to die for.

The vaguest hint of roses lingered in his car. He sucked her scent deep into his nasal passages. It was a weird floral smell but he loved it. And he loved her body naked. And he loved that she was a hell-raiser. He missed her hell-raising the most. The kind of woman no man would ever take home to meet Mother.

He'd come to realize this since their break-up, even though his own mother died when he was barely twelve. Slipped off a narrow hiking trail and plunged to her death during a family camping trip. He was labeled an angry adolescent back then by teachers and school counselors and there'd been a full scale investigation. Yes, officer, I heard a noise like pebbles going down the cliff. Yes, she screamed. I don't know, she might've called my name. It happened so fast. By the time I looked over my shoulder she was going. Slipping, I mean. Slipping sideways. Fingers clawing the air. That weird look on her face, her mouth open almost like a goldfish. It was too late. There was nothing I could do. Nothing.

So Priscilla would never meet his mother. Hell, he didn't even want his nosy neighbor, old Mrs. Blakney across the road in Coker, to meet her. But he'd had a lot of time to dissect what went wrong in their relationship. He'd blown it when he said he loved her. When he gave her the clock. He'd searched all over Alabama for that damn clock and then she broke up with him almost while she was unwrapping it. But it all made sense now and she was right. Actually he never really loved her at all. He loved the way they partied together. He loved sex with her. He loved that she was intoxicating, exhilarating, and so self centered and pig headed she could never be trusted. This intimidated him before, but no longer. There'd been lots of nights to think it through. She was in it for herself. He picked up his phone to reschedule an afternoon appointment with a grove of poorly bearing pecan trees. He'd go to Metamorphosis, park outside and wait. He'd be the only Romeo on her balcony. And no more Mr. Nice Guy, Mr. Southern Gentleman. From now on they'd play by her rules.

31

He called in sick for the rest of the day. Headache, chills, fever he told his gum chewing receptionist. He'd never confronted her with Priscilla's concern that it looked crass and unprofessional to be chomping on gum and blowing pink bubbles through her plumped-up lips at the front desk. It was enough that she could answer the phone and handle credit card payments. It was hard to get good help these days.

"Can I do anything, Doc?" she asked.

"Just call my appointments and reschedule," he said. "I'll be okay by morning. Has to be just a virus. Flu season's over."

He was on the couch curled up under his grandmother's quilt. Stitch by stitch she'd sewn it, the pine frame stretched across their living room floor while he and Grandpa watched TV, almost always something educational. His grandparents weren't ever much for wasting time. "There's a whole world to learn about out there, Harry. Don't need to fill your mind with garbage."

Even as a young kid he got their point. There was enough garbage in his family. Mom never really there. Dad violent until he disappeared. And now, here it was, perpetuated in this very room, loaded into his genes as surely as the terror he felt contemplating the possibility. Never had a woman gotten him so riled up. Not to where he bullied. Not to where he attacked. It went against everything he believed in. Priscilla was right, his grandparents were surely rising out of their graves.

He'd considered following her, cajoling her into returning. But he was too ashamed. There was a minute of hope when he heard her tap her car horn. She was still close by, but when he looked out the window he saw she was honking at birds blocking her way. Turkey vultures, it looked like. And she kept talking about that damn bra she'd made for him. How many times did she invite him to enjoy it? How many fool times did he let it go?

The smell of her perfume, some cheap alcohol-based rose scent, hung too heavy in the air. She splashed it everywhere on her body, especially in the crook of her elbow and on her neck and around her ankles. And if he happened to lick it off her skin his tongue tasted like chemicals for hours. It was an awful taste. He'd tried to replace it with more desirable scents on several occasions but the rose never stayed gone long. Still, she had dainty manicured toes. He could fit them easily inside his lips, his tongue probing between them, his teeth barely nipping at her nails. Damn, she was hot.

He liked dating older women. He made a habit of it whenever he could. They weren't looking for marriage or trying to define themselves through their relationships. It was less complicated than dating women his own age. They got what they wanted. He got what he wanted. A gentleman's agreement so to speak. But that was before he got tangled up with Priscilla. Something about her drove him totally, absolutely, undeniably insane.

He rolled onto his side and hugged a rectangular velour pillow. It was Auburn orange, he actually never liked the color, but its texture was comforting. He'd send her flowers. Asiatic lilies, her favorites. But were flowers such a good idea? It was bizarrely comical to be so predictable. He knew all about the domestic violence cycle. His school counselor drew a big circular picture of it on a piece of pink construction paper with a black marker when he was in third grade. All she had left in the pack were pink sheets and she said she was sorry because she knew he'd probably rather have a different color. And he'd said, 'no ma'am, pink is fine' and he folded it up and stuffed it deep in his front jeans pocket when she was through and all the rest of the day he prayed none of his friends would find out what he was hiding. The counselor was his grandmother's idea. The counselor drew the circle using arrows and she talked about the pattern he'd seen again and again between his parents. Violence and promises and flowers and forgiveness and honeymooning and calm and rising tension and violence and promises and flowers and forgiveness and honeymooning and calm and rising tension, like a giant tire moving faster and faster down the interstate.

But, he was truly sorry. And he would promise to never do it again. And he would beg for forgiveness and he'd plead for another chance. And he would tell her she was wonderful and that he missed her already and that there was no excuse for his behavior but she made him certifiably crazy jealous. He knew the school counselor, if she were still alive, she looked really old even then, would correct him and tell him jealousy was really "insecurity" and "poor self esteem" and "need to control." The words were burned into his memory even though at the time he had absolutely no idea what she was talking about. But her arrows did help put some predictability into his life.

He looked at his watch. Too late to send flowers to the school. Flowers at school weren't a good idea anyway. He'd send them to her house with a cryptic message. She had a son at home so it had to be cryptic. He picked up the phone to call the florist. No. He'd deliver them himself a little later in the afternoon. She was sure to go home before she went to meet her old lover, Red. Maybe he could still dissuade her from going. He owed her the chance to model that bra.

32

Andrew sat at the head of the long rectangular table in a room the old lady called the Green Room.

The table was made out of some kind of wood but it was unnaturally shiny, almost like plastic.

"Hi. Sit wherever you feel comfortable," a thirty-ish man with a ponytail said when Andrew and Joey first got there. Andrew sat at the table's end. Shrinks. They should get the message. Joey sat two chairs away and the ponytail man sat two seats down from Joey. There were twelve chairs around the table. Andrew counted them. He was glad the ponytail guy gave them some space. The old lady sat across from the ponytail man. She looked really old, probably eighty or ninety or something, but her arms still had big muscles like she was a weightlifter. It was weird to him because most old people had skin that flapped around and hung all loose on their upper arms. She was trying to be sly. Even though she was fussing with papers and writing stuff down he knew she was watching him. Like a raptor, in fact, beady eyes. But oddly wise and kind-looking, too. And she smelled like a swimming pool.

"Yes, an iguana! Andrew named him D-Tail. He always was very clever with words."

Andrew's jaws clenched, molar against molar. His fists, too. Their mother was halfway through the door talking to a friendly looking woman, sort of cute. She was smoozing her way into the room even though it looked like she was limping a little bit. He wondered what that was about. Smiling, laughing, ever so charming. She could really turn it on. Talking about his damn iguana like it was still in his room. Like she hadn't stolen it. He rolled his eyes in Joey's direction. His brother's face was darker than usual, his posture too straight. When Andrew looked back toward the ponytail man he saw the man staring at his clenched fist, the one that wasn't in his lap. He forced his fingers outward, letting his palm and fingertips rest on the table. The man with the ponytail watched this then looked him straight in the eyes and smiled. It was an I-saw-that-your-fist-clenched-when-your-mother-walked-into-the-room smile. It pissed Andrew off. But at least it wasn't a smart-ass smile. He cleared his throat. He could feel the astringent rose smell moving down his windpipe.

The sort of cute woman had a bouncy step. Her clothes were nice. The kind of style Bethy'd like. He'd never say it out loud but his mom looked good too. He didn't like women in suits, too formal and uncomfortable. But she had flair, like she belonged in New York or Atlanta. She was all about appearances.

Two more adults followed behind his mother and the sort of cute woman, including a taller woman with a Victoria Secret body and a face that looked like a horse's. She sat down and the other adult followed suit. He was a Mexican-looking dude. He stretched his arm and half his body across the table to shake hands. "I'm Rico," he said. "I work day shift in the male Luna cottage." The skin on the man's hand was rough. Andrew had no idea. Day shift, whatever that meant. Luna cottage, wherever the hell that was.

He nodded slightly. "Andrew," he said.

Rico looked toward Joey. "So this must be your brother, Joey."

He was surprised Rico knew Joey's name. He didn't like it.

The man with the ponytail looked at the old lady and at the sort of cute woman. The old lady nodded and ponytail man and the sort of cute woman smiled at each other with familiarity. Close friends. Maybe more. The man wore a wedding band. The sort of cute woman didn't.

Ponytail man grinned a nerdy kind of smile. "So, Andrew. Today's meeting is to help familiarize you and your family with Metamorphosis so you'll feel more comfortable when you're admitted, which at the current time looks like it'll probably be Monday. My name is Dr. Luke Bramson and I'm the clinical psychologist for the cottage where you'll be living. There are two Luna cottages, one male and one female. Ms. Shelby McDonald, the lady right over there, and I are both therapists for the Lunas. Ms. McDonald is a clinical social worker. She will primarily work with your mom while I work with you."

"My mom'll need both of you to work on her bullshit."

"I'm sorry, I caught the first part of that sentence about your mom, but I didn't hear the end," said the ponytailed man Bramson.

Andrew smiled. He'd intentionally mumbled. "Doesn't matter."

His mother apparently did hear him. Her stare was fierce. "He said, if I may paraphrase it for you, Dr. Bramson, that I need both you and Ms. McDonald to concentrate on helping me. But of course as I'm sure you can surmise, he said it far more rudely and there is nothing further from the truth."

Andrew saw Joey roll his lips inward onto each other and bite down. He could tell he was biting because the area around his mouth was getting splotchy, pale in some places, red in others.

"No one person is ever to blame," the sort of cute woman named Ms. Shelby McDonald said, looking first at Andrew and then at his mother. "It's the *relationships* between people we try to help change." Her voice was gentle and positive and her intonation reminded Andrew of a pebble skipping on the water. He could make them skip four or five times. Once he'd even managed six.

"But surely," argued his mother, "for any relationship to change, a disrespectful teenager has to learn respect and responsibility."

The old lady shifted positions. "You bring up very valid points. And there'll be time to sort through all of that in detail once Andrew is in residence." She turned to face him. Her face was filled with little lines and wrinkles. "Andrew, I've spoken with your mother on the telephone and I met her in the hall several minutes ago, but you and I've not met. I'm Dr. Lydia Hutchinson, founder of this Center. I'm a psychiatrist, too. It's good to meet you and your brother, Joey."

Andrew watched Joey relax his lips as Dr. Hutchinson turned toward him. He couldn't believe it. His brother had drawn blood. Not a lot. It wasn't dripping or anything. But his lip was cut and there was a line of blood sitting on his lip, like magma along a crack in the Earth. Just sitting, not flowing. The old lady saw it, Andrew was sure. Her raptor eyes went straight for it. For a minute he thought she'd say something about it. But she didn't. She turned her attention away from Joey.

"And let me introduce you to Ms. Moffiti. She'll be your teacher," she said.

Ms. Moffiti, with the fine body and the horsey face, looked up from her notebook and nodded curtly. "I'll have some questions about your academics in a minute."

"And this is Rico, like he's already told you. Rico is what we call a Mentor, meaning he'll be with you and the other Lunas helping you learn to make better decisions."

"Luna, as in moth?" Andrew asked. As in kindergarten? As in kiddie camp? He already knew the answer. There were moths, butterflies, cocoons and caterpillars painted and posted all over the building, at least what he'd seen so far. Tony'd warned him. A place for pussies.

"Yes, that's right," said Dr. Hutchinson.

"So, kids come in here as disturbed caterpillars and leave with wings?"

Dr. Hutchinson's eyes danced and the man with the ponytail, Dr. Bramson, laughed out loud.

"Andrew!" said his mother.

"We like to think so, young man," said Dr. Hutchinson. "The symbolism certainly hasn't escaped you."

"Yeah, well, that's easier to figure out than why everything's orange in the Green room."

It was the sort of cute, perky woman's turn to laugh. "I see green," she said. "Lots of it." Everyone in the room except his mom smiled. Dr. Bramson and the guy named Rico sort of chuckled. Even Joey laughed.

"Yeah," said Andrew. He actually felt a little shy. Everyone was looking at his apple-green hair. It was streaked with just a little magenta over his left ear, and braided to look like dreds.

"I don't know that I've ever seen quite that color before," said horse face Moffiti. "How'd you do it?"

"Lime green gelatin," he said. "The powder stuff in those little boxes."

"Ha!" said Dr. Luke Bramson, adjusting the ponytail on the back of his neck with his hand.

"Well," said old Dr. Hutchinson. "I guess that's as good a use for it as any."

His mom looked pissed. Her eyes were squinty. "Personally I find it embarrassing for him. For me, too, actually."

Andrew looked at his brother and rolled his eyes. Joey was clearly enjoying the gelatin talk. Andrew laughed a little too loudly and leaned back in his chair. These people were okay.

"All right," said Dr. Bramson. "Let's try to get serious for a few minutes so we can wrap this up before the party tonight. One of our Luna boys, Benjamin, is having a birthday party after dinner. You're all welcome to stay if you'd like."

"Thanks," said his mother, "I've got another commitment."

"A date, she means," said Andrew. He actually mumbled so softly he didn't think anyone would hear.

"Well, Andrew, your mom's single," said the sort of cute woman Ms. McDonald. "Do you object to her dating?"

Joey shifted in his chair and Andrew heard him sucking air. "So, are we being honest here or polite?" Andrew asked.

"It's possible to be both," his mom said tersely. She was furious. Andrew smiled.

"Sometimes it is. Sometimes it's not," said old Dr. Hutchinson.

"Do you object to her dating?" This time Dr. Bramson asked.

Joey rolled his chair backward. "Excuse me," he said standing. "Which way is the men's room?"

"Down the hall to the right. First door."

"I'm not feeling well," said Joey. "Probably something I ate. I'll grab a few minutes of fresh air before I rejoin you. I'm sorry."

"Can I get you anything?" asked Dr. Hutchinson.

"No . . . thanks. I'll be okay."

Andrew watched his brother leave. Escaping. The whole dating question was too much.

Dr. Bramson turned expectantly toward Andrew. His eyebrows were raised, sort of the same way Bethy did when she was waiting for an answer. He thought about laying it all out on the table. His heart beat faster, harder, up into his throat right beneath his Adam's apple again and his stomach sent food back up his esophagus. See, my brother's sick because our mom sleeps around and he just found out today she's sleeping with his new boss. It was a real important job to him, and anyway, the guy's almost Joey's age. She always does stuff like that.

"Andrew does seem to have difficulty with my dating," said his mother formally. "Much more trouble than Joey does, actually. I think it has to do with Andrew's underlying problem and I can certainly understand his feelings. He has always had to struggle with not knowing his father's identity. But like I tell Andrew all the time, he is still responsible for his behaviors."

Andrew sat forward. "Like you, Mother?"

"Don't you dare use that tone of voice with me! You will be respectful!"

"Why?" Andrew countered. "You disrespect Joey and me all the time."

"That's enough," said his mother.

"No," he said. "I don't think so. You need help, not me." He wanted to go on, but it was all too embarrassing and too painful, and for a reason he didn't understand and didn't want to admit, he was afraid of her. There were rules. The line was very clear to him and to her, invisible to those outside the family. He dare not say what he was thinking, *or else.* Or else what? He had no idea. But ever since he was little he understood that things he said during arguments at home couldn't be repeated in public. *Or else.* "This is stupid," he said, pushing away from the table. "I'm going to find Joey."

"You stay in here, young man!" His mother started to stand but Dr. Hutchinson touched her arm.

"It's okay. Let him go check on his brother and cool off a little himself."

Andrew crossed to the door in four strides. His face was flushed, he could tell. He shut the door too heavily behind him. As it shut he heard his mother's voice. Her sad victim voice. "He's so angry. I have to put up with tantrums like this all the time. I'm sorry you had to see it."

"It's important for us to see it," he heard the old lady answer in a muted fuzzy voice.

The hallway was well lit. It was covered with some kind of paneling, a yellowy wood smothered in shellac or something. And there were cut-outs of caterpillars and moths and butterflies stuck everywhere. Permanently crawling and flying, never moving. Like flies on fly paper. The floor was white linoleum with glittery specks in it. It smelled like ammonia and pine. Joey wasn't in the hall. Neither was anybody else. "Bitch!" he yelled as he stalked toward the exit.

The metal bar on the exit door was sticky like it was caked with dried hand sweat. The door opened onto a sort of garden area, and beyond that, what looked like a multi-use athletic field. Joey was sitting on a bench beneath a huge tree with thick dark leaves. Nestled in the tree's branches were three beach ball sized globs of sticks and pine straw and leaves. Squirrel nests. He waved and Joey waved back. Andrew saw that he was on the phone.

"She *did* know I'd be working with him this summer," he was saying as Andrew sat down. The bench was black metal and contoured to be comfortable. Andrew leaned back and listened. "I specifically told her about it. That's what makes it unforgivable. I swear to God I'll never forgive her."

The exit door opened. Luke Bramson stepped outside. They were both there, sitting on the bench. He felt relieved they hadn't taken off.

Joey was on the phone. He smiled and headed toward them. The toes of his boots overlapped cracks in the sidewalk as he walked. It wasn't that he believed in the old step-on-a-crack-break-your-mother's-back stuff, he was a clinical psychologist for goodness sake, but still he lifted his toes inside his boots as he walked.

"Thomas, hold just a second." Joey stared at the approaching Dr. Bramson and covered his phone's mouthpiece. "Andy, go back inside to the meeting. I'll be in after I finish talking to Thomas, okay?"

"I just came to check on you. Anyway, Mom's in there talking bullshit."

"Yeah, well, they can tell. They're used to people like her, I'm sure."

Dr. Bramson stopped about four yards away. He glanced at Joey's phone. "You have a few minutes to talk?" he asked Andrew in a quiet voice. "We can sit right over there at the picnic table if you'd like."

"Go," said Joey. "I'll wait here until you guys are through and then we'll go back in together."

Andrew stood and squared his shoulders. He was nearly as tall as the man standing before him. Dr. Bramson didn't speak as they walked across the grass toward the concrete table. Andrew smelled peppermint. The man was rolling something around on his tongue.

"Want a peppermint?" he asked pulling one out of his pocket.

Damn, the guy was good. He'd obviously been studying people a long time. "No thanks." He sat on the concrete bench across from Dr. Bramson. He put his arms on the table. It was littered with leaves and had little sticky dots on it that reminded him of syrup but he guessed were tree sap. The concrete was gray, stained darker in places, and jagged on one corner. There was white bird poop with little black lines in it near one edge. He watched an ant skirt the white. Winged seeds rotored down like little helicopter blades from one of the trees above them.

"So," Dr. Bramson said. "There were lots of people in there and it's hard to concentrate with so much going on. In case you didn't catch it, I'm Dr. Luke Bramson and I'm a clinical psychologist. You can just call me Dr. Luke if you want. That's what most folks call me."

Andrew watched his brother. He was walking back and forth near the bench still talking to his father.

Dr. Luke followed his eyes. "Is your brother feeling better?"

"I don't know. He's talking to his dad."

"Oh . . ."

"So what do you need to talk to me about?"

Dr. Luke looked him directly in the eyes. Direct but somehow nonchalant. He had smart eyes. Damn, they were blue. They looked kind. "So, part of being a clinical psychologist is that what you tell me, unless you tell me you have plans to seriously harm yourself or someone else, is confidential. That means I don't repeat what you say without your permission. Not to your mother. Not to your brother. Not to anyone."

"Joey and I don't have secrets," said Andrew.

"I can see you're close," said Dr. Luke scratching his neck behind his ponytail. "But having said that, it's sometimes helpful if I can represent your thoughts and feelings to the rest of your treatment team. It makes progress faster and easier. They have to keep everything confidential, too."

He had no idea who was on a treatment team. "You mean, tell them what I tell you?"

"Only with your permission. And you can tell me what I can say to them and what I can't."

"I guess I wouldn't care if you told that lady Shelby and the old lady who owns the place."

"Dr. Lydia? That's what we usually call her. I think she told you her name was Dr. Hutchinson."

"Yeah, I guess."

Luke smiled and nodded. "Good choices," he said.

Andrew studied the brown leather string that tied the man's hair back. He wondered how long Dr. Luke had been growing his hair. "So how long has it been since you cut your hair?" he asked.

Dr. Luke chuckled. "About a year and a half," he said. His attention followed Andrew's stare back over toward Joey. "You seem really worried about your brother today."

It was more a statement than a question even though Andrew knew it was really a question. He rubbed his eyes and forehead hard with his hands and sighed. What the hell? It didn't really matter. He was never coming back to this place anyway. "My brother's seeing a shrink at Auburn," he said. "I just found out today."

"He told you?"

"Yeah." Andrew slouched.

"Sounds like what he said surprised you."

Andrew leaned over and picked up a stick. He snapped it into pieces, uneven short pieces, and let them fall back to the ground. "He's scaring the hell out of me. He smashed a lamp at the house right before we came here today."

"Because you're being admitted?"

"No." Silence. He wanted to say it. It was so damned embarrassing. The man named Dr. Luke waited. It was a patient wait, not a demanding one. "Can you talk to him?" Andrew asked. "He needs someone to talk to."

Dr. Luke motioned toward Joey with a slight nod of his head. "Looks like he's talking to his father right now. Do they have a good relationship?"

"Yeah. Thomas is cool."

"And, he's obviously talked to you."

"Yeah, but he needs someone who can help him."

Dr. Luke paused, smiled slightly. "Do you know his counselor's name at Auburn?"

"Some guy named Asa."

Dr. Luke nodded. "I think your brother's in good hands. I've gotten to know Asa over the years at professional meetings. If you'd like, I can relay your concerns to him. He won't be able to say he knows your brother because of confidentiality, but he can still listen and what we tell him might help."

"It really pisses me off."

"What does?"

"Our fuckin' mother. It's all because of her. My bad. I didn't mean to curse."

"What's because of her?"

"All of it."

Silence again. He could feel Dr. Luke waiting. What the hell? Why not say it? "Joey found out today and I'm the one who told him that she's been screwing the man he planned to work with this summer. The guy's a vet and that's what Joey wants to be and the man has some great reputation so Joey wanted to work with him. And he was already hired. Supposed to start in about four weeks, I think. And, his girlfriend's coming home for the summer so he wants to be in Tuscaloosa. And our mother knew all this and still went out and started screwing him and the guy is young enough to be our brother. Joey says she's got a sexual addiction."

"Hmm . . ." He saw Dr. Luke's eyes narrow. He could tell he was sorting through everything.

"She's always done crap like this to us."

"So, it's about a lot more than not knowing who your dad is?"

Andrew laughed. "Like I give a shit about him. I gave up on him about the same time I stopped believing in the Easter bunny."

Dr. Luke nodded slowly.

"Don't call Asa," said Andrew. "Never mind. I don't want Joey to think I'm in his business."

The man nodded again. "That must have been a tough way for both of you to grow up," he said.

"It was fucking messed up. Still is." He picked up a pine cone and threw it across the lawn. "Sorry, my bad for cursing."

Dr. Luke nodded again.

The guy sure nodded a lot. It was weird but not in a particularly bad way.

"Okay," said Dr. Luke. "So, I'm going to change the subject for a minute if that's okay. But it's all like a big circle and it's all related and it will help me understand. Okay?"

Andrew shrugged.

"In your records it says you have a history of a lot of things. Like stealing and lying and truancy and using cigarettes, maybe other substances, too, and being defiant."

He didn't know he had a record. He wondered what it said. He wondered where it was. He wondered how it got to Dr. Luke. It embarrassed him to ask about it. Not now. "Only with her," he said. "Her and a teacher at the Magnet school last year who looks like an iguana and was always on my case."

Dr. Luke laughed. "So did he have a long tail, or what?"

"Who? My iguana or the guy?"

Dr. Luke laughed again. "The guy. But I heard your mom say you have an iguana."

"Had. His name was D-Tail. I came home one day and the whole damn aquarium was gone. Mom'd taken it to her school for the science teacher. That's the way she is. It really pissed me off." That was really only partly true. He'd flown into a rage and punched three holes in his walls and threatened to dump Winx in the woods but he knew he'd never really do that because the dog was really Joey's and anyway, it wasn't the dog's fault. Anyway in some ways it was a relief. Taking care of D-Tail could be a hassle especially when the lizard crapped in the aquarium and his whole room stank and he had to clean out the tank and clean the heat rock and the water dish and the food bowl. Still, he missed him and the way he draped his body across his dresser or the couch and stared with alien eyes. And the way he sat on the top of his head and just stayed there, heavy, toes wrapped into his hair, pulling. "The teacher had a hangy down lizard neck," he said. "Just like my iguana."

Dr. Luke's face scrunched up like he was trying to imagine it.

"And I don't do drugs unless you count alcohol. Tried beer three or four times and had vodka once. One time I did take a few hits off a marijuana cigarette at a party but that's it. Didn't like it."

"Regular cigarettes?"

"Yeah. When I can get them."

"Sex?"

Andrew tensed. "What?"

Dr. Luke smiled. "Strange questions psychologists ask, huh? But, it's an important question we ask all teens, if they're sexually active I mean."

He did feel embarrassed. "Not now," he said.

"In the past?"

"Once at a party with like an eighteen year old girl." On an old yellow couch with dirty foam rubber crumbling out of one of the cushions. Afterwards he fled the party and never saw her again. She had fat thighs and her hair covered his bare shoulder and her boobs were shaped sort of like fried eggs and he kept staring at her closed eyes and he wanted to slap the shit out of her. She had a reputation for wanting sex and his friends pushed him to go for it, he was thirteen, what was he waiting for? But even while they were doing it all he could think was that she was just like his mother and it made him want to puke and beat her up.

"So, are you with anyone now?"

Andrew squirmed. The concrete was getting hard, digging into his tailbone, and Joey was off the phone. "What is this, twenty questions?"

Dr. Luke chuckled again. "I'm sure it feels like it," he said. "I'm just trying to get to know you better. Sorry if I've kept you too long."

Andrew shrugged. "Yeah, I'm with someone," he said. "And it may sound crazy but I'd never disrespect her like that." The sentence dangled hollow in the air. He felt sick to his stomach again. He knew he sounded lame and he tried to block all emotion from his face. It wasn't normal. Not for a guy. Sex, even the thought of it, made him want to vomit. He could dream about it okay but in real life it was too much. He wondered what this doctor guy would think about that.

"That doesn't sound crazy at all. Sounds like you really care about her."

It wasn't about caring even though he knew he did. It went much deeper. He wasn't about to say anything more.

"Want to go check on your brother?"

"Yeah."

Dr. Luke looked at his watch. "I suspect the meeting's broken up by now, anyway. Rico will've left to pick up the kids from school, and Ms. Moffiti's probably back in her classroom finishing up. Your mom's probably talking to Dr. Lydia Hutchinson, and probably Ms. Shelby McDonald's with them too. It's been good talking with you, Andrew. Once you're admitted you and I can meet at least twice a week if you want."

"Sure," said Andrew wondering if Dr. Bramson knew, like he knew, that it was never going to happen.

33

He was sitting on a boulder outside the male Luna cottage beside Birthday Boy Benjamin. That's what Dr. Luke called him. It was kind of stupid but Andrew could tell it was meant kindly. Birthday Boy Benjamin was short, skinny and freckled. His hair was an anemic looking red and was shaved close. His eyebrows were anemic too and it looked like he didn't have any hair to shave off his chin. His hands were big, like they belonged to another body.

"Hey Dr. Luke, what time's my party?" the boy asked.

"Right after dinner."

"You coming?"

"Wouldn't miss it."

"How about Ms. Shelby?"

"She wouldn't miss it either."

The boy turned to face Andrew. He was grinning. His mouth was also too big for his body. "You wanna come?"

"Um, thanks, but I'm going home soon." Even though the others were keeping their distance, he felt the entire group checking him out. Eighteen staring eyes, not counting Birthday Boy or the Mentor guy Rico. Andrew couldn't see the girls' cottages but he heard laughter and chatter coming from somewhere through the trees. A squirrel ran across the lawn. Run, pause, sit, twitchy tail, run, pause, sit, twitchy tail, and up a nearby pine.

"Shit, your hair's green," a boy with lots of pimples said too loudly. He had broad shoulders and braces and the build of a tackle. "How'd you get it that color, anyway?" Someone across the yard laughed.

"No cursing, Ernie," said Rico the Mentor. "Think of a word to express yourself that works better than shit."

"Golly-jeez, your hair's green," the pimpled boy said, giving a thumb's up when the other kids laughed.

"This is Andrew," Dr. Luke announced. "You fellas remember how it was to visit campus before you moved in, so be sure to come up and introduce yourselves." He turned toward the boy named Benjamin and said more softly, "I'm leaving him here with you, Benji. I've got to do some work in my office. That okay?"

"Sure, Dr. B."

"How about with you?" Dr. Luke asked Andrew.

He shrugged. "Sure, I guess." It wasn't his idea to visit the cottage in the first place. In fact he balked at the idea. "I'll wait out here," he said, motioning toward the little park and the picnic table where he and Dr. Luke sat earlier. That was after Joey announced Thomas was on his way to Metamorphosis to talk with him face to face. Thank God for Thomas. He wondered if Thomas knew about Joey's gory dreams and about the time he cut himself and about the counselor Asa. He wondered if Joey'd told him about sneaking knives up to his room when he was little and about the smashed lamp today. So he was sitting beside Birthday Boy Benjamin waiting for Joey and Thomas to finish talking so he could catch a ride back home. There was no way he was getting into the car with his mother and walking was out of the question. Way too far. Joey wouldn't hear of it. But it was quarter to four. He had so much to do before sunset.

"So when are you moving in?" asked Benjamin, nibbling around the edge of a chocolate chip cookie.

Andrew glanced around. No one was near. "I'm not."

"I thought . . ."

"Yeah, I'm supposed to sometime in the next few days. But I'm not."

"Ha! You runnin'?"

"Maybe."

Benjamin shrugged. "I was like that at first. But it's not bad here. It beats the hell out of a lot of places I've been."

"Good."

"Why're you bein' put here?"

"None ya'."

Benjamin licked one of the chocolate chips, his tongue moving slowly, digging, scooping the chocolate. "Yeah, maybe. But once you get here it'll all be out. You have to talk about all that shit. They call it taking responsibility for your actions."

"Whatever."

Benjamin turned his wrist holding the cookie upside down. He stared at his watch. Laughter flickered through his eyes. "Are you fast?"

"What?"

"Can you run fast?"

The guy was starting to annoy him. "Fast as anyone else, I guess."

Benjamin pushed the cookie into his mouth and glanced toward Rico. Andrew looked that way, too. The man was busy helping Ernie with the pimples re-inflate a football. In fact, Rico was squatting and his back was toward them.

"I'm gonna show you something," said Benjamin. "I usually charge a dollar for my excursions, but I'll give it to you today."

"What the hell you talking about, excursions?"

"It'll make you want to be here. I can promise you that."

Andrew glanced toward the parking lot where he knew Joey and Thomas were meeting. He wished they'd hurry. "That's okay," he said.

"Don't be an asshole. All you have to do is chase me. Cuss me out if you want. But follow me and run like hell."

Andrew shook his head. "Naw. I'll be leaving in a few minutes."

"This won't take long. I swear. Trust me." He stood up. "Are you in?"

Andrew shrugged. He was a little curious. "Whatever," he said.

"Bastard!" screamed Benjamin. He shoved Andrew sideways on the boulder, pushed past him and sprinted up the hill toward the main buildings. "Bastard!" he yelled again over his shoulder.

Andrew paused. The dumbass had stepped on his toe. The baby toe on his right foot. He wiggled it inside his tennis shoe gingerly. The guy was clearly psycho. But, what the hell? It was his birthday. He leaped off the rock and took off in pursuit. Out of the corner of his eye he saw Rico swivel around, still squatting, then stand.

"Benjamin!" the man yelled after both of them. "Stop! Come back! Don't get in trouble today! It's your birthday!"

"Come back, Benjamin!" one of the boys chimed in. "Come back, dude!"

Andrew was breathing hard by the time he reached the main building complex. His tee-shirt stuck to his back in a circle of sweat right above his waist. He put his hands down into his pockets to reassure himself his treasures were still there. Benjamin was nowhere to be seen. "Damn!" he said. What was he thinking, anyway? Following a crazy SOB God knows where.

"Hey! Over here. Hurry!"

Andrew saw the boy's red hair and freckled face peeking through a tall unkempt bush. His mother made him shape all their bushes at home. "What the hell are we doing?" he asked.

"Shut up," the kid said in a hoarse whisper. "Come on. Hurry! We're almost there."

Benjamin pushed his way along the brick wall behind the row of shrubs. Andrew was annoyed. The branches were scratching his arms and poking him in the face. It wasn't like the shrubs were really thick enough to hide them. Benjamin shoved his hand into his back pocket and pulled out a key. He put it in the lock of a gray metal door framed by the shrubs. "I stole this months ago from the janitor," he whispered. "Best thing I've ever stolen anywhere." He pulled the door open and grabbed Andrew's arm. "Come on!"

For being so skinny and short, the kid was strong. Andrew was jerked into a dark room. It wasn't much bigger than a closet. It was piled high with suitcases. It smelled like hot plastic and dust.

"Where the hell are we?"

"Shut up," Benjamin whispered pulling the door closed.

"What the hell is this place?"

"Talk soft!" Benjamin whispered. "It's an observation room. They stand in here and watch us sometimes. We can see her but she can't see us. It's a mirror on her side." He slowly opened a set of Venetian blinds hanging along one side of the dark room, the side not piled with suitcases. "*Yes!*" he said. "She's still here."

Andrew moved toward Benjamin and peered through the blinds. It was the teacher, Ms. Moffiti. She was sitting behind her desk writing something in a green book. They watched her pick up the phone. It was hard to hear what she was saying but Andrew heard a garbled mumble about leaving soon and she'd keep a look-out for "them."

"I'd turn on the sound but she probably won't be saying much," whispered Benjamin. "I think that call's probably about us."

"No duh," said Andrew.

"Watch, dude."

Andrew wondered if Joey were ready to go. "I need to get out of here."

"Not yet," said Benjamin. "Watch! We all call her Mo-titti."

Andrew watched her open her bottom right hand drawer and pull out a pair of shorts, a jogging bra and a white tee-shirt.

"Oh, yeah!" whispered Benjamin. "Oh, yeah! Here we go! Mo-titti! Mo-titti! Damn, she's hot!"

Andrew watched her cross her arms and pull her blouse up by its hem until her stomach was exposed. Tight and tan. Up over her bra. White lace. Nipples poking. Her blouse went inside out over her head and she stood facing them, turning her blouse right side out, folding it neatly, placing it on a corner of her desk. She moved her hands around to the right side of her waist and he watched her unzip her slacks. With a little wiggle of her hips they fell to the floor.

"I'm in love," whispered Benjamin. "I swear to God I'm in love. She's the hottest woman I've ever seen. Look at those titties. God, what a body!"

Andrew watched her step sideways out of her slacks, bend over, pick them up and fold them.

"Damn what an ass!" whispered Benjamin.

She held her jogging bra out in front of her. She turned it around. Andrew swallowed nervously. This was like an animated version of his mother's lingerie catalogues. He started stealing and stashing them in his room when he was about twelve.

"Man," he whispered. "This is totally messed up. I'm out of here. I'm not a fucking peeping Tom."

"You crazy?" Benjamin said a little too loudly.

"I'm out of here," Andrew said again.

"You can't! Not 'til she leaves. If you open the door she'll be able to see us."

Andrew moved against the suitcases. They were light. Empty. Easy to push around. He wondered why they were there. He got to the door and turned the knob. "Then close the blinds," he said. "I'm gone."

"Dammit!" said Benjamin, again too loud, grabbing the plastic rod, twisting quickly. The blinds closed. "You out of your fucking head?"

Andrew cracked the door and peered outside. Coast was clear. "See ya'."

Benjamin followed Andrew out of the observation room. Both boys blinked in the sunlight. "You're an idiot," Benjamin said, shoving Andrew backward.

Andrew barely moved despite Benjamin's shove to his chest. "Keep your hands off me, dude, I mean it." He balled his fists.

"Yeah," said Benjamin walking toward him, squaring his shoulders. "Try it."

"I don't want to fight," said Andrew. "Just keep off me."

"Forget ever coming up here with me again. I'll bring the other guys who appreciate it."

Andrew relaxed his fists. "Fine by me."

"Benjamin! Andrew! Hold up!" It was Dr. Luke. He was turning the corner of the building, jogging toward them on the sidewalk. Behind him, jogging in the opposite direction was Ms. Moffiti.

"You're one crazy sonofabitch," said Andrew.

"Don't say anything," said Benjamin quickly. "Let me handle it."

"Whatever."

Dr. Luke was breathing heavily by the time he reached them. He turned toward Benjamin. "What's all this about? Rico says you guys ran from the cottage."

"He called my mom a bitch," said Benjamin. "And I overreacted, Dr. B. But then I remembered the technique we learned in group, you know, the Stop, Think, Choose, Act. And so I did that and it worked just like you said it would. I told myself he doesn't even know my mother, and even if he did, just because he called her a bitch doesn't make her one. And I chose to not fight. So we're on a quick tour of this place on our way back to the cottage. You know, so he can learn his way around."

Dr. Luke raised his eyebrows and shook his head slowly. "And what's the rule about running off from the cottages and wandering around without permission?"

"Don't do it. I'm sorry, Dr. Luke. We were on our way back when you found us."

"Well, when you get back you need to serve a half hour room restriction before dinner. I'm going to trust you to tell Rico that yourself. I'm sorry you both broke the trust I placed in you."

"Me too, Dr. Luke."

Andrew stared at Benjamin. The kid looked totally remorseful.

"But I'm proud of you for using the Stop, Think, Choose, Act technique, Benji. I'm glad you chose a better solution than fighting."

"That's progress for me, isn't it, Dr. Luke?" asked Benjamin, flashing a coy smile.

Dr. Luke Bramson looked toward Andrew and then back at Benjamin. "It's good you recognize progress in yourself," he answered.

"Andrew, once you settle in here, try hard to think for yourself. Don't follow bad leads, okay? There will always be bad leads in our world. We have to learn to think responsibly."

There was that word, just like Benjamin promised. "Yes, sir."

"Okay, well, I think your brother's ready to leave. He's been waiting on you down at the Luna cottage."

Damn! He told Benjamin he didn't have time. Joey was waiting. There was so much to do.

"Now you guys go straight back to the cottage. No more sightseeing, got that?" He had a no-nonsense expression on his face.

Benjamin nodded solemnly before he cracked a lopsided grin. "Yes, sir. But I did show him some amazing parts of our campus. Didn't I, Andrew?"

Andrew shrugged. He thought about the weird room with the suitcases. And Ms. Moffiti and her white lace bra and her tight tan stomach.

"It's not okay to break the rules, Benji," said Dr. Luke. "I want you to think about what you could have done differently while you're in your room, then talk to me about that before your party."

"Yes, sir."

"Okay, now get out of here. I'll call Rico and let him know you're on your way."

"See you tonight, Dr. Luke," said Benjamin. He turned and took off running.

Andrew looked Dr. Luke Bramson straight in the eyes. The guy was okay. Totally clueless but okay. "Thanks for talking to me about my brother earlier," he said.

Dr. Luke nodded and extended his hand. "Sure thing," he said.

Andrew shook it. Dr. Luke had long fingers. He'd have good reach on the keyboard. An octave and a half maybe.

"See you Monday," said Dr. Luke.

Andrew didn't answer. He liked the guy. He didn't want to lie.

Even though Benjamin had a head start, Andrew's legs were longer and he caught up with him halfway down the hill. "You lied," he said. "I never called your mom a bitch."

"You called me a sonofabitch."

"I called you one crazy sonofabitch."

"Well, my mom *is* a bitch so you're right." The kid was loping along with that lopsided grin on his face.

"Yeah?" Andrew said. "My mom, too. With a capital B."

"That was funny as hell, dude, Ms. Mo-titti jogging right past Dr. B's back while he's talkin' to us."

Andrew threw his head back and laughed from somewhere deep inside his belly. "You're one crazy-ass dude, Birthday Boy Benny."

34

She pushed the worn metal bar and stepped through the door onto the sidewalk. The metal felt sticky and she rubbed her fingers together as her eyes adjusted to the sunlight. The sidewalk was decorated with chalk, a green horse, or maybe it was a dinosaur, three suns of various sizes, two yellow and one orange and all with lined rays sticking out of them like porcupine quills, and the names Sophie and Amandica written in bubble letters. She glanced at her watch. Four forty-five. She didn't have much time. As soon as she got home she'd get rid of her green shoes, thank God, and find that black lace underwear.

Ms. Shelby McDonald chuckled softly. "I see the younger kids have been expressing themselves with chalk," she said.

Dr. Beaty stepped onto a blue lake with a group of black V's flying above it. "I can't see Andrew ever getting into sidewalk art," she said.

Ms. McDonald smiled again. "He's a little older than the group that was out here, but you never know. You might be surprised."

"I doubt it."

"Well, Dr. Beaty, it was good to meet you," she said. "And I look forward to working with you when Andrew's admitted next week."

Dr. Priscilla Beaty glanced up the hill toward her Lexus and tried not to breathe deeply. Her side still hurt. She hoped there were no visible bruises. She dreaded the walk up the hill in her shoes. She'd take them off as soon as the McDonald lady left her alone. "I just hope you can help Andrew," she said. "Who knows how he'll react when I identify his father?"

Shelby's breath caught in her throat. She hoped it wasn't noticeable. "I understand," she said thinking of Molly. Of Steve. Of the day she'd be facing the same problem. "But we'll all try to help Andrew together. Like we said in the meeting, Dr. Bramson will be Andrew's individual therapist and I'll be your primary contact, and hopefully together we can begin to get things straightened out for your family."

"Andrew's the only mess. Joey and I are fine."

"It's always a family effort, Dr. Beaty." She said it gently, softly, but there was no mistaking the implication. And the implication angered Dr. Beaty. Shelby saw it quiver across her lips.

A car door swung open about a hundred feet away. "Damn!" Dr. Beaty exclaimed before she could catch herself. "What the hell is he doing out here?" Bob. He really had followed her. He really was waiting.

Shelby looked at her with surprised concern. "Do you know that man?"

"Yes," she said. She didn't want this McDonald woman in her business. "It's not a problem. He's a friend. But I told him not to come."

The two women watched him stride toward them.

"I asked you not to come," said Dr. Beaty coldly when he was close enough to hear. He continued to close the gap between them.

"I know, darlin'. But you gave me quite a scare this afternoon. I'm just here to see you home. I'll follow you. Make sure everything's okay, that's all."

Dr. Beaty cast an awkward glance toward Shelby. "I told you I'd make it home by myself just fine, Bob."

Shelby stepped backward. "Do you want me to wait over there? So you two can talk?"

"No need." She tried to make her answer sound light, conversational. "This is my overly concerned friend, Mr. Bob Tulane. Bob, this is Ms. Shelby McDonald. She'll be one of the people helping Andrew."

Shelby extended her hand and he shook it. His palm near the knuckles was calloused and his skin felt rough. "Hello," she said.

"Good to meet you," he said but he was clearly not paying attention. He turned back to Dr. Beaty. "I'm sorry, Priscilla. Just let me do this and I'll get out of your hair."

The tension between them was palpable. "Well, if everything's okay, I'm going to head back toward my office," Shelby said watching Mr. Bob Tulane take another step toward Dr. Beaty. "I'll phone you Monday morning before work, Dr. Beaty, so we can discuss details. Call me before that if you'd like."

Dr. Beaty didn't look in her direction. "Fine," she said, narrowing her eyes at Bob.

"Nice meeting you," the man said. It was obviously formality only. Dr. Beaty's narrowed eyes appeared to amuse him. There was a cockiness, an arrogance in his smile.

Shelby turned and walked slowly back toward the buildings. She had an icky feeling. She was unsure about leaving Dr. Beaty with this man.

"How dare you show up here?" Dr. Beaty asked in a raspy whisper that was meant to exclude Shelby but did not. "Who knows what that lady thinks with you showing your ass like this?"

"I'm sorry, Kitten," Shelby heard him say. "But that really was quite a scare you gave me today. And then you needed rescuing again from Mr. Angry Dad this afternoon. That's twice in one day."

"Dammit, Bob, get lost, and from now on when you talk to me use my name. I hate damn cats."

Shelby couldn't see it but Bob looked confused for about thirty seconds. Like he was trying to connect cats to something. She did hear him laugh. "Sure, honey," he said. "But just let me follow you home then I swear to God I'll leave. You don't know about guys like him. He's gonna show up, I promise you that. You don't think he'll let you just walk out of his life? Come on, Priscilla. Let's get out of here. Stop by the Walk of Champions and talk a bit."

She hadn't been to the Walk of Champions since last football season. He knew how much she loved it. The neatly tailored plaza leading into the football stadium was lined with larger than life sized bronze statues of the coaches who'd led Alabama to national football championships. There was Wallace Wade from the 20's, Frank Thomas from the 30's, Bear Bryant, who coached from the 50's through the 80's, Gene Stallings from the 90's and Nick Saban after 2000. "Bob, I have six o'clock plans. I've got to go."

Pause. "Plans? Not with that jerk . . ."

"You're acting like a damned stalker, Bob. And I don't remember inviting you all up into my business. I'm meeting with Red about Andrew since you're so intent on knowing. Now get lost."

"Okay. Okay. I don't mean to . . ."

"Screw July, Bob."

"Come on, Kitten. I mean, Priscilla. I'm sorry. Really. I just . . ." His voice blended into the calls of birds and the hum of the building's air conditioner.

"Curious," said Shelby aloud as she neared the building's corner.

"Curious?" echoed Luke. He was headed the other way and nimbly jumped aside right before they collided.

"Oh, hi. Really curious actually." Shelby nodded toward the pair. They were still involved in animated discussion. As she nodded Mr. Tulane took five or six steps backward, apparently moving toward his car. Dr. Beaty turned and headed up the hill toward hers. It appeared that she was limping, and she had her elbow pinned against her rib cage. Suddenly she stopped and took off one of her shoes. Just one. "That man out there, his name is Mr. Bob Tulane, apparently he showed up uninvited. She was really pissed but identified him as a friend. He kept alluding to needing to protect her from another guy, maybe even two guys, or maybe from something else, I don't know. Something about her giving him a real scare today. But clearly they weren't talking about Andrew. And she kept telling him to get lost."

"Hmm," said Luke. "Well, actually that fits with what Andrew told me about his mom's relationships. I think he'll work out just fine here. He gave me permission to talk to you, verbal, not written, but we'll get written permission next week."

"Good."

"He's opened up a little bit already. Mainly seems worried about his brother. Says Mom's been having an affair with his brother's summer boss despite knowing the conflicts this might cause. Andrew apparently thinks his brother's destabilizing. I think Joey shared some personal stuff with him today that sort of freaked him out."

"Mom really sticks to her opinion that Andrew's the only one with a problem."

Luke watched her nearing her Lexus. "Why's she limping with her shoe off?" he asked. "Looks like she's holding her rib cage, too."

"I noticed that," said Shelby.

"Andrew describes her as having real problems with promiscuity. He didn't put it that way. He called it sexual addiction. He apparently learned that term from his brother."

"So the ladies at Reverend Lincoln's church might have been right?"

"Andrew's certainly got lots of anger directed toward her behaviors. He denies struggling much with the unidentified father issue. Sounds like most of his behaviors are fueled by his maternal relationship."

"So, we're looking at a Monday admission?"

"The bed's free tomorrow, but I think it's better to wait until after the weekend."

"Works for me," said Shelby. "Looks like he isn't backing off," she said as both cars turned the corner and disappeared, Mr. Tulane's car following close behind the Lexus. "Strange." She glanced at her watch. "Hope she'll be okay. Well, I guess I'd better head back in to make some calls."

"Oh, Shel, one more thing."

"Yeah?"

"I caught Benjamin and Andrew running around up here. Actually saw them on the sidewalk outside the classroom. Don't know where they'd been. Benji said he was taking Andrew on a tour of some of the amazing parts of Metamorphosis. That's what he said, 'amazing'."

Shelby laughed. "Sounds suspicious for sure."

"Absolutely. Benji concocted some story about why they ran from the cottage but I don't believe a word of it. You know, this is about the eleventh time we've caught him running around the building at about the same time of day, sometimes with a buddy, sometimes alone. He's up to something. I just can't figure it out."

"The snack machines maybe?"

Luke shrugged. "Maybe. But staff never catches him with anything."

"Transition problems between the structure of the school day and free time at the cottage?"

"Possible," Luke said. "He does have problems with transitions. But I think there's more."

"Well, we'll catch him eventually," she said. "We always do."

Luke laughed. "As good as all of us are at sleuthing, I suspect these walls could tell stories to forever make us humble."

Her eyes met his. His were dancing with vicarious mischief. "I'm sure you're right about that," she said.

"I told Benji he'd earned room restriction so he's serving it now, before his party."

"That's only about an hour from now. I need to get to those phone calls. See you at the party."

"I'll bring down the cake." He'd been in too much of a hurry when trying to apprehend the boys, but now he could use greater care. He strategically lifted the toes of his boots and was careful where he placed his heels as he negotiated the cracks in the sidewalk, headed back to his office.

35

"I'm screwed on my test tomorrow," Joey said. Andrew looked straight out the windshield, earlier glances at his brother had freaked him. It was a side of Joey he'd never seen. Sitting straight like he had a rod up his ass, hands purple-tight on the steering wheel, his brow thickened in a deep frown.

"You still have time to make it back," Andrew said. "I bet your study group'll still be there."

Silence.

"Joey . . ."

His brother's hands lifted, slammed against the steering wheel. "You can't make this better for me, Andy."

"I hope . . ."

"Thomas wants me to confront Mom today, before I go back to Auburn. He wants to be with me. He says that's the best way to get past my anger."

"Where?"

"Where what?"

"Confront her where?"

"Thomas said he'd come to our place. But I haven't been able to find her. She must have her phone off."

"Maybe she's already home." He knew this was improbable. She never showed up until around ten o'clock. Sometimes not at all.

Joey yielded to the right as he came to a tight traffic circle. There were several on Queen City Avenue to slow vehicles. "Forget it," he said. "I don't want to talk about her anymore."

Andrew stared straight ahead. He didn't know what to say. They were getting close to home. He could see the park with the splash pad fountain. There was an eccentric woman they used to see in the park when it was still part of the school playground. She had a pet blackbird, a starling she called it. It sat on her shoulder and flew free in the air and landed high in the pines and then flew back to her. And it talked like a mynah bird. Joey was mesmerized by it. He liked when it landed on his shoulder and ate dog food from a spoon. About then, Joey decided for sure to become a vet. Andrew stopped himself from mentioning the bird. It would remind Joey of his problem.

"I didn't even ask," Joey said breaking into Andrew's thoughts. "What'd you think of Metamorphosis?"

Andrew felt relieved to talk. He shrugged. "It was okay. Who cares for real?" He thought about telling Joey about the boy Benjamin and the teacher but it wasn't the right time. That was a story for a better day. Joey turned onto Dearing Place. Andrew was glad to be home, wanting to get out of the car and the tension and awkwardness as fast as he could. Wanting to not get out of the car. To stay and make sure Joey was okay. To help make him okay. The Lexus wasn't in the driveway.

"Nope, she's not here," said Joey, it seemed more to himself than to Andrew. "I don't think I should be near her right now anyway. I might beat the crap out of her." The car stopped in front of their house.

"Joey . . ."

"Get out, Andy," Joey said. "Go on. I'll call you."

Andrew's hand paused on the handle. "Where you headed?"

"I'm not sure. I really don't know."

"Go to Thomas' house, Joey. Forget the study group. Go eat dinner with Thomas."

*   *   *

There was a wicker basket the size of a basketball hoop snuggled in the bushes beside the front door. It was overflowing with flowers. As he neared he could see a little white envelope with "Priscilla" scrawled on it. It stuck out of the basket on a red plastic spike. Around the outside of the basket was a white ribbon with Roll Tide Roll Tide Roll Tide printed all over it and a huge crimson and white bow that had little gold colored A's hanging down on streamers. Probably from Harry. Either she and Harry argued or Harry was about to get the boot for somebody new. Maybe both. Her relationships were boringly predictable and notably short.

He turned the key in the lock. Winx greeted him at the front door, his back half and tail thrashing side to side. "Hey, boy," Andrew said bending forward to pet him. Winx's tongue slathered his wrist and watch face with saliva. "Sorry. Joey's already gone." Five after five. He hadn't planned on being so late getting back. Past the broken lamp, up the stairs two at a time, into his room. His actions were precise, planned, quick. He grabbed his clothes, back pack, phone charger, the stuff under the sink, shoes, snacks, a pair of scissors, the Book of Mormon, and hair dye. He confirmed his money and stuck his hand in his front pocket. The stuff he'd stolen from his mom's room was still okay. He grabbed his black duffel bag. Packed efficiently, economically. Stuffed the rest in his back pack. His bike was out back leaning against the chimney. He pulled a towel off the rack as he passed his bathroom and threw it around his shoulders.

"See ya'," he said to Winx. The dog tried to keep up with him on the way back down the stairs. Front half, back half, front half, back half. Andrew opened the front door and paused. "Here," he said to the dog, placing a concrete elephant on top of the front threshold, leaving the door open about half a foot. "No telling when she'll get home." He stepped outside, dropped his black bag, picked up the envelope in the flowers and pulled out the card. She always shrieked at him for getting in her business but he checked every time. There was a snowball's chance in hell but it was always possible. *Please come back tonight. Wear what you made. I was a bigger ass than O.T. today. I'm sorry. We need to talk.* Who the hell was O.T.? Had to be from the veterinarian guy Harry. Not from Red.

He pulled out his phone to text Joey. *They had a fight.* His fingers paused. He hit Delete. It wouldn't help. Joey needed a lot more than that. He knew that short of the most horrendous, unthinkable, but oddly titillating solution, nothing would help. He dropped his backpack against an azalea, bumped his shoulder against the front door and carried the flowers into the downstairs guest bathroom. He lifted the seat, held the basket over the toilet and flipped it. Flowers plopped, water splashed onto the toilet seat, onto the floor. "Dunk shot!" He watched the white envelope and flower heads drown in blue toilet water, blue creeping slowly along the Roll Tide ribbon, wicker snapping, cracking as he crammed it deeper into the bowl.

*   *   *

She couldn't believe it. The door was propped open. "Damn it, Andrew!" How many times had she specifically told him not to leave the door propped? She didn't bother pulling the elephant back into its place among the snapdragons. It was heavy. Her ribs hurt. She was in a hurry. She pushed the door fully open and stepped over the raised concrete tusks and trunk. "'Drew!" she yelled. "Andrew!" She glanced hurriedly toward the den as she passed. What was that? A broken pot? She took two steps back and stared in disbelief. Her lamp. Her very favorite lamp, smashed to bits, scattered everywhere. "Oh, no!" she wailed. "Andrew! Andrew Lyle Beaty!" No answer. Not even Winx. She heard the icemaker clink a piece of ice into the tray. Even as she stared she was unable to make sense of it. All the tantrums, all the years, even at his wildest he'd never touched her lamp. She'd honestly stopped worrying about it. It was an unspoken pact between them. A line he wouldn't cross. He wouldn't smash her lamp. He wouldn't smash her. She heard Winx's tags jingling. The dog yawned from the top of the stairs, rear end wagging. She dropped the green heel she'd carried into the house, kicked off the other. There was no time to do anything about the lamp. She'd take a picture of the mess when she got home and e-mail it to that Shelby McDonald woman. Prove to her that Andrew was the only one with a problem. She tossed her purse on a hallway chair and started up the steps, half pulling herself along with the handrail, beige carpet slick beneath her stockinged feet, her ribs and arm and blister still aching. "I thought you'd be outside," she said as she limped past the dog. He didn't follow. Soft thumping. She knew he was headed downstairs, front legs, back legs, front legs, back legs. In less than a minute he was outside barking. Cats. Chipmunks. Squirrels. Even a possum or two. There were always creatures invading his territory. And he was a lousy hunter.

Because of that long-winded Shelby McDonald woman and because Bob was such an asshole, she had no more than ten minutes to change clothes. It was at least a fifteen minute drive across town to the Moon Winx. No time for a shower. No time to paint her nails. She peeled off her suit jacket and blouse and reached under her skirt to pull down her pantyhose. When the elastic rolled to mid thigh she sat on the edge of her bed. Taupe. Not her favorite color for nylons but suitable for work. She rolled them further down and off one foot, turning the stocking inside out. It was dirty on the bottom. She looked at the sole of her foot. It was filthy. She absolutely had to scrub her feet before she got dressed. If they had time, if *he* had time, maybe she'd take a shower at the motel. Maybe they'd take one together. Doubtful. They hadn't done that in sixteen years. Slowly, very slowly, she pulled the stocking off her other foot. "Ow!" she said. The bandage peeled off with the hose but dried blood stuck the nylon to her blister. The stocking was embedded in the scab. "Ouch, ouch, ouch." It was going to hurt to wash it.

Outside Winx was still barking. Must have treed it, whatever it was. He'd stand beneath a tree for hours, stubbornly, stupidly really, barking incessantly, demanding that the animal come down. She'd throw him in the house on her way out. There was a three minute continuous bark law in Tuscaloosa. No one ever had, but one of the neighbors could complain. She walked to the window and looked out. Nothing. She couldn't even see the dog. She raised her left arm and sniffed under her armpit. Still okay. She checked the right one. Okay, too.

Her jewelry cabinet was beneath the window. She opened the bracelet drawer. She fished around in the back of it, searching with both her fingers and her eyes for Red's bracelet. She kept it hidden beneath the other pieces. Where was it? She opened the drawer above. Below. The other drawers, scanning them, moving things around. Where had she put it? She crossed to her dresser and opened the drawer filled with underwear. She dug her hands into the cottons and silks, porpoising under them with her fingers. Her hand found a cool metal object and she ran her fingers across it. No, it was the silver rim of her hand mirror. The one that belonged to her grandmother and had the engraved initials MLR. Madeline Rosanna Lyle, but on the mirror the L was in the middle and was a little larger. Lyle. Andrew's middle name. The bracelet wasn't there. No time. She'd have to go without it. That seemed bad luck. She always wore the bracelet when they were together. *Everlasting love.* He'd had it inscribed for her. She never wanted him to forget it.

Her black bra and panties were imports from Spain. The lacework was exquisite. She'd paid a fortune for them. Red adored them. She lifted them out of the drawer. It was quiet outside now. Apparently Winx had given up. She held the lace up to her face and sniffed. She reached for her perfume. A spritz of rose. She inhaled. The perfume burned her nose deep inside and left a floral alcohol taste in the back of her throat. She wanted to spit.

"Roses. I'll forever think of you when I smell roses."

She wheeled to her right and gasped. Her rib. She'd forgotten to support it. "What . . ." Disbelief, confusion across her face. Metal arched toward her head. Her arm jerked up. The blow hit above her wrist, smashed into her temple. She heard a loud crack, felt electric pain, saw starburst light. She was unconscious before she hit the floor.

The intruder straddled her body, pounded again and again. The lace bra draped over her middle finger, her underpants lay crumpled beside her hand. Great looking black lace, the antithesis of the bra she was wearing. Crudely hand painted, ugly, in definite bad taste. Like her rose perfume. Blood on her face and her neck and her shoulder and splattered on her breast and on the carpet and on that ugly bra. Her eyes frozen wide. What the hell was she thinking wearing such an ugly bra? The murderer paused, scanned for evidence, moved toward the bedroom door and quickly down the stairs to the kitchen. The oven door opened, the weapon clunked into the bottom, blood-splattered jacket followed, oven racks slid out, the door shut. It was set on self clean. It clicked. Locked. The oven handle was wiped clean. Out of the kitchen, down the hall, moving quickly toward the front door, the doorknob opened using an antibacterial wipe.

"Roll Tide!" the murderer said as way of a prayer, pausing only a second to scratch the dog's head before stepping nimbly over the concrete elephant's trunk. This time Winx didn't bark. Instead, with a wagging tail he followed, rabies and identification tags jingling together as he jaunted happily along.

36

Even green dreds didn't draw much attention on the University campus. Riding his bike, a sports bag tied behind the seat and wearing a backpack with a towel draped around his neck, he imagined he looked like any one of the thirty-something thousand students who made The University of Alabama home. He felt at home too. He rode his trike, flew his kites, learned to skateboard on the sidewalks that criss-crossed the Quad. He placed his miniature hands, his toddler tennis shoes, in worn cement imprints of Alabama team captains, captured like the famous imprints on Hollywood Boulevard in sidewalks beneath Denny Chimes. Sometimes the cement was scalding against his palms, other times the indentions were filled with rain and leaves. But always it was fun. He'd gone to Homecoming parades and bonfires, Easter egg hunts and basketball games, rock concerts and international festivals. During summers he swam in the outdoor pool pointing head first down the curvy blue slide, and at Halloween he trick-or-treated on sorority row where co-eds dressed like witches and black cats, fairies and pirates and fussed over him and Joey and the other kids. Ooooooh, you're so cute! And ohhhhhhhh, you're so scary! His childhood took root on The University of Alabama campus. It was a beautiful place, green and friendly and easy to negotiate by foot and by bike.

It was almost six as he rode across the Quad toward the main library. There were clusters of students playing soccer, throwing footballs, playing Frisbee golf. Students going to class, jogging, walking their dogs, eating, skating, riding bikes, lying in the grass, and a handful even studying. He was headed to the men's bathroom in the library basement, or he guessed it was called the basement. Almost no one used it. Sometimes there was one weird guy hanging out down there, sitting on the floor in his shorts, no shirt, playing the worn tiles with drumsticks. He usually disappeared somewhere into the hall when Andrew came in. Andrew even reported him once. "Ah, I don't know if you guys already know this but there's some weirdo sitting in his shorts in the men's room downstairs playing drumsticks on the bathroom floor." The librarian assured him he'd take care of it. He really looked like a grad student but he phoned security while Andrew was there. "It's that drummer again," he said into the phone. "Yeah, we've had a report he's back." It didn't take long to figure out the guy always came back. Andrew decided it wasn't worth freaking out about. The guy sucked as a drummer but seemed harmless enough.

Denny Chimes made a sort of mechanical whirring noise then played Westminster Chimes before bonging the hour. As he pedaled he counted. One. Two. He simultaneously realized he didn't know if there were an electrical outlet in the bathroom. Five. Six. Six o'clock. Bethy'd already be crazy with worry about him. His phone screen was grayish black. Dead battery. He parked his bike, snapped on the lock and untied the sports bag. He'd tied it with yellow nylon rope. He wrapped the rope several times around his handlebars before heading into the building, towel still draped around his neck. An Alexander the Great term paper in eighth grade, the moons of Jupiter term paper in seventh, a probability research project for the science fair in sixth. There were at least eight libraries on campus but he knew this one best. He knew how to skirt the busier areas, how to weave his way downstairs without attracting a lot of attention. He smiled at a pretty brown haired librarian, probably another grad student, and she nodded back.

He pushed the heavy wooden door open. The light was out. He flipped it on and looked around. Thank God. The weird guy wasn't there. He scanned the walls for outlets. There was one near the sink. Lucky. He propped his bag on the sink, rummaged through until his fingers found the charger and connected his phone. *All's good. Luv u.* He pressed Send then propped his phone against a sink faucet and wriggled out of his back pack. Sports bag open, scissors out, green hair falling, severed braids on the grayish white tile. They were never real dreds, just braids. Short. Shorter. Uneven around his ears. He needed the electric shaver bad but Joey'd taken it to Auburn. He worked fast. Footsteps in the hallway. He paused, scissors pressed to his scalp. Oh no, not the weird guy. He held his breath, listening. The footsteps passed.

Ammonia in the black hair dye assaulted his nostrils. He stood in front of the mirror and squeezed it out of a bottle with a narrow cap. He was wearing the provided plastic gloves, ripped down the sides to enlarge them, flapping open around his palms but protecting his fingernails from stains. A little black line trickled across his forehead toward his nose. He grabbed a paper towel, wet it and rubbed the line away. Twenty minutes and it'd be done. He scrubbed the black marks off the side of his face in front of his ear and on the side of his neck just to the left of his chin. His skin turned from black to gray. He scrubbed harder. His skin stayed gray. He peeled off his gloves and pushed the aluminum knob of the soap dispenser with his palm, pumping it, directing yellow goo onto a paper towel. The dispenser was one of the old ones. His phone vibrated. He hurried toward it and rubbed his hand back and forth across his leg before picking it up. :-) *Come over! Mom at yoga til 9:30.* He pressed Reply. *K. But don't freak when u c me.*

At 7:22 a young man with cropped black hair, black glasses, dressed in a pair of dark pants and a short sleeve white button down shirt, wearing a plain brown tie and brown loafers, and clutching the Book of Mormon picked up his back pack and sports bag, ditched his dye-stained towel in the trash, opened the men's room door and headed toward the right rear exit. He felt the bulges of the treasures he'd transferred from his jeans into his dress pants pockets. As he turned the hall corner there the guy was, the weirdo with his drumsticks, headed toward the bathroom. Andrew nodded a missionary's recognition. The weird guy averted his gaze as they passed shoulder to shoulder, thereby missing the smile creeping onto Andrew's lips. The guy'd have little green hairs stuck all over his ass after drum practice tonight. Andrew pushed on the exit door feeling titillated, alive, and very clever. He'd pulled it off. The perfect disguise. He threw his head back and howled at the moon.

* * *

She was wearing a turquoise tank top with skinny straps and no bra and her nipples pointed toward him through the cotton. Her shorts were short, really short, and white and made her long legs seem even longer. She wore no shoes. He tried hard, really hard, to not look at her breasts. And her legs. And her butt. He stared directly into her face.

"Oh my God! Andrew? Is that you for real?" she asked opening the screen door. Her eyes wide, she stared at him, grinning in a strange sort of way.

"Andrew in disguise." A wave of regret swept through him. He shouldn't have come. "I shouldn't have come," he said. He hadn't considered that she might think he was a geek. He took off his fake black glasses.

Her smile leveled into a more normal one. She reached for his hand. "It's just, well, you caught me by surprise, I guess. Oh my God, you look so different. What happened to your hair?"

"It had to go."

"Well, you're disguised for real."

He was still standing right inside the door. He dry swallowed. "Is that okay? You still want to go with me?"

Her laugh filled the hallway, soft, like butter melting on warm toast. "You'll take some getting used to." She pulled on his arm, the one holding the Book of Mormon, and led him through the hallway toward the den. He liked her house. There were three framed paintings in the hall and a wood framed mirror. The paintings were landscapes, all farm scenes. A field of sunflowers, huge petaled flowers bending forward on their stalks toward him. A field of rolled hay bales. And a field of some crop growing, probably soybeans, with a herd of deer grazing in the background. There were six deer. The one with the deer was his favorite. The first time he visited her house Bethy told him her mom painted them. She's really good, he'd said. She's doing more of it now with Dad gone, she'd said.

He caught a glance of himself in the hall mirror. Shit! Was that him? He looked away quickly. He couldn't think about how he looked.

"Hungry?"

"Starving."

"We've got jalapeno potato chips, pretzels, maybe a banana, I know we have apples."

He'd get a burger later. "Naw, that's okay."

She pushed him backward with her fingers and he plopped into a corduroy recliner. She sat on the chair's arm for a second before her shorts slid across the ridged upholstery and her bottom found his lap. She curled her legs, shins resting against the padded arm. She laid her head on his shoulder. "I've been worried sick about you," she said.

He couldn't think. Except that her butt was against his groin and he was getting a hard on and he didn't want to be walking around her house like that but it felt so good and he didn't want to ask her to move. He tried to shift positions so she was sitting more on his hip. It was crazy. She was saying something. He struggled to focus.

She tilted her head and her lips grazed his neck and chin. Oh my God she smelled good! And different. Not like citrus tonight. Like something else. He inhaled slowly. Maybe cloves and honey.

"You smell good," he said. "Like honey, or something."

"You like it? It's honey soap. Mom and I went to the farmer's market at the Episcopal church last week. A beekeeper makes it."

He stroked her hair. "Yeah, I like it a lot."

"Well, so how was that place?"

"Where?"

She giggled. "Metamorphosis, dummy."

He shrugged, sort of embarrassed. "There were some okay people there. A guy named Dr. Luke and a woman named Ms. Shelby McDonald, and a really ancient lady who owns the place. And they had a pool and horses and stuff. I guess they have horses, I didn't see them, I think they were in a field behind the buildings. And there was a totally insane kid named Benjamin who lives there and today was his birthday and they were having a party for him tonight."

"So does your mom know you're gone?"

Andrew leaned his head back. The headrest was pillowed, bumping his head forward, throwing his neck into a forty-five degree angle. He shut his eyes. "I don't want to talk about her, okay?"

She curled up tighter in his lap and snuggled deeper against him. Silence. Silence and honey and cloves and her ass and her hair tickling his chin. Her hand found his and she interlocked their fingers. Her thumb rubbed softly back and forth against the base of his.

"You feel so good," he said, eyes still closed.

"Where will you go tonight?"

He'd been asking himself the same thing. His plan was a tried and true one, he'd gotten away with it before. He'd crash in the lobby of one of the campus dorms. Hang out on one of the sofas with an open book like he was pulling an all-nighter. Move from dorm to dorm for a few days until he found something more permanent. "Shhhh," he whispered. "Let's not talk about that, not now anyway." In truth he felt tired, exhausted all the way to his bones. It'd been a long, complicated day and he still was trying to make sense of everything Joey'd said and the bracelet he'd found in his mother's drawer. He ran his free hand along the outside bottom of his pocket. It was still there, the other stuff, too. He thought about telling Bethy about the bracelet especially, but he was too tired to complicate the moment. He breathed in slowly. "I think there're cloves mixed in with the honey," he said. "It smells sort of like Christmas."

She wiggled her body into a more upright position and pulled at his wrist until she could read his watch. "Mom'll be home in about fifty minutes," she said. She leaned her face forward, lips skimming his, mouth parted slightly, tongue flirting. "I love you," she whispered, deepening the kiss. He wrapped his arms around her, tongue meeting tongue. She was great at kissing.

"I love you, too," he murmured. "God, Bethy, I really do."

She cupped her small palm around the back of his hand and slid them along her rib cage, under the knit cotton of her top, pressing his palm against her belly and up. Up toward her nipples. Her skin, warm, a little damp from sweat. A gasp caught somewhere in his throat. His eyes popped open and he jerked his hand away like he'd been scalded. He held her by her upper arms. "No," he said gently.

Her eyebrows narrowed. Confusion. Hurt.

He felt like a dork. A total asshole. How the hell crazy was he? "I . . . I don't want that, I mean I do, but I can't . . . it isn't . . ." He straightened his back, eased her off his lap. He saw her stare at his crotch, a smile form on her lips. The smile, but still confusion and worry. "It's getting late. I need to go."

"What happened?" she asked. "Why? I didn't mean . . . I'm sorry." She was standing in front of him, hair messed up, her turquoise shirt folded over a little at her waist.

He stood, hugged her. "It's not you," he said. "It's just, I've got a lot on my mind. I can't . . . I dream about us, um, about us doing it all the time and I wake up and I'm all horny, but . . ."

She put two fingers to his lips. Her fingernails were scratchy they were so bitten off. "It's okay," she said but it didn't sound like she meant it.

"It's not you," he said again. It was the truth. The truth, the fucking truth, was it was his mother. His damned mother. Somehow she bled into his relationships, into Bethy's hand guiding his toward her sweet little titties. It was all messed up. "I need to go," he said. "To find a place to stay tonight. I'll call you when I get there."

She shrugged, her clavicle forming a little indented triangle intersected by the spaghetti strap of her top. Her lips rolled inward, pressed together.

"Please don't be mad . . ."

They unrolled. "I'm not. I just . . ."

He pulled her back against him. "Thanks," he said. "I'm just so tired, baby. It's been a helluva day." She stayed perfectly still in his embrace. Her hair tickled his nostrils and he was afraid he would sneeze but he fought against it. "You're so beautiful, so perfect. Like an angel, or something."

Her chest moved against his gut, she was chuckling softly. "I don't know about the angel part."

He felt doubt sneaking in. "No," he said to paralyze the thoughts.

"No what?"

He didn't realize he'd said it out loud. "Nothing." But the monster was in the room. The way she slid into his lap and the way she wore her clothes and the breast thing. The way she sometimes smelled edible, like honey and cloves. It was bugging him. "Gotta go, baby," he said kissing her forehead. "I'll call later tonight. And remember, no matter what, don't blow my cover, all right?"

37

Detective Adelaide Joanna Bramson pulled up behind the line of squad cars, six to be exact, and took a deep breath. Dead bodies disturbed her. She pulled her phone from the glove compartment and texted Luke. *Better eat without me.* She tossed her phone back in, glanced at her watch, and opened the car door. The time actually surprised her. Already a little past seven. She'd stuck around the office to catch the investigating officers of the fatal Whitesmythe crash. Curious situation they'd said. Four yellow jackets were still bumping around against the rear windshield of the car when they arrived on the scene. Two more were underneath the front passenger's seat in an empty drink bottle. Looked like the wasps startled Ms. Whitesmythe whose attention was diverted long enough to send her careening off the road and into the trees. Four drivers in different vehicles reported seeing no cars passing nor approaching around that time, and they denied seeing deer or other wildlife on the road. And they reported seeing no suspicious looking persons walking the sidewalk. Just the usual joggers and dog walkers and parents accompanying bike riding children. One of the officers was checking with the vehicle's owner to see if the wasps were easily explained.

The yard was cordoned off with yellow crime scene tape. She pushed it down and stepped over. A Black rookie detective, R.J. Morrow, met her at the front door of the Beaty house. He caught her just as she was sticking her hand into the Animal Cracker bag to fish out several. He shook his head when she offered them, then smiled. "Man, you sure do like those things," he said.

"I'm totally addicted." She liked R.J. a lot. She was glad they were often assigned to work together.

His eyes narrowed, his jaw worked back and forth as she stepped past him into the hall. Smoke assaulted her nostrils. She wondered if there'd been a fire.

"There's a fresh bouquet of flowers stuffed face down in the toilet down the hallway to the left," he said. "We fished the florist card out of the toilet already. Blue and blurred but still readable. An apology note apparently for something that happened earlier today. Whoever sent the flowers knew the victim was a Bama fan. A lamp is smashed to smithereens in the living room, and she's only partially clothed upstairs. Unusual underwear she's wearing. Apparently was changing clothes at the time of her death. No preliminary signs of sexual assault. And something's in the self-cleaning oven, sure as hell smoked up the house. It's still on lock cycle. Cooling down. It'll take a while but whatever was in there's long gone I'd bet. Stinks pretty bad in here and the smoke's hell on the eyes."

She swallowed the dissolved cookies and a nose full of smoke. "Ick," she said.

"Windows are all open," he said. "We have a call in for box fans."

"Neighbors?"

"Nothing yet. There's only one so far who claims to have been at home around the approximate time of death. An elderly lady across the street. She says she was napping in her bedroom late this afternoon when the Beaty's dog woke her up. She says she didn't look out. Apparently the dog barks at squirrels a lot. She did state that it wasn't unusual for people, males especially, to come and go from Dr. Beaty's house all hours of the day and night.

Addie's eyes burned. "Time of death?"

"It's preliminary, of course, but the coroner's best guess is between five thirty and six."

"Who else lives here?"

"One son aged sixteen according to the next door neighbor. Andrew Beaty. Green dreadlocks, may be troubled. The neighbor says that's the way Dr. Beaty has always described him, as troubled, even though the neighbor himself has never witnessed anything disturbing in the boy's behaviors. And there's an older son, Joey, attending Auburn University. Another neighbor four doors down says he saw both boys in the neighborhood earlier today, a little after lunch, when he dropped by his house to feed his cat. He said Andrew and Joey were walking toward their house and it looked like maybe they'd been walking around the neighborhood. He said Dr. Beaty wasn't with them."

"So did her younger son find the body?"

R.J.'s forehead wrinkled. "No. It's actually somewhat concerning. Neither son has been located. The man who found her was a Mr. Bob Tulane, a self-described friend of Dr. Beaty's. He called 911. We asked him to stick around until you arrived. He's in the sun room at the back of the house with Dr. Beaty's dog, I think he said the dog's name is Winx, little wiener dog. We have Emilia sitting with him until you can get to him."

Addie nodded. Coughed. The rims of R.J.'s eyes were pinkish, irritated. She was glad he was there to brief her. He was young, serious, extremely thorough. "Winx," she said. "Cute name for a dog." She straightened her posture until the muscles along her spine stretched tight. "Thanks, R.J. I think I'll go meet Dr. Beaty first."

"Good plan. Air's better upstairs."

She glanced into the living room as she passed. The room was foggy, smoke hanging like a cloud. Homicide was in the room taking fingerprints and photos and putting pieces of smashed lamp and other items in evidence bags. An officer named Amy raised a hand in greeting. She was wearing a paper nose and mouth mask. "Hey, Addie. We've finished dusting upstairs. Still have to get the bathroom down here."

Addie detoured into the living room. "Hear we're thinking crime of passion, but could you dust for theft as well?"

"Already did her jewelry chest and dresser drawers and her purse. Anything else?"

"Not right off hand," said Addie. "Thanks."

"Wait 'til you see the underwear the deceased is wearing. If it can't lead us to the killer, I doubt anything can."

*   *   *

Amy wasn't exaggerating. "Wow!" Addie said staring at the semi-clad body sprawled on the cream colored rug. Maybe it was closer to a beige. It was hard to tell in the light. Blood splatters, some already browning, and a larger pool of blood beside Dr. Beaty's left temple suggested numerous strikes by the murder weapon. Blood even on the ceiling. Some sort of blunt force instrument. Addie focused on the bra. It was impossible to concentrate fully on anything else. "How wild," she said. The corpse's brassiere was clearly hand painted. "Do you imagine she wore this to school today?"

A rookie of about two months, Lee somebody or other, Garrento she thought was his name, glanced toward the corpse and chuckled. "We wondered the same thing," he said. "It'd sure make front page headlines if the press got a hold of this." His laugh escaped from his throat as a giggle. Addie pretended not to notice. He was so young. Hardly looked out of high school. "Looks like she was changing into the black one when it happened," he added with compensating gravity.

A pair of black lace panties lay crumpled approximately two inches from her right hand. A black lace bra was nestled against her left ear and draped on her middle finger. Fingernails and toenails in matching pink polish. Chipped polish on several of her fingers and on her left baby toenail and right big toe. Addie studied the position of the body. Right arm stretched out, left curved toward her face, legs indicating she'd spun around to meet her assailant. Green skirt still on. Twisted around her thighs. Pantyhose rolled inside out on the bed. Something, it looked like a dirty bandage on the top of one of the nylons. There was a bloody blister on the top of her foot. At least eight assault marks on her face, six near her temples, one on her forehead, one at the bridge of her nose. There was another on her neck. At least two on her outstretched arm. The rib cage looked a little discolored too. She crouched down to get a closer look. Lee crouched beside her. She smelled garlic on his breath.

"Damnedest thing I ever saw to be honest with you," he said. "I mean, I know I'm new and everything but who'd ever think she'd be wearing something like *this* under designer clothes? My grandmom used to say, 'Lee, the only thing that separates the people inside Bryce Hospital from those outside is the door.' She worked at Bryce as a mental health aide for twenty-five years before institutional down-sizing got her job."

Addie smiled. "My husband'd probably agree," she said. Lee still had peach fuzz on his chin. Maybe three little whiskers on his upper lip. If she remembered right he lived at home with his mother and younger sister. "Lee, would your mama want you getting such an eyeful? This verges on porn in my way of thinking." Lee laughed. She laughed. The other officers in the room laughed. Sometimes a little levity made the job more tolerable.

She stood and walked slowly around the room. The deceased's green suit jacket on the bed, the heaped up pantyhose with the bloody bandage stuck to the nylon, shoes nowhere to be found. "Where are her shoes?"

"Forensics got them," said Lee. "They were downstairs. Headed away from the door. Like she kicked them off when she got home."

Addie inhaled.

"Some sort of flower smell, I think," said Lee.

"Roses," said Addie. Smelled like dollar store perfume. Dr. Beaty was an odd bird for sure.

Flash! Crimson light. Addie jumped. Lee wheeled around, hand at his holster. Crimson light blinking in a little plastic football. *Rammer Jammer Yellow Hammer. Give 'em HELL Alabama!* A plastic football player connected to a clock beside Dr. Beaty's bed cradled the ball. His legs were moving in circles. Running. Moving nowhere. She heard a click. The football stopped blinking. Addie looked at her own watch. Seven thirty.

"It plays the Alabama fight song on the hour," said Lee. "Or at least, it played it at seven. But that red light spooked me. This lady's full of surprises."

"No lie." She turned back to the corpse. Somebody sure beat the hell out of her. Kept beating long after she was dead. "Beautiful though, wasn't she?"

"Quite a looker," said Lee.

"That saying's a tad old fashioned, Lee," teased Addie. Probably came from his grandmother too. "Okay, I guess I'm done up here. I'm going down to check out the flowers in the toilet."

Broken stems, lilies mutilated, upside down in toilet water tinted with blue tablet cleanser. Wicker basket shoved into the bowl. Water tinged light blue on the toilet seat, on the floor. One of those cushioned toilet seats that hissed out a little bit of air whenever someone sat on it. University of Alabama elephants parading around the oval, stuck with the fate of strangers' butts temporarily smothering them. Crimson tide floral ribbon now purplish blue. Little A's resting on the toilet bowl's bottom. R.J. was right. Whoever sent the flowers obviously knew her fan status. There was a pale blue florist's card sitting soggily on the tank. Blurred but readable. *Please come back tonight. Wear what you made. I was a bigger ass than O.T. today. I'm sorry. We need to talk.* An argument almost certainly. What she made. The bra perhaps? Who was O.T.? Even more to the point, who was the bigger ass? Looked like two dozen Asiatic lilies. One of Addie's favorites. She hated to see any flowers, especially lilies, meet such demise. The sender obviously had some cash or at least a healthy line of credit. Except for the splashed toilet water no signs of an apparent struggle. She turned and headed toward the living room.

Amy was snapping the last photographs of the room. She'd pulled her mask down around her neck. The smoke had dissipated significantly. "Honestly, Addie, except for the lamp it doesn't look like a struggle went on in here," she said. "Everything else is in place." Addie walked toward the mantle. Three photographs in pewter frames sat amidst Crimson Tide knick knacks. One frame held a photo from a beach somewhere. The younger boy had a blonde crew cut, chubby cheeks and a green frog float around his belly. Eight or nine probably. The older boy, by maybe four or five years, looked sunburned and was squinting into the camera. One of his arms draped around the younger child. Andrew and Joey she guessed. The second photo was maybe even a year earlier. The young boy was sitting on the knee of the Crimson Tide mascot, Big Al, blond hair a little longer, bangs combed out of his face. The older child was standing beside the elephant mascot holding a football. The third looked like a copy of a high school yearbook photo and was a photograph of a majorette. Her leotard was covered in sequins, her booted foot raised in spirited march, her baton poised above her head. She had sequin-gloved arms. She guessed it was Dr. Beaty. "So sad," said Addie.

"She was beautiful," said Amy.

There were male voices in the hall. R. J. and Lee. R.J. already had Dr. Beaty's purse in an evidence bag. Addie joined them. "Anything?" she asked.

R.J. shook his head. "Not really. Purse still has her wallet in it. Her money and credit cards appear untouched. A few receipts that might help track her recent comings and goings. Five bottles of partially used nail polish, one with gold speckles in it. Part of a bracelet. Looks broken. That's about it."

Addie studied the purse through the plastic. Dr. Beaty probably dropped two hundred dollars on that bag. Maybe more. So she carried animal cookies and Dr. Beaty carried nail polish. She opened her own purse and ferreted out the bag. R.J. and Lee shook their heads. She pulled out a headless giraffe and a zebra. The zebra was as close as she could get to an ass. She stared at it, hoping for insight. None came. She popped the zebra onto her tongue. "Still no word about her sons?" she asked.

"'Fraid not."

"Then home invasion's still a possibility."

"The murder's being released to the media just in case. It'll hit the ten o'clock news. Chief's decision."

Addie slowly sucked in air. It was a big gamble. "Let's hope the boys are safe *and* that they don't learn of their mother's death via TV," she said.

"That'd be a bummer," said the rookie Lee.

R.J. Morrow turned toward the bathroom down the hall. He still had to collect evidence from the toilet dunked flowers. "I don't know which would be worse, a home invasion where they're in danger or discovering one of them is the murderer. Maybe even them both."

"I've been thinking about that," said Addie. She'd worked two cases involving child murderers in the past. They gave her the willies. One kid was only nine. Adopted. Reportedly couldn't form, in fact couldn't even tolerate, healthy meaningful love bonds. She'd been hiding knives in her mother's potted plants, under her mattress, in her toy chest, since she was four. The psychologist who worked with the family testified the mother'd frequently awaken in the night to find her young daughter standing over her bed staring a hole in her. She started locking her bedroom door. The daughter started setting fires. Little fires that were more worrisome than dangerous. The daughter was hospitalized. She came back from the hospital playing with poisons, pouring rubbing alcohol into the lemonade and so forth. She was sent to residential treatment. She came back cutting on herself and was described as more withdrawn. By the time the girl was eight the mother was a nervous wreck. Ultimately the daughter shot her during an argument related to eating broccoli. Shot her right through the forehead. The girl testified in juvenile court she bought the gun from another kid in the neighborhood. Thirteen dollars and a pack of cigarettes. After the mother's death the girl alternately shrugged off her mother's demise and curled up in a fetal position and sobbed like a baby from the depths of her tortured soul. Her husband Luke often complained that the Reactive Attachment Disorder diagnosis was overused in mental health circles, used to describe too many types of attachment problems, but this girl's inability to attach was the real thing. The girl was sent back off to a juvenile treatment center. Addie heard she was behaving well with staff because there was no pressure to form lasting bonds. And she wore a picture of her deceased mother in a locket over her heart.

And then there was the fifteen year old who backed over her mother in the driveway when her mom went to collect the mail. Girls were statistically less prevalent when it came to committing murder and she almost got away with it. Lots and lots of tears and wailing that it was an accident. But the girl's best friend called in an anonymous tip that the murder had been planned for weeks. Had e-mails to prove it. It was about her mother saying no when she wanted to go to a motel with her boyfriend. Impulse control disorder, the clinical psychologist explained on the stand. The e-mails were fantasy, not serious plans. Backing over her mother was an impulsive act, done without conceptualizing the impact of her actions. At the time of trial the girl was diagnosed with Post Traumatic Stress Disorder. She was reportedly blocking on almost everything that happened related to the death. Couldn't remember what happened. Couldn't sleep. Couldn't eat. Reported paranoia. She was tried as an adult and sent to Tutwiler Prison. Addie knew that kids could get themselves into all kinds of serious messes.

"Hey, Addie," R.J. said over his shoulder. "Just wanted to remind you that fellow Bob Tulane is waiting for you in the sunroom."

"On my way right now. Oh, and can you start the paperwork to seize Dr. Beaty's computers, home and work, and we'll need her phone records too."

R.J. pivoted playfully on his heels and threw a salute. "Already on top of it, ma'am."

Addie smiled. "And the murder weapon?"

R.J. shook his head. "Not sure," he said. "If it's in the oven, it's a four hour cycle. Still cooling."

*   *   *

When Addie was little, most early mornings were spent in a tall slatted chair at her father's gigantic cherry desk. The wood was smooth and cool and a soft color of reddish brown and when she ran her hand across it she could feel little dents from years of use by her father and his father and his father before him. At first her dad had a silver and black electric typewriter that softly and consistently chugged when it was on, and there'd be the click, click, click of keys striking paper and a little 'ding' at the end of each line. Her dad was a successful novelist whose books were favorites in mall bookstores and airport kiosks, but when she was little she didn't know any of that. She only knew that he wrote something called mysteries and that she loved to watch his fingers dance across the typewriter keys and the cottony smell of the paper and the special time they shared while she helped him with important jobs like counting the paper clips in his white plastic penguin holder and putting all the rubber bands into a special box, sometimes even arranging them by color. "It's so great to have such a helpful partner," he'd say, "someone who can keep my desk so neat and organized. I don't know what I'd do without such important help." And she'd curl up in his lap and bask in his praise.

As she grew older and his typewriter retired into its gray-green case, an almost silent keyboard took its place and his paper clips and rubber bands lay in disorganized heaps all over his desk. And he bounced storylines off her, outlining crimes, delving into suspects' minds, developing motives, detail upon detail, clues carefully woven, subtly hidden throughout. When she grew up and joined the force, there was hardly a real life crime she hadn't already encountered one way or another through her father's imagination. He was the reason she'd earned Detective so young. She still got ideas, insights, from his novels. In reality his plots were more complicated than her real life murders. And his guilty characters, much more clever.

Mr. Bob Tulane stood as she entered the room. The brown dachshund lying on the couch beside him stood as well, stretched, and plopped down again. Fiftyish, thinning brown hair, receding hairline, wiry with muscular biceps, hard to tell through his slacks but his thighs looked muscular too, about five foot eleven. His gaze met hers initially, then skipped like a smooth pebble on a lake across the room. Luke was great at skipping pebbles. It was all in the flick of the wrist he told her. She still didn't quite have the hang of it.

"Mr. Tulane?"

"Yes, ma'am."

Addie nodded toward Emilia. "Thanks, Emilia, I've got it from here."

"Yes, Detective Bramson. I'll be heading home then."

"Please, Mr. Tulane," said Addie as Emilia departed. "Have a seat. I apologize for keeping you so long."

Mr. Tulane wavered momentarily before sitting. The dog stood, circled three times on the pillow, plopped again. "No problem," he said calmly. "Priscilla was my dear friend. Anything I can do . . ." His voice trailed away.

"Of course," said Addie. "Maybe you can start by giving me more details about your friendship?" She fished around in her purse until she located her digital recorder. She pulled it out, fingers brushing against the Animal Cracker bag, and placed it on her knee. "Our conversation will be recorded," she said. "That way I don't have to waste your time or mine taking notes."

His eyes flickered, lids blinked, he looked off to his right and down at the floor briefly before clearly forcing himself to stare her straight in the eyes. "Um, sure," he said. "We dated briefly last football season, too briefly for my liking, to be honest. She was a football fanatic, Priscilla was. I'm afraid I became too serious, moved too quickly if you know what I mean, told her I loved her. She broke it off that very week."

"And yet you remained friends?"

"Yes and no. Hadn't spoken to her or seen her in an age until today. But that didn't mean I hadn't been thinking about her. She was, how should I put this . . . she was sexually voracious. It drove me crazy, really, thinking about her with other men. And I had no delusions about her activities. I knew there were always other men." He coughed softly. It seemed to Addie a cough of nerves, not phlegm. "So today I called her out of the blue and tried to convince her to go out with me again. I promised to keep it lighter, no strings attached, but that would've been a crazy arrangement to be honest with you. Not sure I could've done it."

"And what did she say about dating you again?"

His shoulders visibly slumped. His chin jutted forward. "She said she'd think about it."

"So is that why you stopped by the house? To further this conversation?"

Mr. Tulane shook his head quickly. His hand dropped to the dog's head and his thumb moved back and forth near its muzzle. "Oh, no, by no means. Although had I found her alive I might have broached the subject again." He smiled weakly. The smile wilted. "No, there was something else happening with Priscilla. Something worrisome. She was with some man at lunch, he didn't identify himself to me but he was abusive, or at the very least, controlling. He obviously checked her phone messages because he called me on her mobile. Real aggressive call. Told me to back off. Priscilla was clearly frightened of him. I made it my business to discover his identity."

"And did you?"

"No."

So maybe the aggressive guy was the flower guy. The one who called himself an ass. Or maybe Mr. Tulane was sending up a smokescreen. Maybe he sent the flowers himself. "Tell me, Mr. Tulane. Did you send Dr. Beaty flowers today?"

A smirk floated across his lips. "The mess in the toilet, you mean? I overheard your buddies talking about the swimming flowers. No. No, I didn't."

"And where were you this afternoon. Say, from two o'clock on?"

Another flicker of his eyes. He cleared his throat. Looked her in the eyes. "I went to her school right as the school day ended. She always stands outside on the sidewalk in the parking lot, um, to make sure the buses load smoothly and the children's car pick-ups are safely executed. She was almost done with that. I convinced her to get into my car with me. I was afraid the lunchtime guy would show up and cause a scene. Abusive males are more predictable than people think."

He was right about that. "But, correct me if I'm wrong Mr. Tulane, dealing with abusive males isn't your line of business . . . ?"

Mr. Tulane's brows lowered. He broke eye contact. "No. I'm a tree surgeon. I own a business out in Coker. Mainly I spend my days removing diseased and unwanted trees if you want the long and short of it."

"Yet you have experience with males who abuse?"

A negative shadow of emotion, bitterness, anger, perhaps, passed across his face. "Yeah, you could say I've had my own experiences with abusive males," he said. "Enough to know they can't stand to lose control and if their egos feel threatened they can be violent."

Addie stared. She guessed he'd learned that in childhood.

"Anyway, Priscilla had a lot on her plate. Something about her younger son, Andrew, and a meeting this afternoon at a place called Metamorphosis."

Addie jerked forward. She felt certain it was noticeable. "Metamorphosis?" she repeated.

"Yeah, it's some residential treatment place out on the lake for kids who have problems."

"Yes," said Addie. "Yes, I'm familiar with it."

"Well, Priscilla's had problems with Andrew since he was just a little bug, you know, smashing and stealing her stuff, running away. When we were dating he was always giving her grief in one way or another. I don't know. Something about a rejecting father or something. A guy she called Red. She still kept in contact with the man. Anyway, she met with those residential folks today after school."

"Okay."

"But there was some other guy bothering her, too. Some disgruntled parent. He showed up this afternoon in the school parking lot. Seemed to be hanging out in his car, watching her. She was trying to avoid him. Appeared to dread the idea of talking to him. He never got out of his car though. I saw to that."

Damn, it was too small a world. First Metamorphosis. Now almost certainly Larry Ryan. "Can you describe the parent? His car?"

"Sure. He was driving a blue Escort. From what I could tell maybe stocky, at least broad shoulders. In his thirties probably. Looked pissed off. Seemed like Priscilla felt a little threatened by him even though she denied it." He chuckled softly. "Let's just say she appreciated my efforts to keep him at bay."

"Hmm . . . So you're saying they had no contact in the parking lot? To the best of your knowledge?" She struggled against playing out the scenario forming in her mind. Larry Ryan was pissed off when she left him at DHR. He was on his way to confront Dr. Beaty, determined to get results. An ex-cop knew how things worked. How to get away with murder.

"Nope, she was in the car with me. We watched him leave. I stared the sucker down."

She felt just a tad of reassurance. "So, then what?"

"So she got out of my car and went back into the school."

Addie's stomach growled, a loud growl like the ones that created hysterics in her elementary school classmates when she was little, especially in Penelope Wimmerton who giggled one time nonstop all the way until recess. She'd always had very assertive stomach juices. "I'm sorry," she said. "I haven't had time to eat dinner." She reached into her purse and got her bag of Animal Crackers. She extended them toward Mr. Tulane who stared at them curiously before shaking his head.

"Haven't seen those since I was a kid," he said.

"No kidding?" said Addie. She poured five or six animals into her hand and threw them all into her mouth at once. "So is that when you last saw her?" she asked with a full mouth. "In the parking lot?"

Maybe he was thinking about the cookies. Or maybe he was like Penelope Wimmerton and was thinking about her stomach noises. But the question appeared to unbalance him. Just slightly. She'd been in the business long enough to sense when someone was uncomfortable.

"Um, no. I was worried about the lunch time guy showing up at that place Metamorphosis and following her home. So around four-thirty I headed out there. I parked and waited for her to come out of the building. Andrew and her other son, his name is Joey, they were both there. I saw them walking around. And there was another man I didn't know who showed up and spent time talking to Joey."

"Another man? Can you describe him?"

Mr. Tulane paused then shook his head. "No. Didn't pay him any attention to be honest. They weren't with her. She came out of the building later with some woman, a young girl, she introduced herself as McDonald or McDaniel or something like that. She works there, anyway."

McDonald. Shelby. So Andrew was Luke's intake client today. "Did you talk to her? Dr. Beaty, I mean."

Eyes darting again. Addie sat forward, zeroed in. Eye darting made her pulse quicken. His hands moved slowly to his face and he rubbed his eye sockets. "Sorry. I'm pretty wasted. The shock of finding her . . ."

The dog stood, turned more circles then snuggled complacently against the man's thigh. If she went by the science of canine instincts, Mr. Eye Darting Tulane wasn't the murderer. But that was assuming the dachshund was endowed with sharp canine instincts. Its eyes were shut. It was definitely missing the visual clues.

"Yes," said Addie although she wasn't truly convinced. "I'm sure it's been an awful shock. I appreciate your cooperation. We're almost finished, Mr. Tulane."

"Anything I can do to help. Now, what was the question again?"

"Did you talk to Dr. Beaty at Metamorphosis?"

"Oh. Yes. Yes, I did."

"And what was her state of mind? Did she seem worried or distracted or anything else out of the ordinary?"

He paused. Breathed deeply. Swallowed. "Basically she was angry with me for following her out there. Furious, really. She couldn't understand my point. That the guy at noon was going to return. Statistically, I mean. Abusers do that, no secret there."

"Did you see signs of domestic violence? Was she bruised, cut . . ."

"No, but the stuff that went down at noon, that I heard on the phone, was abusive."

Addie nodded. "So you say she was angry you followed her to Metamorphosis."

"And she wouldn't let me follow her home. That's what I wanted to do. Just make sure everything was okay at her house."

Addie frowned. "So you thought this guy might be waiting for her at home but she didn't?"

Mr. Tulane put his hand on Winx's back. It traveled from collar to tail. "That's right. And she was in a hurry. Said she had a six o'clock meeting with Andrew's father."

She leaned forward. "Did she say where? Did she give you a name?"

He laughed. "Never ever a name. Nothing substantial, I mean. Just Red. Like I said before, that's what she called him. I got an earful about him when we were dating last year. She was forever complaining that he wouldn't step up to the plate. That he refused to claim Andrew, publicly, I mean. She said he did provide financial support. Apparently, generously. The deal was he'd cut off all monies and publicly disown Andrew if she ever revealed his identity. She talked a lot about that. I don't think the financial end of it was that big a deal. She was more concerned about how public rejection would affect Andrew. She made pretty good money herself."

Addie nodded. "And she told you they were meeting at six?"

"That's what she said. But she didn't say where."

She wanted another Animal Cracker but she didn't want to look insensitive. Unprofessional. She'd already downed a handful in front of the guy. She jiggled her knee. She'd wait. "Then, how'd you end up finding her here tonight? Since she didn't want you tailing her home?"

Was his face flushed? Hard to tell in the light. The new compact fluorescent bulbs played eye tricks. Especially when she was tired.

"Honestly I didn't plan to stop by here," he said. "I was so pissed off when I left Metamorphosis. She could be such a pig's butt. Basically she called me a stalker and told me to get lost. So I did. I drove back through town, grabbed a burger and took it to the park over near City Hall. Sat on a bench and watched a family with young children walk the circle reading all the historic markers. Nice park. I hadn't been there before. Then I started home toward Coker. But I couldn't shake the feeling that something was wrong. That something was going down. Don't ask me how. Just one of those intuitions. So I decided to drive by, not stop or anything, on my way out of town."

"What time was that?"

Mr. Tulane glanced at his watch. "Um, I'm guessing a few minutes after six is when I pulled up outside. I didn't get out at first. It looked like she was still home. The dog was walking around on the sidewalk and the front door was propped open."

"The front door was open?"

"Yeah. And her car was in the driveway. So I waited. No other cars were around. So I guessed the Red guy wasn't with her. I wasn't sure about Andrew and Joey. Of course Joey goes to Auburn and Andrew's like most teenagers to hear her tell it, stays away from home a lot and up in his room by himself the rest of the time."

"So, you saw no other cars?"

"None. I mean, there was one parked down the street at a neighbor's house and some out on Queen City in driveways, but none here."

"And then what?"

Mr. Bob Tulane closed his eyes, sighed deeply, stroked the dog's neck. "And then I began to worry. Things just didn't compute. Priscilla was a punctuality stickler. If she said six, she meant six. Not one 'til six. Not one after six. Six. So I got out and went to the door. Called out. Knew she'd curse me like a sailor if she were home. But she didn't answer. Called out again. No answer. Went inside and there was all this smoke. And I saw the broken vase, a broken flower. The smoke smell was God-awful. I called her again. No answer. Then I got scared, uneasy-like. It was all crazy. I could feel it. So I went upstairs and into her room and . . ."

Addie waited. He jammed his fists into his forehead. Yellow pools of forehead encircled by red skin.

"I loved that damn woman."

"So, you went into her room and what, Mr. Tulane?"

Mr. Tulane stared at her incredulously. His pupils dilated. His breathing increased. "Then what?" he asked much too loudly. "Then what? She was there on the floor. Blood everywhere. Damn rose perfume sprayed all over her, I could smell it. She had on a bizarre bra. Ugliest thing I'd ever seen. Totally out of character for her. Black lace underwear near her body on the floor. Dead." He choked. Let out a kind of punctuated sob. "I bent down, touched her neck. No pulse. Still warm. Still warm, just dead."

Addie pursed her lips. Bizarre didn't even begin to capture the essence of that bra. She could appreciate Mr. Tulane's point. Black lace seemed much more in keeping with Dr. Beaty's image. "I understand this must be very difficult for you, Mr. Tulane. But please think carefully. What did you do next? After you found her dead, I mean? Did you see or hear anyone else in the house?"

"No, nothing. I looked. Searched every room after I called 911. Wanted to kill the SOB. Would have done it, I swear to God. But no one was here."

"So you're saying your fingerprints will be all over the house?"

Mr. Tulane appeared startled by the question. "Well, yes. I mean, yes, I guess that's right."

"And you have no idea where her boys might be?"

He shook his head. "I guess Joey's back at Auburn. But Andrew . . . I have no idea."

Addie studied him quietly. She liked to stare at suspects after they completed their stories. Kept them cooperative. Guessing. Intimidated. Her back ached. She straightened it. Her stomach growled. She ignored it. Warm oil. Candlelight. Soft music. Luke's long fingers walking up her spine. "Thank you again for your cooperation, Mr. Tulane," she said. "Is there any information I failed to elicit that you think might be helpful to this investigation?"

A flicker of uncertainty. Discomfort almost certainly. There was definitely something. Something he wasn't saying. "No," he said.

She expected that. She stood and arched her back.

He stood, too. "Oh," he said suddenly. "Oh, there is something."

Ha! "Yes?"

He scooped up the little dog. "I, um, I was planning to take Winx home with me until things settle down."

No surprises. Nothing of significance after all. "Thanks for offering, Mr. Tulane. But he'll go to the vet for boarding until the boys are found. I'll let them know you offered though."

A dark look. "I understand," he said. It was clear he didn't.

"If you don't mind, what does his rabies tag say? Who's their vet?"

Mr. Tulane's fingers fumbled with the dog's tags. He squinted and Winx wriggled and trembled a little. Addie didn't get it. Little dogs trembled at the strangest times.

"It's okay, boy," she said.

Mr. Tulane put the dog back on the couch. "Dr. Greene," he said. "The tag says Greene's Veterinary Clinic."

38

Mr. Vic Abernathy sat kicked back in his brown leather recliner, shoes off, hairy toes wiggling beyond the edge of the footrest. He was watching Wheel of Fortune. Something that smelled like bacon and onions wafted from the kitchen, a creative concoction by his wife of thirty-two years. Tonight she was making a casserole for tomorrow's pot luck luncheon at the B.F. Goodrich plant where she worked. Lois liked to experiment with food and most of the time that was a good thing. Sometimes her flavor combinations were a little over the top like when she added a whole lemon to her vegetable soup. "It's good to live on the edge, Victor," she'd say. He smiled just thinking about it. The truth was their lifestyle was smack dab in the center of a very broad plateau, not an edge in sight. He heard the refrigerator door open and close and squawky voices and static from the police scanner. She was an avid police scanner hobbyist. She loved getting the scoop on what was happening around town. He couldn't stand to be in the same room with it.

He studied the lettered puzzle on the screen. _ _u _r_ _ _ cu_ _ _ t_ _. The challenger was about to buy another vowel. Vic loved the show. It kept his synapses snapping. He'd already figured this one out. One day he hoped to be a contestant and win his way right into retirement. No more bored pimply faces with bored zombie eyes. No more algebraic equations buried beneath giddy mountains of testosterone and estrogen.

"Vic, honey?"

"Okay, be right there. I just want to see if I got this right."

The guy bought an "e." _ _u _re _ _ cu_ _ _ te_. Yep, he was right. Had to be. Lois appeared at the door. "Honey?" she said. Her forehead was furrowed like she was about to say something serious. "There was something on the scanner just then. There was a murder today. An elementary school principal. Fifty-three years old. I think they said Beaty." She wiped her hands on the dishtowel she was carrying. "They're looking for her sons."

Vic Abernathy's toes stopped wiggling. He pushed the footrest down and sat arrow straight in his chair. "Dr. Beaty?" he asked. "They're looking for Andrew?"

His wife shook her head, her right shoulder moving just a little. "They didn't give a boy's name. But they're looking for both her sons. So there must be two. There's concern they could all be victims of a home invasion. And they didn't say it but it sounded like they may also be suspects in their mother's death. Is one of them your student?"

"Not now. Andrew was. Difficult kid, sort of, but bright, not too bad, really, lots of potential."

"It'll be on the news at ten, I'm sure," she said glancing at her wrist. "About eight minutes."

He picked up the remote and switched channels. There was a crime show ending. His brain felt stuffed with cotton. He'd never personally known a murder victim. It had to be a mistake.

Priscilla. Sixteen. Her long arms wrapped around him, her fingers locked together at the top of his spine. Alabama summer and he was sweating like a pig and her damp wrists stuck to the sides of his neck right at his hairline. She had pretty eyes and she smelled gaggingly strong of roses and she smiled and showed straight, white teeth and he knew it was okay to be sweaty because who cared when you were seventeen and about to get laid? She was wearing blue eye shadow and the stuff she put on her eyelashes was glopped up into little balls in one or two places and he remembered wondering if she'd put on too much. She was the most sophisticated girl he'd ever met.

And Andrew. Kidnapped? Was he alive? Dead? Hiding? Had the boy even heard the news? A thought formed on the cusp of Mr. Vic Abernathy's cerebral cortex. No way. Andrew was much too smart for that. He couldn't possibly be the murderer. It was no secret his relationship with his mother was troubled. But still. Obnoxious, yes. A murderer, no. Vic didn't really know Andrew's brother. He'd met him a time or two but never taught him in school.

"Did you know her, honey? The Beaty woman?"

Lois' voice zapped him back to the room, his recliner, the television. He hoped she couldn't see the lie. "Um, not well," he said. "We went to high school together. Unhappy girl as I recall. A majorette, though, as I remember. I've see her around town several times. Last time was in December, I think, at the post office. She said she was mailing something off to her boy at Auburn. Joey, I think she called him. She told me Andrew, that's the one I had in class, was still giving her grief."

His wife laid the dishtowel across her shoulder. "Well, I hope they get it all sorted out quickly."

"Yes," he said. "And that Andrew and his brother are safe."

The local news didn't have a lot to add. The anchor, a doe-eyed University communications major who talked too slowly, enunciated too carefully, and kept her hands locked cardboard style together in front of her at her waist, led off by announcing breaking news, details to be elaborated upon as they became available. She announced a tragic afternoon in Tuscaloosa. The murder of Tuskaloosa Gardens Elementary School's principal, Dr. Priscilla Beaty, and a one vehicle accident on Northridge Road that left one woman, twenty-nine year old Dana Whitesmythe, dead at the scene. According to preliminary reports, Ms. Whitesmythe was in her first trimester of pregnancy. A video of an overturned vehicle with a bashed in hood and fender that was flipped sideways against a pine flashed onto the screen. Law enforcement came on asking any witnesses driving in the area between two and three o'clock to come forward with information, no matter how seemingly inconsequential.

"There should be plenty of witnesses," Vic said to his wife. "That's when Verner Elementary gets out, and some kids were probably leaving Northridge High early, too."

"You'd think so," she said.

The death of Dr. Beaty expanded into about five minutes of coverage. The police captain explained she was found by a man identifying himself as a family friend. Preliminary reports indicated she died of multiple blows to the head and body, delivered by a blunt force instrument. Her home was in apparent disarray at the time of police entry. Some of the evidence had apparently been calculatingly destroyed. Details were being withheld. Police were looking for Dr. Beaty's two sons, Andrew, aged sixteen, last seen leaving the Lake Tuscaloosa area, and Joey, aged twenty-one, an Auburn student also last seen leaving the Lake Tuscaloosa area with his brother. Andrew was described as a Caucasian male, approximately five feet eleven inches and one hundred sixty-two pounds, with green braided hair, last seen wearing jeans and a black tee-shirt. Joey as a Caucasian male, five feet, ten inches, approximately one hundred eighty-five pounds, brown hair, last seen wearing jeans and an Auburn tee-shirt. He was driving a green Jetta and was believed to be returning to Auburn University. There was no evidence to suggest he arrived. There was concern the boys had been abducted. Anyone with information about either of these males, or with information related to the murder of Dr. Priscilla Beaty, was asked to phone the Tuscaloosa City Police Department immediately. Information could be provided anonymously. The cameras then transitioned into a shot of a tidy brick two-story home with a well-manicured lawn in the Dearing Place neighborhood. A man who identified himself as Mr. Bob Tulane stood out in front of the home with a dachshund in his arms. He told the young male reporter he'd been worried about Dr. Beaty's safety earlier in the day and dropped by to check on her. When she didn't answer the door he found his way inside. He was not at liberty to describe what he found inside the house. Authorities estimated Dr. Beaty was killed slightly before six o'clock. More information would be provided as details became available. The news anchor then wiped the serious look off her face and offered a lighter story about a kayaking marriage held earlier in the day down at Riverwalk.

"I'm restless," said Vic turning off the TV before the wedding story was over. "Think I'll go walk around the Quad with Mozart. Want to come?"

"No," said Lois. "That casserole's in the oven and I'm right at the end of the novel I checked out of the library. It's due back day after tomorrow. But Mozart will be thrilled."

Vic unhooked the yellow leash with little black dog bones on it from the hall pegboard and whistled to their Chinese Crested. Weird little fellow, their dog. Bred to be naked. Just a few black freckle markings on his brown skin, and plumes of wheat colored fur on the top of his head, on each foot at the ankle and on his lower tail. That was it. Never did grow many teeth, either. Not at all like a normal dog. They'd purchased him during a trip to Louisiana when they ventured out to the annual frog festival in Rayne, the self-proclaimed Bullfrog Capital of the World. His wife named the dog Mozart because of the way he sang whenever the phone rang. She misidentified his howling as melodious.

"Come on, boy," called Vic. "Let's go for a walk." Mozart knew the word. He slid around the corner, banking against the kitchen cabinet, slid to a stop just short of the dishwasher. Vic didn't bother leashing him. Mozart followed him down the front steps and jumped into the backseat almost faster than the car door could open.

"Let's pray Andrew and his brother are okay," Vic said to Mozart as they drove toward the University. "Truth be known, I've always liked the boy." Mozart hopped into the front seat. "In the back," said Vic. "You know the rules." Joggers and walkers dotted the Quad's perimeter sidewalk. Lights cast shadows all across the thirteen acre park. The perimeter sidewalk was a healthy work out and he tried to walk Mozart around it at least four times a week after dinner. For every step he took, Mozart had to take five.

He parked at the School of Social Work across the street from Denny Chimes just as the computer operated bells indicated the quarter hour. There was myth surrounding the brick tower. When a virgin walked beneath it, a brick was supposed to fall. All the bricks were intact and had been for as long as anyone could remember. Certainly there was no danger of one falling on poor Priscilla. He fastened Mozart's leash to his matching collar and guided him safely beside the Social Work building and across University Boulevard, the white columned President's mansion at their backs. He paused only long enough to decide whether to walk clockwise or counterclockwise, chose clockwise, and Mozart trotted happily along beside him. A female wearing white shorts and a long sleeve tee-shirt passed.

"Hey," she said a little shyly.

"Good evening," Vic replied. He remembered being her age, not her father's age, and he scowled as he considered the fleeting nature of time. A man jogged past wearing a US Marines tee-shirt followed by two guys in Chi Phi frat tees. They weren't much older than Andrew. He'd always assumed Andrew would make it to college. Surely Andrew was still alive. The boy's wits were lightning quick. Mr. Vic Abernathy breathed in deeply and looked into the sky. There was a nighthawk calling, circling higher and higher into the darkness, spiraling until it was just a dot, a tiny dot barely discernable to his eyes. All of a sudden growing larger, free falling, plummeting like a boulder toward the ground. A daredevil, pulling out of its dive with a whoomph just in time to avoid a disaster of gravity and ground. Somewhere nearby Vic knew a female nighthawk sat on a rooftop watching. He chuckled to himself. Amazing what males were willing to do to impress their lady loves. Hormones and procreation and survival of the species. It reminded him of his classrooms. There was never a dull hormonal moment. It kept him on his toes.

A young couple holding hands approached and Mozart pulled frantically on his leash. They were walking a husky. It was pulling too. They veered off into the lawn toward a grassy mound. It was where the remains of the University were heaped after the campus was burned by Federal troops at the end of the Civil War. A grassed mini-plateau of history, the University Mound. After heavy rains Vic and his wife found exposed pieces of pottery and melted glass around its base. Another bike approached, this one with a young Mormon riding it. Neat white button down shirt, dark pants, a tie flapping off to the right below the tie clip, a bulging dark backpack. The Mormon's feet stopped pedaling, coasted, then appeared to brake before starting to pedal again. Vic nodded in greeting and reined in Mozart. The missionary passed without speaking. In fact, he appeared to lower his head to prevent eye contact. Odd. Vic had never known a Mormon missionary who avoided eye contact. He stopped abruptly and Mozart coughed as his collar pressed against his larynx.

"That's Andrew," he said to his dog. But that didn't make any sense. Andrew had green dreads just this morning. Andrew wasn't a Mormon and he wasn't a missionary. But he was extraordinarily creative. It would be just like the boy. Vic spun around. "Andrew!" he yelled at the departing figure. "Andrew! Wait! Wait! It's important!" Mozart's little toenails clicked along the sidewalk as he ran to keep up. The Mormon was pedaling faster than Mr. Vic Abernathy and Mozart could move. "Maybe I'm wrong," Vic thought. It made a hell of a lot more sense for him to be wrong. "Andrew!" he called. "Stop! It's important, son!"

The handlebars of the bicycle wavered. Two black dress shoes moved toward the pavement and the boy stood straddling the bike, as straight and still as Denny Chimes. Mr. Abernathy slowed his pace, gasped for breath, wondered if Andrew knew his mother was dead, and wondered for what earthly reason the boy was disguised as a Mormon riding around the University of Alabama campus in the dark. Andrew was always the one to paddle upstream when everyone else was floating peacefully down. He was so relieved to find Andrew alive and unharmed that he hadn't considered the enormity of the task ahead until he had nearly reached the boy's side.

Son! Andrew's stomach felt like it had dropped into his intestines. Oh my God! Son! So his fears were right after all. Mr. Abernathy, the man who had red hair in the slides Bethy's class saw this very day, the

Iguana Man, just yelled out the one word that bound Andrew to him irrevocably forever, even if they never saw one another again. In some ways he'd always suspected it would end up being somebody like Mr. Abernathy. Old Iguana Man was breathing hard and his face was flushed with beads of sweat on his forehead and sweat lines trickling down the sides of his face. His little dog, what a totally weird looking dog, was panting even harder.

"I'm so glad I found you," said Mr. Abernathy with effort, still catching his breath.

Andrew couldn't help it, his eyes were drawn toward the hangy down lizard neck. Oh God, was it hereditary? He swallowed in an effort to redigest the glob of whatever it was he felt suspended below his Adam's apple. He reached toward his throat. The skin was reassuringly tight. "So," he said in a voice he didn't recognize as his own. "So, I guess you're bi- or something?" His words hung awkwardly in the air as a question.

"I'm what?"

It was too much to think about. "Nothing," said Andrew. "Never mind."

Mr. Abernathy stared at him while his weird little dog lifted a leg and peed on the trunk of a gingko tree. "I have absolutely no idea what you're talking about."

Andrew rolled his eyes. He dug into his front pocket and identified the bracelet with his thumb and forefinger. He pulled it out and handed it to the man. "Look familiar?"

Mr. Abernathy held the bracelet in the palm of his hand and moved off the sidewalk to allow several joggers to pass without appearing to even notice them. He turned the bracelet over in his hand and his forehead furrowed. "No. Um, sorry."

"To my beautiful Prissy with everlasting love. Red," said Andrew. He reached for the bracelet and jammed it back into his pocket. "Damn! I can't imagine it. You're not her type." The words dangled. It was a stupid thing to say and he knew it. Every man was her type. "All the kids say you're gay."

The man shook his head. He looked very confused. His neck skin flapped. "No, but if I were? . . ."

Andrew's eyes rolled again. "Son," he said. "You called me son. I'm sure you don't like it any more than me."

Mr. Abernathy's eyelids narrowed, then widened, then narrowed again. A subtle smile played on his lips. When he spoke his eyes were soft and kind. "Are you trying to tell me you think I'm your father?"

Andrew put one foot back on a pedal. He was starting to feel pissed off. "You used to have red hair. You showed your class old slides today. And you just called me son."

The man's face scrunched up like he was trying to recall what he'd said. His iguana neck wiggled back and forth again. "It was just a figure of speech, Andrew. I'm sorry if you misunderstood. You can be sure I'd already have told you something that important."

Andrew moved his right shoulder and adjusted his backpack. It was heavy and the straps were digging into his clavicles. Neanderthal. Dumb-ass stupid. Of course it was just a figure of speech. Thank God it was just a figure of speech. "So why'd you stop me?" he asked. "How'd you even figure out it was me?"

"You don't really think a disguise like this could fool me, do you? But why are you masquerading as a Mormon missionary, Andrew? When I saw you kissing Miss Bethy Smithson this morning you looked like the Andrew I know."

He'd told her Old Iguana Man was watching them. He could just feel those beady eyes. "Gotta go," he said. "But leave Bethy out of it. She has nothing to do with any of it."

Mr. Vic Abernathy took a step toward him and grasped the handlebars. "Nothing to do with what?" he asked. It was inconceivable Andrew might have murdered. But why the disguise? And why was he biking around the Quad at this time of night?

"Let go of my freakin' bike," said Andrew.

Vic Abernathy held on. He had no idea where to start. In 'Nam it had fallen to him to break the news of soldiers' deaths on several occasions. He was barely older than Andrew then. Nineteen, drafted, and he grew up fast. Be succinct. Bare bone facts. Let him ask questions to fill in the details when he's ready. But this was murder. His mother. Assuming he didn't already know. Assuming, and Vic did assume, Andrew wasn't her murderer. "The police are looking for you, Andrew. It was on the ten o'clock news."

"Already?" It caught him by surprise. "Yeah, well, they've looked for me before."

Vic Abernathy moved the toe of his shoe in front of the bike tire. "You need to call them. They think you're missing."

"I am. And I'm gonna stay that way." He pushed forward with his grounded foot. The tire bumped against the man's toe and rolled over it. "Let go and move please."

Mr. Abernathy didn't budge. "The news said they're looking for your brother, too."

Andrew's foot, the one on the pedal, returned to the ground. "Joey? Why would they be looking for Joey? He should be back at Auburn by now. In a study group."

Mr. Abernathy let go of the handlebars but reblocked the tire with his shoe. "Maybe that's where he is, then. Maybe they just don't know about the study group."

Andrew pulled his phone out of his pocket. "Why are they looking for Joey anyway?" He pressed speed dial. His brother's answering message came on. He tried again. "Pick up," he said, but Joey didn't. He scrolled to Thomas. Thomas answered on the second ring.

"Thomas, it's Andrew. Sorry to call so late but I just heard they were looking for Joey on the news tonight. Is he okay?"

"Andrew, where are you?"

"Here on the Quad. Is he all right?"

"Where on the Quad?"

Andrew looked around. "Um, on the sidewalk near the Mound."

"Don't move. I'm on my way."

*   *   *

Luke massaged her feet with warm oil scented with jasmine. Her toes wiggled gleefully as his thumbs worked along her soles, circling again and again beneath her arches. It felt heavenly and she was almost successful in ignoring her impatient backbone and shoulder blades and her mind that was working overtime. She was a long way from feeling relaxed. She could sense tension in her husband, too. Deep thought at least. She knew he was thinking about the missing Andrew Beaty and probably about his dead mother and missing brother, as well. She'd told him right away that she knew the Beatys had visited Metamorphosis. That Andrew was being considered for life with the Lunas. And that the homicide was her case to solve. He'd rubbed warm oil on his hands and laid a towel on the bed and motioned for her to lie down and mumbled something about confidentiality unless Andrew was in mortal danger or worst case scenario, if he'd murdered his mother. Neither of them reached eagerly to answer the phone when it rang. Luke squinted at the caller ID while his fingers continued their circles around the pressure points of Addie's feet. "It's the department," he said.

"Darn!" she said. "Better take it." He handed her the receiver. She rolled onto her back and sat up. "Bramson," she said.

"Detective Bramson?"

"Yes?"

"Cartwright here."

"Oh, hi Butch."

"Sorry to bother you so late. But we've found the kid. Andrew Beaty. He called from the house where he's staying tonight. The family of a Mr. Thomas Chalot. We spoke to Mr. Chalot. He guaranteed he'd keep the boy settled until it was determined what to do with him."

Addie's eyes locked on Luke's. She smiled and gave him the thumbs up. "So he's safe?" she said.

"Yes. Mr. Chalot reports he appears to be in shock related to the news of his mother and all. Says he's curled up in bed with a blanket over his head. Keeps asking for his brother. Refused dinner."

"Who is this man?" she asked. "How does he know Andrew?"

"He's apparently a close family friend. Mr. Chalot says he's actually the father of the other missing boy, Joey Chalot. We were able to confirm that."

"So Joey's still missing?"

"Not accounted for, but he could easily be back at Auburn. Probably hasn't gotten word yet that he's missing. That his mother's dead. That's what Mr. Chalot's assuming. It might take a while to locate him, him being a college kid and all."

Addie wiggled her toes and nestled her head into the crook of Luke's elbow. "Well, thank goodness Andrew's alive and safe. Maybe we'll know Joey's whereabouts by morning."

"Yes, ma'am. We'll be working on it."

Ma'am. What was it with these young guys? Ma'am sounded old, like she was fifty. "Where will Mr. Chalot and Andrew be in the morning? I'd like to talk with them first thing."

"Mr. Chalot says Andrew's told him he's suspended from school for cigarette possession. He'll confirm that with the school tomorrow. He plans to call into work and stay home with Andrew until he hears from our department."

"Good work, Butch. I'll get over there first thing tomorrow. Thanks."

"Oh, Detective Bramson?"

"Yes?"

"One more thing. Something odd."

"Yes?"

"When Andrew was located he was disguised."

"Disguised?"

"Affirmative. According to Mr. Chalot."

Addie's nose and forehead wrinkled and light flickering from the candles danced through her eyes as she listened. She still wore a puzzled look when she hung up the phone. "It seems," she said to Luke as she stretched her feet lazily back toward him, "your newest Luna pupa has metamorphosed into a bicycle missionary for the Church of Jesus Christ of Latter Day Saints."

39

He was taller, cleaner cut than she'd anticipated. He sat at the Chalot's glass top breakfast table in a wicker chair stuffed with green gingham upholstery cushions. He was staring in what she interpreted as a hostile manner at her digital recorder as she placed it on the table, its little green light in the far right hand corner blinking steadily. Mr. Thomas Chalot, also a tall thin man, sat beside him. Mr. Chalot's face was memorable. High cheekbones, a long narrow nose Luke would admire, and almond shaped kind-looking eyes. Kind-looking but astute nonetheless.

She pulled her badge from her purse pocket and flashed it quickly as way of formal introduction. "Detective Adelaide Bramson," she said. "Andrew, I'm sorry for your loss."

The boy's eyes darted toward her, away, back again. "Bramson? That's weird. As in Bramson at that place Metamorphosis?"

"Yes. Dr. Luke Bramson is my husband."

Andrew put the palms of his hands against the table top and shoved backward. His chair squeaked across the tile floor. "That's screwed."

"Andrew!" Mr. Chalot chided. "There's no place for that attitude in this house." Addie was impressed by the man's firm, calm reprimand.

The boy's shoulders slumped ever so slightly. "Sorry, Thomas," he said.

"Apology accepted," said Mr. Chalot.

"Absolutely," said Addie. "But just for the record, Andrew, Dr. Bramson never tells me anything about the people he sees. He didn't even let on he knew you last night. Even with you being in the news. I told him about you but he said nothing. I'm sure he talked to you about confidentiality. Now if you were in real danger, like if you'd been kidnapped . . ."

Andrew tossed his head and scoffed. "Like anyone'd have the balls to try that."

"Andrew . . .," warned Mr. Chalot again.

"Or if he knew you'd murdered someone or even hurt someone deemed more vulnerable by law." Her mind was running circles around her words. He hadn't acknowledged her condolences about his mother. "So," she said. "I need to ask you some questions. I'm sorry that some might be hard to answer under the circumstances. And as you've already noted, I record all my interviews." She nodded toward the small recorder.

Andrew shrugged. Actually, he felt odd, like he had an entire roll of toilet paper crammed between his ears. He'd lain in Thomas' guest room queen-sized bed last night and stared at the ceiling even though he couldn't see it in the dark and he'd cried and even laughed once or twice. The sheets felt like tee-shirts against his skin and he wasn't sure when he'd finally gotten to sleep or if he'd slept at all. It was surreal. And where was Joey? Right at daybreak he'd heard Joey's half-sibs in the bathroom getting ready for school. One of them was singing 'Row Row Row Your Boat.' It was annoying. "I hated my mother," he said evenly and his voice sounded foreign and hollow to him.

"Go on," Addie said gently.

Andrew didn't look up from his hands. They were still positioned on the edge of the table. "That's it. I hated my mother."

"Enough to kill her?"

A contorted smile played across his lips. He glanced up. "Sometimes."

"What about yesterday?"

"I don't remember."

Addie saw Mr. Chalot shift in his chair almost imperceptibly. He was clearly trying to be invisible. They agreed before Andrew joined them that he'd probably be more responsive with Mr. Chalot present. "Okay," she said. "Let's start at the beginning."

"Of my life?"

She smiled. "Well, we could but that's not really what I had in mind. Why don't you start with yesterday morning and try to remember the sequence of your day."

Andrew rolled his eyes. "Okay. Mom came upstairs yesterday morning before she went to work. I pretended to be asleep so she'd leave me alone. She planned to stick me at Metamorphosis because she called me out of control. That was bullshit, I can control myself. But after she left I got up and she'd left me a whole list of chores. I ripped up the paper and left to, ah, meet with some folks before I ran away."

"What were the folks' names?"

Andrew flexed his biceps. He put his elbow on the table and turned his attention to his flexing muscles.

Maybe he was the kid spotted with Tony. It might fit. Tony was seen at the park close to Andrew's house. "You wouldn't have met a guy named Tony by any chance?"

Andrew's arm froze in mid-flex. He continued to stare at his biceps. "Tony, who?" he asked but he wondered if his voice were convincing. "Never known a Tony."

"And why weren't you at school?"

He rolled his eyes again. "Suspended for cigarettes."

"And do you have a girlfriend?"

"She's not in this," he said sharply. "Leave her alone."

"Andrew . . ."

Addie nodded reassuringly toward Mr. Chalot. "That's okay for now. Okay, so you met some unidentified folks. And then what?"

"I went back home. Packed. Thought about smashing her goddamn football clock. Smashed her first one but then one of her . . . um, admirers gave her its evil twin." He frowned at the recorder. "Do we have to have that damn thing on?"

"'Fraid so," said Addie. She waited. She wanted to tell him she understood about the clock, that she'd surely smash it too if she had to live with it. "But you didn't smash it?"

"Nope."

Silence. "And then?"

"Then I met my brother, Joey, right after lunch. We walked around the neighborhood. Talked. He's the one who drove me to that Metamorphosis place to meet your husband. But before we left we went back to the house. I was pissed off at my mom about all of it. Before we left I smashed her favorite lamp. It was from Chinatown or somewhere. It felt great smashing it. Wanted to see her face when she came in and found it all over the floor."

So that accounted for the lamp. Not part of a domestic struggle if he were telling the truth. "And did you get to see her face when she came home?"

"Nope. I was gone by then."

She was letting him get ahead of himself. Actually guided him that way. Back on track. "Okay, so you smashed the lamp. Was your brother still with you?"

"Yeah. He tried to keep me calm. Joey always tries to keep me calm."

"Okay, and then?"

"Um, then we went to Metamorphosis. Did all that stuff. Rode home with Joey. He dropped me off at the house. He was in a hurry to get back to Auburn to study for a test." Andrew looked toward Mr. Chalot for confirmation. The man nodded subtly.

"So when Joey dropped you off, was there anyone else at home?"

"Nope. There were, um, flowers out front. By the door. I stuffed them in the toilet."

Addie leaned forward. "And why would you do that?"

His eyes narrowed. His face seemed to change shapes. She'd seen it happen before with other suspects. Leaner looking, harder, colder eyes. "Because my mother's a whore," he said.

"Andrew!" Thomas chided.

Andrew's back straightened, shoulders tighter. "You know it's true," he said turning toward Mr. Chalot. "And she hurt you, too. Dr. Priscilla Perfect, that's what she made herself out to be. But we all knew somebody'd kill her one day. Joey said that just yesterday."

"Exactly what did he say? Can you remember his words?"

Andrew stared coldly. Same hard, lean look. "Luck of the draw. Odds play out. Something like that."

Luck of the draw. What a concise way to explain unforeseen demise. She softened her tone. "Andrew, do you have any idea who sent the flowers?"

He threw one shoulder forward in a half shrug. "Yeah, sure. I read the card. I'm sure it was that vet dude she's been seeing. The guy who hired Joey for the summer. He was young enough to be our fucking brother. But he had a penis, that's all it took."

"Andrew! This is your last warning. Stop being disrespectful." Mr. Chalot's tone was sharper. His almond shaped eyes had morphed into slits.

Silence. "So," she said finally when it was obvious Andrew wasn't going to offer more spontaneously. "You went into the house and then what?"

More silence. Well, not true silence. There was the sound of the dishwasher on wash cycle and the hum of the refrigerator and outside what sounded like a small jet overhead somewhere. Not too many aircraft flew into Tuscaloosa except during football season when corporate jets and planes of all sizes and shapes, and occasionally the Goodyear blimp, filled the airspace and the tarmac. And when the Blue Angels brought their precision flying skills to the city and cars were bumper to bumper and people were shoulder to shoulder for as far as the eye could see. There were several corporate and charter jets and some recreational aircraft and law enforcement helicopters around town too, but not enough to become accustomed to the sound of things moving around overhead.

He shrugged again. "Like I said. I drowned the flowers. Then I got my stuff together, already packed most of it earlier, and split. I left the door cracked for Winx. Propped open."

Addie squinted. "So you're saying you didn't lock your front door?"

"It's no big deal. I've done it before."

It fit with Mr. Bob Tulane's story. The front door was open. He was concerned. He walked in to check it out. "So," she said. "Why'd you choose to disguise yourself as a missionary?"

A smile flickered across Andrew's lips, danced through his eyes. He was obviously pleased with himself. Clearly saw himself as clever. "These missionary dudes knocked on the doors in our neighborhood a while back. I let them in just for the hell of it. I listened to their spiel and they gave me the Book of Mormon. They were nice guys. Dorks but okay. So one night when I was almost asleep and I knew I was gonna run it came to me. No one'd ever recognize me dressed like that."

There were little smeared spots of blackish gray skin unevenly distributed around the base of his hairline on his neck and behind his right ear.

"There's no evidence of your hair dying activity at home," said Addie. "Where'd you do it?"

"I couldn't do it at home," he said. "That'd blow my cover. I did it at the University library. The bathroom in the basement. No one bothered me. I don't even think anyone noticed me."

"And what time was that?"

His jaw moved sideways, back and forth, back and forth. "I have no idea. Why?"

"It's important to establish where you were and when."

"Well, I was there getting ready until I went onto the Quad and rode around waiting until it was time to go hang out in a dorm lobby. To stay overnight. But then old Iguana Man found me." He laughed. He was actually impressed. "Sonofabitch recognized me like I'd been a Mormon all my life."

Addie glanced at Mr. Chalot with a puzzled look on her face. "Iguana Man?"

"Not him," said Andrew. "Not Thomas. It's one of my old teachers. He looks like an iguana." But the name didn't really suit Mr. Abernathy anymore. Andrew wasn't sure what to do with that yet. Mr. Abernathy'd been nice, hadn't hassled him at all. Had stayed with him until Thomas could pick him up. And he'd called him son. Andrew'd thought about that last night all night, off and on while he was staring into the dark. Of course Mr. Abernathy would deny being his father. He'd denied it all along. But maybe he really was. Why else would he be so concerned?

"So you ran into this ex-teacher and what time was that?"

Andrew shrugged again. "Like ten-thirty, I think, a little later."

"Andrew called me a little after eleven," offered Thomas. "I told him to stay exactly where he was until I could get over to the Quad to pick him up. I called the police to inform them he'd been located and then headed off to find him. Mr. Abernathy stayed until I got there."

"And what's Mr. Abernathy's first name?"

"Vic," said Andrew. "Vic-tor." He burped for emphasis.

"Excuse me," said Thomas.

"Yes," said Andrew. "Excuse me." He was smiling and totally insincere.

"And where does he teach?"

"The Magnet school. Eighth grade math."

Addie stared at Andrew and cleared her throat. Bad Cop time. "Andrew, yesterday there was a report of a guy with green dreds meeting at the park behind your house with an older guy named Tony. We've got a lot of information on Tony. We know he's a fence. We've heard he's offering kill-for-hire services."

He could barely think. He forced himself to keep his eyes open, focus on her, breath evenly, sit up straight. He shook his head. "Like I said, never heard of him," he said.

"You're sure about that?"

He dared not look at Thomas. He cupped his hand across his forehead. "If you have to know, but it's really none of your business, I went to see my girlfriend. Had to bike over to her school, the Magnet school. Saw her during her morning break. Then I met up with Joey."

"What's your girlfriend's name?"

"I told you, leave her out of it."

"Answer her question, Andrew," said Thomas.

"No," said Andrew. "She doesn't have anything to do with any of this."

"Well," said Addie slowly, deliberately. "Maybe something will come to mind over the next couple of days. Just let me know when it does."

Andrew rolled his eyes. He still dared not look at Thomas.

She backed off. Back to the role of Good Cop. "Andrew, can you think of anyone who might want to murder your mother? Did she have any enemies? Anyone hassling her? Stalking her?"

His laugh was sharp. It stabbed through the quiet kitchen. "My mom was the original drama queen," he said. "Someone was always pissed at her. Living on borrowed time, that's what she was doing. I mean, just the chances of her dying of AIDS or hepatitis or something like that, not to mention all the dudes she's been with."

"What about this last guy?"

Andrew rubbed his chin. Light stubble. Still not enough growing there for any kind of respectable beard. "No idea. I've heard them fight on the phone a couple of times. Once he wanted her computer password. I told her she was crazy to give it to him."

"So he knew her password?"

"Yeah, me too. I overheard it."

"Really?" said Addie. "Do you still know it?"

Andrew moved his bottom forward and up off the chair. He leaned back and slid his hand into his back pocket. His wallet was nylon and Velcro. He smiled at Thomas. It was last year's Christmas present from the Chalots. He wondered if Thomas recognized it. He opened it and tugged at a scrap of paper. "Here," he said. "This is it. Keep it. I know it by heart."

Addie reached for the crumpled notebook paper. She unfolded it, smoothed it with her index finger and nodded. "Thanks," she said. "Do you think it's current?"

Andrew wanted to hock a loogie but he swallowed it instead. "I have no idea."

She gathered her thoughts. He shut his eyes while he waited. "So," she said. "No murder suspects come immediately to mind?"

"I stayed away from her as much as I could."

"Yes," she said. "It sounds like you've been angry for a long time."

"No shit."

"Andrew!"

"Sorry," Andrew said. He wasn't. Not really. He waited. He knew what was coming next. He knew because she'd been leading up to it all morning, dabbled with it, danced around it.

Addie leaned toward him. An intimidation tactic. Bad Cop. Bluff Cop. In for the kill. "Andrew," she said in her best no-nonsense tone. "Did you kill your mother when you got home from Metamorphosis yesterday afternoon? Killed her then ran? Thought you'd escape with that elaborate disguise?"

He sat very still. Very quiet. Thoughts tornadoed through his head. "No comment."

"The smashed lamp, smashed flowers. Things got out of control fast," she continued.

"No comment." Out of the corner of his eye he watched Thomas scowl.

"And how about Joey?" she pressed. "How was he involved?"

Andrew leapt out of his chair. "Go to hell! No way! Joey'd never kill anybody!" He stalked across the kitchen, jerked on the yellow kitchen door and let the cool morning air smack against his face.

*　　*　　*

"Andrew!" called Mr. Chalot. "Andrew! Get in here immediately!"

Andrew paused, his back to the house. He'd never heard Thomas raise his voice like that. He could hear him even outside in the yard with the door shut. His stomach cramped. He'd never disrespected Thomas before. He leaned over and vomited before taking off across the lawn, through the neighbor's back yard, front yard, across the street, into a front yard, back yard, back yard, front yard, across another street. Dogs barking. Don't mess with Joey. Why the hell had she mentioned Joey? And where the hell was he? He couldn't hear Thomas yelling for him anymore. In his mind's eye he saw his breakfast sitting all gelatinous and blended on the Chalot's side lawn with blades of green poking like little swords all through it.

Addie fished for her phone, her eyes meeting those of Mr. Chalot. "I guess I'll have to call for a pick-up on him," she said. "We can't have him running off."

Thomas bent his head forward and ran his fingers across his scalp. "I'm sure that's what you're required to do," he said. "Knowing Andrew though, he'll be back before the squad cars get near the neighborhood. He's not going anywhere. He's impulsive sometimes. He'll cool off and head back. May not come back in until you leave though."

Her phone was poised in mid-air. "Hmmm . . .," she said. "Impulsive isn't a word I like to hear when an angry adolescent's parent has been murdered."

"I know," he said. "It doesn't look good. But, I'll be honest with you. I just don't think either of the boys has it in them. Not murder. I've known Andrew since he was born. I've spent a lot of time with him. I would have spent even more but Priscilla never forgave my wife for marrying me."

"So is the plan for Andrew to stay here with you until things get settled?"

"No," said Thomas with evident sadness. "Actually a Miss Zenah Elenrude from DHR called this morning. She said just by coincidence she was involved in staffing his case at Metamorphosis, yesterday I guess, and so she knew his history. Apparently DHR's already filed an emergency hearing to take custody of him since he's a minor. The way she explained it he's a minor with no known parent. She plans to go ahead and place him at Metamorphosis until it can all get sorted out. Priscilla had him all set for admission so he'll probably be there by tonight."

Addie stared at the refrigerator door. Construction paper projects held in place by plastic alphabet magnets. There were a few red and yellow and green number magnets clinging to the door of the fridge as well. "You have younger children?"

"Three. All girls."

So DHR was proceeding with the plan to place Andrew at Metamorphosis. Probably a late night for Luke then. "I take it Andrew doesn't have any idea . . ."

"No. No. I was waiting to tell him. 'Til I had all the details. His emotions are pretty raw right now. He acts like Priscilla's death is no big deal but of course it is. I heard him crying in his room most of last night. And we're all worried about Joey. It's not like Joey to disappear off the face of the Earth. It's really out of character."

Addie watched strands of hair fall into a part of sorts as his fingers combed through it. "So he's never run off before?" she asked.

Thomas continued to finger comb. "No, never. I'm afraid something bad's happened. And it's my fault, really. He was so distraught yesterday. That news about Priscilla having an affair with the veterinarian he planned to work with this summer really threw him for a loop. I even met him out at Metamorphosis to spend time with him, help him calm down, come up with a plan. He was out there for Andrew's meeting but he called me and said he felt like he was about to lose it. I wanted him to spend the night here at the house but he said he had to get back for a big exam today. But I called his professor. He never made it to class. I've been calling around. Even have a call into his girlfriend's parents to get her mobile number."

"Is she local?"

"No. Well, yes. But she's up at Amherst. A sophomore." He paused, stood and walked toward the kitchen window. His lips turned upward. "There he is. Andrew I mean. I knew he'd be back."

Addie joined him at the window. She watched Andrew stop at the property's edge and stare toward the house before sitting on the grass. He leaned back on his elbows.

"Good," said Addie.

"He's a good kid, a real good kid, just like his brother," said Mr. Chalot. "In fact, I'm not saying anything to him yet, but my wife and I want him to move in with us. I wanted him to come here instead of going to Metamorphosis but Priscilla said no. He's never given me a lick of trouble."

"Why did Dr. Beaty choose Metamorphosis for Andrew over your home?" asked Addie. She remembered what Andrew'd said, about his mother hurting Mr. Chalot, too. She wondered what that meant.

The man's lips curled into a tight smile. It didn't look like a real smile. There was something almost sinister about it. "You had to know Priscilla," he said. "She couldn't stand relinquishing even a microbe of control."

She knew about adolescents with controlling parents. Luke talked her ear off when he got going on the topic of oppositional defiance. It wasn't the only reason kids became oppositional, some kids just seemed to be born spitting like llamas, but it went a long way toward explaining their behaviors sometimes. "Well, that might account for some of the oppositional and defiant behaviors in him," she said.

Mr. Chalot left the window and returned to the table. He pushed Andrew's chair back in place and sat down. Addie followed. "He certainly can be oppositional," he said. "There is something though, something he said . . . something he told you, it doesn't make sense. He told you he broke the lamp. But Joey told me he was the one who smashed Priscilla's lamp, the one in their living room. He said he did it after Andrew told him about their mom's affair. Joey told me Andrew insisted on taking the blame for it."

"Interesting . . ." The two of them might have killed her together. It was hard to be dispassionate about it. She wanted Thomas Chalot to be right. Good kids incapable of murder. But sometimes even good kids derailed the rest of their lives. She and Luke talked about it often, new research mapping the adolescent brain, why teens didn't always consider consequences, why they engaged in risk taking, why they made serious life altering choices.

"Andrew idolizes Joey," said Thomas quietly. "He'd do anything for him."

Addie stood. Angry, impulsive, would do anything for his brother. None of that sounded good. And where was his brother? Out of character for him to disappear. The real lamp smasher. That didn't sound good either. "Oh," she said. "I almost forgot. Their dog's boarded at Dr. Greene's veterinary clinic."

"That's the guy, I think. Dr. Greene. Dr. Harry Greene. That's what Joey said."

"What guy?"

"The one he planned to work for this summer."

"So that would make him Dr. Beaty's romantic interest?"

Mr. Chalot nodded and shrugged simultaneously. "To hear the boys tell it."

Addie studied the man's face. It seemed peculiar the way he talked about Dr. Beaty, Priscilla as he called her, like she was some distant acquaintance, like he was talking about the rise or fall of the stock market, not about his ex-lover's murder. "Just out of curiosity," she said, "how would you describe your relationship with the deceased?"

He stretched his feet forward. Long narrow shoes. Size twelve, thirteen perhaps. Brown loafers. Leather scuffed in a few spots around the toes. "We were friends," he said. Calm voice.

"Before Andrew left he mentioned that she'd hurt you."

His gaze was still steady. He was looking somewhere between the bridge of her nose and her forehead. "She did," he said evenly. "When we were younger, of course. I wanted to marry her. Begged her in fact. She was pregnant with my child. She said no. We hurt each other, I guess." He stared directly into her eyes and smiled dolefully. "But isn't that what most young lovers ultimately do? Inadvertently?"

Addie frowned. "How would you say you hurt her?" she asked.

He allowed a subtle smile to creep back onto his lips. "I married Holly. Priscilla never got over that."

"Meaning?"

His smile kept growing, detached, like a paste-on mustache. "I guess you could say I was always Priscilla's best friend. She confused that for romantic love sometimes, even when she was with another lover. And to be honest, no lack of respect for my marriage or my wife, but I never stopped loving Priscilla. She was like a child. A bird with a broken wing. I don't know. It was always complicated. Priscilla was like that."

Addie moved her purse strap further onto her shoulder. She glanced sideways out the window. Andrew was lying on the grass, legs apart, arms straight out from his sides, palms facing the sun. "Mr. Chalot," she said. "Please recognize that I have to ask. Were you and Dr. Beaty still romantically or perhaps sexually involved?"

His eyes seemed to register surprise. Then amusement. "Certainly not," he said. "I am very married, Detective Bramson."

She nodded. Maybe true. But she'd heard it all before. "And where did you go after you left Metamorphosis yesterday afternoon?"

Calm detachment again. Amusement flickering in his eyes. "I called my wife. Told her I'd grab a pizza or two on the way home. I had to order them and wait." He reached into his pocket, pulled out his wallet, opened it and produced a folded receipt. "Here," he said. "Luckily I kept it. As you can see I was all the way across town from Priscilla's place."

Addie studied the receipt. Six o'five. One pepperoni and one barbeque chicken with pineapple and peppers. One hand tossed, one thin crust. She handed it back to him. She was suddenly hungry. But it was too early for pizza. She thought about the animals in her purse. "Thank you, Mr. Chalot," she said. "I'm sure you understand that I have to ask."

"Certainly." Voice still oddly detached. "Just doing your job. But please believe I would never in a million lifetimes consider harming Priscilla."

She reached for her recorder, turned it off and dropped it in her purse. "Please keep Andrew closely supervised," she said. "Let me know immediately if he goes running off again. And also please call immediately if you hear from Joey."

"Definitely," he said.

She opened up the kitchen door, paused and turned to face him again. There was just a slight chance but it was still worth asking. "One more thing."

"Yes?"

"Do you have any idea, or did Dr. Beaty ever confide in you, the name of Andrew's biologic father?"

He crossed his arms on his chest and stared at the tiled floor. A pregnant pause, awkward, difficult, closed off body language too. The aloof smile reappeared. "Priscilla had her ways," he said. "There were always men. Even when we were dating there were men. Some for weeks, some for hours. I don't think anything I could offer would help you."

"Red," she said. "The man I'm looking for goes by the name Red. Or she called him that anyway. A private nickname perhaps."

Air escaped from Thomas' nose. A non-laugh laugh. "Yes," he said. "Red. The mysterious Red."

Nothing. But something. She was certain he knew. Or at least had strong suspicions. She'd get back to him on it. "Well, thanks for your help and time, Mr. Chalot," she said. "Contact me if you think of anything that might be helpful to our investigation." She opened the side door and stepped onto the carport. Andrew stood and brushed off the seat of his jeans.

"Will do," said Mr. Chalot. "And please find my boy alive and safe. We're all worried sick. I don't think any of us slept more than five minutes all night."

"Yes," said Addie. "We'll do our best. Bye, Andrew," she called waving casually in his direction. She'd catch up with him soon at Metamorphosis.

40

Shelby McDonald curled her legs in Luke's leather office chair, tucking her heels against her bottom. She leaned her shoulders and head against the chair's puffy headrest and raised her chin slightly. Her fingers reached to massage her temples. "I can't believe she's dead," she said. "When I heard the news last night I didn't know what to think."

He looked at her closed eyes and her short upturned nose and waited.

"It's been a long time since I felt so freaked," she said. She reopened her eyes and stared at the long strip of gray paint that ran the length of his office wall. Gray bookended with a black square on the left and a white square on the right. It was one of Luke's favorite therapy tools. Sort of like Dr. Hutchinson's Assume Nothing signs. "She seemed so confident and assertive. Like she could take care of herself. And even though things weren't great, I could tell she loved her boys."

Luke opened his top drawer and removed a Swiss army knife. He clipped off a thread hanging from his sleeve. "Now my button'll probably fall off," he said before turning his attention back to her. "I understand DHR's taking custody of Andrew today in an emergency hearing and he'll probably be admitted here tonight. I just got the call from Zenah Elenrude. She'll be his caseworker."

"Man," Shelby said. "Another long night . . . I miss Molly," she added softly.

"There's no need for you to stay," Luke said. "I can handle it. It'll just be Andrew and Miss Elenrude. Perhaps the family who's keeping him, the Chalots."

Shelby shifted her knees around until she was sitting cross legged. "Did Zenah say how he's doing?" she asked.

"She hasn't seen him yet."

"Oh."

"But Addie probably has," Luke said. "The murder's her case. She's got a pretty full plate right now."

Shelby's fingers found her temples again. She made little circles on the sides of her head.

"Have a headache?"

"No. It's just . . . I mean, I know it's crazy thinking." Her cheeks flushed. Shelby rarely ever cried. He could remember only three or four times since they started working together. She rubbed her cheeks with her palms. "It's just last night I kept thinking I could have saved her. Dr. Beaty, I mean. That guy, the one I told you about. I think he was stalking her. He kept on and on about following her home. And she was really pissed at him, you could tell, and she was telling him to get lost. And I heard him say something about needing to protect her from some other guy or guys. I should have called the cops, or at least threatened him with it. I keep thinking she'd be alive if I'd done something."

Luke reached toward the corner of his desk and pulled a tissue out of a little cardboard box. There were bluebirds printed on it. Eternally flying on cardboard. He handed the tissue to her. "Shelby, we have no idea what was going on in her life. The guy might have been totally legit, just concerned and too Cro-Magnon in his way of handling the situation. But why don't you call Addie and tell her what you heard? Maybe it'll help in the investigation."

"I'm glad it's Addie handling it," she said. "I really am having a hard time with this. I mean, I didn't have time to get to know Dr. Beaty but I identified with her and her feelings about Andrew and his father."

Luke's eyes softened. A gentle smile played across his lips. His body leaned forward ever so slightly. The intimacy in the room was palpable.

"She just seemed too strong, too professional, no, I guess I mean too capable and independent to be a victim," she said. "I don't know. It doesn't make sense but I felt sorry for her when she was talking about that guy Red. It really seemed to bother her that Red wouldn't claim Andrew. That she couldn't make everything okay. I understood that. It'll be that way for Molly. I mean, she'll want to know her father, at least know about him, and I don't know what I'll say. I'll never let them meet."

Luke's phone rang. He stared at it.

"Go ahead," Shelby said.

"No," he said. "They'll leave a message." Three rings, four. Silence. They both looked at the phone for several seconds. "You know, Shelby," said Luke. "You've never told me about Molly's father."

Shelby pulled her knees up to her chest and wrapped her arms around them. "I don't talk about him," she said.

Luke nodded. Waited.

She rocked back and forth for several minutes, arms still wrapped around her legs. "I was working out at a gym when I met him," she said. "Actually, I'd been watching him for a while." She chuckled. "He was a hunk."

Luke looked at her, surprised. He hadn't really ever considered that Shelby thought in hunks. He smiled.

"And he'd been studying me, too. Little silly flirtations, that kind of thing."

He could see it. Shelby was hot, sexy in a gymnast kind of way. And she had that pixie nose.

"But what really drew me to him were the kids. There were several older teenagers he brought with him almost every time he came. Street kids. He mentored them and they adored him. So I was thinking he was this great guy making the world a better place, keeping kids off the streets, building their self- esteem, all that."

Luke nodded.

"But now I know it was their adoration that motivated him. It was never about them. It was about him and a fawning audience. But I didn't see that then."

Luke nodded again.

"So we started dating and we hit it off great and it was like, this is going to sound crazy, but like I'd finally found my soul mate. He was romantic and funny and loved to go jogging before work in the mornings. He worked with amputees at the V.A., helping them move toward independent living. He told me he'd gotten interested in that population after his wife was killed overseas. He said she'd caught some shrapnel in her neck. Hit her carotid artery and she bled to death before the medics could get her to base. Her name was Adrianna, he said. They'd been married four years. She'd been deceased for two. He was still grieving he said but meeting me made him feel alive again. He kept Adrianna's photos up around the house and didn't want to change any of her decorating or anything, and I was really okay with our threesome. From the pictures she was a striking woman. Blond sort of kinky hair, freckles, tall. He said she was a visual artist and joined the National Guard to supplement their income. She planned to open up an art center for special needs kids one day he told me. He said one day he planned to establish a center like that in her name. There was a lot of her art work

around the house, too. She painted abstract, bright colors. I liked it."
Shelby paused, swallowed. Luke waited.

"So anyway, I was totally smitten. And in the middle of all this
Molly was conceived. We planned to move in together first then get
married before Molly was born. But about a month after I told him I
was pregnant he got cold feet. Said he wasn't ready. Needed space. Asked
for a three month separation with no contact while he worked out his
feelings." She cleared her throat and shifted her legs around to the floor.
"I was devastated. I mean, totally. I'd had relationships get screwed up
in the past, but this was different. All I wanted was to marry him, have
our little family. And he was poof, gone. But then, just as quickly as he
popped out of my life he popped back in. Thanks for giving me the time
to sort it all out, he said. I guess I ignored my gut, I just wanted so bad
to believe him, and so Molly was born and he was the most attentive of
fathers and I was happier than I'd ever been even though I kept bringing
up the subject of marriage and he kept putting me off." She glanced
down sheepishly.

Luke smiled. "I know a lot of women do it alone," he said
supportively. "But you ought to know by now that I'm a champion for
marriage."

"Well, anyway. Everything was moving along. He was still working
at the V.A., and I went to work at a domestic violence shelter running
groups for the children there and counseling with the women." She
paused, sighed deeply, bit her upper lip, pulled her knees back up toward
her chest and wrapped her arms around them. "Then one day I was
home with Molly. She was sick with an ear infection, a high fever. And
all of a sudden I heard someone pushing on the front door. It wasn't
locked. The door opened and this woman walked in and dropped her
duffel bags and said really quietly, almost whispering because she was
looking at Molly who was sleeping, "Who the hell are you?"

"Adrianna?" Luke guessed.

Shelby buried her head against her knees. The tears surprised her.
She thought she was way past tears. She'd almost drowned in her bed and
she'd cried watching TV and while she was mopping and driving and
cutting up potatoes. It was months before she could think about Steve
without feeling raw emotion.

"She was really nice," Shelby said. "Believe it or not we became
friends over time. In fact we still keep in touch. She said she wondered

why Steve'd stopped writing regularly while she was gone, and why he'd gotten a P.O. box, too. She said he asked her to use it and made up some story about stolen mail. We only used mobile phones so she couldn't call. He'd changed his number. She said he would e-mail sometimes. Never let on he was seeing someone else. She told me she got R&R Stateside and then was redeployed. She only got to stay home about three months. Things seemed normal between them while she was home she said. Was I dating her husband then? And then the whole separation thing made sense. Well, anyway, we both ditched him that afternoon before he got home from work. We co-wrote a nasty letter and left it for him between the sheets of his bed. I abandoned most of my stuff. She told me later he threatened to kill her if she didn't stay with him. And she said he ranted on and on about hunting me down if I tried to leave with Molly. She filed for divorce right away and I took off for Alabama with Molly. I know it's just mind games but sometimes I think I see him here, like driving down McFarland Boulevard or in the grocery store parking lot. It scares the hell out of me."

Luke's face darkened. "It's hard to hide nowadays, Shel."

"Adrianna tells me he's living in Arkansas with some new victim. But who knows? I don't take anything for granted. I watch my back every day. Only thing that keeps him at bay is knowing I'd bleed every last penny out of him for child support."

"Understandably."

She smiled weakly. "So Molly's dad is a narcissist, a sociopath. A sociopath who played me. Talk about messing with my head. I still don't understand. How could I have missed it?"

"We don't practice therapy on our friends and lovers, Shelby. You know that. It's a perfect situation for a sociopath to waltz into."

She filled her lungs and belly with air, released it slowly. She made direct eye contact. His eyes were unfathomably blue. Blue and clear and intuitive. "Thanks," she said. "I needed to talk about it. I don't know why exactly, but this thing with Dr. Beaty reminded me of my situation so much. That guy named Red did sort of the same thing to her from what she told me. I mean the situation was different but he sounds like a sociopath, too, the way she described him. And she told me yesterday she still loved him, no matter how much she wanted to hate him, somehow he still had a hold over her. And I think that scared me the most because I understood where she was coming from."

"Maybe Red's the killer," Luke said. "Maybe it wasn't this Bob Tulane guy or Andrew or Joey or that veterinarian or whoever she's been sleeping with most recently."

"I don't know," she said. "That guy Bob Tulane still has my bet. I hope Addie can untangle it all." As she stood she glanced out the window, craned her neck forward, then walked toward the glass. "Isn't that a phone in Benjamin's hand?" she asked.

Luke joined her at the window. "I'm not believing it," he said. "How many have we confiscated from him? Where's he getting them all?"

"Stealing them maybe?"

Luke frowned. "Maybe, but none of them are new, that's the thing. He has to be trading for them or swiping them used. But where's his source?"

"He's a clever one," said Shelby.

Luke smiled. There was something irresistibly endearing about scrappy little Benjamin Ball. In therapeutic lingo Luke knew what he was feeling was countertransference. All therapists studied it. Most, if not all, experienced it. "That Benji's a wheeler-dealer for sure," he said. "If we can help him stay out of the correctional system he'll own a multi-million dollar corporation one day."

"The two aren't always mutually exclusive," said Shelby. "Want me to go confiscate it?"

"Do you mind?" Luke raised his arms, turned his palms toward the ceiling and stretched. He was only about half an inch from the acoustic ceiling tiles. He moved toward his desk phone. He wanted to check for messages. "I've been waiting to hear from Addie," he said. He felt a thin muscular arm sweep across his back and hug him at the waist.

"Thanks for listening, Luke," Shelby said. "It really helped."

He grabbed her hand as she passed and squeezed it gently. She was wearing a jade band that felt cooler than her skin and her fingers were thicker and shorter than Addie's. "Thanks for trusting me."

Shelby opened the door. "When you talk to Addie please let her know I need to tell her about Mr. Tulane."

"Will do," said Luke. He felt some trepidation as he retrieved his messages, hoping Addie would not have news that Andrew killed his mother. He crossed his middle fingers over his indexes and his ring fingers over his baby ones and made an X by bridging his thumbs as soon as Shelby was out of sight. It was grade school and superstitious, and he knew psychologists didn't do such crazy things. He crossed his eyes for extra luck. Then he made the silent wish that Andrew and his brother Joey, too, had nothing, absolutely nothing, to do with the murder of their mother. There was a marketing message from the American Psychological Association on his phone. Nothing more. Addie had not called.

41

He kept a very busy calendar, he'd told her. Just this morning he had three surgeries and a farm call for a sick horse. Murder took precedence, she countered. And by all indications the victim was a close friend of his. There were questions in need of answers. One o'clock then, he said. Good, she'd be there. Could they meet somewhere else, he inquired. Not at his practice. Not enough privacy, the walls had ears. Where then? Possibly at his farmhouse in Fosters, he suggested. That was actually preferable, she thought. Gave her a chance to scope out his place.

She looked at her watch. Eleven fifteen. She'd go by the school. Talk to Dr. Beaty's school staff. Secretaries were treasure troves of information. She turned left onto McFarland and headed toward Tuskaloosa Gardens Elementary School. Her phone rang. It was her work-related drill sergeant ring tone. *Left, right, left, right. March in place. Step quick. Pick 'em up. Left, right. Halt.* She'd gotten the idea from some woman's magazine. Exercise ring tones to break up a sedentary day. A reminder on a desk job to stand up and walk. "Bramson."

"Yes, hello?" A question rather than a statement. A young voice, unsure, hesitant. "R.J. here."

"Hey, R.J. What've you turned up?"

"Several things of interest, ma'am."

She smiled to herself. She'd told him at least a hundred times. "R.J., call me Addie. Everybody else does. We're colleagues, partners."

"Sorry. Right. Hard habit to break." She heard him swallowing. And even though he was too polite to say it, she knew he was thinking he always called older people ma'am and sir. It was the Southern way. The way his mama'd taught him. "Several things, Addie. Turns out the person who owns the car Dana Whitesmythe was driving leaves her car windows open frequently according to one of her neighbors. And the wasps were our regular Alabama yellow jackets according to one of the University entomologists, um, a Dr. Henry Caralola. Ms. Whitesmythe'd been stung multiple times according to the coroner. One sting sends a lot of people off the road. Dr. Caralola says the wasps are attracted to sugar and to liquids in general, but he thought it unusual for several to have congregated in and around a bottle underneath the car's passenger seat. He says they live in colonies, actually in nests underground. He says there seem to be more of them this year for some reason. And they'll come after you if you agitate them. We have people looking for a nest out at the car owner's house right now. No luck yet."

"Curious . . ."

"The coroner had some news on Dr. Beaty, too. Seems the bruises weren't all the same age. The bruising on her rib cage and upper arm was older, maybe by a day or less. Like she'd been punched maybe. Not much more news on that foot blister though."

"Hmm," said Addie. "So it's possible those bruises you were talking about, they might have happened that morning or at lunchtime?"

"Exactly. Outside chance they came from the night before."

"That fits with my hunch," said Addie. "Good work, R.J."

"There's more. That password you phoned in, the one for Dr. Beaty's computer. It's still good. We haven't gotten it all sorted out yet but it looks like she was communicating with some guy named Red about meeting somewhere last night at six. Looks like he's the one who asked her to wear the black lingerie. I guess she was changing into it when she was attacked."

"Do you know where they were meeting?"

"Not really. It's all pretty cryptic. Something about a crescent moon."

Addie smiled. R.J.'d mispronounced cryptic so the word cry was in it. "A crescent moon," she repeated. She'd have to check the moon phase. "And the meeting, was it about her son, Andrew?"

"That appears to be the original purpose."

"Original?"

R.J. paused. "Well, ma'am, there is the black lace . . ."

Addie chuckled. "You've got a point, R.J." That was ultra sexy underwear. Probably cost as much as the refrigerator she and Luke bought last summer. If she wore something like that Luke's tongue would hang to the floor. He'd be licking up the cat hair. Save her having to vacuum. "Anything else?"

"That's about it for now. Oh, wait, one more thing . . . Looks like the alibis check out for Ms. Erma P. Wallenskowski related to the DHR bomb threats, just like you guessed. I've completed a report on her and put it on your desk. Seems like she can be scratched off as a suspect, at least it looks that way to me."

"Thanks, R.J. See what you can dig up on that Mr. Neil Lamphurte. He's Larry Ryan's favorite candidate. Larry was an ace policeman while he was on the force and he's DHR security now. I trust his gut." She didn't tell R.J., didn't even dare verbalize it completely to herself, but it was there. Trepidation hanging backstage in her mind, dark, formless. *If Larry Ryan, himself, isn't the murderer.* She saw him with her own eyes. Agitated, almost purple-faced yesterday when he got the news about his children.

"Yes ma'am."

Addie laughed. "Addie, R.J. Just call me Addie."

"Oh, sorry. Okay. I'll get back to you soon, um . . . Addie."

"'K. Talk to you later." She hit her left turn signal and pulled into the elementary school's parking lot. One of the first lessons she'd learned in detective work, victims' secretaries almost always knew more than spouses and best friends combined.

There were three of them perched in varying degrees on the chairs in Dr. Beaty's outer office. Doris, a sort of unassuming woman in her early twenties, identified herself as Dr. Beaty's secretary of about four years before she pulled a key out of her desk and opened the door to the inner office so the group could speak privately. The two other women identified themselves as Erin and Alice. It was Erin who ambled across the hall and recruited some temporary office help. Doris was dressed in black. Her hair was short, almost crew cut length, and spiked. Very New York. Addie noted an empty spot on Dr. Beaty's desk. The computer was gone. Forensics worked fast.

"When did they pick up the computer?" she asked.

Doris glanced toward the empty spot on the desk. "About ten, maybe ten thirty this morning," she said. "They came in and searched through her desk and said they'd be getting her phone records. They took some papers from her desktop, her daily schedule book too." She seemed to be sitting unnaturally straight. Addie was accustomed to inadvertently making people nervous.

She pulled Dr. Beaty's office chair around to the front of the desk and sat down. She removed the digital recorder from her purse, turned it on and laid it on the corner of the desk. "Please," she said to the three women. "Sit down." Erin and Alice sat in the leather chairs facing the desk. Doris backed up against an end table and leaned her bottom against it. "Okay," Addie said. "As you can see, I record my interviews for later review. And please excuse me if I ask some questions you've already answered, but I'm trying to create a clear picture for myself of what was happening in Dr. Beaty's life in the days, maybe even in the weeks or months, prior to her death."

Doris nodded. Erin appeared oddly amused, well, perhaps amused was too strong an adjective, titillated might better fit her demeanor, but certainly it looked as though all of this would become part of her evening telephone calls to friends. Juicy gossip material. And the woman Alice appeared noncommittal, a little disinterested maybe, like she didn't want to get involved.

"How much did Dr. Beaty share her professional and private life concerns with any of you three women?" asked Addie.

The woman named Erin chuckled. "Intentionally? Not at all, I'd say. Unintentionally? She left a trail a mile long."

The woman named Alice looked at her coworker and nodded ever so subtly.

"Great," said Addie, crossing her right leg over her left knee. "Can you give me some examples that relate to recent events?"

Silence. A quick glance at each other before Alice looked down at her feet, Erin looked over at Doris and Doris closed her eyes and bent her head backwards as though in thought. Addie waited. Outside the room she heard the office phones ringing. The substitute office workers appeared to be marginally managing. She heard another voice too, probably that of the nurse, telling a mother about a sick child.

"Does anything come to mind?" she prodded gently.

Doris opened her eyes and rubbed the palm of her hand across her forehead before she spoke. "Ah, I guess Erin's referring to the strange calls she'd get sometimes and even when they didn't seem strange at the time, her reactions to the calls seemed, well, odd, to put it mildly."

"Good," said Addie, still prodding. "Did she get any calls like that yesterday?"

"Yes, ma'am," said Doris. "I mean, maybe they won't sound strange when I describe them, but, well, for example, there was her dog's veterinarian. He called yesterday, before lunch it was, and maybe I'm speaking out of turn but he sounded stressed and maybe even irritated and he was almost like demanding to speak directly to Dr. Beaty. But she kept putting him off."

"Good," said Addie. "Can you remember his name?"

"Yes, yes, I can because he's phoned a lot of times recently and he always leaves the same message that he wants Dr. Beaty to phone him back about her dog. And he almost always sounds frustrated, sometimes even angry when he calls, but when I ring her to say he's on the line, she never wants to talk to him. She always wants me to give him some message. Usually it's to let him know their earlier plan is unchanged. Like yesterday she told me to say she still planned to take her dog for treatment during her lunch hour. But, it's always sort of like she's really irritated, too. Like she doesn't even like the man. And then I think to myself, but it's none of my business really, why does her dog need so much treatment anyway and why does she go to a veterinarian who irritates her so much?"

"And," added the woman named Erin, "it's none of my business, either, but whose veterinarian calls so much, anyway? I mean, I have five cats and three dogs and I only talk to my vet a few times a year."

"And what's the vet's name?" asked Addie, already knowing the answer.

"He calls himself Dr. Greene. Dr. Harry Greene," said Doris.

"And he phoned wanting to talk to Dr. Beaty yesterday morning?"

"Yes, ma'am. Insisted on it. I mean, he's always real polite, but it's just something about the way he says it. It's in his voice. When you answer phones for a living, you learn to hear more than what people actually say."

Doris was sharp. "Good," Addie said. She wanted an Animal Cracker. She reached into her purse and pulled out the bag. She offered them around. All three women declined. She shook three into her palm, a lion, some other sort of cat, maybe a cheetah, and a buffalo. She put the buffalo on her tongue and allowed her saliva to dissolve it. "So," she said after it turned to a sweet goo in her mouth, "Dr. Beaty didn't talk to him when he called, but asked you to relay a message?"

"Yes, ma'am."

"Can you remember exactly what she asked you to tell him? Please think carefully as it may be important."

Erin's eyes widened. "Really? You think maybe he had something to do with it . . . the murder, I mean?"

Addie dropped the cookie bag back into her purse. She bit off the back legs of the cheetah. "No, that's not what I'm saying. I wish solving crimes were that easy. But all facts are important to the puzzle, and it's important to get everything as accurate as possible." She popped the rest of the cheetah in her mouth.

The woman named Alice nudged her coworker. "That makes sense," she said. "Honestly, Erin, this isn't a television script. It's real life. It'll be complicated."

Doris leaned forward, her body at around a sixty-five degree angle. "I don't remember the exact words," she said. "But she asked me to tell him she still planned to take her dog to him during her lunch hour, like I said a minute ago. And when I told him that, he still sounded frustrated and stressed, but he said okay and thanked me and hung up the phone."

"And, do you know if she really did make that appointment? The one with Dr. Greene?"

Doris ran her teeth across her top lip and slowly shook her head. "No, not really. But, she was real late getting back to the office. Almost didn't get back in time for the bus runs after school. And she was limping, said she had a bad blister on her foot."

"Yes," said Alice. "I noticed her limping a little bit that morning."

"She put on those slippers of hers," said Erin. The three women looked at each other and all three laughed. A shared joke. Addie bit off the head of the lion and waited. "See," said Erin, "we heard them make that weird trumpeting sound while she was meeting with one of the parents."

Addie laughed too. "You've totally lost me," she said, finishing off the lion.

Doris giggled. "She had these slippers in her office drawer. Alabama elephants, Big Al slippers, I guess, and they made elephant noises if she stepped on the heels a certain way."

"Computer chips," said Erin.

"And she wore them here at school?"

"She loved to wear them whenever she could. There she'd be, all dressed up in some three or four hundred dollar outfit, some designer deal, padding around the office in Big Al slippers. She was a strange bird, for real."

Addie laughed again. "So, you say she was limping and got back late?" she asked returning her attention to Doris.

"Yes, ma'am. And, Alice noticed she was walking sort of funny when she returned, I don't know, maybe it was the blister, but she was walking sort of crab-like. Sort of like this," she said, demonstrating.

"And did she say where she'd been? Was she generally late like that?"

Doris looked toward Erin and then toward Alice and then back toward Erin who chuckled cynically.

"Not usually," said Erin, 'but if there was a man involved . . . she was, um . . . she was sort of like an unchaperoned teenager if you get my meaning . . . and she would show back up whenever they were through with their, um, their *lunch.* "

"So, you think she may have been with somebody yesterday during lunch?"

"Well," answered Erin, sweeping her gaze around the room to include her coworkers in her answer. "We certainly thought that. But then she phoned and said she'd had car trouble, isn't that what she said, Doris?"

"Yes, yes she said she had car trouble. When she called she said the car was fixed and she was on her way back in. She'd scheduled an appointment to get her nails done but had to cancel that because she was so late."

"So something serious like car trouble must have held her up," said Erin. "Nothing ever got in the way of her nail appointments. Even if we were in the middle of a tornado warning I think she'd be out in the hallway sitting in her office chair with her bare feet propped up for Leah to work on."

"Leah? . . ."

"She's a manicurist or pedicurist or both, whatever that's called, who works at a place called Heavenly Feet. She drops by, well, ah, used to drop by the office during school work breaks to do Dr. Beaty's nails," explained Doris.

"So all three of you are assuming she did have car trouble?"

"Well, maybe not her car, but some kind of trouble for real," said Erin.

"And then another man called," said Doris. "A man I know about because he lives across the road from my aunt, her name is Mrs. Corine Gretchen Blakney, in Coker. His name is Mr. Bob Tulane. And his call was strange, too. He sounded worried, nervous-like. And he was really anxious to talk to Dr. Beaty. He wanted to know where she was and he wanted her to call him as soon as we found her. He was jittery almost. It gave me the willies . . ."

"Why?" asked Addie. "I mean, why did his call give you the willies?"

Doris paused. Addie waited. Children's voices in the outer office. Ringing phones. "Well, I don't know if it's right to say anything," she said. "I mean, they're just rumors and you're with the police and maybe there's no truth to any of it, but there're all kinds of rumors about Mr. Tulane going around Coker."

Addie's eyes widened. "Really?" she asked.

Doris nodded.

"Well," said Addie. "Sometimes there's truth in rumors and sometimes there's not. But it always helps to know what's being said, true or not."

"Well then," Doris said in a kind of breathy voice. "Word around Coker is that Mr. Tulane was jailed for the murder, or at least for the disappearance of his fiancée a few years back somewhere in North Alabama. Lamar County I think it was. But they let him go. I think because they didn't have enough evidence. And rumor has it another girlfriend disappeared, just fell off the face of the Earth, in Wyoming, no not Wyoming, it was Nevada, I think. One of the Western states, anyway. But they never could prove anything wrong there either. So people sort of steer clear of him if you know what I mean. But my aunt says he's always real nice around her. A good neighbor. A gentleman of sorts. None of it may be important at all."

Aha! She'd suspected it. Mr. Tulane did withhold important information. She'd phone it in to R.J. as soon as she left the school. Get a background search on him. It would fit, all right. He was just a little too confident, a little too smooth. First one on the scene. Holding the dog like they were great buddies. We were good friends, he'd said. Lovers in the past. Ever so helpful.

"That's great information," said Addie to Doris. "Thanks." She looked toward Erin. "You described Dr. Beaty as being like an unchaperoned teenager . . . are you inferring she was promiscuous . . . flirtatious?"

Erin cocked her head to one side. "I don't think that's any secret," she said. "It was a joke around school, among staff, I mean. She was always on the make. Either on the make or PMS-ing, striking terror into the hearts of some of the kids and even their parents sometimes. She pissed off a lot of people, I can tell you that."

Addie nodded. Larry Ryan, for one. Terrorized his kids. Pissed him off royally. She looked all three women directly in the eyes, aimed her question toward all of them. "Were there any people, staff or parents or others, who might have wanted Dr. Beaty dead?" she asked.

Erin laughed out loud. "Like us, you mean?"

The woman named Alice scowled at her coworker. "Leave me out of it," she said.

"Like you didn't hate her, too?" Erin asked. "I'm not saying we killed her, Alice, just telling it like it is. She was a royal B. Treated a lot of decent children and their parents awful."

"Only some, though," said Doris quietly. "She was like two sides of a coin. Some parents sang her praises. Others despised her. She bullied some people, at least that's what it looked like to me, to us I mean."

"She was a bully," said Erin. "An old fashioned bully."

"Like yesterday with that poor Mr. Ryan and his boys," said Doris. "She always picked on those boys. The sort of timid boy left the office almost crying. She went after them just to get back at their dad."

"Mr. Ryan?"

"Yes."

Addie felt her neck tighten. Larry Ryan. She didn't want him involved in this. And yet he was knee deep in it already. "Tell me about it," she said. "I mean, about Mr. Ryan and his boys and Dr. Beaty."

"Well," said Doris. "Mr. Ryan had a meeting with her yesterday morning. They've had heated meetings in the past. About her attitude, I mean, the way she treated his kids. I don't know how to explain it. It was like it was personal for her."

"She was a bully," said Erin again.

Doris looked toward her coworker and nodded. "Well, anyway, it was a bad meeting. We could hear yelling in the room."

"And then the elephant slippers trumpeted," giggled Erin.

Doris ignored her. "And in the middle of the arguing, Mr. Ryan stormed out."

"Sweet kids," said Erin. "Nice man, too. Any good father would be livid, the way Dr. Beaty carried on about his sons, the kinds of decisions she made about them."

"So," Addie said, her neck tightening more. "Mr. Ryan stormed out of here yesterday morning?"

"Yes," said Doris. "And his car was in the parking lot yesterday afternoon, too. We all saw it parked there. While she was out doing bus duty. He sat in his car in the parking lot and watched her. I know because I was watching him."

The tension crawled down Addie's spine, branched out the other direction across her shoulders. "Why were you watching him?"

Doris shrugged one shoulder and looked down at the floor. "I don't know really. I felt sorry for him, I guess. I wanted to see if he'd get a chance to give Dr. Beaty a piece of his mind."

"Do you know if he did? Get a chance to talk to Dr. Beaty, I mean?"

"No," said Doris. "I know he didn't. Dr. Beaty got into a car with somebody for a while. I guess Mr. Ryan got tired of waiting. He drove on off."

"With somebody?" said Addie. "Did you recognize that person? The car?"

"No," said Doris. "All I know is the car was sort of a real dark reddish color. The school buses were blocking my view."

"And do you know Mr. Ryan's first name?" asked Addie. Larry of course.

"Mr. Larry Ryan," said Erin. "Lawrence, really, but he always says to call him Larry."

"He's a good guy. A security guard at DHR, I think," said Doris. "He said he used to be a policeman. We think he must be a single father. Their mother's not listed on the boys' contact sheets for emergencies or anything. He has a bunch of kids, four or five, all young."

"I admire single fathers," said Erin.

"Me, too," said Addie. She swallowed, wanted another cookie but refrained. She dreaded asking the question. "Did any of you hear Mr. Ryan threaten Dr. Beaty or act threatening toward her in any way? Anything like that?"

Doris looked toward Erin and Alice. Alice's expression remained impassive. Erin shrugged. "They were yelling at each other for sure," said Doris. "Maybe he said something threatening, but I couldn't swear to it."

Maybe Larry'd end up in the clear so she could scratch him off the suspect list. Permanently. Totally. There was really nothing of significance so far. A loud argument with the victim. Storming out. Hanging around without success later on in the parking lot. But she knew none of that really mattered. The real question was whether he dropped by Dr. Beaty's house later in the afternoon. It really wouldn't be unlike him. Addie shifted her weight to stand. It was time to head toward Dr. Greene's farm. "I'd like to ask each of you to come up with a list of parents and others who held grudges against Dr. Beaty," she said. "I'll come back early next week to collect them. Any leads you offer will be appreciated."

"Grudges? Like half the city of Tuscaloosa?" laughed Erin. "I mean, Dr. Beaty was no fairy princess."

"Just list those who come to mind," Addie said. "And just a few more things for now . . . do you know, or have any of you heard her talk about a man named Red?"

The three women looked at each other. Doris spoke first. "No."

"She had a son named Andrew. Did she ever confide the identity of Andrew's father to anyone, that you know of?"

Again the women looked at one another before Doris shook her head. "No."

"Did any man or woman contact her at school on personal business that seemed curious to you? Other than those things we've talked about I mean."

Doris shrugged. "She talked a lot on her mobile phone," she said.

Erin frowned. "Don't get us wrong. Lots of people called, men I mean, but they never left messages. Usually they said they'd call her back. Most of them were real polite-like."

"That's true," said Doris. "And educated."

Probably Thomas, Joey's father, was one of them. "Do the words 'crescent moon' mean anything to you?" she asked.

Again, a quick glance among themselves. "No."

"And do you know if Dr. Beaty spoke to either of her sons yesterday at any time during the school day?"

Doris shook her head. "No calls came through the school phone from them," she said. "But, again, she had a personal phone. So, it's possible."

"O.K. Thanks," said Addie.

"Um," said Doris.

"Yes?"

"There was one other unusual call, I mean I thought it was unusual. I put it through and the line stayed busy a long time. It was quite a lengthy conversation. The man identified himself as a Dr. Bramson. Luke, he said." Suddenly Doris' head jerked up and forward. Full attention. She stared, blinked, and her face flushed. "Oh," she stammered. "I just realized . . . is that, I mean, is he . . .?"

Adelaide Bramson laughed softly. "Yep," she answered. "He is. It's a small, small world."

42

"Hey, R.J.," Addie said when she settled back in her car. "I've got a possible lead for us."

"Shoot." He was eager. He'd picked up on the first ring. She envisioned his fingers poised above his electronic tablet, ready to enter notes while they talked.

"I just learned our Mr. Bob Tulane might have a history of disappearing women. Supposedly a fiancée from Lamar County disappeared several years ago and another girlfriend out West, maybe in Nevada, several years before that. Might have been jailed for the Lamar County disappearance and then released for lack of sufficient evidence. Can you follow it up?"

"I'm on it."

"Any news on Dr. Beaty's son, Joey?"

"Nada," said R.J. "Still searching."

Addie started the car engine and looked in her rearview mirror. "Anything else?"

"Nothing significant."

She left her foot on the brake and opened her purse. She found her cookies and moved the top ones around with her pinkie. She chose an elephant and a gorilla and held them between her thumb and forefinger. Only a few left. "I'm headed out to Dr. Harry Greene's farm in Fosters," she said. "Our meeting's in about twenty-five minutes."

"How about some back up?"

"Not necessary," said Addie.

"Well, strap on your pink holster . . ."

She smiled. Her pink holster. A gift from the guys. "Planned on it," she said. "I'll check in afterwards. An hour tops."

"Still don't like it . . ."

"See ya," said Addie. She knew Luke would like it even less. A farm. A rural area. A murder suspect. No immediate back up.

She unzipped a red corduroy CD holder and searched for disc Numero Uno. Beginning Spanish. She slipped the disc in the narrow slot below the car's radio. "Buenos días," the CD greeted as she pointed the car toward McFarland Boulevard and Fifteenth Street. "Buenos días," she repeated. "Me llamo es Señor García. ¿Como se llamo?" Addie moved into the left lane and let the speedometer inch toward fifty. "Um . . . ah . . . Me llamo es Señora Adelaide Bramson," she said. Increasingly people she needed to interview spoke only Spanish. Interpreters were helpful but it wasn't the same as interviewing alone. She'd get in at least the first whole lesson before she reached the farm.

* * *

She got out of her car, strapped on the holster and slipped her Glock into it when she reached Dr. Harry Greene's gate. It was closed but unlocked. He'd given efficient directions and she'd made good time. She ran her fingertips along the gun's smooth handle. She'd only used her gun, really shot with it, once over the past year and that was to kill a rabid fox. It'd sunk its teeth into a woman's front bumper and had eaten off half its tail. She just happened to be in the park that afternoon. Not even on duty. Shot the pathetic thing dead and then called animal control. Radioed for a consult about the infected bumper. Animal control picked up the carcass and cleaned the area. Didn't want other wildlife to become contaminated, they explained. She surveyed the land in front of her as she closed the gate behind. Flat green fields. Spring wild flowers. Horses. Cows. A solitary donkey grazing among the cattle. She guided the car toward a wooden frame house across the pasture.

He looked younger than she anticipated. Tall, really tall, six foot six, six foot seven probably. Broad shouldered. Beautiful straight white teeth and braided hair pulled back on his neck. He greeted her at the door as she walked up the wooden steps. The steps were old and gave slightly as she climbed them. The screen door creaked. He extended his hand. A firm but not intimidating handshake. "Dr. Harry Greene," he said. "Any trouble finding the place?"

She followed him inside. "None. Your directions were good." The living room was small, cozy. Looked a lot like Luke's grandmother's living room. Doilies on the coffee table. Crocheted sofa arm covers. Couch pillows. Flowered wallpaper. Green heart shaped leaves, little purple flowers. Looked like violets. Interesting decor for a single man. "Do you crochet?" she asked.

He looked confused at first, eyebrows arched slightly, then he smiled as he followed her gaze. "This was my grandparents' home," he explained. "They raised me. She crocheted."

"My husband needlepoints," she said. She always made it a point to mention Luke when she was interviewing a single man.

"Guess it's not too different from stitching up animals if you think about it."

Something bumped against the door at the end of the hallway. Addie's hand traveled reflexively toward her gun but stopped short. "What's that?" she asked.

Dr. Greene motioned toward a wing backed chair. He sat on the couch extending his very long arm across the couch's back. Very muscular arms. He was obviously into fitness. "That's Bart," he said. "My dog. I put him up so he wouldn't jump in your lap and beg for a belly rub." A broad smile. Cool. Confident. So young. Couldn't be too much older than Dr. Beaty's children. He motioned toward the chair again. "Please, have a seat."

"Thanks," she said. "I will shortly." It was always important to establish dominance. She opened her purse and fished out her recorder. She held it up and turned it on. "I'll be recording our conversation today," she said. "Helps me keep all the facts straight later."

"I understand," he said but it was clear from his expression he didn't like it.

"I wanted to start by thanking you, Dr. Greene, for taking time away from your practice to help address certain areas of concern."

His eyelids blinked quickly several times before he remasked. "Concern?"

"Yes," said Addie. "As you know Dr. Beaty was murdered last night . . ."

He leaned forward ever so slightly. "It was a horrible shock!" he said. "I heard about it on the ten o'clock news. I didn't sleep at all last night. I kept seeing her in the wall, at the window, and I heard her voice calling me. She was everywhere."

"You're speaking figuratively I gather?"

"Grief does strange things you know. She and I were . . . well, we were close . . . well, more than close. We were lovers." He stared at her intently. "But I'm sure you've learned that by now."

The dog, if that's what it really was, bumped hard against the door.

"Bart! Stop!" Dr. Greene reprimanded.

"Yes," said Addie. "We've learned that you and Dr. Beaty were romantically involved. She was a good bit older than you, was she not?"

"Yes, um, twenty one years actually."

Addie continued to scan the room. Ceramic frog collection, probably his grandmother's. Oval rag rug on the floor, perhaps made by his grandmother. There was something glittery wedged against the leg of the couch. Behind the leg actually. Maybe just part of a foil candy wrapper. On the end table, a converted brass oil lamp. "Is that age difference not somewhat unusual?" she asked.

He wiggled long thin fingers along the back of the couch. "For most people I'm sure it is," he said. "For me, to be honest, not really. I prefer relationships with mature women. The arrangement is cleaner for the most part, cut and dried, if you follow my meaning. There's that element of understanding in them. Marriage is not an issue."

"Ah," said Addie. "So, good times, good sex, no muss, no fuss?"

He shrugged. "Yeah, I guess you could put it that way."

From what she knew, probably a true account. "So, how did you two meet?"

"She came into my office with her dog in tow. Manufactured a reason to be there. She, ah, basically came on to me. To this day I don't know why."

Addie frowned. "Even though her son, Joey, was planning to intern with you this summer?"

Dr. Greene's eyes widened. Genuine surprise. She was sure of it. "Joey Chalot's her son?" He cupped his face in his hands. "Damn, I had no idea . . . That's poor."

Addie heard what did sound like a dog plopping down on the floor against the door. She cleared her throat. "So, when was it that you last saw Dr. Beaty?" she asked. Silence. She watched him roll his forehead back and forth in his cupped palms. He was maybe still digesting the information about Joey, but she sensed there was more, too. She'd seen it a thousand times, well, maybe not a thousand but at least several hundred. Stalling, thinking, trying to figure out what she already knew. "Dr. Greene?"

He raised his head only slightly, peeking at her. "Mmmmhh," he said. "Yesterday. Here. At lunchtime. We often had lunch together. Not much time to spend but it was private. Both of us needed the privacy. For our professional positions, I'm sure you can understand."

She could certainly understand. "So how long were the two of you here yesterday?"

"Mmmmhh. Let's see. I got here a few minutes before her. She got here a little after twelve, I think. We both had to be back shortly after one. Back in Tuscaloosa. So not a long lunch. Just enough time for the chicken salad I made the night before. My grandmother's recipe. It uses feta cheese. One of Priscilla's, ah, Dr. Beaty's, favorites. Then we walked around outside a little bit."

"And how would you describe your interactions?"

He shrugged again. "Like I said, rushed but pleasant. We grabbed time as we could. Both of us had busy schedules. Lots of demands. I'm sure you understand."

"Certainly. But yesterday was different, wasn't it? She was extremely late getting back to school, indeed the school day was virtually over."

He swallowed. She'd seen that kind of swallowing before. Dry swallowing. Nervous swallowing.

"Really? I didn't know . . . Usually we leave here together but yesterday I stayed behind. I was ill, actually. I called into my office sick for the remainder of the afternoon. You can check with my secretary."

"Dr. Greene, we have a witness reporting knowledge of an argument between the two of you during the noon hour."

Denial. A look of puzzlement. Recognition. Scrambling for an answer. She'd gotten pretty darn good at reading the language of eyes.

"Um, yes I suppose that's true. Nothing major, of course. I was angry because she wouldn't answer my phone calls earlier in the day. I . . . I was trying to reach her to say I felt ill. She was somewhat of a germaphobe and I knew she'd want to know."

"We're pulling the phone records, Dr. Greene, but just for the sake of convenience, how many times would you say you tried to reach her yesterday morning?"

"Um, I've got no idea. She does that a lot, not answer the phone I mean, and that does get to me. And the more stubborn she is about not answering it, seems like the more stubborn I get about calling. So, quite a few times I'd say."

"And finally you phoned her secretary and got the message about her dog?"

A flicker of surprise crossed his eyes but he hid it quickly. "Yes, but of course, the dog's just a cover."

"Of course."

Dr. Greene stretched his legs forward and crossed them at the ankles. His heels rested a third of the way across the rag rug. The living room seemed too small for him. "Look, I don't know what you're getting at, but I cared deeply for Priscilla."

"Where were you last evening . . . say, around five thirty, six o'clock?"

He shut his eyes. "Let's see. Let me think. Um, I would have been on my way back into my office."

"Even though you were sick?"

"Ah . . . yes, I felt better by then for the most part. Queasy stomach stuff. I just wanted to run in and check the status of several of my surgical patients."

"And can anyone verify your movements?"

Pause. "Um, no, no I guess not."

Addie waited before going on. It was all about tempo. Authority. "Are you aware, Dr. Greene, that Dr. Beaty had several bruised areas on her body, bruising that most likely occurred yesterday around lunchtime?"

His legs twitched. "No, I had no idea. We didn't have time to . . . I mean sometimes we had time to be . . . intimate. But not yesterday. And of course I felt sick. She, ah, didn't mention bruises or anything. But I can tell you that she was very sensitive about her relationship with her younger son. Andrew is his name. Perhaps they fought earlier in the day."

It was true. A distinct possibility. "Perhaps." She leveled her stare, focused directly on the intensity of his brown eyes. It didn't explain the bouquet with the apology note. "Did she say anything to you about feeling threatened by anyone, about having trouble with anyone?"

He blinked several times. It was always like poker, these interviews. Trying to figure out each other's cards. Highly intelligent suspects like Dr. Greene were her favorites.

"Um, yes," he said, lowering his outstretched arm to look at his watch. "Yes, actually, she told me she was having a terrible day. She said there was some deranged parent she feared might stalk her, some guy she'd met with earlier in the day. And there was some other guy she talked with on her phone while she was here. A Bob somebody. A tree surgeon, I think. Seemed like he was crowding in on her, bothering her.

And of course like I said she was having trouble with her son, Andrew. That's a constant. And she was going to a meeting at a residential treatment center for him and she was stressed about that, too. And there was a meeting with the boy's father, with a guy she called Red. It was last night, I think. I think she said around six. I never felt comfortable with their relationship to tell you the truth. Seemed like he always had the upper hand. She still loved him even though she swore she didn't. I could see it in her eyes. She played lousy poker."

Addie smiled to herself. Funny he should say that. "Did she ever divulge Red's identity to you?"

Dr. Greene cleared his throat. "Not a chance. And I dug for it, I'm embarrassed to say. It was like a pact between them. That's the way it appeared to me anyway."

Addie stood and walked toward the leg of the couch. When she bent down she'd be vulnerable. She stooped quickly, warily, keeping her eyes on him for movement. He remained perfectly still. She pinched the shiny object between her fingers, felt the coolness of metal, straightened and backed away. "Interesting," she said studying the jewelry. A little silver mask, a weiner dog, a small disc of silver with a generic boy's profile on the front. All attached to six or seven silver links. She turned the disc over. "Hmmm," she said.

He remained statue still, a frozen look of social appropriateness on his face. "What's that?" he asked.

She'd forgotten an evidence bag. She unzipped a side pocket of her purse and dropped it in. "I was hoping you could tell me," she said. "But if it helps jog your memory, it's a piece of a charm bracelet. Looks like it might be sterling. It's engraved with Andrew's name and date of birth. The rest of the bracelet is in her purse. So now the real question is why I found part of it underneath your couch. And how did it break?"

Dr. Greene stood. "I have no idea." He looked mystified. He was good, really good.

"So you don't recall a struggle with Dr. Beaty that might have resulted in bruising and a broken bracelet?"

"A struggle?" he echoed. "No struggle here. Surely you don't think . . ."

"That your relationship with her involved domestic violence?"

Still the frozen look. "We'd never . . . I'd never . . . My grandparents raised me better than that."

"Hmmm," she said. She opened the front door. She heard his dog stand, whine, scratch on the bedroom door. Just one scratch.

Cadence. It was all about cadence, rhythm. "Nice place you have here," she said. "Beautiful countryside."

"Yes. Yes. It's my haven," he said. "It was Priscilla's haven, too. She said that all the time. It's, um, it's going to feel different out here now. With her gone, I mean."

"I bet," said Addie.

"Yes." Silence. He was studying her. She waited. "She wanted to learn how to ride," he said, nodding toward three horses in the field. A roan, a palomino, and a white horse that looked Arabian. He chuckled to himself. "But to be totally honest, she was lousy with the horses. Better with O.T. and Bart. Bart was totally smitten with her."

Addie turned. "O.T.?" she repeated.

"Yes. The donkey out there."

Ha! She tried to keep her response steady. "The donkey's name is O.T.?"

"O.T. for short. Donkey-O.T. in full. My granddaddy was a witty man. A lover of puns."

Donkey-O.T. It was funny. "That's a good one," said Addie. The flowers and apology note. The bigger ass than O.T. It was confirmed. "You're sticking around the Tuscaloosa/Fosters area for the next couple of weeks, right?" she asked. She negotiated the steps, all senses focused on his physical presence. He made no move toward her. "I suspect there'll be other things we'll need to clarify."

"Yes, of course," he said. "And please do call if there's anything I can do to help with your investigation. Priscilla drove me crazy sometimes, I'll tell you the truth. But I cared about her deeply. Anything at all you need, I'm right here."

"Good to know," said Addie as she opened her car door, adjusted her pink holster and eased into the seat. "Thanks for your cooperation and your time, Dr. Greene. We'll be in touch."

Soon. She turned off the digital recorder and dropped it onto the passenger's seat.

*   *   *

"We may have him," she said to R.J. as soon as she made it back to the highway. "A piece of the broken charm bracelet we found in the victim's purse was underneath his living room couch. And O.T. is his donkey. So he's at least the one who sent the flowers and apology. It all supports domestic violence, like Mr. Tulane suggested. Dr. Greene denies any problems with violence in their relationship but admits they argued at his home during lunch. And he says he traveled back to town on the evening of her murder. Says he was checking on the animals at his clinic, but has no one to verify his story."

"A veterinarian murdering an elementary school principal. It'll be pretty high profile if it turns out to be him," said R.J. There was static on the line. Addie shifted ears impatiently.

"There's static on the line," she said. "Can you still hear me?"

"Yes, ma'am," said R.J. "Oh, sorry. Addie."

She giggled.

"But since you brought up Bob Tulane, let me fill you in." He paused.

"Go ahead," she said.

"Looks like your information was spot on," he said. "Our Mr. Tulane spent three weeks and a day jailed for the murder of a woman named Sheila G. Woodcock nearly eight years ago. She was a cosmetologist up in Lamar County. Records indicate she was considerably younger than he was. She was barely twenty-seven when she disappeared. They'd been engaged for three months or thereabouts. Her family told police they were certain he murdered her. Bail was set at 100,000 dollars. Seems Mr. Tulane's sister lived near Anniston at the time and bonded him out. Charges were dropped approximately seven months later. Lack of sufficient evidence. I haven't been able to follow up on the Nevada girl's disappearance yet. But I've got something else. Damnedest thing. His mother was killed in a fall from a cliff while hiking on a trail with young Mr. Tulane. When he was only twelve. Ruled accidental. No witnesses other than Bob Tulane, himself."

"My gosh!" said Addie. "So we might be looking at a serial killer going back into childhood. Thanks, R.J. Great work." Great work, but where did that put Dr. Greene? She'd been close to slapping the cuffs on him.

"No problem. I'll get on the Nevada disappearance as soon as I get back from a Whitesmythe inquiry for the Chief. He wants to wrap that case up as accidental as soon as possible. Yesterday, to tell you the truth.

But he's sending me out to talk to Ms. Whitesmythe's next door neighbor first. Flora's her name. Apparently she was like a mother to the deceased."

"Okay," she said.

"Oh, and I've checked out Neil Lamphurte. His alibis for the bomb threats. Looks like the alibis are legit, Addie. I don't think he's your man."

"Hmmm," said Addie swerving to miss a road kill skunk. "Eewwwh!" she said as pungent odor permeated the air. "Dead skunk." She tried not to breathe through her nose. "Too bad about Lamphurte. Larry Ryan seemed so certain. I was hoping he'd pegged him for us."

"Yes ma'am."

"Addie . . ."

"Addie. I'm sorry. It's hard . . ."

"You'll get used to it," she said. "Okay, well, I'm famished. I'm grabbing a bite and then I'll try catching up with Mr. Victor Abernathy at the Magnet school since he found Andrew last night."

"Over and out," said R.J.

The phone went dead. Addie moved the speedometer up past seventy. Did anybody really say corny things like over and out? She imagined R.J. as a little boy glued to cop reruns on Saturdays. Eighty. It still felt like she was crawling on the straight empty road. A hundred, even a hundred twenty was more like it. Speed was one of the perks of the job. The TV cops she watched as a kid always drove like NASCAR racers. There were several sheriffs' cars including two canine units semi-hidden along the grassy median. She slowed considerably and flashed her headlights in greeting. Drugs. This part of the interstate was a drug corridor. Sometimes they got lucky. She ran her index finger across her phone's buttons and punched speed dial.

"Bramson," said a husky male voice.

"Hi, Bramson. Bramson here." Luke chuckled. She giggled. "I could sure use the input of a brilliant clinical psychologist."

"I've been waiting to hear from you," he said. "I didn't call, I knew you were in the middle of your investigation. How's your day been?"

"Well, I can assure you that your child, Andrew Beaty, wasn't very cooperative this morning."

A warm intimate laugh. She imagined him leaning back in his chair, his bluer than blue eyes full of mischief. His eyes were almost always full of mischief.

"Somehow that doesn't surprise me," he said.

"Have you eaten?"

He paused. "Gosh, Addie. It's almost two o'clock. I ate hours ago."

She glanced at her car's clock. He was right. "I was hoping I could spirit you away for awhile."

"Don't think it's possible, honey. I have permission to tell you we've scheduled Andrew's admission for later this afternoon. Sort of an impromptu thing. DHR's taken temporary custody. At least until this murder thing's cleared up. After that he'll probably go live with his half-brother's father, Mr. Chalot. But the judge wants him in a stable facility until we know he's innocent."

"He didn't deny killing her when I talked to him this morning, Luke."

Dead phone space.

"Luke?"

"I'm sorry. I'm here. What do you mean, Addie?"

"I mean that when I asked him if he killed his mother he told me he had no comment."

"Damn. I hope he didn't."

"He didn't look broken up about her death, either. But the man you mentioned, Mr. Chalot, did tell me he heard Andrew crying during the night."

"His crying could mean anything, I guess. But remember, Addie, kids grieve differently. Not like adults. And adolescents often hide their feelings. Act out, get moody, become irritable, that sort of thing."

"Well," she said. "He was certainly irritable. What time's his admission?"

"Four thirty or thereabouts. He's not a happy camper from what I understand. He's apparently threatening to run away as soon as he gets here."

"He ran this morning."

"Really?"

"Yeah, but just around the neighborhood. Mr. Chalot wasn't concerned. He seems to have a good handle on Andrew and his ways."

"I think so too."

"Well, I love you. I'm passing a barbeque joint. Think I'll drive through and grab a sandwich."

"I'll be late getting home. Depends how long it takes to settle Andrew."

"You'll still beat me," she said. "There're several people left to interview today."

"Be careful, baby. Remember, you're keeping company with a murderer, a potential bomber and a teen gangster."

Tony. There weren't enough hours in the day. "We haven't had time to spend on Tony since all this murder stuff erupted," she said. "And there's a soda bottle of yellow jackets in the mix as well."

"What?"

"That woman, Ms. Whitesmythe. There was a drink bottle underneath the passenger's seat in the car she was driving. There were still yellow jackets crawling around in it. She apparently got stung multiple times. Chief thinks it was accidental, but I'm not convinced. R.J.'s trying to wrap it up."

"I like it better when you're attending kayak weddings."

Addie laughed. "Me too," she said but it was a lie. "See you tonight. There's a spinach and chicken pizza in the freezer." She pulled up to the drive-through speaker. *Welcome to Shorty's. Can I take your order?* "Gotta go."

"Bye. Eat some fries for me. With loads of honey mustard."

"No fries. Bad for the thighs," she sang. She pushed end call. Barbeque. Mr. Abernathy. Then Larry Ryan. That should finish off the afternoon.

She ordered a pulled chicken barbeque sandwich, spicy coleslaw and water. Shorty didn't use mayonnaise in his coleslaw. He used vinegar, chopped onions and his own secret pepper sauce. The barbeque was different, too. Spicy vegetable juice, he told her once between winks. Gave it that extra fullness and zing. She'd tried it at home but it came out tasting like vegetable soup. Luke said the old man was spoofing her. A young woman handed her a paper bag out the drive-through window. The window had grease smears across it and a crack running its length. Spices wafted through the car. She was hungry. She parked in Shorty's lot, opened her windows, exchanged disc Numero Uno for an acoustic guitar CD and opened the sack. Yum. She'd try to catch Mr. Victor Abernathy and Larry right after she ate.

43

Mr. Abernathy was around five foot, ten with an angular nose Luke would admire, wire rimmed glasses and a huge double chin. His face was thin and his head was basically bald which made the flaps of skin around his neck more noticeable, odd looking in fact. She suspected that at one time in his life he'd been heavyset and as the weight came off, the skin stayed put. He stood as she entered his classroom and then doubled behind her to close the thick wooden door.

"How can I help you?" he asked, extending his hand. A firm but genteel handshake. Addie sat at the student desk closest to his metal one. She fished the digital recorder out of her purse and turned it on. "I hope you won't mind," she said. "I record all my interviews to help jog my memory later."

"Of course," he said.

"Thanks for making the time to see me," she began. "I understand you're the one who found Andrew last night. I wanted to hear about it first-hand."

"Yes," Mr. Victor Abernathy said, pushing his chair with the backs of his knees before sitting. He picked up a pencil and quietly rotated it, top, bottom, top, bottom on his desk blotter. "Actually," he began, "it was because of Andrew that I went out walking last night. Not to find him, you understand, but because the news of his mother's death was disturbing and I was concerned about his well-being when I learned he was missing."

"I assume you knew Dr. Beaty, then?"

Mr. Abernathy crooked his elbow up towards his mouth and coughed quietly. "Yes, but not well. We were classmates in high school. I knew of her, you might say."

"I understand she was a school majorette."

"Yes, as I recall she was." He stopped the pencil and let it rest on its eraser. There was about half an eraser left and it was rubbed uneven around the edges. "But I did have a more recent relationship with Andrew. He was my 'difficult child' in class last year. Likeable fellow and smart enough to attend any university in the country if he'll apply himself. But I guess you could say he wrote the book on oppositional behaviors. I think that's what they call smart alecks and disobedience these days."

Addie laughed. "Yes, I think so."

"Well, Andrew had a regular seat out in the hall and a regular pass, so to speak, to the principal's office, but regardless, he endeared himself to me. Perhaps because I suspected his home life was likely, um, disruptive."

"How so?" Addie asked.

Mr. Abernathy put his hand up to his mouth and cleared his throat. His neck skin wobbled. "I'm sure you've learned through your investigation that Dr. Beaty was quite interested in the opposite sex."

"Promiscuous, you mean?"

He cleared his throat again. "Some rumored that."

Addie nodded. "That might make it difficult for an adolescent, for sure. But the question is, difficult enough to kill?"

Mr. Abernathy's eyebrows lowered. The pencil fell to the blotter. "You know, honestly, Detective Bramson, I just can't see it. Not the Andrew I know, anyway. Obnoxious without a doubt, but I can't remember a time when his behaviors even remotely hinted of violence. Quick temper, yes. Aggressive, no. More the type to smart off or withdraw completely if he could get away."

Like this morning at the Chalot's. Smarted off and then escaped. No threat of violence. It fit.

"So what was he doing when you found him last night?" she asked.

"I took Mozart, that's our dog, for a walk on the Quad. Andrew was there riding his bike on the sidewalk. Weird thing was, he was dressed like a Mormon missionary. I barely recognized him. But his eyes tipped me off. I'd know them anywhere. Angry, inquisitive, bright. And I could tell he recognized me although he tried his best to disguise it."

"What time was this?"

"I'm guessing around ten fifty. After the ten o'clock news for certain because that's when I learned about his mother and about his disappearance. Well, actually that's not true. My wife came upstairs and told me first. While I was watching television. She likes to listen to the police scanner. It's a hobby of hers."

Addie nodded. "And did he say where he was going or why he was disguised as a Mormon?"

"No." Mr. Abernathy's forehead wrinkled and his glasses slipped halfway down his nose. He pushed them back up with his finger. "Another odd thing, though. He appeared to be under the assumption I was his father."

She looked at him with sharpened interest. "Really?" It might fit. He certainly appeared to have a bond with the boy. "Did he say why he was operating under that assumption?"

"Not completely. Perhaps because I used the generic term, 'son,' when I was trying to get his attention. Or maybe because he heard that I showed my class slides earlier in the day. Slides of me at their age. My hair, I had more then of course, was red. I'm not totally sure what the connection is there, but the red hair seemed to hold a lot of significance for him."

"Hmmm," said Addie. "How'd he find out about the slides? He's over in Northridge now, isn't he?"

"Yes, but his girlfriend, Bethy Smithson, is currently in my class. In fact, I actually saw him earlier in the day yesterday, when he still had his green dreds. He was talking to her on the fringe of campus during morning break. I don't know why he wasn't in school. He was on his bike then, too. I thought about writing her up. Saw them kissing. Her initiation, not his. But I let it go. Bethy's a good girl and a good student and her mother is extremely active in our PTSO. In fact, I saw Ms. Smithson in the office just before you arrived. I'm sure she's still around if you need to speak to Bethy. She might be able to shed some light on your investigation. Over the years I've learned that kids this age know a heck of a lot about their peers, more than their parents usually."

It was true. When she was Andrew's age she'd poured out her soul to skinny little Joseph LaMonte, the boy she was certain she'd love forever. Four months of fantasizing about a relationship, three weeks of ecstatic going steady before she decided he was a jerk. Her girlfriends told her that from the beginning. "Yes," she said. "It'd be great to talk to Bethy and her mother if they're still around."

Mr. Abernathy pushed an intercom button on the wall behind his desk. The speaker squawked to life with a fuzzy female voice. Yes, she'd just seen them in the hallway. They were probably on their way to the library for the Spring fling fundraiser meeting. She'd try to get word to them.

"Thanks," said Addie. She returned her attention to the previous night. "So he never explained why he was dressed as a Mormon? And did I hear you say he had green dreds earlier in the day?"

"No, he didn't explain why he was in disguise, I guess it was a disguise, I don't guess he's converted. To be honest I didn't consider that possibility. And yes, he did have green dreds earlier in the day. Andrew has always played with his appearance, for as long as I've known him. Different hair colors, hair styles, fake tattoos, goth and punk jewelry, peculiar clothes for this region of the country. That kind of thing. He doesn't conform to the mainstream, I guess you'd say."

"Did he say anything about his mother last night? His brother?"

"To tell you the truth we didn't talk about his mother. I was prepared to when I ran into him, but it appeared he had no idea she was dead. So I just told him the police were looking for him and for his brother. That I'd heard it on the news. When I mentioned his brother he immediately called his brother's father, Mr. Thomas Chalot, I think was his name, and Mr. Chalot asked him to stay put with me until he could get there to pick him up. Mr. Chalot assured me he'd contacted the police to report Andrew was no longer missing."

Addie considered what he said carefully. "What made you think Andrew knew nothing of his mother's death?" she asked.

Mr. Abernathy pursed his lips and shook his head. His neck skin wiggled. She couldn't help it. Her stare was drawn toward the skin and the whiskery stubbles dotting it. "I don't know exactly," he said. "Just intuitive observation and my knowledge of the young man, I guess."

There was a tentative knock on the door. "That must be the Smithsons," he said.

Addie slid out of the desk and walked toward the door. She cracked it open. A young girl wearing striped tights, a thigh length skirt and a quilted vest stood beside a woman with short frosted hair and muted peach lipstick. "Hi," she said. "You must be the Smithsons."

"Yes, that's right," the woman said.

"Thank you and your daughter for coming." She opened the door wider but blocked their entrance with her body. "I'm Detective Adelaide Bramson. I need to ask the two of you a few questions."

"About my daughter's friend, Andrew Beaty, I'm sure," said Ms. Smithson. The daughter had a deer in the headlights look. Except her eyes were gray. Almost pewter.

"Yes. That's right. Just routine."

Ms. Smithson nodded and smiled. A strained smile, one extremely familiar to Addie. "Of course."

"I'm just wrapping it up in here," said Addie. "Please give me several more minutes."

"Of course," Ms. Smithson said again.

"Thanks." Addie shut the door and returned to face Mr. Abernathy.

"Can you think of anything else that might help in my investigation of Dr. Beaty's murder, Mr. Abernathy? Anything I may have failed to ask?"

Mr. Abernathy's elbow went back up to his mouth. Another soft cough. There was something. Something he wasn't saying. She felt sure of it. "No," he said. "Nothing I can think of at the moment. It's just, I know anything's possible with adolescents. And you see this kind of thing on the news sometimes. But, I just can't see Andrew as a murderer. I don't think he's the one."

"I sincerely hope not," said Addie. "But I'm sure you know teenage brains are still developing. Consequences don't always enter into their decision making processes. I'm sure you see that every day."

"There's truth in that," said Vic Abernathy.

"And, just for the record. Where were you around five, six o'clock last night?"

Mr. Abernathy jolted forward in surprise. "Well, I actually have no idea. Not without some thought." He shut his eyes. Addie noted his respiration rate increased. "I, ah, I believe I was at the grocery store. Picking up some lemons and potatoes for my wife."

"How did you pay for it? Cash? Check? Debit? Charge?"

"Ah, I can't remember. Surely . . ." He didn't finish his thought.

She decided to go for it. Right to the jugular. The jugular underneath all those skin flaps. "One more question," she said.

"Yes?"

"Was Andrew right? Are you 'Red,' the man identified by Dr. Beaty as Andrew's father?"

Her question appeared to catch him completely off guard. He swallowed hard, a peach pit of an Adam's apple bobbing up, then down inside his neck. "Heavens, no!" he exclaimed, picking up the pencil and tapping it, eraser to point, point to eraser, eraser to point, point to eraser. "No, of course I'm not. Whatever would give you that idea?"

Addie watched the flipping pencil and smiled. "Just have to cover all the bases, Mr. Abernathy. I'm sure you understand."

* * *

Bethy Smithson entered the room shielding herself with her mother's body, nearly holding onto Ms. Smithson's turquoise print jacket and following like a caboose. She reminded Addie of a kindergartener on the first day of school. Mr. Abernathy excused himself quickly and Ms. Smithson took his place behind the desk. Bethy stood behind her mother to the left, eyeing Addie nervously. If Ms. Smithson were nervous, Addie couldn't see it. The woman leaned forward, concern in her eyes, a slight smile on her peach colored lips.

"How can we help you, Detective?" she asked.

"Thanks for being willing to help," said Addie. "As you can see, this interview is being recorded to help me remember things accurately later."

"I'm sure that's the best way to keep the facts straight," said Ms. Smithson. Her gaze rested only briefly on the recorder before she made full eye contact with Addie again.

"I understand that your daughter is a very close friend of Andrew Beaty's," said Addie.

Ms. Smithson smiled a maternal adult-to-adult kind of smile. "Yes. That's true. Of course I don't let Bethy really date yet, but she and Andrew, I think the word they use is 'talk.' They've been interested in each other about, ah, let's see . . . , how long has it been, Bethy?"

Bethy curled her lips inward, pressed them tightly together, cocked her head to one side and shrugged one shoulder. "I don't remember," she said at long last.

A good girl Mr. Abernathy'd said and a good student. But not telling the truth. "Bethy," Addie said. "You're not in trouble. I'm just trying to get a clearer picture of Andrew and what's been going on with him."

"We understand," said Ms. Smithson. "I'm very protective of my daughter, Detective. I watch her and her friends carefully. Andrew is a very polite and intelligent young man. He's always been extremely respectful around my daughter and me."

"He has," said Bethy.

"Very good," said Addie. She decided to let her first question go unanswered. "Bethy," she said, "has he ever talked to you about his relationship with his mother?"

Bethy shifted from one leg to the other. She stared out the window. Squinted. Addie followed her gaze. Nothing there of immediate interest. "Not really," she said. "I mean, he was upset about having to go to that residential place. You know, Metamorphosis. She was putting him there. But nothing else. I mean, nothing important."

"Did he ever talk threateningly about it? Like did he say he was going to stop his mother from putting him there? Anything like that?"

Bethy paused. Stared out the window again. Lips pursed again. Silence.

"Bethy, honey, the detective asked you a question."

Silence.

"Bethy . . ."

Anger? . . . fear? . . . flashed through her eyes. "I don't want to talk about him."

Ms. Smithson pivoted the chair to face her child. "Bethy, you need to answer the detective's questions. It'll help Andrew, I'm sure it will."

Silence.

"Your mother's right," said Addie. "I need to know anything you can tell me. Even if you think it's something little. Or bad. Or embarrassing."

Bethy moved sideways toward her mother until their arms touched. "He said he wasn't going to that place," she said softly. "He ran away."

Withdrawal, just like Mr. Abernathy said. "When did you see him last, Bethy?"

Her gray eyes darted to the right, to the ceiling, to the floor. "Ah, sometime last week I guess. We talk more by phone and computer than in person."

Addie frowned. A lie. But she wouldn't have done better at that age with her mother in the room. Wasn't she thirteen when she went to the mall with friends and shoplifted a small palate of eye shadow? Six greasy little blue and green and metallic colored rectangles. The bronze one attracted her attention in the first place. It sparkled like it had mica in it. She went home that day and went straight to bed and her heart felt like it was going to jump right out of her breast every time the phone rang. For days. She never even used the stuff. A week later she threw it in the lunchroom garbage can and globbed her spaghetti lunch on top of it.

Whenever she interviewed teenagers she tried to frame it against her own foray into crime. "Bethy," she said firmly. "You're not telling the truth. I have a witness who's told me you were together yesterday."

Navy eyeliner. Bethy's eyes grew larger, rounder. Lips pursed again. She glanced down at her mother.

Ms. Smithson's forehead creased. She looked confused. "Yesterday?" she asked. "Bethy, why would you lie to the detective about that? Tell her everything you know. You're not helping Andrew a bit if you don't."

"And," said Addie gently. "You may not know the law. It's a crime to lie or withhold information from an officer."

Bethy shifted her weight. Her fingers skirted the edge of the desk, bitten fingernails skittering like little water spiders on top of pond water. "Okay," she said. "He came over last night but I guess you know that already."

Nope, thought Addie.

"Last night?" Ms. Smithson repeated. Surprise in her face. Her voice. So he probably didn't use the front door, Addie thought. In through a window maybe. The way teens usually did it.

"He just dropped by for a minute while you were at yoga, Mama. He wanted to show me his, ah, his disguise."

Not a window after all. "His Mormon missionary disguise?" asked Addie.

"Yes, ma'am," Bethy nodded. "It sort of weirded me out."

Addie laughed. "I bet. Quite a change from green dreds. What time was that, Bethy?"

"Um, I don't know. Sometime around 8:45 I think."

"Did you let him in?" asked her mother.

Pause.

"Did you?"

"Just for a second, Mama. He, ah, he couldn't stay. He had to go find a place to sleep."

"And did he say anything about what was happening at home?" asked Addie. Ms. Smithson was not a happy camper. Bethy was standing ramrod straight. She'd backed away from her mother's side.

Bethy shook her head.

"Nothing about his house?"

"No, ma'am. Just that he wasn't going to that place Metamorphosis."

"Did he talk about his mother? About them having a fight? About an accident or anything?"

"No. No, ma'am. Nothing like that."

"How about his brother?"

Bethy closed her eyes. She reopened them very slowly. "No."

"Did he behave differently? Look nervous? Was he short tempered? Crying? Anything like that?"

Pause. "No, ma'am. Nothing like that. Nothing I noticed." Her eyes met Addie's. Worried. Confused. Beautifully gray. "He's okay, isn't he?" she asked. "I mean, he's not arrested or anything is he?"

"No," Addie said reassuringly. "He's safe and staying with friends of his family today. But I want you to think really hard. Is there anything you can tell me, anything at all, that might help me figure out what's been going on?"

Bethy's eyes made earnest contact. Mr. Abernathy was right. A good girl. "No. No, ma'am. Nothing except I know Andrew's a nice person. He was mad at his mother but he'd never hurt her. He'd never hurt anybody. I'm sure of that."

"And when he came over here to visit you at school yesterday morning he didn't say anything I should know?"

Ms. Smithson pivoted toward her daughter again. "Andrew came to see you here at school? He came here *and* to the house?"

Bethy seemed not to hear her mother. "No, ma'am. Not really. He came to tell me he was running away. He promised he'd stay in touch."

Young love. Painful always. "Thank you, Bethy," Addie said. "I guess that's it for now. But if you think of anything, and I mean anything, that you think I should know please ask your mother to contact me immediately."

"Yes, ma'am. But I know Andrew didn't do anything bad."

Addie looked toward Ms. Smithson. "Thank you, Ms. Smithson," she said. Ms. Smithson's jaw had jutted forward. The smile on her peach lips was strained.

"Certainly," she answered. "Believe me, Detective Bramson, this has been a learning experience for me. Bethy knows she's not allowed to let anyone in the house while I'm gone, particularly a male. And I had no idea they were meeting at school." She glared at her daughter. "We have a lot to talk about on the ride home."

Bethy's ragged nails disappeared into the palms of her hands, a nervous sort of gesture, but to Addie she didn't look particularly worried. She switched off the recorder. So Andrew went to visit Bethy at her house the night of his mother's murder. It was a piece of the puzzle, one of many pieces her intuition told her, that he'd chosen not to share.

44

"I'm not staying. I'm outta here at dark."

He was standing behind a conference room chair in the Green Room. The psychologist guy, Dr. Luke, the sort of cool looking woman named Shelby McSomething, the old lady who owned the place, the woman who told him she was his social worker, Miss Elenrude, and Thomas were all looking at him. He'd told Miss Elenrude he didn't have and didn't need a social worker and if he did ever need one which he wouldn't, he wouldn't want an old lady with blond porcupine hair and a name like Zenah Elenrude anyway. What kind of messed up name was that? Thomas had fussed at him but Miss Elenrude didn't. Instead she smiled in a way that suggested she'd probably had kids call her all kinds of things and so it didn't really get to her. Then she told him she knew he'd been through a lot and she understood why he wouldn't want a social worker and why he wouldn't want to stay at Metamorphosis, but the judge had made the decision, not her, and anyway, it was a safe place for him to be until they could get everything sorted out.

Thomas pulled Andrew's chair back from the table. "Sit please, Andrew," he said.

Andrew could see the stress lines running across Thomas' forehead and he knew they were both worried sick about Joey, and that neither had slept well last night because they both expected Joey to answer his cell phone messages and he hadn't. And he knew Thomas had taken on the responsibility of helping arrange his mother's funeral but the two of them were waiting until they found Joey before making any final plans. It was something the three of them needed to do together.

"Please do this for me, Andy," said Thomas in a conciliatory tone. "Do what you need to do right now and we'll get it straightened out as soon as we can. Acting up won't help you or me or Joey, and it won't bring your mother back or get you out of here, unless you misbehave and wind up someplace like juvenile hall."

"He's right, you know," said Dr. Luke. "There're worse places to be."

Andrew stared into Thomas' eyes. They were tired, flat. "This is so screwed," he mumbled but he sat.

"Good decision!" said the woman Shelby McSomething. It was annoying.

He shoved his legs outward underneath the table and crossed them at the ankle.

"Why don't we do a contract?" suggested Miss Elenrude. "An agreement that if you behave responsibly and comply with the judge's order and the rules of Metamorphosis for a week, I'll go before the judge and ask that she consider an alternative placement for you, assuming you're cleared of wrongdoing in your mother's death."

Andrew's back stiffened. "Screw the judge," he said.

"Andrew!" warned Thomas. Surprise. Thomas never raised his voice. Not like that.

"Sorry," said Andrew.

"Where would you want to live if you could go anywhere?" asked Miss Elenrude.

Andrew rolled his eyes. He and Thomas had already talked about it. It was the only reason he'd agreed to get in the car to come to Metamorphosis. "With Thomas and Holly," he answered.

"That's what I thought you'd say," said Miss Elenrude. "And Mr. Chalot has told me he and his wife want you to live with them. So that's the goal we'll try working toward. But understand, Andrew, I'm not saying you'll move in with Mr. Chalot in a week. I'm saying we can work toward that. It's up to the judge when and where you go."

"And the judge," said the old lady who owned the place, Dr. Lydia Hutchinsomething, "will make her determination based on your behaviors here as well as other factors. So ultimately, young man, a lot of the decision about when and where you go is based on your choices. It's not the only thing that enters into the decision making process, of course, but it's a big factor in it."

"Do you understand what everyone's telling you?" asked Thomas.

"Yeah. If I behave maybe I can come live with you."

"Right," said the woman Shelby McSomething. "And how do you feel about that?"

Stupid question. "Honestly?" he asked.

"Yes." Her eyes were bright. Shiny, happy little eyes. One of those pixie-like ski lift noses. He didn't like that kind of nose. Annoying. But for some reason he did like her.

"Honestly I don't think it's anybody's damn business but mine and Thomas' where I live."

"That may be the way you feel," said the guy Dr. Luke. "But it's not the reality of the situation. And you'll have to deal with realities of this situation if you want to negotiate it successfully." Straight up. Dr. Luke was an okay guy.

"And young man," added the old lady who owned the place, "if we're worried you're going to run we'll have to remove privileges to keep a better eye on you. We can always put staff one on one with you if need be."

"Do you hear that, Andrew?" asked Thomas. "Stay put."

Andrew sighed and laid his head sideways on the table. Where the hell was Joey?

"Andrew?"

"Yes, sir. I hear it," he said. "And I'm here, aren't I?"

"How about the contract idea?" asked Miss Elenrude.

Andrew shrugged a sideways shrug. Head still on the table. "Yeah, okay, whatever."

"Yes, ma'am," corrected Thomas.

Miss Elenrude looked toward the lady who owned the place, then toward the Shelby McSomething woman and finally toward Dr. Luke. "We went through his clothes and personal items while he was packing," she said. "Everything's in order."

"Good," said Dr. Luke. "We'll have Rico help him unpack just to double check that everything's allowed on the unit. What about your pockets?" he asked Andrew.

"What do you mean?"

"We need to see what's in them. Just to make sure you don't have cigarettes or a lighter or a phone, that kind of stuff."

"No way you're getting my phone," said Andrew.

"I'll take it home," said Thomas.

Bethy. She'd be worried about him. He could endure anything as long as they could talk. And text. "Why can't I keep it?" he asked Dr. Luke.

"I'm sure you wouldn't misuse yours," Dr. Luke answered. "But we have folks here who'd be texting fellow gang members, or sexting, all kinds of things. And we can't make exceptions for new people entering the unit. We do allow phones on our highest trust level but if things go as smoothly as we all hope, you'll be home with the phone in your pocket before you have time to reach Level Four."

"How long does it take?" asked Andrew.

"With excellent behavior, following the rules, all of that, about a month."

Andrew snorted. Forget that. A month without his phone. No way. He shoved his hand into his pocket. He wrapped his fingers tightly around it. "Joey might phone. He might text."

"I'll keep an eye out for that," said Thomas. "You know I will." He reached an open palm toward Andrew.

Andrew sighed. "I need to call a friend first."

"Who?" asked the pixie-nosed McSomething woman.

None of your damn business.

"Andrew, Ms. McDonald asked you a question," Thomas said.

"Um, a friend of mine . . . Bethy."

A slight curl of the lips from the old lady who owned the place.

Dr. Luke nodded. "Sure," he said. "You can call her in just a minute. Thanks for your cooperation, Andrew."

The woman named Shelby McDonald leaned back and reached deep into her front pocket. "Speaking of contraband phones," she said to Dr. Luke. She pushed a black flip phone across the table toward him. "Here's the one I confiscated today from our friend. I forgot to give it to you earlier."

"Thanks," said Dr. Luke, sticking it in his shirt pocket. "Now, will you please empty your pockets, Andrew?"

The bracelet. And the pendant and the ring. Damn, how could he have been so stupid?

"I don't have cigarettes or a lighter on me. No matches, either. Nothing but a few dollars and my driver's license in my billfold."

"Good," said Dr. Luke. "Then you won't mind following my directions."

"Everything," said the old lady who owned the place. Hutchinson, it was Hutchinson. "If it's not contraband you can probably have it back."

Andrew's fingers curled around the bracelet. His knuckles rubbed the ring and the pendant with the photo. He pulled them out. The jewelry clinked against the wood table. The tissue paper halfway fell away from the pendant. He saw Thomas' eyes grow larger, then fill with concern, then curiosity. Andrew reached into his back pocket and took out his wallet. He reached into his other front pocket and removed his keys. His house key, a spare key to the Lexus, hey, maybe it was his now. Joey already had a car. Bethy'd love it. All his friends would be freaking. He'd talk to Thomas and Joey about it. When they found Joey. Finally, he removed his phone. "That's it," he said.

"Can you turn your pockets inside out please?" asked the social worker lady, Elenrude.

He rolled his eyes but pushed his hands back into the linings of each pocket, pulling them inside out one by one. "Great to be trusted," he said.

"Just standard procedure," Dr. Luke responded.

The woman named Shelby McDonald leaned forward and examined the bracelet and the ring and the pendant by touching them with her index finger. "What are you doing with these?" she asked. "Whose are they?"

He straightened his back and shoulders. He dared not look at Thomas. "My mother's," he answered. "She gave them to me about a week ago. The bracelet is from the man she called my dad. It has writing inside it, cut into the metal. She wanted me to have it."

"Are you sure you didn't just take them?" asked Dr. Luke.

"Good question," said Thomas. "Andy, why would she give you these things? You can't wear them."

"I can't wear them but she said I could carry them, like I'm doing. It's all I've ever had of my dad's, whoever he is." He heard the pleading in his voice. He lowered his eyes. Sad. It was important to look sad.

"And the ring and pendant?" asked the woman Shelby McDonald. Her voice was noticeably gentler. "Were they from him, too?"

"I don't know," he said. "She just said they were clues. So I guess they must be."

Thomas frowned. "Let me see," he said.

Andrew picked up the three items and deposited them carefully in Thomas' palm. The tissue paper sat empty on the table. "I have no idea," Thomas said after turning them over in his hand and holding them up toward the window for better light. He studied the pendant's photograph and frowned slightly. He ran his tongue across his lips and held the bracelet sideways to read the inscription. "I wish it *had* been everlasting love," he said glancing toward Andrew. "She always loved your father, you know? Never stopped loving him. Maybe things'd be different if their relationship had worked out."

Andrew pursed his lips. Or yours, he wanted to say. How many nights had he lain in bed, eyes wide open, red lit numbers reading three o'clock, four, four thirty, wishing, praying when he used to pray, that Thomas and his mother would get back together? The man named Red was persona non grata to him.

"Normally we don't allow jewelry like this on the unit," said Dr. Luke. "The reason is it's likely to get stolen. But," he looked toward the Hutchinson and the Shelby women and Andrew saw both nod ever so slightly, "under the circumstances . . . Given your situation . . . If you can promise you won't flash it around and that if it's stolen you'll cope, then I'd say we can make an exception in your case."

Thomas handed the items back to him, still frowning slightly. "I hope you're telling the truth, Andrew," he said. "That your mother gave you these, I mean."

He stared at his social worker, the Zenah Elenrude woman. There were little patches of gray above her ears where the blond dye didn't take right. No way would he look at Thomas. "I wouldn't lie about something like that. Not now . . ."

Dr. Luke stood. "Okay, young man. Let's see what's in your wallet and then you can put everything back where it came from, except of course the phone."

Andrew's wallet was gray nylon with black Velcro. Thomas had given Joey a matching one the same Christmas. He wondered if Joey still had his. The Velcro crackled. He handed it to Dr. Luke. Eight dollars. That was it. He'd taped the rest of the money in a plastic baggie inside the toilet tank in the guest bedroom suite at Thomas' house. It'd be safe there. They'd given him that room for the time being.

They wouldn't snoop. Even if they did, which they wouldn't, they weren't the type to think about hiding anything in a toilet tank. He watched Dr. Luke go through his wallet. His driver's permit, an emergency ID card, his student ID, an old library card. A photo of Joey acting crazy with Winx. Another of Thomas and his family taken at one of those studio places. One of Bethy. Her class picture. It was good but she was prettier. And it didn't smell like her, either. He saw Dr. Luke glance at the photos, eyes pausing on Bethy for just a millisecond longer.

"Eight dollars," Dr. Luke said. "Just ask Rico to write that in the records when you get down to the unit. He'll put your cash in the safe. That way, nobody'll steal it."

"When can I have it?"

"You really won't need money until we go off campus. Like to the mall or something," said the woman Shelby McDonald.

No money. It was like being five years old again.

"In fact," said old Dr. Hutchinson, "we recommend you leave your wallet at home. We unfortunately do have thieves at times. You won't need any of those cards while you're here."

"I want my photos," said Andrew. He reached for his wallet and pulled out the photos and the money.

"Here," he said to Thomas handing him the billfold.

"Sure you don't want me to take the jewelry home?"

Andrew moved his chair backward without even thinking about it. He could tell. Thomas didn't believe his story about the jewelry. "No," he said. "No. I want to carry them for a while. They were the last things Mama gave me." He tried to ignore the look of skepticism on Thomas' face. He wrapped the pendant back in the tissue paper.

"Well," said Dr. Luke. "Why don't we all step out of the room so you can make your call? Then you and I will meet alone with Mr. Chalot before we go down to the unit, okay?"

Andrew shrugged. Whatever. He was in no hurry to get down to the cottage.

"Five minutes tops, okay?" said Dr. Luke. It was said as a question, but Andrew knew it was a direction.

"Okay," said Andrew. He waited until old lady Hutchinson was out of the room, she was the last one out and she was definitely not in a hurry. She was talking to his social worker about some kind of meeting they'd be attending next week. When the door closed, he dialed Bethy's number. The phone rang only once. She was waiting for his call. Had to be.

"Andrew?"

"Hey. I just have a few minutes. They're waiting for me in the hall."

"Are you okay? Where are you?"

"At that stupid Metamorphosis place. Sucks big time."

"For how long?"

"A week, two maybe, I think. Too damn long, oh, sorry, too long, anyway."

"Have you found Joey?"

"No. Nothing."

"I love you, Andrew."

His pulse pounded in his throat. It still felt awkward to say. He'd told her before, a lot of times now, but still it was a struggle.

"Well?" she said. "Do you love me back?"

"Of course," he said. "Yes. It's just . . . everything's so messed up."

"Not us."

"They're taking my phone. I won't be able to text you. I'll try to use the phone at the cottage."

"Are the girls cute there?"

"I don't know."

"Better not be."

"Wouldn't matter. I'm putting your picture beside my bed."

"My picture? Which one?"

"The one in my wallet. You know, from school."

"Oh no," she halfway whined. "I look so gross in that one!"

"Not hardly." He paused. "But it doesn't smell good like you," he said.

Silence. Andrew imagined her lying on the bed in her room, hair loose on her pillow, smelling like fresh citrus.

"I need to tell you," she said finally. "Some lady detective asked me questions today at school. My mom was there, too. She knew you came by last night. And somehow she knew about your coming to the school, too. And she already knew about your Mormon thing."

"Was she short with curly brown hair and a bunch of earrings, like six or something?"

"Well, two were ear cuffs," said Bethy. "Yeah, that's her."

"She came to see me, too. Her name made me think about math. Addie. Addie uppie."

A soft giggle. He thought about her tongue on his lips. Flavored lip gloss. Frenching.

"Yeah, I think so," she said. "She called herself Detective Adelaide Bramson, or Bransom, or something. I'm not exactly sure."

"Wanna hear something crazy? My shrink here is her husband. Dr. Luke they call him."

"That's weird."

"Yeah. So what did she ask you?"

"Questions about what you've said about your mom and stuff."

"What did you say?"

She made a funny noise.

"What was that?"

"What?"

"That noise you just made."

She paused, giggled. "Oh, I was just turning over onto my stomach."

He imagined her lying on her stomach, knees bent and ankles crossed, her hair draped across her pillow. "So what did you say?" he asked again.

"That you don't talk about her much. And she wanted to know if you'd been making threats or anything and I said no except for threatening to run away. Nothing much, really. And I told her there was no way you'd ever hurt your mom."

Andrew turned toward the window. A group of girls was walking along the sidewalk toward the building. Three of them were smokin' hot looking. "I'm sorry, baby, that you had to get involved in all that," he said.

"No biggie," she said. "And even Mama didn't fuss too much about me letting you into the house while she was gone. I'm grounded for a week, can't go out with friends or have friends in, but who cares since you're out there? And I'm grounded from the phone, too, but that doesn't really matter. She's gone so much I can talk anyway."

"I'm sorry," he said. "It was stupid of me to stop by."

"You'd better have," she said.

Pause. One of the girls, the one second from the end of the line, with fine looking legs and long blond hair and a pretty face, saw him in the window. She poked her friend with her elbow and that girl, not so pretty, turned to look. They both waved and started laughing, bumping against each other's shoulders and hips like they were trying to knock one another off the sidewalk. A third girl said something to them and laughed and waved, too. He smiled, held up his hand but decided against it. No waving. No complications. He turned away. "I've got to go, baby," he said. "I'll call you later tonight if they'll let me."

"I miss you," she said.

"Me too."

"Love you."

"Me, too. Bye." He pressed end call and opened up the back of his phone. He slipped his fingernail under the metal strip and removed his sim card. He'd hide it behind one of the framed pictures, lodge it in the brown paper backing behind one of the frames. He moved toward a poster edged with black wood that read, ***Take a step forward everyday and it becomes your life journey.*** He stopped, stared at the words. Green letters printed on a fluffy-cloud sky. Clouds as white as marshmallows. Some sort of butterfly in the right hand corner. They were wearing out the metamorphosis theme. Butterflies and caterpillars everywhere and he hadn't even moved in yet. He was pulling the frame off the wall when he realized it wouldn't work. He'd have to erase everything on his phone instead. Thomas needed his phone in case Joey called it. He slipped the sim card back in and sat down at the table. He'd erase all his texts, all his calls, all his messages and his phone directory. An empty phone. That's what Thomas would take home.

*   *   *

He was waiting in the hallway for Andrew. Mr. Chalot had excused himself to the men's room. The women had departed, Shelby to her office and Miss Elenrude to Dr. Lydia's office. A dog barked, a huge German shepherd sound. Luke smiled at his cleverness. He liked to change his phone's ring at least every other day. It kept the kids amused. "Hello?"

"Hello, Dr. Bramson? I'm in need of mental health. Can't wait till tonight after all." There was levity in Addie's voice.

"Hi, honey. Where are you?"

"That's a good question. Feels like Mars the way the investigation's going. I think they're all guilty, I swear they are. Everyone of them's lying, I'm sure of it. They all have motives and several have histories."

"I'm with my intake right now," he said. "But if you have time to hang out a bit, come on by. I'll make us some coffee."

"Think I will," said Addie. "I've got another interview today, with Larry, you remember the guy who used to be on the force? Security guard now at DHR? I'm stopping by his house after work so I have some time to kill. Anyway, I'd like to get Shelby's impressions of Bob Tulane's interactions with Dr. Beaty on the afternoon of the murder if she's got a few minutes."

"Want to try catching her by phone right now?"

"No. I'll wait 'til I stop by. I need a kiss."

Luke smiled. Mr. Chalot was approaching from down the hall. "Me, too," he said. "It's a date."

"See ya." Dial tone.

He knocked on the conference room door. "Andrew? Ready?" Andrew opened the door almost immediately. "Wow," said Dr. Luke. "That was faster than I expected."

Andrew dropped his phone into Thomas' hand. "Please keep on the lookout for Joey," he said. He knew it was a dumb thing to say. Joey was on Thomas' mind twenty-four seven.

Mr. Chalot put the phone in his front pant's pocket. "I've got a call into his girlfriend up at Amherst, calls into his roommate, his psychologist, and several of his identified friends at Auburn. I promise I'll be watching. If he texts or calls, you'll be the first to know, Andy. The police will be second."

Andrew nodded. It felt good for Thomas to call him Andy, just like Joey did sometimes. It was a sign of family. Only Joey and Thomas could call him that. To everyone else, even Bethy, he was Andrew.

"Excellent," said Dr. Luke. It was concerning from a lot of perspectives the way Joey'd gone missing. There were multiple ways to interpret it. He was sure both Andrew and Thomas had considered most of them. "Let's go to my office," he said. "We'll tie up a few loose ends and then we'll be through."

Down the hallway, around the corner. Closed office doors. Posters with inspirational sayings all over the walls. *Invest in change, one decision at a time. If you can't change a situation, change the way you react to it. Don't recycle mistakes. Learn from them instead.* Dr. Luke stopped in front of a honey colored wooden door with the brass name plate LUKE BRAMSON, Ph.D. screwed on at eye level. He pulled his keys out of his pocket, Andrew guessed there were at least eight on the ring, maybe more, and slipped one into the lock. Andrew wondered if Birthday Boy Benjamin's stolen key opened all the doors in the building or just that observation place near the classroom. He'd have to ask.

"Sit wherever you're comfortable," Dr. Luke said.

Andrew looked around. It was a tidy, man's office. No frills. A computer and a phone, some kind of rock and some magnetic metal men clinging acrobatically to a post on the desk. Some tissues in a little cardboard box. A green recliner, an office chair, two leather straight back chairs, a long black, gray and white stripe painted along one wall, and several framed pictures made out of thread. Probably from his mother or wife or a sister. He walked over and looked at one with a hawk, wings outstretched, catching the currents above the treetops. The threads in the hawk were muted all the different shades of a hawk in real life. It was sort of cool that thread came in so many colors like the colors of crayons in the big box he used to buy as a kid.

"I may as well admit it right now," laughed Dr. Luke, "'cause you'll hear it from the guys on the unit. I'm a closet needlepointer."

Andrew turned to look at him. "What's that?"

Dr. Luke nodded toward the hawk. "That's called needlepoint. I make my own designs from photos I take and then I needlepoint them. It's one of my hobbies."

Thomas sat in one of the straight backed chairs, attention focused on the picture. "Interesting," he said.

"You sew? That's weird," said Andrew. "For a guy, I mean. I thought your mother or wife or sister or somebody did them."

Dr. Luke laughed. "My wife could never sit still long enough to needlepoint."

Andrew sat down beside Thomas. "She's that detective lady who came to see me this morning," he said.

Dr. Luke lowered himself into his office chair and swiveled to face them. "If her name was Detective Adelaide Bramson, then yes, you're right."

"I didn't even know there were lady detectives, I mean for real, not on TV, until I met her."

Dr. Luke leaned back. "Having a detective for a wife keeps me out of trouble, I can tell you that." He laughed even though it sounded to Andrew like he told that joke often. Thomas laughed, too. "Actually, Andrew, that's one of the things I want to talk about. She is the detective assigned to your mother's death. I want to help catch your mother's killer. It would help a lot if I could talk to her about what I think, especially what I think about your situation."

"Makes sense," said Thomas.

Dr. Luke opened his bottom left desk drawer and pulled out a file. He removed several forms.

"These are called release of information forms. You remember the other day we talked about them and you said I could share information about you with several people here on staff, including my partner, Ms. Shelby McDonald and the owner, Dr. Lydia Hutchinson, and probably our teacher, Ms. Moffiti, too. Well, I'd like to fill out forms with their names to make it all legit, and if you agree, I'll add Mr. Chalot to one so I can talk to him about how you're doing here, and if you agree, one with my wife's name so I can help her better understand you."

Andrew shrugged. "Whatever," he said.

"But are you comfortable with that? I don't want you to feel under any pressure."

"Yeah, sure." He wasn't going to spill his guts, anyway. He'd never talk, especially not about his mother. Or his brother. Or Bethy. Or himself.

"Good," said Dr. Luke as he wrote things on the forms.

"Damn, you guys have too many forms," said Andrew. "How many have I signed already? Ten? Fifteen?"

Dr. Luke glanced up and laughed. "You're right about that. I didn't know until I graduated from college that it's all about the paperwork. It makes the world go round."

Mr. Chalot laughed again. It was easy to tell Thomas liked Dr. Luke. Andrew settled more comfortably in his chair. He leaned his head back. He was exhausted. And worried. What was Joey doing anyway? Fear, dark shadows rising from the pit of Andrew's stomach, glided over his rib cage into his throat. Last night the shadows smothered him, slithered over his face until he couldn't catch his breath. He stared at the black and gray line to distract himself. "What's that line for, anyway?" he asked. Black on one end, white on the other. It ran the distance of the wall, the gray growing increasingly lighter as it transitioned from black to white. At one point the line was a sort of silvery gray, the color of Bethy's dog, Sterling. But none of the grays were as pretty as Bethy's eyes. He wondered what she was doing. He wondered if he could call her from the cottage. He wondered how many nights her mother went to yoga.

Dr. Luke opened his middle drawer and removed a sheet of paper with the same line on it. "It's a relativity line," he said.

"And?" Andrew asked. He really didn't want to take the paper but he took it to be polite. He was pretty sure Dr. Luke was an okay guy.

"Well," Dr. Luke said. "Lots of people get into absolute thinking about things. Hot, cold. Thrilling, boring. Love, hate. Black, white. But what if we talk in shades of gray instead? It's the same concept as a scale from one to ten, basically. So, at one time in my life I probably would have told you I hated cats. But when I think about my wife's cat, my emotions are probably somewhere around the middle of the line, in the gray. I might be closer to the black square when I think about the cat shedding all over my clothes or when I have to change the kitty litter or when she scratches the furniture, but I'd be closer to the white square when she curls up in my lap at night and purrs or when I think about how happy my wife is to have her as a family member. So it's about dissecting our responses, training ourselves to see both the good and bad of things. When people can see both the good and the bad rather than thinking in absolutes, do you think they might be experiencing life more maturely?"

Andrew wished he'd never asked. He knew Dr. Luke wanted him to say yes. He shrugged. "I guess," he answered. He wondered what the cat's name was.

"Just mull the concept over, Andrew," said Dr. Luke. "See if you can apply it to your relationship with your mother."

Andrew frowned. "That *is* absolute. No gray there," he said, but he knew he wasn't fooling either of them. Not himself. Not Dr. Luke. Not Thomas, either. He hated his mother but there was something else, that thing that wrenched at his gut when she was alive and even now when he thought about her being dead.

Dr. Luke rolled his chair slightly closer. "Andrew," he said gently. It was weird but somehow not too bad weird to have a man talk so gently to him. "We all hope you'll be here a very short time. From my own perspective, the best place for you is with Mr. Chalot." He nodded toward Thomas. "But while you're here it might be helpful in our therapy to explore the anger you express toward your mother."

Andrew shifted in his chair. "She's dead. Waste of time." He saw Thomas look toward the floor and his eyes looked sad. Really sad. And tired. In some ways he was sure Thomas had never stopped loving her. But she'd screwed that up too, she always screwed up the good things.

"Well, choosing to always be angry is your prerogative, of course," said Dr. Luke, pen poised above the forms. "But to me it seems like anger is a healthy emotion that tells us something or some things need to be changed. Positive change to help reduce or eliminate anger is a good thing. Getting stuck in the negativity of anger itself, staying there, is unhealthy. Like a tire spinning around and around in the mud."

Andrew thought of the time he went mudding with Joey in their friend's Jeep. Mud flinging everywhere, tires digging deeper and deeper in glop. The sucking sound around their tennis shoes when they tried to push it out. Mud splattered all over him, the gritty taste in his mouth. He never went mudding again.

Thomas cleared his throat. When he looked up he had a strange expression on his face. His eyes even looked watery. Andrew's stomach churned. Thomas was strong. Thomas never cried. "Andy, what Dr. Bramson's saying is true," he said in a husky voice that didn't sound like Thomas at all. "You and your brother have a lot of legitimate anger stored deep. I understand that. But there's something you don't know. Something I need to tell you. It may help in your journey toward forgiveness."

Andrew moved toward the front of the chair. The silence was heavy. He didn't want to forgive her. He could feel food pressing upward against his Adam's apple again. Food and his pulse. He wanted to get away. Stick his finger down his throat. Throw up.

"Your mother never told you," said Thomas. "She needed help. It was her responsibility to get it and she never did."

Andrew wanted to say that was a no-brainer. "Cause she liked being that way . . ."

"Hear me out, Andy," said Thomas, the odd expression still there. "The way she was with men. Something bad happened when she was a little girl. I'm the only one she ever told. She was ashamed, I think. Your grandfather, her father . . ."

Andrew saw recognition in Dr. Luke's eyes. Like he knew what Thomas was going to say. He wanted to put his hands over his ears and make noise and drown out Thomas' voice.

"She was an incest victim, Andrew. Repeatedly. And, like Dr. Bramson will tell you, when that happens to children they get, well, it messes with their minds, and . . ."

Andrew saw Thomas' mouth moving but he no longer heard the words. He felt dizzy. Sick. "I'm going to the bathroom," he said jumping out of his chair, bumping into Thomas' leg as he moved toward the door. "I won't go anywhere else. I promise."

45

"I have some concerns about that young man, Lydia" said Miss Zenah Elenrude. The office smelled like spicy mint tea and Miss Elenrude inhaled deeply. Over in the corner of the room on a little brown table was the pitcher of tea with mint leaves floating in it.

Dr. Lydia followed her stare and smiled. "I like the smell of freshly cut mint in my office," she said. "Amazing how something so simple can lift one's spirits. Would you care for some, Zenah?"

Miss Elenrude considered it. The truth of the matter was tea always made her bladder overactive. "No," she said. "But it smells divine."

Dr. Hutchinson cleared her throat. "But you were talking about Andrew. Yes. There's certainly conflict bubbling around inside him."

Miss Elenrude ran her fingers through her short hair. "Conflict is one thing, but he seems so, I don't know, so cold to his mother's death. I don't see grief. It worries me."

"Sometimes in adolescents, younger kids too, grief is hard to read," Dr. Hutchinson said.

"I know he could be in shock, but on the other hand, he might have killed her. He hasn't denied it, not to me anyway. It's possible he and his brother are in it together. He acts like he doesn't know where Joey is, but who knows? I've certainly worked with other teens who tried to murder their caretakers. You would have asked any one of them to baby-sit your own children. That's how normal they looked."

"You're right," said Dr. Lydia. "Anything's possible. There's no denying the anger's certainly there. I guess we'll know in time. Luke tells me his wife, Adelaide, has the case."

Miss Elenrude chuckled. "A family affair," she said.

Dr. Hutchinson smiled too. "I can't think of a better team to crack it," she said. "I'm sure among all of us we'll at least figure out whether Andrew had anything to do with it. I'm so glad Andrew's assigned to your caseload, Zenah. And Jerry Lincoln's the minister on call this week, too. So he'll be coming out tomorrow or the next day unless he sends his youth minister. He does that sometimes. James Harraday. Excellent mentor for our children. Young, energetic. They adore him."

"He doesn't like me much."

"Who?"

"Reverend Lincoln."

"Why would you say that?"

Miss Elenrude looked embarrassed. Her lips were drawn into a funny shaped oval. "I trust this will never leave your office," she said. She paused. Swallowed. "About four years ago Jerry and I were working a case together. A lady dying of cancer from his congregation. In her seventies or eighties, probably closer to eighty. Anyway, as we were leaving her daughter's home one night, Jerry's hand brushed my rear end, well actually Lydia, more than brushed against it. I was sure it was intentional. I was taken aback. I waited until we were out of hearing distance from the house and then I let him have it."

Lydia leaned back in her chair, careful not to interrupt.

"He was shocked, of course. Denied any such intention. He went on and on about being devastated that I would accuse him of anything untoward. If he'd bumped me at all it was an accident, he said. He was a man of the cloth. A man of God. How could I even think such a thing? Then he apologized for being angry. He called it a gross misunderstanding. The more I thought about it the more I decided I did misinterpret what happened. I work with so many male clients who disrespect women. I think it just clouded my judgment. It was embarrassing. I ended up apologizing but our relationship hasn't been the same since. It's like we're walking on eggshells, so to speak."

Lydia Hutchinson drummed the fingers of her right hand on her desktop. Her hands were large knuckled and there were raised purple veins tunneling the backs of them. "Hmmmm," she said, fingers still drumming.

Miss Elenrude nodded toward the front window of the office. "There's Addie," she said. "And I have to take off in a minute for DHR. We're holding a treatment plan meeting at six o'clock for three children all under five who are coming into care tonight. The mom's been arrested for crystal meth."

"So unfortunate," said Lydia but she smiled. She was watching Detective Adelaide Bramson approach. Addie's step was full of bounce. She was the perfect life partner for Luke. It was good to see smart young people together. "I know you don't have long, Zenah," she said. "I'm sure

Addie doesn't either. But, let's invite her in. I suspect Luke's still involved with our young Mr. Beaty."

* * *

Addie wiggled her rump backwards and settled into the chair. She felt a stream of air escape from the leather cushion. The chair didn't fit her. Her feet didn't touch the floor.

"Does Luke know you're here?" asked Dr. Lydia.

"He knew I was coming. But actually I'm hoping to catch Shelby when she's free. The receptionist said she's leading group therapy for twenty more minutes, and Luke's still with his intake."

"Yes," said Miss Elenrude. "My new fellow. I believe you spoke with him this morning."

"To the extent he'd talk to me," Addie said.

"Well if it's any consolation I'm in the same boat."

"How's the case going?" asked Dr. Lydia. "Sad situation, that's for certain."

"Murder's always sad," Addie said. "There're lots of possibilities. I think I've got all the suspects lined up, just a matter of ferreting out the one who actually did it."

"You've got our bomb threat case too, don't you?" asked Miss Elenrude.

"Yes. Actually, I was hoping to get your take on that, Zenah."

Miss Elenrude shook her head. "I'm beginning to get paranoid, to tell you the truth. Do you know there weren't any threats the whole time I was on vacation? And then within just days of my returning, here we go again."

Addie's eyes widened. "That's an interesting observation. May not mean a thing, but it's worth thinking about."

"And now my sweet little client, Dana Whitesmythe, has died in that car accident. I'll tell you, that just about broke my heart."

"I'm sure," said Addie. "I was in the DHR lobby when she left your office. Can you shed any light on her situation, Zenah? We're still treating it as accidental. But there're some loose ends, I think. She apparently phoned our department several times recently to report threats from an unidentified male acquaintance."

"I don't know what to think," said Zenah. "You know, the news reported she was pregnant. Well, she'd just been talking to me about that. Her common law husband, the man she's lived with most of the time for years and years, his name is Rayne, isn't the father of any of her other children. We've run DNA tests on all of them. She said he wasn't the father this time, either, and they'd split up again. The split would have been temporary, I'm sure. She told me the father of this baby was the same guy who's fathered all the rest. All I know about him is he's employed, according to her, and he's always pushed her to end her pregnancies. She never has."

"Where are her other children?" asked Addie.

Dr. Lydia and Zenah glanced at one another. Addie caught a smile on Dr. Lydia's lips. There was something they weren't saying. She was obviously out of the loop.

"Parental rights were terminated on them all," said Miss Elenrude. "Dana was able to learn simple parenting skills and I think we did everything we could to help her learn how to safely keep her children. But unfortunately her decision making was always seriously flawed. Rayne's problem solving wasn't any better. Ultimately, the children were put up for adoption and adopted as a sibling group."

Addie glanced at the clock on Dr. Lydia's desk. It was a porcelain clock with pink flowers climbing around a brass clock face. It had been dropped and broken into tiny fragments and painstakingly glued back together again with glue that had yellowed over time. The repair job was far from perfect. There were gaps in the fit and absent porcelain chips all over it. Four minutes until Shelby's group ended. The rest of the loop would have to wait. "Zenah," she said. "Did Ms. Whitesmythe mention who was threatening her?"

Miss Elenrude's eyebrows lowered. Addie liked her eyebrows. They were almost black even though her hair was bottle blond. It made for a unique look. "Yes, actually," said Zenah. "She said it was the father. But she didn't appear to take him seriously. She never did. I cautioned her about that when we talked yesterday."

Addie frowned. "Do you have any ideas at all about who the father might be?"

"No ideas with any substance. I've always had a suspicion, but it's not grounded in any tangible proof, that the father might be the same man I suspect is behind the bomb threats. Mr. Neal Lamphurte. They lived in the same trailer park and knew one another. Dana always seemed, well, smitten by him, for lack of a better term. And he certainly has a temper, and he has a good job as a welder as I'm sure you already know."

"Hmm," said Addie. "You're one of several who suspects Mr. Lamphurte," she said. "But so far his alibis check out, at least as far as the bomb threats. My colleague, R.J., has been working that angle. He's pretty thorough in his investigations. We'll go back and check it out again though. Are you saying you think the bomb threats and Ms. Whitesmythe's most recent pregnancy might be connected?"

Zenah Elenrude shrugged. "I don't know, Addie. It's just a gut feeling. But it might make sense. A way to intimidate her maybe. To keep her away from DHR. I don't know. I might be completely off base. But I'll tell you this for sure, Mr. Neil Lamphurte is a wily man. I'd check and recheck his alibis. He'd be a whiz at covering his tracks."

Addie uncrossed her legs to stand. "Thanks," she said. "I've not met the man at all. But you've suggested a fresh way to look at the situation. Might be about time for Mr. Lamphurte and me to become acquainted."

"Addie," said Dr. Hutchinson. "You're not slipping out of here without some green mint tea, are you?"

"Thanks," said Addie. "Next time, when there's more time to visit."

"I'm on my way, too," said Miss Elenrude. "Lydia, would you mind sending word to Andrew that I'll drop by to see him sometime late tomorrow afternoon, just to see how he's settling in?"

"Happy to. I hope he's still here tomorrow. The only thing keeping him here this very moment is his relationship with Mr. Chalot. We'll see how well that sticks as the night wears on."

"I have a feeling you're spot on," said Zenah Elenrude.

"He'd better stay put," said Addie. "He's still got a lot of explaining to do."

*   *   *

She moved a silk-screened throw pillow that read *Life is a two way street. You can u-turn* and sat down. She laid the pillow in her lap and let her fingers run back and forth across the fabric's weave. "Thanks for sparing a few minutes, Shelby," she said. "I know you and Luke are swamped."

Shelby closed her office door, exposing a poster entitled **RESPONSIBILITY** and sat across from her. "Luke tells me you're the one who's swamped right now, Addie."

Addie reached into her purse and dug out her bag of Animal Crackers. The broken charm bracelet she'd found underneath Dr. Greene's couch came out with it. "Poor woman," she said dropping the bracelet back in. She held the cookies out toward Shelby.

"No thanks."

Addie fished out a zebra and a gorilla. "It is a pretty crazy group of cases I have right now," she said turning the cookies over in her hand. The gorilla looked like it was smiling. "But I guess none of us will ever complain about our jobs being humdrum." She popped the creature into her mouth and chomped. Her finger ran along a ceramic picture frame painted with little roses and hearts as she chewed. It was a photograph of Molly taken at Easter. She was sitting in the lap of a white buck-toothed Easter bunny at some mall kiosk. "This is so cute," she said.

"Thanks," said Shelby. "She's growing up fast."

"I was just thinking that," said Addie. "Gosh, Shelby, she sure does have your eyes." Sometimes late at night when her mind was finally relaxed and Miss Agatha was purring on her chest, she'd lie with her eyes open listening to Luke's soft, regular snoring, wondering whom their children would resemble. "She's beautiful."

Shelby knew it. "Thanks."

Addie cleared her throat and pulled out her recorder. "I appreciate your call yesterday about Dr. Beaty and your concerns about Bob Tulane," she said. "Could you go over it one more time for me, filling in any details as they come to you? I'll be recording it just to help keep my facts straight."

"Yes. Of course." Shelby briefly closed her eyes as though this helped formulate her thoughts. "Like I explained yesterday, Addie, I was walking Dr. Beaty out to her car. We were talking about Andrew and the program, you know, the typical stuff we do for new parents. But then she suddenly stopped in her tracks when she saw him, Mr. Tulane, and I think she said, 'Damn.' Anyway, she wasn't happy to see him and she made that very clear to him. I gathered from what they said to each other that she'd told him not to come to Metamorphosis but he kept saying something about feeling like he had to protect her."

"Did he say from whom?"

"It was a little confusing. Seemed like there were two guys, he had a pretty bizarre name for one. I think he called him Mr. Angry Dad."

Larry Ryan. Almost for sure. What on earth was his part in all this? "Hmmm," she said, studying the zebra. There were little wavy indentions to make its mane. "Can you remember more details?"

"Um, no. Not really. It was all sort of vague. But the guy they were really arguing about was somebody else. Mr. Tulane kept saying *that* man would stalk her. He wanted to follow her home, make sure she was safe. He said something about her giving him, Mr. Tulane I mean, quite a scare earlier."

"And she didn't want him following her?"

"Not at all. She basically accused *him* of being the stalker. She was getting angry, I heard it in her voice, but he kept on and kept on, reminding her of some incident that happened earlier in the day. It sounded like Mr. Tulane was involved in her rescue somehow."

Bob Tulane certainly wanted to be seen as the rescuer, he'd made that clear enough. She bit down on the zebra's haunches. "Did you get the sense Dr. Beaty and Bob Tulane were romantically involved?"

"I don't know. Maybe. He was sure invested in her. But she was dismissive of him. And she was in a hurry to leave. I overheard her tell him she had a meeting with the man Red. That's the man she claimed in our meeting is Andrew's father."

"Yes," said Addie letting her mouth engulf the zebra's head. "So what eventually happened?"

"She got in her car and left. Oh, first she took off one of her shoes. She was, um, limping a little bit I think. And she was maybe holding her rib cage a little funny with her arm. I don't know, maybe not but it looked like it. Then he got in his car and followed her out. But she didn't seem scared of him at all. In fact, she didn't seem scared of any of them. And she seemed totally unimpressed with Mr. Tulane's belief that she was in danger."

"Hmmm," Addie said again. "Danger perhaps because of Bob Tulane, himself."

"He did seem controlling, Addie. Looking back, he probably *was* stalking her."

"Well we know he followed her home at some point because he claims to have found her body."

303

Shelby's shoulders slumped. She stared into her lap. "I feel like I missed it, Addie," she said quietly. "I should have reported his behaviors right away. If I had, she'd probably still be alive. But she said he wasn't a problem, that he was a friend, and like I said, she didn't seem intimidated by him in the least."

Addie collected her recorder and purse, stood, put the pillow back on the chair and grasped the doorknob. They both stared at the pillow. Its message seemed trivial and false. There was no U-turning for Dr. Beaty. Murder was one way. "What is it you mental health folks call it? Client self- determination? It sounds like she didn't want your help. Anyway, Mr. Tulane may have nothing to do with her death, Shelby. We'll just have to let it all play out."

Shelby appeared unconvinced. "I know," she said.

"Thanks. I appreciate your time."

"Were you wanting to see Luke?"

"We did hope to catch a few seconds together."

Shelby picked up her phone. "Last I heard he was sitting in front of the cool-down room talking to somebody," she said as she dialed. "I'll check. Hi, Ms. Moffiti? It's Shelby. Is Luke around?" Addie watched Shelby's forehead wrinkle as she listened. "O.K. Thanks. Well," she said putting the phone back on the receiver, "Andrew's apparently the one in cool-down. Says he's leaving to go search for his brother. Luke's working with him and Mr. Chalot's in the classroom waiting to go with them to the cottage to help settle him in."

Addie absorbed the information. Search for Joey or go meet him? She poked her lips out in disappointment. "I guess I'll go on then," she said. "Luke'll be tied up for awhile."

"Most likely," said Shelby.

"Say hi to Molly." She turned and headed down the hall toward the front door.

Seeing him walk into the building caught her totally off guard. He glanced sheepishly in her direction, raised his left hand slightly from his side and waved, his hand jutting out at a ninety degree angle. He stepped quickly into Dr. Hutchinson's outer office before she could respond. Larry Ryan. She couldn't wait to ask him. What on earth was his connection to Metamorphosis?

46

"Hello?" Addie said.

"R. J. here. Just checking in."

"Hey, R.J. Got anything?" Addie maneuvered her car into the grocery store parking lot. She parked so her car faced away from traffic. There were wild flowers in the field beyond the asphalt. Black eyed Susans and small wild sunflowers, or were they coreopsis, she wasn't sure, and a purple flowered plant she'd never identified. The Queen Anne's lace was still green. It'd be white in a week or so.

"I visited a neighbor of Ms. Whitesmythe, her name's Flora. It was Flora's car that Ms. Whitesmythe was driving. She said the deceased hadn't been living at the trailer park for a while, apparently Ms. Whitesmythe and her boyfriend broke up. She said they split up and got back together a lot. A Mr. Rayne McNeeley, that's the guy's name. I'm running a background on him."

"I learned that today, too. She apparently was staying with her sister."

"Anyway, this Flora woman did say Ms. Whitesmythe cleans, ah, cleaned houses on the side."

Addie's eyes widened. "That might be helpful. Can we get a list of her customers?"

"Don't know. Most of them apparently paid cash under the table, so it'll take some sleuthing. But Flora knew two by name. I'm hoping they can supply the names of others."

"Any luck finding a yellow jacket nest?"

"None. Still looks like a freak accident to me."

"Probably. But the threats she reported and the fact she was pregnant still bug me."

"Me too. I hate coincidences. You never know when to leave them alone."

Addie cleared her throat. It was true. Sometimes coincidences were just that. Life was full of them. "R.J., I talked to Ms. Whitesmythe's social worker today. Zenah Elenrude. She suspects Neil Lamphurte is the biological father of Dana Whitesmythe's children and that he's behind the bomb threats, too. Larry Ryan still thinks Lamphurte's behind the

305

bomb threats. I know you've found his alibis credible, but do you mind going over them one more time? See if you can find anything that doesn't jive. Apparently Lamphurte's a clever fellow. Might try to throw you off track."

R.J. didn't answer immediately. Addie sensed his frustration but knew he'd never voice it. He'd checked out Lamphurte twice already. "Yeah, o.k.," he said finally. "Third time's the charm."

"Thanks," she said. "Oh, and another coincidence for you. Zenah Elenrude says the bomb threats stopped the whole time she was on vacation."

"Hmm. That might be relevant." Addie imagined him adding the information to his electronic notebook. "I was able to get some interesting stuff on Bob Tulane," he finally said. "Apparently his fiancée, the one who disappeared from Lamar County, isn't really missing. She eventually turned up in the Vegas area. Took her mother's maiden name as I understand it. Ashby. Sheila Ashby. Has some kind of performance art going on there. Free spirit type I'm guessing. I've been trying to locate her by phone. Get her take on him. Find out what happened between them."

Addie's jaw dropped. "You're kidding." So Sheila G. Woodcock, AKA Sheila Ashby, wasn't dead after all. And Bob Tulane obviously had no idea she'd reappeared on the other side of the continent. "Amazing," she said. It changed things. Still, it didn't clear him of bashing Dr. Beaty's head in.

R.J. paused. "Um, there's another peculiar development in this case, Addie," he said. "Seems the Department got a call today from one of the teachers at Dr. Beaty's school. A Mrs. June Allencot. She doubted any relevance but stated that on the day of Dr. Beaty's murder she was in the vicinity of the school office and overheard three staff discussing their dislike of Dr. Beaty and talking about murder."

"Talking how about murder?"

"Mrs. Allencot couldn't remember their exact words, she said she was actually in the hallway when she overheard them, she'd apparently just left the office, but she said they were laughing and talking about Dr. Beaty and murder. Said she didn't think anything of it at the time because those women gossip and are catty. Her words. But in light of what happened she wanted to let us know."

"Sounds unlikely. But all three were pretty clear with me that Dr. Beaty wouldn't win their boss of the year award."

Another pause. Addie imagined him typing notes on his keypad. "I checked on Dr. Greene," he said after several minutes. "No priors or complaints on record. His office staff denies knowledge of any domestic violence in his private life. They claim he's pretty even keel at work."

"Hmmm," said Addie. She was unconvinced. The bruising on Priscilla Beaty prior to the time of death, the broken charm bracelet under his couch, the flowers and apology note, the frequent phoning. All of it pointed to a batterer. "I'm not ready to give Harry Greene a clean bill of health," she said.

"I'll keep working on it."

Addie curled her toes and felt the stretch in her calves. "Well," she said. "Andrew's at Metamorphosis now but I don't expect to find him there in the morning. He'll run, I'm sure of it. Any word on Joey?"

"Nada."

She remembered Andrew and the park and her hunch. "R.J., was there a description of the guy who met in the park with our friend, Tony, yesterday?"

Pause. He was scrolling through the notes on his tablet. She was sure of it. "Yes," he said after several minutes. "Tall, thin. The distinguishing descriptor was long green hair, braided maybe."

She had him pegged. "Andrew Beaty," she said. "Pre-Mormon missionary disguise."

"Shit, that's not good."

"My thoughts exactly. Hopefully he didn't avail himself of Tony's murder for hire endeavor."

"Tony didn't stray much from home today according to reports. Yesterday afternoon he had a meeting at CHANGE and from there ended up at one of the local churches doing yard work."

Addie shook her head. "Wish change were that simple," she said. "That it?"

"One more thing. Forensics confirms the Beaty murder weapon was a hammer. Possibly from her home. They found metal zipper parts in the oven, too. Burned clothing apparently. Not sure of the significance of that yet. I went by there this afternoon. Couldn't find a hammer in the obvious places so maybe it was the one in the oven. Problem is, there're thousands of hammer heads just like it."

She figured so. "O.K. Good day's work, R.J. Why don't you call it a night? I'm off to interview Larry Ryan and then I'm done myself."

"Don't mind if I do. I'm totally bushed," he said. "Buenos noches, Señora."

"Adiós, Señor. Hasta mañana." She smiled. He knew she was working on her Spanish. "Bright and early."

47

His living room resembled a hybrid man cave, day care center. Overstuffed brown furniture, microsuede fabric, anchored the room. Addie was swallowed up comfortably by an armchair and Larry Ryan sat beside Leah, Leah of Heavenly Feet, on the couch. They were holding hands although it appeared to Addie a little awkwardly. Larry was sitting back deep in the cushions with his arm resting on a pillow between them. Leah sat on the edge of the couch, feet squarely on the floor, with her hand twisted backward entwined in his. Her presence at the house caught Addie totally by surprise.

Leah was probably no more than five feet tall with angular features and hair that cascaded down her back like category five rapids. The rapids. Both she and Luke loved white water and it'd been so long since they'd been. She'd book a cabin up near the Ocoee, raft the river by day, lock the bears out by night, as soon as this investigation ended. She watched Leah wriggle her fingers deeper into Larry's interlocking ones. Leah's nails were meticulously shaped, painted silver and accented in a shade of midnight blue.

Addie had to ring the doorbell twice when she first arrived. And then it wasn't Larry who answered the door. She'd introduced herself as Leah, Dr. Beaty's nail professional and Larry's girlfriend. The children were out getting pizza with their sitter and the sitter's teenage daughters, she'd said. She and Larry wanted to have an adult conversation with her without being interrupted. She bent over to pick up a handful of stray plastic building blocks near the coffee table and her hair fell like Niagara Falls toward the floor. Have a seat, she'd said. Larry'd just gotten home and was changing into something more comfortable. Wasn't it an awful thing about Dr. Beaty? Such an intelligent woman. And she loved to look her best. Rarely ever missed a nail appointment and always wanted both her fingernails and toenails done. In fact, she'd just been telling Larry that on the day Dr. Beaty was murdered something seemed odd. Yes, Dr. Beaty called after lunch and cancelled her appointment for the day. The receptionist said she sounded strange. Stressed, maybe. Vague. Didn't even try to reschedule. And that was the oddest thing of all.

She was about to ask Leah if there were anything else unusual about the call when Larry had walked into the room dressed in cargo pants and a striped pullover. He appeared intent on Leah's words as he joined her on the couch. Addie noted that Leah's fingers found his immediately. A nonverbal statement of solidarity. The receptionist said it sounded like Dr. Beaty was driving when she called, Leah continued. The number showed up on caller ID as her mobile phone.

Larry reached toward the coffee table with his free hand and picked up a stuffed animal, a Halloween-orange orangutan. He put it in his lap. "Welcome to my castle, Addie," he said. "I know you're wondering, I could see it in your face when you ran into me at Metamorphosis, what was I doing there?"

Addie smiled. "It did whet my curiosity."

"I needed to talk to my mama," he said, combing the orangutan's hair with his index and middle fingers.

"Your mama?"

"Dr. Lydia. Dr. Hutchinson. You know. I'm sure I told you back when I was on the force that I grew up out there at her place."

Addie pushed deeper into the cushions. What a crazy, crazy day. "No. No, Larry, I had no idea. I don't remember ever hearing that before."

He didn't really appear surprised. "Yep," he said. "I went there when I was eight years and fifty three days old. I used to keep track of it like that when I was a kid. I left when I joined the service. My parents were, well, not available to raise me. I had a pretty tough time of it for a while. I had a temper, well, I still have it, but I learned from Dr. Lydia how to manage it."

Addie knew she was staring. She tried to envision Larry as an angry, institutionalized eight year old.

"I don't really advertise all that," he said. "It's quite frankly nobody's business. We all have childhoods. One way or another, we grow up."

"True," said Leah, wiggling her fingers free, moving her hand to his arm. Addie watched her massage his wrist gently, reassuringly.

"Anyway," he said. "I went to see Dr. Lydia because I just didn't know where else to go. I've been so upset by Dana's death. I needed to get some things off my chest. But I didn't expect Miss Elenrude to be there. I didn't expect you to be there either."

"Tell me about Dana," Addie said. "Ms. Whitesmythe." Most of the time she preferred using surnames. It was more professional.

He searched Leah's eyes. They were passing information back and forth. Secrets. Decisions. Addie waited. Thirty seconds. Maybe forty five. Still he paused. Leah nodded subtly. Larry nodded back. Subtly. He turned his body on the couch to more squarely face Addie. "Well, I may as well tell you everything," he finally said. "It's not that I mind you knowing, Addie. It's just, well, I don't talk about it much."

"Okay," said Addie glancing at the recorder she'd set up on the coffee table.

Larry Ryan glanced toward it, too. "You see," he said, "Dana's the biological mother of all of my children. And Miss Elenrude's been involved, of course. She was Dana's worker. I adopted the whole sibling group. That's the way they try to do things at DHR nowadays, keep the family as intact as possible."

Addie looked at Larry in wonderment. She'd never considered that he was an adoptive father. Adoptive single fathers were actually still pretty rare in Alabama. And to adopt a sibling group with so many little children. "I never knew," she said, her voice trailing off. "I mean, I guess I always assumed your relationship with their mother just didn't work out somehow or another."

"Right," said Larry. "I think that's what everybody assumes. And, that's okay, of course. The children have the right to grow up as normally as possible." He brushed his index finger against his right eyelid. His eyes were watering. "But that'll be a lot harder now. Now that their mama's dead."

Addie cleared her throat. She hoped Larry wouldn't lose it in front of her. It'd feel awkward. "So do they know Ms. Whitesmythe was their mother?" she asked.

His hand moved from his face to his scalp. His hair parted against the sides of his fingers. "No," he said. "We agreed to wait until the youngest reached eighteen before telling them. But they did know her. She was our cleaning lady. It was actually Miss Elenrude who came up with that idea. A way for Dana to get to know the children, watch them grow, all of that, without giving them the kind of information that might confuse them. At least I got pictures of her with them, with all of them together."

"I had no idea." It was a situation not too unlike Andrew's. All of them growing up with no idea of their birth parents' identities. Like picture frames with nothing in them. "Where are the biological fathers of your children?" she asked.

He shrugged. His shoulders were massive. He clearly still worked out. When he was on the force he kept a Russian kettle bell in his locker. "Dana always claimed one man fathered them all," he said. "Parental rights were terminated when he or they didn't come forward to claim them. And Dana never named names. You know, in these types of situations sometimes the mother doesn't even have a clue. Not for sure. Not without testing."

"I'm sorry," said Addie. "I'm sorry for your children's loss."

"I'll miss her, too," he said. "She was special in her own way. Rough around the edges for sure, but as good hearted as they come."

"She was sweet," Leah added. "And she had a lot more sense than most people gave her credit for." She leaned sideways and rested her head on Larry's bicep. It was a movement of comfortable familiarity. They'd obviously been a couple a while.

"I understand she cleaned for other people, too," said Addie. "Do you happen to know who they were?"

"A few she talked about," he said. "I can give you three or four names. And a bank and several doctors' offices. A couple of churches, too. And occasionally she mentioned cleaning new homes for a realty company. Leah and I'll jot down the names we remember."

"Good," said Addie. "That'll help."

"So you're suspecting foul play?" asked Larry.

"No. Not really. It's ruled accidental so far. But I'm curious to hear what you think."

He moved his hand back to the orangutan. Black yarn stitched into a comical grin. Brown felt eyelashes. "I don't know," he said. "She had an insect phobia, you know. Bees and such. I mean, if one was even in the same county she'd freak. If some showed up in her car . . ."

"She was afraid of bees?"

"And hornets, wasps, anything else that remotely looked like them. Dirt daubers, dragonflies, you name it. It didn't help to tell her things like dragonflies are harmless. She just couldn't deal with any of them." He smiled softly. "I remember her running out of this very room screaming at the top of her lungs one morning when she saw one of those carpenter bees, you know the ones that drill holes in wood, flying all around the ceiling. I had to chase it out the window with a broom before she'd come back in."

"Was she allergic to their stings?"

Larry paused, obviously pondering the question. "She never said she was. Just phobic."

Leah shifted positions, winding her right foot under her body and stretching her left foot outward toward the floor. Like a cat. Addie wondered if Luke were home, and if he'd fed Agatha kitty. It was past Agatha's dinner time. She'd be pacing on the countertop. "She was such a nice person," Leah said sadly. "And how she loved her children!"

Larry lowered his head. "So that's why I went to see Dr. Lydia. She's the world's expert on loss, in my opinion. I just didn't know what else to do."

"I understand," said Addie. The three sat in silence, Addie mulling over the information she'd been given, including the presence of Leah. There were times, she'd encountered them before, when random informational bits got sucked up together to create new dimensions of reality. She'd worked on the force with Larry for five years before he quit to take the security job. Reliable, responsible, steady. It was difficult to imagine him as troubled and living at Metamorphosis, growing up to adopt the children of Ms. Dana Whitesmythe. And how did he get involved with that specific sibling group? Unless maybe he was secretly the biological father of the children. He obviously kept a treasure trove of secrets. Why else would he adopt five? Most single fathers would opt for one, maybe two. She glanced at a photograph of Larry and all five children taken somewhere at a lake, framed in plastic molded to look like wood. It was sitting on the table beside her. The oldest boy and the little girl did look remarkably like him. "They're beautiful children," she said.

"Yes," said Leah.

"Thank you," said Larry.

So Ms. Whitesmythe had a stinging insect phobia. A fear, anyway, from Larry's description. "Larry," Addie said finally. "What do you make of Miss Elenrude's observation to me today that there were no bomb threats whatsoever while she was away on vacation, and that they resumed upon her return?"

His eyes shifted. Cop eyes. Security guard eyes. "Funny," he said. "I hadn't put that together but she's right, you know. May not mean anything at all. But what if someone has it in for Miss Zenah herself? Or maybe she's working a case that's hitting a raw nerve in somebody. I don't know. Does she feel in danger?"

"Not really. But she's noticed it. Like you say, it may mean nothing."

Larry stood, went into the kitchen, got three mugs from brass hooks hanging under the cabinet. "Leah's made some decaf," he said sticking his head around the refrigerator. "Fresh right before you got here. Can I pour you a cup?"

Normally she wouldn't. It made investigations less complicated to keep things cut and dried, clear boundaries. Business only. But Larry was different. "Be great," she said. "Just a little milk. You can add it."

"Leah?"

"Sure, honey, since you're pouring."

He returned with the three mugs, two in one hand, index and middle fingers looped through the handles and balanced against his thumb and baby finger. He handed Addie a mug with John Deere tractor logo on it.

She inhaled slowly. The smell was the best part. It always soothed her. It smelled good even before the bitter taste became delicious, back when she was helping her father in his office, sorting paper clips. "We need to shift gears," she said. "There may be other questions about Ms. Whitesmythe and the bomb threats later, but there're some questions that need to be asked about Dr. Priscilla Beaty."

"Yes," said Larry, holding his mug only inches from his lips. The mug was blue ceramic and Alabama Post Adoption Center was printed boldly across it in cream colored lettering. "But to be honest, Addie, there's not much you don't already know about my relationship with her. I hated her for picking on my kids. I think she picked on them as a way to needle me. Sounds crazy, but that's the way I feel. You know I wanted her gone, and to be honest I didn't really care how. Fired. Dead. Incapacitated. Promoted to another school zone. I didn't care. Just as long as she disappeared from my kids' lives."

Dead. Disappeared. It was a poor choice of words. Assigning R.J. to this interview would have been smart. She'd considered it but minimized the conflict she thought she'd feel. She pressed on. "I know she's gotten on your nerves for a long time, Larry. I remember how angry you'd get at her when you were on the force." She studied his face. A few deep lines across his forehead. Honest eyes. He'd always had honest eyes. "And I saw your anger again the other day when we were at DHR."

"Yes." He was sitting erect. Coffee mug down in his lap now, his thumb rubbing back and forth against the handle. Eyes leveled on hers, steady, unguarded. "And you know I left DHR to go back to the school to confront her again."

"That's right."

"But I didn't get the chance. Just my luck, she got in a car with some man. He was in a crimson colored BMW. Crimson and white, actually. White trim. He was obviously on to me. He kept staring at me, sending me the message to get lost."

"Right," said Addie. "I've spoken to him. And what did you do?"

"I got sick of waiting for her to get back out. Pissed me off, giving up more work time, having to ask for special favors like that from my supervisor, just to drive around a parking lot waiting for my chance to tell her what I thought of her bullying little children. But it became evident she was staying put. So I left."

"And where'd you go?"

Larry put his coffee mug on a plastic coaster. "I took off driving," he said. "Out past Lake Tuscaloosa spillway, past Lake Nichols, turned off onto the Lake Harris road. Drove all the way down to the water. Car's still got red clay on the bumpers. The rims, too."

"Can anybody corroborate that?"

"I called Leah from around Lake Nichols, told her I was driving around until I calmed down, but no, not really. There were some kids out at Lake Harris. Young couple. Drove up on them kissing. They had a black lab. They were driving one of those little VW bugs, an electric green one as I recall. Obviously they weren't real happy to have me there chaperoning. I watched them throw sticks in the lake for their dog for a few minutes and then took off. Headed out further, toward Holt Lock and Dam but I knew it was time to get home to the kids. Turned around probably about two miles from the dam and headed back."

It was a pretty drive. She and Luke hiked those areas often. The University ski team used Lake Harris to practice. There was a ski jump there, a wooden structure jutting up out of the water.

"So you got home when?"

Larry looked at Leah. She stared at him blankly. "A little before seven thirty," he said. "The clock on the oven said seven twenty eight when I handed the sitter the money."

"I'll need her contact information to verify that."

"Of course," said Larry smoothly. "Then Leah came over around eight thirty. She stayed until after the ten o'clock news. That's when we heard, that's when we learned about both of them. To be honest, I didn't pay much attention to what all they said about Dr. Beaty. When I heard about Dana . . ."

"Yes," said Addie softly. She moved the mug to her lips, drank about half the cup. The coffee was lukewarm. She'd let it sit too long. Coffee tasted like dishwater when it was lukewarm. And the good smell, gone too. She put her cup on the side table.

"I planned to talk to Dr. Beaty the next morning, you know. I'd already decided to be late for work again. And that pissed me off, too. Putting my own job in jeopardy because she couldn't do hers. I mean, I'm sorry she's dead, Addie. I'm sorry for her sons. But, I won't lose any sleep over her murder."

"And," Addie said again. "No one can account for your whereabouts between the hours of five and seven? Except for that unidentified kissing couple with the dog, I mean?"

"That's right," said Larry. "And that makes me a suspect with motive and opportunity. And I certainly have means."

"Larry!" Leah exclaimed.

"I'm afraid Larry knows his police work," said Addie. "He indeed is a suspect with both motive and opportunity. And I assume he refers to his gun as means."

"Don't be asinine!" Leah swung her foot from under her, jumped up, and moved closer to Addie to make her point. "Larry would never . . . You know him well enough . . . I mean, we joked about ways to get rid of her all the time, but he loves his kids too much to ever do anything stupid."

Addie stood. It was curious, she reflected, that she came to interview one suspect and ended up finding two. "I know this is difficult," she said evenly. "But Larry, I'm sure you understand my position." She wanted him to have a rock solid alibi. He had no alibi at all.

"Of course, Addie," he said, standing to face her. He was smiling. But not a happy smile. Not the smile of a friend. More a smile of irony. "I certainly do."

Addie returned her attention to the framed photograph. Children attached to his arms, sitting on his knees, sitting cross legged at his feet. They were in their bathing suits. The boys all with skinny untanned chests and the little girl missing two front teeth and wearing heart shaped pink sun glasses. "How did you come to adopt your children?" she asked.

"I had reasons to adopt," he said, "as I'm sure you can understand. I found my family through a DHR adoption fair. It was at the Tuscaloosa Public Library. When I saw their photographs, they were posted on a sort of room divider surrounded by photos of lots of other kids, and when I read their little interviews, I just knew . . . Sort of like falling in love, I guess." He glanced, Addie thought somewhat shyly, toward Leah. Leah walked over, took his hand. Big short-cropped fingernails and dainty ones of midnight blue and silver. "Anyway, the very next day I went during my morning break to sign up for the adoption training classes." He smiled at the photo. "And, I praise God everyday for them. Once I met them in person, I never looked back."

Sweet story. He was, Addie felt certain, absolutely certain, a good man. But she'd learned being a cop, had it rubbed in her face at times, that good men, even cops and ex-cops, misstepped. She was anxious to hear the story of how he met Leah. A pedicure? She coughed to stifle a chuckle. Leah was dainty and well-groomed and would clearly protect Larry with the tenacity of a Chihuahua. She'd learned over the years to be wary of those little dogs. Better to be met at the door by a German shepherd or a Rottweiler than by a feisty little Chihuahua who yipped and yapped and sank needle sharp teeth into her ankles.

"Leah, I need to ask you as well," she said. "Where were you between five and seven on the night of the murder?"

Leah's mouth dropped open but she didn't truly look surprised. It was more a kind of sassiness. "You've got to be kidding me. You don't actually think I . . ."

"It's a routine question. Where were you between five and seven that evening?"

Leah glanced quickly at Larry. Addie caught his subtle encouraging nod. Leah rolled her eyes and turned back toward Addie. "Well, let's see," she said. "I left work around four thirty that day I think. Had to make the Heavenly Feet bank deposit. It's actually the Alabama Credit Union where we bank, so I went to the branch over on New Watermelon Road. Then I went to the grocery store across the street since I was in the neighborhood. Bought some cat food for my three cats and then headed to the Mary Ann Phelps Activity Center, you know, the one overlooking the lake, where I take Pilates twice a week at five. Only I'd forgotten the class was cancelled that night. So I drove home, took a shower, unwound and then, like Larry told you, I came over here."

"Can anyone confirm your movements?"

Leah rolled her eyes again. "Yeah. My cats." She put her hands on her hips and took a step back. "I understand you have a job to do, Detective Bramson, but this is bordering on absurd. I'll tell you right now that I didn't particularly like Dr. Beaty. She was egocentric and arrogant and I hated the way she treated Larry's children. Not only his children, either. There were others. But even if I'd wanted to kill her, how could I do it? She was taller by almost a head and outweighed me by at least thirty pounds, maybe more."

The size differential was accurate but Addie knew, and she was certain Leah knew, there were other factors to stir into the mix. Like passion. Leah certainly had the spitfire personality. And the element of surprise. Dr. Beaty wouldn't be guarded around her. And what better motive than protecting her man and his family? She cocked her head to one side. "Did Dr. Beaty realize you didn't like her? Did she know about your relationship with Larry?"

Leah laughed condescendingly. "You *are* kidding . . . right?" she asked. "Not hardly. And she was so egotistical it was easy to hide things from her. She'd go on and on about her stressful day this and her stressful day that and about a difficult parent who had difficult children and I knew she was talking about Larry but I never let on. I just said, uh-huh and um-hum every so often and she went on and on and on. And I'd listen and then," she stopped herself and smiled sideways toward Larry.

Addie caught the look of warning he flashed. "And then what?" she asked.

Leah jutted her chin forward and laughed again. The same laugh. "And then I came over here at night and engaged in creative fantasies with Larry once the children were safe in their rooms asleep."

Addie wondered. Adults always said, always assumed, the children were sleeping. But she'd learned from Luke that children's ears frequently worked overtime. "Fantasies like what?" she asked.

Leah's hands were down off her hips now but there was still a real cockiness to her stance. "Like looking up poisons we could slip into the nail polishes I used on her nails. The Internet's great for that kind of thing. We found one chemical agent," she said, looking at Larry as if she needed coaxing.

"It's not important," he said.

"Yes it is. We did it, looked it up I mean, why not tell her? We didn't poison her so what the hell difference does it make? It was four letters, DSMO, I think. It'd go right through her nails, right through her skin. So then we researched different poisons that would dissolve in the polishes with the DSMO so she'd never be the wiser. A garlic-like smell, that's all she'd notice, and I could cover that with her obnoxious rose perfume, and slowly over time she'd die. No one would ever figure it out."

Addie cleared her throat, afraid to look at Larry. She was weary. Ready to go home. It wasn't a crime to indulge in fantasy. It was a crime to plot murder. Where did Leah draw the line? Where did Larry?

Leah's haughty laugh again. "What are you thinking?" she asked too loudly. "I told you it was all fantasy."

Addie glanced at her watch. She was way past fatigued. And there was too much to digest. She moved toward the door. She reached out to shake Larry's hand. Then Leah's. "Thanks for your time," she said. Larry's hand was cold and his skin was rough. It wasn't cold in the house. "You'll both be around if I need to question you further?"

Larry nodded. Leah smiled her sassy smile. "If you're looking for me, come to Heavenly Feet. I'll shape those nails and work on your cuticles while we talk. Your feet, too."

"Thanks," she said switching off her recorder. Not an iceberg's chance in hell. Poisoned pedicures did not appeal.

48

The door wasn't locked. She pressed her thumb against the handle and pushed it open. The house smelled good. Not just one smell, lots of mingling smells, some type of meat, chicken probably, and broccoli maybe and definitely vanilla candles. "I'm home," she called, placing her right hand against the wall while she kicked off her shoes.

"In here," Luke answered from the back of the house.

"Where?"

"Come find me."

The hall carpet rose up between her toes. Chopin was playing on the Bose. "I'm so exhausted," she said as she walked toward the bedroom. "What a totally insane day."

He was dressed in blue jogging pants and a tee shirt that said Niagara Falls. They'd gone to the Falls two years ago when he presented at a psychology convention near Buffalo. Hyperactivity in Children, Symptoms with Multiple Etiologies, or something like that. The shirt had a half rainbow arching over his chest starting at his pectoral muscle, falling across his abs.

The scent of vanilla rose from four candles Luke had placed on the dressers and a bookcase. He'd spread their camping blanket across their bed. Massage oils were lined up beside one of the candles. "Massage before dinner, Madame?" he asked in a bad foreign accent as he bowed deeply at the waist.

She giggled. "Crazy day and crazier husband," she said unbuttoning her blouse and wiggling out of it. She let it fall to the floor, unbuttoned and unzipped her pants and let them fall as well.

"Does Madame wish to remove her bra?" he asked, warming his hands and a small bottle of oil above one of the flames.

She reached back between her scapulas, fingers on the hooks and eyes. Just a simple white lace bra. It loosened, joined her other clothes on the floor. Extravagant imported black lace. Blood splatters. Stop. Cut it off. No work thoughts in the bedroom.

"Oooh-la-la," he said in an accent even worse than the first. "Madame is more bee-uu-te-ful today than on the day of her marr-igge."

"That'll earn you some points in heaven," she laughed. She climbed into bed on her knees, stretched across the blanket stomach down and rested her head on her pillow. Her eyes shut. Luke's warm, strong hands pressed against her shoulder blades, along her spine, working the light scent of peppermint oil into the pores of her skin, deep into every muscle of her body.

49

When he was a young therapist protracted silence had been the hardest. It took discipline and confidence to be with someone in silence, to sit casually and patiently while still conveying an invitation to speak.

Andrew's head rested sideways, cushioned by his forearms, on the other side of Dr. Luke's desk. Five yawns, six. Obviously he'd had a restless night. No reports of problems logged onto the computer this morning by overnight staff, though. And he hadn't run. At least not yet. Ten minutes. Fifteen. Another yawn. This time Andrew covered his mouth and sat up. "Sorry," he said. "I didn't sleep so well last night."

"It can be hard to sleep in a new place," Dr. Luke said. "Not to mention the major stressors currently in your life."

Andrew made eye contact. He toyed with telling him. It was about that Birthday Benjamin kid. Maybe it was two thirty, maybe closer to three. He was asleep. Dreaming about Bethy. They were at Lake Lurleen and she was in her bathing suit, a turquoise one, and she bent forward to scoop water in cupped palms to splash him, and she was laughing and motioning for him to join her but he was just standing there looking at her ass and thinking it was beautiful and wanting to tell her but knowing he wouldn't. She reached out and grabbed his arm, jerked it playfully, and his body followed. And then her lips touched his and they were kissing, lightly at first then urgently with passion. But it was Benjamin. Shaking him. Pulling his arm. And he had his big hand pressed tight across Andrew's mouth. "Shhhh," he whispered, waiting until Andrew opened his eyes before he removed his hand. "We're sneaking out. Meeting the girls. There's this girl, Esmeralda, she's got the hots for you. Get up. Be quiet."

"No, man," he said before he'd even completely regained his bearings. "Not interested. Remember? I've got a girl already."

"Esme said to bring you," whispered Benjamin a little more harshly.

"Not interested." Andrew rolled onto his side. He stared at the wall. There was a sharp punch to his shoulder blade.

"You some kind of damn psycho or what?" Louder whispering, angrier.

Andrew didn't move. "Hit me again," he threatened.

"Shhh. They'll hear."

"Get lost," Andrew said more quietly.

"Esme's gonna be really pissed."

He'd shut his eyes. Esmeralda was the snake girl. Not too great looking but any girl who liked snakes had to be okay. "Tell her, nothing personal." He waited several minutes. Nothing more. He rolled over, opened his eyes. His room was empty. He'd had a hard time sleeping after that.

He yawned again. "Thomas hasn't called has he?" he asked Dr. Luke.

"No, not yet."

He expelled air through his nose. Where the hell was Joey?

Dr. Luke cleared his throat and sat straighter in his chair. "Andrew, I want to make clear the limits of confidentiality again so everything will stay on the up and up."

Andrew shrugged.

"I want to make sure you understand that if you tell me you were involved in your mother's murder, or if you give me information indicating the guilt of someone else, I will report that to authorities."

"You mean your wife."

Dr. Luke smiled. "Sort of weird, I know, but yes, you're right."

Andrew stared him straight in the eye. "And if I tell you I did kill her, what'll happen to me?"

Calm eyes. Calm body language. What did it mean? "I don't know," Dr. Luke answered. "It'd be up to the judge. Maybe you'd stay here until the justice system dealt with you. Maybe you'd go to adult jail and be tried as an adult. Maybe you'd be moved to the detention facility."

"The one over near the skating rink?" His mom used to drop Joey and him off at the rink on Friday nights when he was about thirteen. One or two times they spent the night there at skating lock-ins.

"Yeah, that's right." Dr. Luke waited.

"Just wondered." Silence again. He wondered what Dr. Luke would do if he knew about Benjamin and the key and Benjamin and his night excursions. He'd woken up a second time during the night to the sound of rain falling against his Plexiglas window. Plexiglas to keep kids with tempers from cutting themselves. Made sense but the Plexiglas was scratched and filmy looking and did weird yellow things to the landscape outside when he looked through it. He remembered wondering if

323

Benjamin and Esmeralda and whoever else were getting wet, but this morning he saw someone'd been throwing dirt up against his window. It was all along his sill and he realized it hadn't rained at all. Benjamin told him at breakfast he and a guy named DeeMarcko climbed out the bathroom window all the time, that's how they met the girls at night, and it was Esme's idea to wake him up with the dirt.

"Andrew," said Dr. Luke. "I want to ask you something from yesterday, about what Thomas said. About your mother and her father, I mean."

Andrew clenched his teeth. He was going to gag. Throw up again. It'd been like a scratched CD all night. Repeating. Over and over and over. And here it was again.

"While you're with us, I'm hoping you'll explore your feelings. Maybe even work toward some level of understanding of her. When children are sexualized, especially by trusted adults like parents, the results can be devastating, lifelong."

"I don't want to talk about it."

"This is a safe place, Andrew. And there are coping skills I can offer if you're willing to learn."

TapTapTap. His foot tapped nonstop against the floor. He saw Dr. Luke watching it but he made no effort to stop. His grandfather was a bastard. And he'd never known. Not until yesterday. PawPaw with the long legs and the superb hook shot who always took them great places. Once PawPaw took him kite flying at Moundville Archaeological Park and even though the signs said to stay off, they climbed to the top of one of the grassed mounds, kite in tow, and ran down the side to get it higher. It was a red kite with a dragon face and it had a long black tail. It flew high, as high as some buzzards circling above the trees, and then it teetered, flipped, and plummeted head first into the branches. Lost. Broken. His PawPaw was gone now. There was a little metal vase, its rim flush with the ground, holding a bouquet of plastic flowers near his headstone.

"Maybe Mom lied to Thomas about him," Andrew said. "She lied about men a lot."

Dr. Luke nodded. "Maybe," he said. "That happens. But, it certainly might help explain her behaviors as you've described them to me."

"People are still responsible for what they do. She didn't have to be that way."

"That's true," said Dr. Luke. "But sometimes people don't know how to stop doing things they know are bad for them."

"That screw up their kids' lives."

"Kids can get a really rotten deal. But they can work toward getting it sorted out. Like you said your brother, Joey's, been doing."

Andrew stopped tapping his foot. "Yeah, well, that counselor guy Asa doesn't seem to be helping Joey much, does he?"

"We don't know that. But I agree that your brother's disappearance is very concerning." Dr. Luke paused, considered the phrasing of his next question. He decided to be direct. "Andrew, are you sure you don't know where your brother is? If you know and you're trying to protect him, it might backfire on you both."

Andrew glared. "Why the fuck would you ask a dumb ass question like that?"

Dr. Luke shrugged. Low key. "Just covering all the bases, that's all. To make sure I'm helping you and Joey as much as possible. And I think you could have expressed yourself better without the cursing."

"Whatever," Andrew said, but his voice was calm. "Something's happened to him. I know it. It's not like Joey to go missing."

Dr. Luke waited but Andrew was through. "Perhaps we'll hear something today," he said. "I'll check in with Mr. Chalot later just to make sure there's nothing new."

"Call him Thomas. We all do."

"Okay, then. Thomas," Dr. Luke said with a smile. Trust was building. He hoped to hell Andrew didn't have anything to do with the death. He glanced at the wall clock. "About ready for class?"

Andrew didn't answer. What was it Birthday Benjamin called her? Ms. Mo-titti? It'd be hard to concentrate. Embarrassing to sit in her classroom knowing what she looked like in her underwear.

50

Detective Adelade Bramson strapped her holster around her hips and inserted her gun. The pink clashed with her burnt orange top but what did the guys at the station know about fashion? Bob Tulane sounded less than friendly when she phoned before eight this morning. Yes, he'd be home, at least until eleven. He had an appointment with a sick tree at twelve in Northport. Could it wait until then? Addie was firm. She'd see him in Coker. What was it about, he wanted to know. He'd told her everything he knew. There appeared to be some omissions, she'd said. She left it at that. Let him sweat, wonder if she'd found out about the two missing women. She had no intention of telling him his ex-fiancée was alive and apparently involved in the arts in Vegas. Sheila, that was her name, might have good reasons for disappearing.

Highway 82 traffic headed toward Columbus, Mississippi was fairly light at eight thirty in the morning. Most of the traffic was headed eastbound into Northport and Tuscaloosa. There was a wide tree covered median between the lanes, and the drive was a pleasant one despite heavily laden log trucks, empty chicken trucks with cages still snowing feathers from delivered cargo, and semis headed cross country. She knew westbound traffic would be bumper to bumper at the end of the work day when residents from the outlying areas of Tuscaloosa County and those from Pickens County made their ways home from work.

The drive to Coker took about fifteen minutes. She turned at the first left leading into town, passed by mobile homes and modest houses, and when she reached the white wood grocery store with two gas pumps, she turned to her left. Four more turns, five more miles, past concrete deer standing vigilant in front yards, concrete geese parading near sidewalks, outdoor tornado shelters built into earthen mounds, and fields plowed and planted with corn, field peas, and okra. The crops were tiny still, barely peeking through the soil. She knew that nearby there was a snapdragon farm that shipped flowers daily throughout the United States and greenhouse tomatoes being grown hydroponically in coconut shells. She turned right and slowed the car to six miles an hour. She was on a narrow dirt lane with potholes.

Bob's Tree Service said a faded, hand-painted sign. It was shaped like an arrow and she followed its point. There were wood frame homes on both sides of the lane, most with open front porches. One had an above ground pool in the backyard, the next had two coon hounds stretched out under an oak. Neither chased the car as she drove past. There was a trampoline sitting empty in the front yard of the next, and a small white sign that read Happy Honey Farm at the house across the street. She saw stacks of hives in the side yard. She stopped three houses down from the honey farm beside a mailbox where *Bob's Tree Service* was painted in cursive white paint. She glanced around. A woman in the house across the lane stood at her picture window, half behind a living room curtain. Addie considered waving but restrained herself.

Mr. Tulane was obviously watching for her, too. His front door opened simultaneously with her car door opening and he descended the five steps onto his walkway.

"Any trouble following my directions?" He frowned, eyes resting on her gun, but regained his composure quickly and extended his hand in greeting. He had a firm handshake. Nothing remarkable about it.

"None," she said. "Didn't even turn on my GPS."

He stared at her awkwardly. But of course a lot of people did. She was accustomed to it. Accustomed to the tightly restrained anger in his eyes, too. "Well, come on in," he said motioning toward his front door, heading in that direction himself. "Everyone in Coker already knows you're here thanks to my neighbor, Mrs. Blakney."

"Across the road?"

Mr. Tulane glanced toward the Blakney house and Addie looked too. The curtain wiggled and the woman disappeared.

Addie chuckled. "Effective neighborhood watch you have for sure."

"You can call it that," he said. "Gets a little tiresome if you want to know. But she's a widow, a nice lady, really." There were wind chimes hanging from his front entrance porch. Little pieces of fired clay in the shape of ducks dangling on fishing line.

The house smelled like bacon and coffee as Addie entered. It smelled a whole lot better than the multigrain honey snack bar and the banana she'd grabbed on her way out the door earlier. The hallway was dimly lit. It was comfortable and comforting the way a lot of old houses were, like worn shoes or favorite sweaters or jeans stretched to just the right shape.

"We'll sit in the back room. It's a sunroom," he said, motioning with his right arm as he closed the door with his left. She dropped her hand and let it rest on the handle of her Glock.

She intentionally chose the chair closest to the back door, a safety precaution she'd picked up during her years as a rookie, and she again brushed her fingertips along the butt of her gun as she sat down. She didn't expect trouble but he was a wild card. She waited until he sat in an oak rocker across from her. It looked scarred and weary, nineteen fifties maybe, thrift store variety. His hands moved to the arms of the chair, thumbs on the inside of the armrests, baby fingers on the outside.

She pulled out her recorder and touched the record button with her index finger. "So," she said. "I'll come straight to the point, Mr. Tulane. A number of interesting facts turned up when we researched your history. Facts you chose to omit in your discussions with my colleagues and me on the night of Dr. Beaty's murder."

The rocker moved ever so slightly. Back, forth. He raised his eyebrows. "Is that so?" he asked. "And to what interesting facts are you referring?"

"Let's start with your neglecting to mention that two different women disappeared in the past, both under mysterious circumstances while dating you. In fact, that you were the prime suspect in the disappearance of your fiancée, Miss Sheila G. Woodcock. We understand the charges were eventually dropped due to lack of admissible evidence linking you to her disappearance. But it's a funny thing about justice, Mr. Tulane. Release from charges doesn't always mean release from guilt. The other woman, of course, disappeared in Nevada some years ago. And we have at least one witness who reports you were behaving like a stalker on the afternoon of Dr. Beaty's death."

Bob Tulane laughed. A harsh, non-amused laugh. "A stalker? Who the hell would say something stupid like that? Protector is more like it. Priscilla was so damned pig-headed and naïve. She thought she could get rid of whoever that jerk was earlier in the day just by breaking up with him, like she was in junior high school or something. I talked to the guy. He called my phone. He was a controlling SOB. I'm sure he hit her that day or threatened to hurt her anyway. She sounded nervous, on edge, intimidated even. When she was with him at lunch I mean. I kept telling her he'd show up somewhere, at Metamorphosis, her house, wherever she was meeting that guy Red, and he'd probably beat the hell out of her.

Get lost, she said. Not exactly in so many words but she didn't want my help. She'd handle it herself." He rocked forward and backward several times before stopping the chair dead center, his heel on the rung. "Hell, she couldn't even handle the angry parent in the parking lot of her school earlier that day. She sat in my car until he finally gave up and left."

"So you're telling me that even though she was angry with you at Metamorphosis and kept telling you to leave her alone, and didn't want you there in the first place . . ."

"I know it's that woman at Metamorphosis who's your witness. The one who walked Priscilla out to her car. How old is she anyway? Nineteen? Twenty? Well, before she goes jumping to conclusions maybe she should get the whole picture, get the story straight." His foot left the rung of the rocker. The chair moved frenetically, all the way back onto the rocker tips, all the way forward, all the way back. "And as far as those disappearing women are concerned, they have nothing to do with Priscilla. Nothing. Nothing at all."

"We might find reason to disagree with you, Mr. Tulane. Doesn't it strike you as odd that two women disappeared during your involvements with them, and now a third has been murdered? And you just happened to drop by and find the body? After appearing to stalk her earlier in the day?"

"I've already explained. I wasn't stalking her. I was trying to protect her from the person who did murder her. And I didn't just happen to stop by. My visit was intentional for that very purpose." His voice was acidic.

"Tell me about the other two women."

He shook his head. "There's nothing to tell. Like I said, nothing relevant to Priscilla's murder, I mean."

Addie straightened her back, sat taller. She called it the puff up her feathers trick. Birds did it all the time. Dogs and cats did it with their fur. Puff up. Look larger. Exude authority. "Nothing?"

His hands clenched. His eyes lost emotion. They were cold, small, hard. Brown marbles. She'd seen eyes like his before. He could kill, she was sure of it. "You're way off base," he said. "There's nothing to tell."

"It's like this, Mr. Tulane. We can talk here in the comfort of your home or we can continue this conversation in Tuscaloosa at the station."

His stare was icy. Her fingers found the butt of her Glock. "What the hell," he said, chin poked out, voice restrained. He stopped rocking.

She waited. Somewhere in the house she heard the ticking of a clock. And a bird outside. And the hum of a refrigerator.

"The first woman, her name was Amanda. Amanda Bullock. I was living in Reno at the time. Working construction. I was thirty-two. She was a mistake. Dating her, I mean. Calling her flaky would be a kindness. She was a waitress. She ran away from home at fifteen, she told me. Lived hand to mouth, place to place, job to job. She was twenty-four when we met. She said she'd been in several violent relationships, was gun shy she said, didn't trust men. Our relationship was never satisfactory because of that. We never even rode in the same car together. She'd meet me in public places, and that was the extent of it. I never went to her place. She never came to mine. One day, she didn't show up for work. Didn't answer my calls. She'd disappeared off the face of the Earth. Moved on, that's all there was to it. I never heard from her again."

"But police reports suggest she left her clothes and other possessions behind."

He shrugged. "That's what they said. I'll tell you the same thing I told them. I have no idea. She was flaky, that's all there was to it. People do crazy things all the time. But you already know that. She was probably spooked by one of her ex's who found out where she was. That makes as much sense as anything."

Addie frowned, absorbing his words. Plausible but suspicious.

His jaw tensed. It moved forward and backward several times. The rocking chair was statue still.

"And then your fiancée disappeared?"

"You say that like I'm a serial killer or something."

"Sheila Woodcock disappeared from Lamar County while engaged to you, Mr. Tulane."

"Yes. Yes, she did. And like you said, I was originally charged and jailed for her murder even though her body was never found. Eventually the charges were dropped, like you said, lack of evidence. In reality the only thing I'm guilty of is getting myself involved with unstable women."

Dr. Beaty certainly fit that pattern. Addie waited. She could imagine domestic violence, threats, stalking. His fingers were squeezing the rocker's arms tight enough to turn his skin a pinky violet color.

He coughed. "I met Sheila while I was hauling logs up in Lamar County, near Millport if you know where that is."

Addie nodded.

"Hardwoods, mostly. She was working in the library up there. She was younger than me by about twelve years. I figured out later she was looking for a father figure. She was nervous-like. Mopped the kitchen floor in her trailer until she nearly wore out the linoleum. And shy. Quiet-like. Cried a lot about things that didn't matter. She lacked self confidence, I think. Good looking though and a fine cook. She spent most of her time with her momma and grandma. They all three lived together. I used to think she wanted to marry me just to escape her living situation. We argued about that sometimes. And one day after we argued about that very thing she up and left town. Never saw or heard from her again. She just ran, I'm sure of it. Disappeared. New start and all that. It happens." His chair rocked forward, backward, forward, backward. Slowly. Calmly.

"And she also left all of her possessions behind."

"Ha!" he said. "Shows what those cops know. I told them she took the damn diamond I'd given her. I checked every pawn shop around. Checked them for more than a year. I figured that's how she funded her getaway. But I never found it."

There was a weed eater decapitating vegetation somewhere in the neighborhood. He was obviously through with his explanation. She considered her options. She could drop the last bombshell. His mother's death when he was twelve. Falling to her death while she was out hiking with him. Alone. Or she could wait. Rattle him with it during their next interview. There'd certainly be another. She shifted her weight to stand. She'd given him enough to chew on already. "Do you own a hammer, Mr. Tulane?"

He read her body language accurately. He stood first and turned toward the front door. "Of course."

"May I see it?"

He scowled. "Certainly." He motioned toward a door at the end of a short hallway to his left. "I'll get it. I keep my tools in the garage, of course."

"Thank you," said Addie. "I'll wait out front."

The light was bright as she opened the front door. There were bursts of pink azaleas blooming in the front yard across the road. Somehow she'd missed them on her way in. The front curtain moved again. She and Luke could never live with a neighbor so nosy across the street. It would drive them both nuts.

331

"Here," said Mr. Tulane as he joined her, hammer outstretched.

"Okay," she said. "Have you recently owned more than one hammer?"

"No. Not like this. I have a tack hammer, if that counts."

Addie shook her head. "Can anyone verify what you're saying? About the one hammer, I mean?"

He spit. She made a mental note not to walk that direction. "Who the hell could verify something like that?" She watched as recognition swept across his face. "So it was a hammer? He killed her with a hammer?"

"How do you know she wasn't killed by a female?" asked Addie.

"I'm telling you, and I don't know why you won't listen. It was that man at lunch. He was a control freak. She was breaking it off with him." He hesitated, stared straight at her, almost through her. "Look. It's like I said already. I loved Priscilla. She'd agreed to give our relationship another try, if you must know. Not until July, but I would have waited."

"July?" asked Addie. "Why three months from now?" But she could guess. College football season began in late August. A relationship defined by football ticket availability.

He spit again, this time to his right. Into the bushes.

"And Dr. Beaty's hammer. Did you ever use it? Do you know where she kept it?"

"All of this is wasting time. I'm telling you to find that man, her last lover, I'm sure he was her lover."

"You haven't answered my question," Addie said.

"No. That's my answer. When I was with her we didn't use a hammer. We were, ah, otherwise occupied."

Addie stiffled a grin. She was sure that was true.

"Just find that damn man," he said.

"I assure you, Mr. Tulane, we're following up on all leads. You'll be around for the next few weeks, won't you?"

"Of course." He shot an angry look toward the moving curtain across the street. "Damn nosy neighbor," he muttered. "As you know, I run a business. I have to stick around. I don't have reason to leave town anyway."

"Thank you for your time, Mr. Tulane." She switched off her recorder.

He stared at it. Smirked. "Pardon my impertinence," he said in a way that indicated he had no qualms about being impertinent. "Who the crap ever heard of a pink holster? Been around the law all my life. Never seen anything like it."

Addie chuckled. It definitely clashed with her burnt orange shirt.

51

She explicitly informed him she wasn't driving all the way back to Fosters. They could meet at his office, at the station in hers, or anywhere else private enough to talk. Dr. Greene suggested Bowers Park. His veterinary office wasn't private enough he said. The park worked well enough for her. They'd be just down the street from the Department of Human Resources. She'd drop by and see Larry Ryan afterwards if she had time. Their interview last night left her mind running mazes. Larry's connection to Dr. Hutchinson and Metamorphosis, to Zenah Elenrude, to the deceased Ms. Whitesmythe, to the deceased Dr. Beaty, and of all things, to Dr. Beaty's manicurist, Ms. Leah Mosselliana from Heavenly Feet, left her brain in free-fall. She wasn't sure where it would land. The coincidences awakened her at four a.m. and she lay with her eyes open working overtime until dawn. Ms. Whitesmythe's fear of stinging insects was a new puzzle piece, too. It helped explain how she might have careened off such a straight, uncomplicated road.

Dr. Greene hadn't yet arrived when she pulled into a parking space near the Minnie Sellers picnic shelter, stained pine beams supporting a brown shingled roof with a poured concrete floor beneath. No one was using it. There'd been a handful of people eating at the nearby Maple shelter. Several preschool children were swinging with their mothers' help and climbing on a jungle gym shaped like a giant centipede on the Maple playground. One particularly athletic child had wrapped her little body all the way around a metal antenna. There were kids on the corkscrew slide further up in the park, and several people jogging with their dogs.

Addie burrowed through fallen pine straw with the toes of her shoes as she walked toward the shelter. The dead needles were probably half an inch thick and they cushioned her steps as she walked. Her toes kicked up squirrel-gnawed pine cones and rotten small branches from which grew all sorts of opportunistic plants, light green fuzzy bromeliads and blue green algae and dark green tree ferns. There were other treasures hidden among the needles as well, a plastic doll's arm, a red button, the wrappings from a cigarette pack, and a nickel. She stooped to pick up the coin and smiled. Tails. If Luke were with her, he'd insist she turn it over before claiming it. Not that he was really superstitious, he'd say. Of course not. She was moving toward the swings, she still loved to swing, when she heard a car door slam. It was Dr. Greene. She turned back toward the picnic tables under the shelter's protective roof.

"You did say eleven, didn't you?" he asked, glancing at his watch as he approached. His gait was easy, comfortable. He was wearing jeans and he'd pushed his shirt sleeves up to his elbows. He had on black boots. He was unquestionably handsome and confident. He'd told her Dr. Beaty came onto him. There wasn't much he'd said so far that Addie believed, but she did believe that.

"You're fine," she answered, not intending a pun, but suddenly feeling like an awkward school girl. "I was early." She moved onto the concrete and positioned herself across from him at one of the tables. She sat with her legs sideways in case she had to move fast. He mirrored her, his long legs stretched out cattycornered and crossed at the ankles. She pulled out her recorder. Her phone, too, just in case.

"I'm due at a farm on the other side of Moundville in about an hour," he said. "Horse purchase check-up."

Addie stared hard. "If you don't waste any more of our time by lying, Dr. Greene, we should finish in plenty of time."

Oddly, she thought, he didn't react badly. No cursing, no jumping up, no threatening behaviors. Not even a protest. Nothing but staring right back at her. Staring a hole right through her as her grandmother used to say. She watched his body language carefully. Shoulders raised slightly, angular chin, back straight and the muscles in his right bicep jerking. Lips tight.

"I'll try to save us some time," continued Addie. "We know . . ."

His shoulders slumped. He broke eye contact. She waited.

"I didn't damn kill her," he said quietly. "I'm a vet, for God's sake. It's taken me years to learn how to distance my emotions when I have to put a dog or cat down. And that still keeps me awake at night sometimes. Especially when people bring in pets they're just tired of. I won't do that, you know. I take in the animal, get them to sign it over to me, try to find it a new home. You think you see crazy-ass people in your job? Well, I see them in mine, too."

"That's not in question," said Addie.

"But you think I killed her."

"There're several witnesses who will testify your relationship with Dr. Beaty was a controlling one," she said in her most assertive voice. "Then there are concerns about Dr. Beaty's safety that noon, phone calls while she was with you that have been reported. Not to mention bruises identified as occurring prior to her death, almost certainly earlier in the day. The broken piece of charm bracelet I picked up underneath your couch has been identified as hers. And the flowers sent to her home with the apology note. How were you a bigger ass than O.T. that day, Dr. Greene? And why were the flowers found drowned in the toilet? Did she stuff them there when the two of you fought on the evening of her death? Or did you stuff them yourself? I don't believe you went to her home with the intent to kill her. On the contrary, you were seeking forgiveness. But she didn't want to see you. In fact, she was on her way to a meeting with another man, the father of her younger son, wasn't she? And that infuriated you. And so you picked up her hammer. Bludgeoned her to death."

His head jerked up. He was staring again, but this time she read pain and fear in his eyes. Deep brown intelligent eyes. "She was killed with her own hammer?" he asked and it seemed to her an honest question of surprise. She'd been fooled before. Psychopaths were excellent actors.

"And as you know, she was wearing a bra that almost certainly was designed for your eyes only. I can think of no other explanation for her wearing it."

He lowered his eyes again. "The bra," he said softly, very sadly. "She did design it for me, for us." He swallowed. "I never saw it."

He was almost convincing. She waited. He put his elbows on his knees and buried his face in his hands. "She was so damned infuriating," he said quietly. "I loved her, but not in a traditional sense. I don't think she ever really felt anything like love for me. She was in love with herself, anyone will tell you that. But it drove me crazy to think about her with other men. I never kidded myself about any kind of fidelity on her part."

"So you killed her."

He straightened. His fist pounded the concrete table. "Damn it! No! No, I didn't. But you're right about that day at lunch, about things getting physical." His eye contact was gone again. He brushed little black ants off the picnic table with the side of his hand. "I was brought up properly by my grandparents. They taught me the respectful way to treat women. And you may not believe it, but I've always been a gentleman.

336

That day, I don't know. I just . . ." He stopped, took a long soulful breath. "But with Priscilla it was different. She got under my skin not answering my calls for hours and hours. She made me nuts. And the more she ignored me the more I called. It was excessive, I know. But I didn't hit her. I never hit her. I shoved her that day at lunch. Bullied her. I went crazy out of my mind. We argued. She left. I felt humiliated. Guilty. I called in sick for the rest of the day. I know it sounds trite but I ordered flowers to apologize. At first I was going to deliver them myself but I changed my mind. Had them delivered. I didn't go to her house. I didn't go near her. I was waiting. Wanting her to call. I knew her well enough to wait. And she would have called in a day or two. Our chemistry was hot. She wouldn't want to lose it any more than me."

Luke's thumbs on her spine, warm oils, candles, hot chemistry. He was right. Hot chemistry would be hard to lose. She cleared her throat. "You obviously got physical enough with her that her bracelet broke."

He shrugged. His eyes watered. Psychopaths could tear up on cue. But sensitive men, men in love, cried too. "I was so angry when she got to my house. She opened the door and I shoved her. I didn't mean to push her hard enough to knock her down. I was just trying to make a point. And then there was that guy on the phone. That tree guy. And some meeting with her son's father that night. Having that jerk still in her life always pissed me off."

Addie's eyes narrowed. "Did she ever give you an idea of who he was, the father, I mean?"

"No. But I'm telling you, whoever he was, all he had to do was snap his fingers and she was there." He snapped his thumb and the middle finger of his right hand for emphasis. His chin jutted forward. "She called him Red."

"Yes. Did she say where she planned to meet him?"

He paused awkwardly. "No. At least not exactly. But I had her computer password. On rare occasions they'd e-mail. Usually her trying to contact him. There was always something about the moon. I figured they were meeting somewhere like this, out in a park, or maybe along the river or out at the lake."

She shook her head. "Possible, but most of the parks close at sunset."

"There're lots of dirt roads around the lake, out in the woods."

Her phone vibrated, inched along the concrete table. She recognized the number. It was Bob Tulane. As tempting as it was, he'd have to wait.

"So," she said. "What you're saying, Dr. Greene, is that you did become physically and emotionally abusive toward Dr. Priscilla Beaty the day of her murder around lunchtime at your farm. You felt so badly about this you called in sick for the rest of the day, sent her flowers, and never had contact with her again."

"Yes," he said quickly. "Yes, that's exactly right. When you get to know me better you'll know I could never harm her."

Addie stood. "But you did harm her, Dr. Greene."

He stared at the recorder, sighed. "And I'll live the rest of my life regretting that, Detective. Thinking that her last time with me went so wrong. But I could never kill her."

She nodded curtly. He was good. She half-way believed him. He was playing to her emotions and she felt them stirring, stripping away rational doubt. "That's it for now, Dr. Greene," she said. "Thank you for your time. Don't leave town for the next several weeks without contacting me first. We'll be in touch."

He stood. "I loved her," he said again. He hesitated and shifted his weight. He appeared nervous. "I've been thinking," he said. "I'll put up a monetary reward if you think it'll help. Ten thousand. It's money I've saved for African wildlife work. But it might flush out a witness or somebody who knows something, something to catch the SOB who murdered her."

Clever. "Thanks for the offer, but you're still high on the suspect list yourself."

"Don't be a damned fool." His voice was measured. His eyes had narrowed. He turned toward his car.

His gait wasn't nearly as confident as the first time they'd met. Not even as confident as earlier when he arrived. He glanced back over his shoulder twice. She sighed. It got to her sometimes. Ordinary people, at least fairly ordinary people, living fairly ordinary lives, caught for one pivotal unordinary moment in an extraordinary situation. She pulled out her plastic bag. It was bulging, lumpy. She'd refilled it before she left the house. A hippo, a buffalo, a monkey. Thankfully, no donkeys. She flipped off the recorder as she dialed the number for Mr. Bob Tulane. He answered as Dr. Greene shut himself into his car and fastened his seat belt.

"Tulane's Tree Service."

She recognized his voice but took no chances. "Mr. Bob Tulane, please."

"This is Bob."

"Detective Bramson. You phoned a few minutes ago?"

"Yes." There was an awkward pause. He cleared his throat, paused again. "I, ah, I needed to tell you."

"Yes?"

"It's not really that important, I mean, not to what you're investigating. But it's important to my recovery." He paused again. She waited. Dr. Greene's car rounded the park's loop and headed in the direction of the outdoor swimming pool and baseball fields and tennis courts. She watched it disappear. "You see, I wasn't completely honest with you."

"Go on."

"I, um, I didn't take responsibility for the two women's disappearances when we spoke this morning, the women we talked about. I'm an alcoholic, I'm in recovery now, have been for seven years. But before that, I couldn't keep stable relationships. Took advantage of both of them, that's the God's truth. That's why they left."

"And your relationship with Dr. Beaty?"

"Like I told you, I've got seven years of sobriety. This has nothing to do with Priscilla. What I've told you about her, about us, is true. But I'm sure you know that one part of being in recovery is taking responsibility. And I put it all on them this morning. That wasn't right. I needed to tell you, I drove them away."

Addie's eyebrows arched. She waited, but he was through. "Anything else, Mr. Tulane?"

"No. No. I just had to make it right."

"Okay." She suspected there was still more. "Thank you for calling. We'll be in touch." She put her phone in her purse along with the recorder, and the hippo in her mouth. She crunched down hard. The swings' black rubber seats beckoned. When she was little she turned herself nearly upside down swinging high, leaning back, letting her long hair sweep across the dirt. And she'd jump, fly from the seat and land what felt like miles from the swing. The landings were hard. They stung her shin bones. Her knees always had strawberries and the palms of her hands were always cut. She was going to have a good swing before she headed toward Metamorphosis. Maybe she'd still stop by DHR to talk

339

to Larry Ryan without his sidekick, Leah. Maybe spend a few minutes chatting with Zenah Elenrude, too. Get her take on all of Larry's disclosures. At least there'd been no more bomb threats. At least not yet this morning.

52

"Bramson."

"R.J. here."

Addie stopped pumping her legs and looped the crook of her elbow around the chain. She held her legs straight out. The swing slowed. "Hey, R.J. Whatcha got?"

"Nothing Earth shattering. But I rechecked Mr. Lamphurte's alibis for the days of the bomb threats. They're rock solid. I still don't think he's our man."

"Person," corrected Addie. "The caller's male but it might be a woman behind the threats."

"True. I stand corrected." He paused. Addie imagined he was consulting his electronic tablet. "Um, I also went back by the elementary school. Talked to those three office workers and several teachers. I don't see any involvement there, although one of the secretaries doesn't have an alibi to speak of. At home by herself watching television. Two of the teachers I interviewed report they've heard office staff joke about killing Dr. Beaty, wishing she would disappear off the face of the Earth, that kind of thing, but they didn't believe they were credible threats. It was worth looking at but I think it's a dead end."

Addie dragged the toes of her shoes in the sand beneath the swing. It surprised her he'd even gone back to the school. She thought they'd agreed to put those possibilities in the freezer. "I agree," she said. "For now let's focus on our strongest suspects. I've reinterviewed Mr. Tulane and I've just finished up with Dr. Greene. Both have motive. Both have apparent control and anger issues. Right now I'm leaning toward our veterinarian. Circumstantial evidence stacks up against him. But Tulane has the impressive history. And there's a new twist. I interviewed Larry Ryan last night. Turns out his girlfriend, Leah Mosselliana, gave the victim manicures and pedicures regularly, and she's as protective as a pit bull of Larry. I'd like to get an extensive background check on her. My gut says she's the type who'd kill for her man."

Silence. Addie waited.

"I'll run a check on her," R.J. finally said. "Gosh! It's a damn tangled web we're weaving."

Addie laughed. "Dr. Beaty did collect more than her share of suspects," she said. Another pause. She waited.

"Well," R.J. said. "Joey's still missing. And Mr. Chalot is beside himself with worry. He feels certain something is gravely wrong. He claims this kind of disappearance is totally out of character for his son."

It was unsettling. If Joey weren't the murderer, he was probably dead. That was how it was shaping up. Raucous cawing diverted her attention. A group of crows swarmed a pine tree down the road. "Teenagers vanish into thin air and reappear in this country all the time," she said in an effort to be positive. The crows were becoming more rowdy. Sassy. She tried unsuccessfully to see what had them riled. Probably an owl. Or a hawk. "Did you know the name for a group of crows is a murder?" she said. "Not a flock, a murder." It seemed a bad omen.

"Ah, no," said R.J.

"Not important." There were at least thirteen of them. One was tearing into a white paper bag in an overstuffed trash can. She and Luke admired crows. Their intelligence was astonishing. "Andrew's on my list of re-interviews for the day," she said.

R.J. sucked in air. It made a weird little whistling noise. "Have we ruled out the possibility that Mr. Chalot, himself, is involved?" he asked.

The question was a good one. It had been tickling the back of her brain. Crazier things had happened. Same with that teacher, Victor Abernathy. There were squirrelly things about him, too. "No," she said. "Not completely. But I'd put him on the back burner with the secretaries for now."

"And that Red guy. He has to be in the mix."

"That's where I'd like you to put your energies, R.J. Identifying Red. Dr. Beaty apparently never made it to their meeting, unless of course he came to her. I keep going back to Mr. Abernathy. I have a strong suspicion he's Andrew's father, even though he adamantly denies it. He intercepted Andrew the night of the murder, and he fits in a lot of other ways."

"I'll pay him another visit."

"Talk to Mr. Chalot again, too. He has a long history with our victim. Hard to believe he doesn't at least suspect the identity of Red. I mean, he was around at the time."

"Right."

Addie braced her feet on the ground and pushed back. She lifted her legs and swung forward. "That it?"

"Except for the lack of activity on our boy Tony's case. He's been incognito for the past two days. One of his homeboys says he's sick."

"Probably busy fencing on the Internet," Addie said.

"We've been checking. Needle in a haystack odds we'll catch him that way though. Oh, and Chief closed the Whitesmythe case. Accidental death. Makes sense she just freaked out over the yellow jackets and ran off the road. Especially after your report of her insect fears. There's still the question of the threatening boyfriend or lover or whoever he was. But life's rarely tidy, is it?"

"Hmm," said Addie. "Rarely." Threats and pregnancy and stinging insects and death. But she had to agree. Life's coincidences were far more likely than they seemed. Case opened. Case closed. Still, accidental rulings left her with gnawing feelings she might have missed something. It was a crazy business. "Well," she said. "That leaves us with the Beaty case and the DHR bomb threats. And of course, there's always Tony."

"FYI, a rape was reported about an hour ago. But that's going to Detective Stralley, I think."

"Good," said Addie. "We need to stay focused." She didn't say more because it was obvious. The more time that elapsed, the colder the trail.

53

She wasn't surprised to spot Miss Elenrude's cherry red Ford Fusion parked in the Metamorphosis lot. Addie parked beside it and pulled down her visor. Her hair was wind blown. Her lip gloss, worn off. She groomed herself quickly before heading toward the reception area, past the dogwood tree Luke bought about three years ago to plant with a teen who was moving away from the Center. It was a way of establishing a sense of permanence for the boy, Luke told her. And here it was, growing steadily, roots expanding every year, adorned in Spring petals. She wondered if the adolescent had fared so well. Luke's kids struggled to establish roots, to grow toward healthy adulthood.

"Addie!" Her husband's face appeared cut in half by the metal window frame. The window was pushed open as far as it would go. He was in Shelby's office. He motioned with his hand for her to join them. She opened the heavy oak doors that led to reception and turned right, then headed toward the third door on the right. Shelby McDonald, LCSW, PIP said the brass sign. The initials stood for Licensed Clinical Social Worker and Private Independent Practitioner. She'd asked Shelby about them several years ago. She knocked and the door opened. Shelby and Luke. Miss Elenrude was with them, too. The window was already shut and locked.

Luke motioned toward the chair beside him and touched her forearm. "Just in time," he said.

She laughed. "I don't like the sound of that."

Miss Elenrude's eyes narrowed. There was an air of seriousness about her. "We were discussing Andrew," she said. "He's playing games with all of us I believe." She looked first at Luke and then at Shelby, both of whom nodded. "He won't deny killing his mother but he won't admit it, either. It's beginning to get to me. He seems too detached from the fact his mother's dead. Murdered, even worse. I just don't see emotion there. It's giving me the willies."

"It's true," said Shelby, "that he really isn't demonstrating a sense of loss or shock or anger or any of the other emotions we'd normally associate with someone who's just lost his mother. I spent some time with him today and when I asked him to draw an ecomap he didn't even put his mother on it. But he did sign a release allowing me to talk with all of you. Complained the whole time he was writing his name, though, about all the 'damn paperwork.'"

"Well, he's right about that," said Luke.

Addie was familiar with ecomaps. Luke had shown her how to use them. They were basically diagrams people drew to help indicate significant people and things in their lives.

"He included his girlfriend, her name is Bethy, Mr. Chalot, Joey and his unidentified father, Red, as supports."

"Red?" asked Luke. "Now that's interesting."

"It felt to me like he was romanticizing his father, the way a lot of kids do with absent parents," Shelby said. "He showed me the engraved bracelet and the locket with the photo again. He's still carrying them around in his front pocket. Interestingly he put Mr. Abernathy, that teacher who found him, on his ecomap as a stressor but then erased his name and said the man was nicer to him than usual when he found him on the Quad. And he wrote "assholes and horndogs" all in big caps, and kept going over and over the words until they were so dark and messy I almost couldn't read them and then he made the comment they were gone from his life now, they wouldn't bother him anymore."

"That sounds ominous," said Addie.

Shelby made eye contact with her. "Except for Bethy he didn't write down any other friends' names either, but after he handed the ecomap to me he said he knows a guy, he called him a ghost, who's helped him out at different times. And he said that maybe our Benjamin is sort of a friend, but he said Benjamin's crazier than we know."

"A ghost, like in supernatural terms?" asked Zenah Elenrude.

"No," said Shelby. "I asked him that and he mumbled something about gang talk. But he wouldn't clarify it."

"I can't see Andrew involved in a gang," said Miss Elenrude.

"You never know," said Luke.

"We already have information suggesting he was with a well-known gang member the day of his mother's murder," said Addie. "And there are rumors that this gang member is offering murder-for-hire services."

"Do you think . . .," began Zenah, her body straightening in her chair.

"It's way too early to speculate about anything like that," interrupted Luke. "I think it's important to keep ourselves from getting ahead of the facts. We could miss important information if we jump to conclusions."

"True," Addie said to her husband. "But brainstorming's helpful to the investigation."

"Well, I'm of the opinion that Andrew's still in shock," said Luke. "I don't think he's even begun to process the murder. The anger he's historically felt toward his mother would indicate a certain level of passion, and I suspect he's got anxieties and embarrassment and guilt and emotional longing all tangled up in that anger, too. I predict it won't be long before it bubbles to the surface."

"If it hasn't already," said Addie quietly, almost as though the group weren't there. Weren't crimes often the result of emotional entanglements?

Miss Elenrude cleared her throat. "I ran into Reverend Lincoln earlier while I was waiting to get a supplies list for Andrew's classroom materials," she said. "He was making rounds. Anyway, he plans to see if Andrew wants to chat before he leaves campus today."

"Good," said Luke.

"Only if I can have him first," said Addie. "I've come out to interview him in greater depth."

Shelby frowned slightly at the mention of Jeremiah Lincoln. She still wasn't sure what to make of their last encounter. She cleared her throat. "Benjamin stopped me in the hall today and said Reverend Lincoln did talk to him about foster care."

"Yes," said Zenah. "But it apparently left Benjamin feeling insecure. He told me he isn't sure about living with a foster family. That maybe he'd rather stay here until he can move into independent living."

Addie shifted in her seat. Awkward. Benjamin was none of her business.

Luke stroked his beard and made a funny little sound. "That truthfully might be best," he said. "Benji can be a handful. Speaking of which," he said pulling a phone out of his shirt pocket, "your child keeps coming up with phones. This is the fifth or sixth one we've confiscated from him. Shelby caught him with it yesterday."

Miss Elenrude stared at the flip phone and frowned. "Is he stealing them?"

"Stealing or trading," said Shelby.

Addie squirmed again.

Luke pushed the on button. "I forgot to check it yesterday. Got so busy. Maybe there'll be a home number, a hint of where he's gotten it." The room was quiet. "No. No identifying number," he said. He scrolled down the call log. He glanced toward Addie, then back at the phone. "You don't happen to know Tony's phone number, do you?" he asked. "Looks like a guy named Tony sent a text to him earlier today."

Addie looked puzzled. "My Tony?"

"Yeah," said Luke, handing her the phone. "Is that it?"

"Oh, my gosh, it is. I recognize it." She paused before hitting the select button with her index finger. "May I?"

"Certainly," said Luke.

Still in the F'n bed. F'n wasps!

Wasps? "Hmmm," she said handing the phone back to her husband.

Luke stared at the message. "So it appears your Tony is somehow connected to our Benji."

"That's not good," said Addie.

Shelby looked at both of them, then at her watch before she scrunched up her face. "Man," she said. "I'm already late for group. Feel free to use my office. Just lock up when you leave."

"I've got to get back to DHR," said Miss Elenrude. "But when you figure out the connection between Benjamin and this Tony guy, Luke, please fill me in."

"Certainly."

The office door closed. Addie jumped up, too.

"Leaving?" he asked. They were alone in the room. He sounded disappointed.

"Not a chance." She walked to the window and turned the clear plastic wand on the left side of the blinds. The blinds closed. The room darkened. She stretched, wrapped both arms around his neck, pressed her body hard against his. He smelled good. But odd. Like pistachio nuts.

"You smell like pistachios."

"Really?" His hands moved across her face, her neck. His lips followed, met hers.

No doubt. Had to be. He tasted like them too. "Ummm," she said lingering briefly, leaning against him with closed eyes. "I needed that."

"Me, too."

She created an acceptable distance between them before reaching toward the wand to readmit daylight.

"Uh-uh. Close the blinds again."

She laughed. "No such luck. We're both on the clock."

"And we both have loads of comp time."

She smiled. "That we do. But I'm here to interview Andrew."

Luke picked up Benjamin's phone. He resumed scrolling down the call and text logs. "It really disturbs me that Benji knows Tony," he said. "That's not a good prognostic indicator for Benjamin's therapeutic progress. Not at all."

"Did Benjamin text him back?"

"No, at least there's that. But of course, the phone's been in my possession." He stroked his beard. "Sure are a lot of stinging insects buzzing around town affecting people's lives these days."

"Coincidence, maybe. It's that time of year. But I think R.J. and I'll pay Tony a visit before I come home tonight."

"Be careful, baby." He stopped before he said more. Sometimes it was hard being married to a cop. "You ready to see Andrew?"

"Sure. But first, where'd you put those pistachios?"

He looked startled. "Sorry. I finished them off about an hour ago."

"I'm starving," she said, wrinkling her nose.

"Me too. What about your cookie zoo?"

She opened her purse and dumped a little pile of animals out of their bag onto Shelby's desk. She popped a cheetah into her mouth. She frowned as Luke indiscriminately grabbed a handful and ate the animals all at the same time.

"You can meet with Andrew in my office," he said as he reached for Shelby's phone to call the Luna cottage. "Oh, by the way. You wrinkled up your nose a minute ago."

Addie wrinkled her nose again and laughed. "What?"

"You know that drives me crazy."

"Dr. Bramson," she said, placing a gorilla on her tongue. "No need to drive you anywhere. You parked yourself in Crazy a long, long time ago."

*   *   *

348

He walked into the room and said he wanted Dr. Luke to stay. What difference did it make anyway, he asked, since he'd given them permission to talk about him together? Addie was glad. Maybe Luke would glean something from the interview she missed. Maybe Andrew'd be more honest with Luke there. He seemed to have real trouble with females in authority. She watched him cross his lanky legs at the ankle and spread them forward until his feet were almost touching Luke's shins. He had his mother's high cheekbones and piercing eyes. He was a good looking boy.

"So," she said switching on the recorder. "We have to go through parts of your story again, Andrew. I'm sorry. I know it must be difficult, given your recent loss."

Andrew shrugged. "I've already told you I hated her." It was true, but he knew Dr. Luke was right. There was black and white and mostly gray. Hate and love and tornado gray whipping around, tearing up his life. Chaos even now, even with her gone. And Joey. Where the hell was Joey?

"Yes, you've said that. But the real question is, did you hate her enough to kill her?"

His stare sparred with hers. "Sometimes."

"*Did* you kill her?"

His stare didn't break. Silence.

Addie waited. Silence. "Andrew," she finally said. "How are we to interpret your silence? It's a simple question. Did you kill her?"

He moved his broad shoulders forward. "Interpreting's your job."

Addie mirrored his movement, closing the distance between them. "It's my job, Andrew, but your life."

He cocked his head. She wasn't sure but it looked like his lips curled up a tiny bit. A smirk. It was hard to tell.

"Here's what I think, Andrew," she said. "I think you and your mother had an argument. A fight. Maybe about Metamorphosis. Maybe about Dr. Greene and the way her behaviors devastated your brother. Maybe she hit you first. Maybe she said something that really got under your skin. But when you struck her, you did it without thinking. You didn't mean to kill her. Just another argument like all the others. But this one ended differently."

It was a smirk. His lip curled defiantly now. "It's a free country," he said. "Think what you want."

"I always think freely," Addie said evenly. "And right now I think you know more than you're saying. Maybe even about your brother."

Silence.

"Okay, then let's discuss your friend, Bethy. You neglected to mention when we talked earlier that you visited her house on the night your mother was murdered."

His jaw muscle twitched. "Bethy's not in this," he said. "It's none of your business."

"Everything's my business when someone's been killed, Andrew."

"She's not in it," he said again. "You already made her tell you I was there while her mother was gone. So now she's grounded. Leave her alone."

"And I have witnesses who place someone of your description in the park behind your house, Annette Shelby Park, the morning of your mother's murder, meeting with a gang member named Tony."

The crooked lipped smile again. His eyes flickered. "I told you. Never heard of him."

"I hope that's true. Your being there raises all sorts of possibilities."

"Aren't there always possibilities?"

She tried to keep cool, to not look pissed off. Luke could call it oppositional defiance or conduct disorder or problems with familial conflict or whatever. She called it being a smart ass.

The phone rang. Luke stood, opened the door. "Excuse me," he said, moving into the hallway. The door closed behind him.

Addie took a long, deep breath. Adolescents. Sociopaths. Sometimes they behaved too much alike. Sometimes, they were one in the same. "You're not helping yourself, Andrew," she said. "I'm trying to help you and you're not helping at all."

"Helping by accusing me of killing my mother?" It was still there. The same obnoxious smirk.

Luke knocked softly and reopened his door. "Addie, would you mind if we took a short break?" he asked gently. "This is Mr. Chalot. He has Joey on three-way. It might help Andrew to talk to them a minute."

Andrew jumped up, closed the distance in one step. "Joey? On the phone?"

Luke smiled, checked with Addie who nodded, and held the phone out toward him. She scooped up her recorder.

"We'll wait out in the hall," Luke said, "so you can talk privately."

"Joey!" Andrew shouted. "Where the hell have you been? God, I've been out of my mind sick worried about you!"

"Well," she said softly as Luke closed the door and she switched off her recorder. "At least we know he wasn't lying about not knowing Joey's whereabouts."

Luke scanned the hall. No one visible but still that didn't mean there weren't invisible ears listening to every word said. "Want to walk outside a minute?" he asked. "Get some fresh air?"

*   *   *

"Joey! Joey, man, where are you? Where'd you go? Damn it! I've been freakin' sick!" Andrew knew he sounded anxious, scolding, even maybe a little like their mother nagging. He recognized this only in a remote corner of his brain and he tried to dismiss the comparison quickly.

"Hi, Andrew."

"That's it? Hi?"

There was a significant pause. Andrew listened to static on the line and from somewhere in the world, mumbled crossover voices bled into their connection. "I'm sorry, bro'. I didn't know everyone was looking for me. I drove up to Amherst to be with Lesa a while." Another long pause. "I didn't know. About Mom, I mean."

Andrew sat down in Dr. Luke's chair. He closed his eyes. Thank God. Joey didn't know. He reopened his eyes and reached his left hand forward toward Dr. Luke's magnet men. He pulled the little figures off the T-bar and repositioned each one upside down. Unless Joey was lying. Maybe he did know. Maybe he was playing dumb because Thomas was on the line. Or maybe to keep from involving them in a cover-up.

"I'll be home late tomorrow night, Andy," said Joey. "Probably sometime after midnight. Thomas says we have a lot to do. To, um, think about."

"Yes," said Thomas. Andrew could hear Joey's step-sisters talking in the background. Something about a TV show. And he thought he could hear Holly opening and closing cabinets and getting out pans. Probably getting ready to cook. "We've held off buying a casket and making the arrangements. That's something all three of us need to do together."

"I thought Mom wanted to be cremated," said Joey.

Andrew's hand paused. The magnet man he was putting on the T-post slipped off the top, brushed against two others and all three cartwheeled off the desk. He picked them up and stacked them again. Something about his mother becoming a container of ashes. Being burned. He leaned back all the way in Dr. Luke's chair. The leather headrest felt cool and sticky on his neck. He rubbed his left temple, then his right.

"We'll talk about it," Thomas said. "It's really up to you boys. To do what she wanted, I mean."

"Andrew?" said Joey. "You okay?"

He felt like he was going to lose his lunch. "Yeah. Sure. I'm great now that we've found you. Now that you're coming home."

"Yeah," said Joey. "Yeah. Me, too."

"Joey," said Thomas. "Please phone your advisor at Auburn right after we hang up. Let the folks down there know you're all right. See if you can somehow make up what you've missed because of the situation, your mother's death, I mean. You don't need to lose the semester."

"Okay."

"Joey?"

"Yeah?"

"You're sure you didn't know Mom was dead?"

Another pause. A long one. Andrew heard a dog barking. Probably Winx over at Thomas'. He wondered if Lesa had a dog.

"Of course I didn't," said Joey. "How could I? You think I'd be up here instead of at home with you and Thomas if I'd known?"

There was an edge of what-a-stupid-question-why-would-you-ask-me-that in Joey's voice. Andrew swallowed and sat forward. He pulled off an upside down magnet man and put him sideways, sticking him onto the T-bar by his forehead. "Stupid question," said Andrew. "Sorry. Just . . . just glad to hear your voice, that's all."

"Yeah," said Joey. "So how's that place, Metamorphosis?"

Andrew pulled another figure off and put it back sideways. "Okay, I guess. Boring. Stupid. There're some crazy-ass kids here, though." He didn't say it. The worst part was missing the hell out of Bethy.

"Well, Lesa and I are headed out to see a movie. The matinee. Then I'll be heading home. Probably spend the night in Virginia somewhere. Start off again in the morning."

Andrew frowned. Going to the movies seemed weird. He wasn't sure why. What did he expect Joey to do? Put on black and sit in the dark?

"Be careful, Son," said Thomas. "And before you leave for the movies, call Auburn."

Another pause. "Right."

"Be safe," said Andrew.

Joey laughed.

"What's funny?" he asked.

"I didn't say it earlier, but sometimes you sound just like Mom."

Be safe. It was true. She always said that.

"Bye," said Joey. The phone clicked. He'd hung up.

"Andrew?" said Thomas.

"Yes?"

"You okay?"

"A lot better now."

"No kidding," said Thomas. "Me, too. Holly, the kids, all of us feel better. Even Winx, I bet." He cleared his throat. "Do you need anything?"

"Um, could you call Bethy and tell her Joey's okay?"

Thomas cleared his throat. It was like a space filler, like he needed time to think, not like he had to spit. "I'll tell you what," he said. "I'll phone her mother and give her the news. I'm sure she'll pass it along to Bethy."

"Thanks. And, tell her I miss her."

"I'll relay that to her mother, too."

Her mother probably wouldn't pass that along. Not while she was grounded, anyway. "Never mind. Forget the last part."

A chuckle. "Okay. See you tomorrow, then."

"'K. Um, Thomas?"

"Yes?"

"Thanks. Um, thanks for finding my brother."

When the line went dead, Andrew sat forward and took all the little men off the T-pole. He put them back the way he'd found them. Except for one. He stood it on its head away from the others before he stood himself. There was a chance Joey was lying, but he didn't think so. He sounded legit. He closed Dr. Luke's door behind him, looked around, stood still and listened, but heard no one. They must have gone into one of the empty rooms or maybe outside. Outside seemed most logical.

Both Dr. Luke and his wife looked like outdoor people. He walked toward the exit door, quickening his pace when he spotted them through the window. It was just a little window, tinted green and crisscrossed with scratches. More Plexiglas. They were sitting on the bench where he and Dr. Luke sat the first day.

"Hi," said Dr. Luke as he approached. "Join us."

Andrew stopped about a foot away from Detective Bramson and sat cross legged on the grass in front of her. He stared straight in her eyes. "Okay," he said.

"Okay?"

"I didn't do it. No matter how much I hated her, I'd never kill her. Never."

Addie squinted. The sun was bright but not squinting bright. It was more like she was sifting his words.

"And Joey didn't even know. About her death, I mean. He just found out. I knew he wouldn't kill her. I knew he wouldn't."

"Thanks for letting me know," she said.

Dr. Luke made some funny little noise. Probably something like a groundhog or a chipmunk would make. "I thought that was it," he said. "You were waiting. Protecting Joey, weren't you?"

Andrew shrugged his right shoulder. Damn the guy was good. It was like he could see inside his brain.

"What I've been wondering," said Dr. Luke, "was if you were planning to take the fall for him if he had killed her."

Andrew wondered himself. It had been bugging him ever since Joey disappeared. Kept him up at night. Messed with his concentration. He didn't want to go to prison. The thought of it pumped dread to the core of his soul. Prison would totally mess up his relationship with Bethy. He'd stuck his finger down his throat twice to get relief. Had diarrhea. "I don't know for real," he said. "Sounds crazy, but he's my brother. I could never watch him go."

54

"What's on your schedule now, Dr. Bramson?" Addie asked Luke as they watched Andrew lope slowly down the hill toward the cottage.

Luke smiled, looked at his watch and stretched his feet forward. "Well, there's always paperwork," he said. "But I'd prefer going into my office and closing the blinds again." She rolled her eyes and he chuckled softly. "Actually," he said, "I have a client session scheduled around five."

"I need to do some mopping. I could use some help if you have time."

"Mopping," he repeated. "Aren't you just the picture of domesticity?"

She punched her elbow into his ribs. "Ha ha." But his cynicism was on target. Even as a kid she was squatting backwards riding her grandparents' rocking chair like a horse, wearing a metallic plastic pistol in a leather holster that felt like cardboard, while her neighborhood girlfriends played house.

"Just messin' with ya'," he said. "Where do you want to mop?"

Addie looked around. A cardinal, a startling red punctuation mark, sat among the white flowers of a native azalea. Honeysuckle azaleas they were called in the South because their blooms bore that resemblance. The wind was calm. There was no one in sight. It was late afternoon and the air was warm and the sun felt good on her face and the sky was as clear and blue as Luke's eyes. She loved his eyes. "This is good," she said. "We can use the picnic table here. But first let me call R.J. I think Tony's grandmother gets home around 5:30. Unless she's taken a second job. Poor woman. I truly think she does her best with him."

"Yeah," said Luke. "She probably does." They both knew it to be true. There was a legion of grandparents raising grandchildren. Parents on drugs, parents in jail, parents in poverty, absent parents, unnamed parents, it went on and on and on. "You need some paper?"

"That'd be great."

"'K," he said, putting his finger up to his lips and then to her nose. "I'll be right back."

"You and your crazy thing with noses."

"Your nose especially," he said, but he was aware that his own nose was itching as he got up to get the paper. It meant company was coming when noses itched. "It's Spring," he said under his breath. Pollen. Grasses. Noses always itched in the Spring.

*   *   *

It wasn't really mopping. He watched her write out the letters MMOPP-BEATY at the top of the legal pad he'd gotten from his office. While he was in there he'd done a quick inventory of the room. It didn't look like Andrew'd bothered anything. Except a magnet man that was standing on its head. Leaving most of the Metamorphosis kids in his office alone would set them up to steal. He rarely ever took the risk. But Andrew was different. He felt it in his gut.

"I'm meeting R.J. at Tony's a little before six," she said.

Luke watched her write the words Motive, Means, Opportunity, Passion, and Past across the paper. She drew column lines between the words. MMOPPing was Addie's personal touch to the old motive, opportunity and means formula. It had proven remarkably helpful to her over the years in solving crimes. He pulled his legs around the wood that connected the bench to the table. "I love to MMOPP with you," he said.

Addie's lips were pressed against one another in concentration. She wrote the name Andrew on the far left hand side of the page. "Let's start with Andrew," she said. "Family first, always."

"Right." He was convinced Andrew's declaration of innocence was valid, but Addie needed to explore the facts as she saw them. It was her case. Her investigation.

"He had motive. Metamorphosis placement. Joey's messed up chance to work with Dr. Greene. Her unwillingness to identify his father. Her sexual behaviors. Plenty of motive, that's for sure." She wrote these thoughts in abbreviated form. "And, he had means. He knew where to find the hammer. He's tall enough and strong enough to bash her in the head. And, opportunity. They were the only two living in the house."

"True."

"And almost certainly he's lying about meeting with Tony. Tony might have actually done the dirty work, or sent an underling to do it. And he had passion. He's conflicted about their relationship, wouldn't you say?"

"Most definitely."

"And it's on record he has a bad temper. A bad tempered teenager and a cool as a cucumber attitude toward her death." Her expression was sharp, no funny business. It was like in the cartoons the way her features morphed into angular lines. When her face got that look Luke believed she could do almost anything but fly. "And, his past? I need help with that part."

"Some reports of runaway and theft of mother's property," he said. "Some truancy. Smoking. But I didn't see anything to indicate domestic violence against his mother. I understood from Dr. Beaty that she was careful around him at times, perhaps felt intimidated to some degree, but basically described him as cursing, tantrumming, some object aggression, you know, breaking things, throwing things, but not threatening her person. As you know, his history is more one of withdrawal. Seems to me a lot of his behaviors were efforts to vex her."

"And I'm sure he did." She leaned back and stared at what she'd written. "The facts do stack up unfavorably against him. But something about the way he seemed so relieved after talking to Joey, something in his presentation, leads me to think he's not our killer."

Luke agreed. It was a gut feeling.

"What do you think?" she asked.

"Well, to quote Dr. Lydia, assume nothing," he said. "But actually I agree. I don't think he's your man."

Addie began to write Joey's name in the left hand corner. "Or woman," she said.

"I stand corrected. Or woman."

"Okay," said Addie. "Joey. He had a most immediate motive. His mother's affair with his identified mentor. Means, he was here in town. He knew where to find the family's hammer. He's as capable as Andrew of bashing in her head. And she'd be more trusting in his presence. I feel like Joey could catch her off guard. Agree?"

He did. "Yes."

"Opportunity was there. No problem to slip into the house on his way out of town, kill her and disappear. But the next one, I'm not sure. Passion. Maybe his anger smoldered, finally exploded in an act of rage. I need your help, Luke. What do you think? You've met him. I haven't talked to him at all."

He stared at the paper thoughtfully. "I'm glad you'll get to meet him in the next day or two," he said. "But based on what Andrew's told me about him and my own limited exposure, I think you're on target. He apparently has been simmering for a very long time, probably throughout childhood."

"For now I'd say he's a stronger suspect than Andrew."

"Agreed."

Addie's pen paused above the paper. "Thomas Chalot isn't a suspect, at least not yet. But there is the mystery man, Red. R.J.'s still combing through Dr. Beaty's e-mails and handwritten journals trying to determine who the guy is. I have a strong feeling it's the teacher who found Andrew for us, Victor Abernathy, but he denies it outright."

"Which makes sense if he wants to remain incognito," said Luke.

"Exactly. The question is, was anonymity sufficient motive for murder whoever the guy Red is? And why now after all this time?"

"Well," said Luke, "we know she intended to identify Red while Andrew was here. She said so. Maybe this fellow Red got wind of that."

"R.J. says her e-mails indicate they planned to meet under a crescent moon somewhere. I couldn't find any kind of moon symbol in her bedroom."

"Crescent moon. What phase of the moon are we in?"

"No, I checked. It's almost three-quarters. The only crescent moon R.J. and I can come up with is the sign at the Moon Winx. Unless it's referring to something like a poster or painting somewhere."

"I don't know. The Moon Winx seems unlikely," he said.

"Maybe. But that could make it the perfect meeting spot."

"I just can't really see . . . but anyway, your point is she wouldn't be alarmed if this Mr. Abernathy or whoever came walking into her bedroom around the time of their planned meeting."

"We know Mr. Abernathy was quite hard on Andrew in class last year, and he appeared almost overly concerned when I interviewed him about Andrew's recent whereabouts."

Luke chewed the rough edge off one of his fingernails. It'd been driving him crazy catching on the fabric of his shirt all afternoon. "Interesting."

"And we know he went to high school with her. So they were at least acquaintances around the time of her pregnancy with Andrew." She studied her notes as she wrote them. "Anyway, I'm planning to re-interview him tomorrow morning." She pulled out her bag of Animal Crackers. Luke held his hand out and she dumped some into it, then into her own. "Yum," she said amputating the leg of a tiger with her teeth.

"Okay," she said. "That takes us to one of my prime suspects, her most recent lover, Dr. Harry Greene." She wrote his name on the left hand side of the paper, over scoring each letter. "We definitely have all the domestic violence emotions. And she was apparently trying to break it off with him. I found a piece of her charm bracelet under his couch. There were fresh bruises on her body that predate her death. And he sent flowers, the ones drowned in the toilet, to apologize for something that happened on the day of her death. He's definitely in great physical shape and he'd almost certainly know his way around her house. So means and opportunity are taken care of. The passion is obvious. But R.J. can't find anything to suggest violence in his previous relationships. No legal history. And he seems embarrassed and perhaps a little intimidated to be involved in this whole situation. That's the part that doesn't fit."

Addie watched the building door open. Shelby emerged and walked toward them. She turned the legal pad over.

"Hey, sorry to interrupt," Shelby said walking to the edge of the table. "Luke, if it's okay with you, I'm going to head home to Molly. I want to go to the park and out for dinner. She's loving the sliding board this year."

"About time you got out of here while it's still daylight," he said.

Addie turned her notes over again as Shelby headed toward her car. "Okay," she said in her serious voice. "Next up is Bob Tulane, ex-lover and romantic hopeful until Dr. Beaty's dying day. He's my strongest suspect." She wrote his name beneath Dr. Greene's. "We have the motive of unrequited love. He was clearly familiar with her house. Shelby described her as unafraid of him and we know he was hanging around, protecting her to hear him tell it. Shelby described his behaviors as resembling stalking and it sounds like stalking to hear him explain himself. So that takes care of opportunity. She was putting him off, he says, despite his romantic overtures. There's the passion. And he's got a treasure trove of a past. Two different romantic partners disappeared while in relationships with him. One's never been found. The other's living in Vegas but he has no idea she's been located. And his mother died when he was a kid, just the two of them hiking together when she fell to her death. Ruled accidental at the time, but still . . . And what happened to make both women disappear mid-relationship with him?"

Luke squinted. He thought about Shelby. About Molly's father, Steve. About Shelby always looking over her shoulder, hoping Steve never came searching for them.

"He's also the one who found Dr. Beaty's body. He went up into her house even though she told him to get lost. He's a slippery one. Harry Greene is smooth but Bob Tulane is slippery. Tulane's almost certainly a sociopath. I'm not sure how to describe Dr. Greene."

"You sure do meet a lot of sociopaths," he said.

She laughed. "They do tend to break the law, you know, Dr. Bramson."

"You've got a point." His nose was itching again. "We're not expecting company any time soon are we?"

"What?"

"Company. We don't have anyone on the schedule do we?"

"No. Why?"

"No reason," he said. "Just asking."

She drew a circle around Bob Tulane's name. "So Tulane's the guy I'll probably slap the handcuffs on, but I've had to look at some other folks, too. Larry Ryan, I don't think he did it, but he certainly had motive and passion. And being an ex-cop, he's wise in ways to cover up his tracks. He says he'd never do anything to jeopardize the well-being of his children and I want to believe that. But when I went out to interview Larry, there was Dr. Beaty's nail professional. Her name is Leah Mosselliana. She's petite, but it doesn't take too much bulk to bash somebody's head in. I keep coming back to the idea that bashing someone with a hammer seems like an impulsive murder you'd expect from a teenager or someone without the resource of exceptional strength."

Addie was leaning forward across the picnic table. Her breasts were pressed against the edge of the concrete, mounded more than usual at the edge of her blouse. Her hair was moving ever so slightly in the breeze. Her eyes were earnest, intelligent. Her nose was always just perfect.

"God, I want you right now," he said.

"What?"

"You're turning me on. Let's make love right here, right now."

"Great idea," she said. "Are you listening to me at all?"

"Totally. Bashing in Dr. Beaty's head with a hammer doesn't seem like a planned manly murder."

"Close but not exactly."

"Yeah," he said. "Makes sense. A man'd probably strangle her or shoot her, although he might not use a gun in that neighborhood. Maybe knife her. He might abduct her. Probably would have raped her, given the suspects you've described."

Addie wrote down a question mark. "And then, of course, our murderer may be none of the above. R.J.'s looked into the possibility of the school office workers. That's a long shot. But Dr. Beaty was apparently very unpopular among her subordinates. Not all of them had alibis. None of the major suspects have strong alibis either."

Luke glanced at his watch. He still had a few minutes. He leaned across the table and kissed her forehead. "Something'll break soon," he said. "You and R.J.'ve gotten a lot done on the case already. I'm betting on Bob Tulane or Harry Greene, possibly Joey or even Leah the manicurist, maybe even the mysterious Red, aka probably Victor Abernathy. But you're right to keep your mind open, Addie. It may be someone like Dr. Beaty's next door neighbor, or if she were having sex with him, maybe his wife. Or even Andrew's girlfriend, Bethy. She must have been distressed Andrew was placed at Metamorphosis."

Addie tore the paper off the pad, folded it and put it in her purse. She stood. "I'll have to give up my job if it turns out to be Bethy," she said. "She seems too sweet and innocent."

"Got to watch the sweet innocent ones," said Luke.

She knew that was true. "It's helpful bouncing it all off you," she said. "I shouldn't be too late getting home. Tony's my last stop for the night. Just need to ask him about the wasps in his text to Benjamin."

"Wear your pink, okay?"

Addie skimmed her hand across the top of his. "Planning on it," she said. She never took chances with kids like Tony.

55

"So are you mad at me?" Andrew asked the moon faced girl with brown pigtails. Her pigtails were long. They hung like bunched curtains halfway down her flat chest, and framed a silver chain with a snake charm dangling from it.

"You're okay," said Esmeralda. "I was pissed when you didn't come out the other night but I get that you already have a girlfriend. You aren't just trying to get a piece of ass like most of the guys here and I respect that."

Andrew smiled. She wasn't ugly but she wasn't anything to snap pictures of either. "Yeah, well, I think it's cool you're into snakes and stuff," he said.

She looked across the yard at the group playing volleyball. Girls against boys. The boys had a narrow lead of three. "Is your girlfriend into snakes?" she asked.

"Bethy's her name," he said. "She doesn't go all shrieky hysterical when she sees one, but she's more into dogs. She's got a big silver dog with cat eyes."

Esmeralda picked up a pebble and threw it toward the woods. It fell about twenty feet short. "Damn, that was lame," she said. "I can do better." She did have pronounced biceps. "I have a Rottweiler named Eve. She's named that because she likes apples." She picked up another stone and threw it. It went about a foot further. "My dad's a minister."

"I don't know my dad."

She threw another stone. It fell short of the first. "That sucks," she said. "My dad keeps snakes in the house. Poisonous ones. He's a snake handler."

"What's that?"

"Long story," she said. Silence. Andrew liked the way she was straight forward and didn't gab all the time. She was like Bethy in that way. "Why aren't you playing volleyball?" she asked.

"Too tired," he said. "Why aren't you?"

She flashed a grin. She had pretty teeth. Straight. White. And he thought he'd seen a tongue ring. "'Cause I wanted to hang out with you."

Andrew's face flushed. He wanted to ask if she had a tongue ring but it seemed too personal.

"Tell me about Bethy," she said sitting down on the grass. Andrew paused. The grass looked soft and long and had little white clover flowers in it. He joined her. He stretched his legs out and leaned back on his elbows. The sun felt warm, the air a little cool. The volleyball kids were laughing and calling each other names. He wasn't sure he wanted to say anything about Bethy.

Esmeralda was sitting about a foot away, cross-legged, picking clover and making some kind of chain with them. Her grandmother'd taught her how to do it, she said. She was dead now, her name was Joanna Sue, died of pneumonia about six years ago. He watched her loop the stem of a clover into a loose knot and stick the flower head of the next into it. She pulled the knot tight and looped the next stem the same way, connecting the little white flowers to one another, and he started to talk. And he told her about Bethy and Joey and how he was worried about him and his mother and how he wished she weren't dead even though he hated her sometimes and about Thomas and the bracelet he was carrying in his pocket from Red. And he told her about how his stomach felt sick a lot and how he stuck his finger down his throat sometimes, and she said that was called purging and a lot of kids at Metamorphosis did it but it would eat the enamel off his teeth and some people even died from doing it and he said he knew it was a dumbass thing to do and he wanted to stop. And she said maybe sometime they could hunt for snakes together to add to the pet center, not poisonous ones, but snakes like king snakes and garters, and he said he didn't think he would be around much longer because he was going to go live with Thomas as soon as things got straightened out. And she listened and concentrated with a furrowed forehead on her clover project until she had tied about fifty of them together and then she looped the chain into a big circle and leaned across the space and put it around his neck. The clover had a fresh, sweet smell.

"There," she said. "It's like Joanna Sue's sitting right here in the grass with us, soaking up the sun, saying, 'Esme, Andrew, life's too short to spend your time frettin'. Don't you worry, baby. Everything's gonna turn out just right.'"

*   *   *

"Hey, man, ya' wanna call Bethy? That's her name, right?" Birthday Benjamin's eyes were sparking with energy. Andrew felt himself being drawn in.

"How?"

"There're some phones, other stuff, too, stashed in the woods. Not far. I'm making a run in about five minutes after Rico gets busy with paperwork. He always does paperwork at the end of his shift. I need a new phone. Ms. Shelby got my last one."

"Where's the stuff come from?" Andrew asked. This guy Benjamin was like a character off one of the survivor reality shows. It was weird but sometimes his mom liked to watch survivor shows at night and he'd walk past and get hooked into watching them too. You've got to know how to think on your feet, she'd say. Outside the box. Rely on yourself. And now she was dead.

Benjamin leaned forward and lowered his voice. Rico was walking across the room, clipboard in hand. "There's this dude named Tony. He buys stuff. Hides it all over town. Sends it up North in his cousin's van about once a month. The guy lives somewhere up there."

"You mean they fence stuff?" Benjamin needed to know he wasn't stupid or anything. But the news was amazing. It had to be the same Tony.

"Yeah, I guess you'd call it that."

He wondered if his stuff were there. "So, when did he bring it out?"

"Tony never comes. But his homeboys brought a garbage bag of shit last night. After the girls sneaked back into their cottage."

"Damn," muttered Andrew. His things were probably there. "Yeah, I'm in."

Birthday Benjamin laughed and smacked him on the shoulder. "I thought so," he said. "See, I can take what I need 'cause I help him out. Keep my eyes and ears open, that's what I do. Make sure staff stays clueless. Let him know if anybody starts to figure it out. He can't have the shit around his house, he's gone down for stealing before."

"Yeah?" said Andrew. His stomach tightened. He didn't like trouble. Especially with Joey coming back and it not being long until he could leave and go live with Thomas. But he wanted his stuff. And to talk to Bethy. If her mother wasn't home. If there really was a phone in the woods.

"So," said Benjamin, "here's what we do." He sounded dramatic, conspiratorial, like he'd watched too many B-rated movies.

"Yeah?"

"We split up right now. Make your way toward the front door, casual like. Maybe bend down to tie your shoe or something when you get there, or turn your back to the door, whatever, so you don't draw attention. But when I run, run like hell and don't get lost. We'll have the jump on Rico and he's the only one who could hope to catch us. We could outrun the other two with weights on our ankles."

Andrew nodded. "O.K."

Benjamin smiled a crooked sort of tight lipped smile that looked totally fake. He winked an eye, too, and then turned and meandered toward the door. Andrew saw him pick up a magazine that was sitting on a beat up coffee table painted white over a sort of pea green, and it looked like before that it'd been dark brown. He watched him pretend to read as he walked three or four steps, paused, pretended to read again. Andrew headed in the opposite direction, making a slow large circle around the room. Rico was sitting at a far table engrossed in typing notes into the computer. Andrew knew the man was summarizing behaviors, each boy's afternoon. He walked casually toward Benjamin. None of the staff were paying them any attention. One was distracted by a phone call. The other by a boy asking for help with some kind of problem in his room, probably a homework thing. Andrew was nearing the door when he saw Benjamin throw him a nod and run full force toward the exit.

"Benjamin's running!" a bone-skinny short kid named Alexander yelled. Andrew didn't really know the kid yet. The door was closing. He shoved against it, blinked at the daylight and looked around. Benjamin was already halfway across the side lawn running like he was on the high school sprinting team. He was headed toward the woods.

"Come on, Andrew!" he yelled over his shoulder.

Andrew pushed into high gear. He heard the cottage door open despite his own fast and shallow breathing. He kept his eyes on Benjamin who was already at the tree line, leaping over a fallen tree, blazing his own path through the pines and hardwoods. Andrew ducked the low limbs as best he could, felt sticker vines snare his jeans, heard footsteps and yelling behind him but he could tell they weren't getting closer. Benjamin was impressively fast and agile. Up a hill slippery with pine needles and last winter's leaves. Through a stand of native bamboo. Past a huge tree with a lightening line down the length of it. Andrew saw him sliding on his feet and the seat of his pants down a steep ravine. There was a little water at the bottom, maybe a creek, maybe an inlet from the lake. The voices behind them were distant now. Benjamin had nailed it. Staff couldn't keep up. He watched little avalanches of gravel and dirt tumble down the hill ahead of Benjamin. Andrew stopped, frowned. He hated to screw up his jeans. He hated to get his shoes wet when he got to the bottom.

"How much further, man?" he called down the slope.

"Shut up. They'll hear us. Come on!"

He sat on his haunches. He imagined being on his skateboard. He pushed off and let the seat of his jeans ride along the dirt. Little rocks jabbed his butt through the denim and scraped his palms. By this time, Benjamin was up and crossing the water. There was a sycamore tree on the other side. Andrew knew it was a sycamore because the tree guy his mom had dated, Bob somebody, told him trees with white bark near water were almost always sycamores. The tree looked like it'd been white washed. Benjamin was headed toward it, fighting his way through the brambles.

"Wait up," Andrew called softly. There was no answer. When he neared the bottom he stood and ran the rest of the way, stumbling, sloshing, splashing, into the water. It was, as he suspected, an inlet of the lake. Ankle deep and lukewarm. Gooey rotting leaves and algae, mud like quicksand sucking at the soles of his shoes. He scanned for snakes. Cottonmouths. Water moccasins. Those suckers would come right up out of the water after a person. "Damn," he muttered.

"Don't be a wuss," said Benjamin.

He followed the voice around the huge tree and through the brambles. "Ouch!" He pulled a sticker vine away from his calf with his fingers. "Shit."

"You are a wuss."

"Go to hell." He watched Benjamin squat in front of the sycamore's trunk. There were holes, holes big enough for a crow to fly into, starting about half way up. Seven in all.

"The stuff's up there," Benjamin said. "It's a hell of a climb. Can you do it?"

Andrew walked around the tree studying its shape. The first limbs were too high. No way to reach them without climbing the cedar next to it and crossing over. "Sure," he said. "But the tree must be rotten up there. Look at those holes."

"Woodpeckers," said Benjamin. "I thought it was rad the first time I saw it. Perfect hiding places. I drew the holes for Ms. Mo-titti and told her I remembered it from when I was little. She looked it up on the computer. Some kind of woodpecker made them. I remember, like pie-a-lated or something."

"Are they in there now?"

"What?"

"The woodpeckers."

"Nah."

Andrew studied the trunk. It looked healthy enough despite the holes. "Not good to climb messed up trees, bro'."

"Guys climb it all the time," said Benjamin. "Can you get up there?"

It wasn't near as high as the magnolia he and Joey climbed as kids. "Of course."

"Good," said Benjamin sitting on a nearby log. There were ants and mosses and lichens all over it. "You climb and throw the stuff down. Take the stuff you want. Not too much or I'll get beat up. But get me a phone."

He studied the tree closely. Yellower leaves on the branches above the second hole. "Where's the stuff stashed anyway? I'm only climbing to the second hole."

"That's all they use. The first and the second holes."

Andrew wiped his palms on his jeans. He swung a foot into the cedar. The needles felt scratchy and a little sticky with sap and the tree's purple blue berries smelled like air freshener when he crushed them with his shoes. He scanned for good footholds. Handholds. His shoes were muddy and slippery and he heard several muddy globs fall to the needled ground below.

"Shit. You're like a damn monkey. Where'd you learn to climb like that?"

He was level with the first thick tree branch. He inched out on the cedar carefully, it bowed and flexed like an amusement park ride. He leaned forward to make the transfer, moving more like a sloth until he felt the sycamore branch beneath him. "It's what we did when I was a kid," he said. He thought about the Union soldiers swarming the grounds underneath the magnolia. Benjamin would never understand. Anyway, today it was Metamorphosis staff he was watching for. He scanned to his left, in front. No one yet. To his right. "Hey, dude," he said just loud enough for Benjamin to hear. "Looks like there're cars over there. Four of them."

"No duh. It's the boat landing. That's why Tony chose this place. Easy access."

"Oh." Park, jump the fence, stash the stuff. He moved his head to get a better look at the landing. He could see two boat trailers hitched to cars through the leaves. No people.

"I hate heights," said Benjamin. "They make me puke. Here's the deal. When I need something, you climb and get stuff you want, too."

Andrew tested each branch as he moved upward, cautious of rotting wood. The tree was actually in okay shape. "I won't be around long enough to go into partnership or anything." Anyway, all he wanted was to get back his mother's jewelry. "Dude," he said. "How many places like this does Tony have anyway?"

"You just got here, sonofabitch. You ain't going nowhere."

"How many places, dude?"

"You crazy?" Benjamin said. "Nobody asks Tony stuff like that. I just heard he has shit all over town. Like I said before, enough for a van to go North regular."

His mother's jewelry could be anywhere. Andrew wedged his feet in tight against the trunk when he got to the first hole. He looped his left elbow around a branch and peered into the darkness. "God knows what's in here," he said. The hole was deep and creepy. Raccoons. Bats. Maybe even a porcupine.

"Don't be a pussy," said Benjamin. "People stick their hands in there all the time. Anyway, there's a cardboard box stuffed inside so things don't fall all the way down."

Andrew laughed. "They wouldn't anyway. The tree's not hollow all the way down you dumbass."

"Whatever. Just shut up and get your hand in there. Find me a phone."

Andrew crooked his elbow tighter, put his cheek against the trunk, clenched his jaws, shut his eyes, and shoved his hand in. He waited for snake fangs, a scorpion barb, the bite of some big ass spider. Instead his fingers touched cardboard and he pulled out a fistful of electronic gear, an electronic reader and several video games. He leaned forward trying to identify the games as his. No luck "So, you say I just take what I want?"

"Yeah, sort of. But don't go all mall-babe about it."

Andrew plunged his arm back in, dropped the fistful, picked up another. "Man, some bad ass thing's gonna bite the hell out of me."

Benjamin laughed. "Hadn't yet."

He brought his fist back out, fingers curled around a phone. A flip phone. "All right," he said, wiping one or two ants, the big black fast ones, off its plastic window and flipping it open. He frowned. "Must need a sim card."

"Toss it down on that pine straw over there."

"Too high, dude," said Andrew maneuvering it into his back pocket. "It'd break." He stuck his hand back in, fished around. No jewelry. "So there's stuff in the second hole too?" He felt the branch give slightly as he stepped upward. "Shit." He'd have to be careful. He grabbed the trunk coconut tree style like he'd seen on T.V. and boosted himself upward cautiously. He peered into the second hole and stuck his arm in. This hole wasn't as deep. "Jewelry," he said pulling out a wad of chains and rings, bracelets and watches, and several mismatched earrings. There they were. One of his mom's rings, her two watches, and all three bracelets. "Hot damn!" he said, and an odd feeling, maybe it was relief or maybe it was something else, he wasn't sure, swept through him. "So, I'm taking some jewelry. Wanna dress up my girl."

Benjamin picked up a pine cone and lobbed it in the air toward Andrew and gave him a lopsided, crazy grin. "She must be some hot piece of ass."

His stomach tensed, his hands too. His right foot slipped on some little green tree ferns and he held tighter to the trunk with his arms. Piece of ass. He wanted to beat the crap out of him. "Is that all you fuckin' think about?"

Birthday Benjamin laughed, stopped abruptly. "Damn! We need to be quiet," he said.

Andrew imagined Union troops swarming toward the sycamore. Still no Metamorphosis staff in sight. He looked toward the boat landing. No one there either. He leaned his body hard against the tree, crammed her jewelry into his front pockets, and stuffed the rest back into the hole. His fingers groped around for the other ring. No luck. He pulled out another handful. A smart phone, a video game, one of his, and somebody else's bracelet. "Smart phone," he said. He pushed a button. Light. A little jingly sound. "It works." He dropped it into his front shirt pocket.

"That's better. Put the other one back."

"Sure." It didn't work anyway. He fished for it, holding the other stuff in his arm that curled around the tree. He put his game and the bracelet and the flip phone back into the hole. His fingers identified the flat cool plastic of some CDs or DVDs. He pulled them to the opening but decided not to get them out. "That's it," he said.

"Okay, get your ass back down."

It was a hell of a long way down. It didn't look so high while he was climbing. An electric shock sensation traveled up the back of his legs, through his spine, tingled in his stomach. Somewhere off in the distance he heard voices of Metamorphosis staff. "So I've got you the smart phone and I've got some jewelry."

It was crazy. But thinking about some dickwad's girlfriend wearing his mom's jewelry around the streets up North pissed him off. It had to go home. Back into her drawer. Into her room with her dumbass football clock. He swallowed, felt oddly weak, dizzy. He held onto the branches tighter, his left hand higher than his right. Somewhere deep inside a thought stirred. And then another. He didn't have a home. His mother was gone. He shut the thoughts out. Not today. Maybe when Joey got back and they had time to talk about everything. "Coming down," he said. His pockets bulged against his thighs. The stuff dug into his legs whenever he got up close to the tree. He maneuvered easily among the limbs like he'd done all his life. He didn't bother transferring to the cedar on his way back down. When he was about twelve feet off the ground he searched for a soft landing spot and jumped. The pine needles jabbed into his palms. The soles of his feet burned. His thighs felt bruised where the stuff jammed into them. He stood and brushed off his jeans, his palms. There was a small cut and a little blood on his right hand. He rubbed it on his shirt.

"Let's see," said Benjamin.

Andrew pulled out the jewelry.

"Way too much. No way you earned that. How you gonna pay me?"

"Cigarettes?" Andrew said.

"How many?"

"A carton?"

"How you gonna get them?" asked Benjamin. Clearly he was interested.

"Not important."

Benjamin slapped the palm of his hand against his side, an absent minded sort of gesture. Thwack, thwack, thwack. "Yeah, okay if you throw in a six pack."

Andrew wondered how he'd convince Joey to buy him a six pack. Cigarettes, sure, but alcohol was a different story. He'd think of something. "Yeah, all right, but that's it."

"You've got a lot of shit there," argued Benjamin.

"A carton and a six pack, that's it."

Thwack, thwack, thwack. "Yeah, okay." Thwack, thwack, thwack. "Deal."

Andrew stuffed his mother's jewelry back into his pockets. He knew some of it was sitting on top of Red's bracelet and the photo in the locket and the college ring.

"When do I get paid?" asked Benjamin.

He shrugged. "Two or three days, a week tops."

"Don't rip me off, man."

"I don't play like that."

Benjamin squinted, nodded, then held out his hand for the phone. He fiddled with it for about a minute. "So, you wanna call your woman?"

"Nah, she's grounded. I'll call tonight. Her mom'll be at yoga. From the cottage."

Benjamin sat on the mossy log again. He brushed a skinny brown and red striped bug off his shirt. It had a forked tail. Andrew wondered if it had a stinger. "You crazy?" Benjamin laughed. "You think you'll have phone privileges after our run?"

"What d'ya mean? What's gonna happen?"

Benjamin laughed again. "Well, they can't chain us to a dungeon wall, dude. But, we'll be knocked down to Level zero for real. Probably grounded for a week."

"Grounded? From what?"

"Anything, everything. No phone, no TV, all free time'll be in our rooms."

It was like he'd been punched in his chest. "What about family? Visits, I mean?"

"Oh, yeah. Family's different. They're the exception. But that doesn't do me a hell of a lot of good."

Andrew relaxed. He could still see Joey. Talk on the phone, too. "Doesn't sound so bad."

"Say that after a week when everyone's outside playing. But we still get P.E."

He shrugged. He didn't hear any Metamorphosis voices. It was like they'd given up. Gone back to the cottage.

"So, what's the number?" Benjamin asked.

"What number?"

"That girl, Bethy. I'll get her on the phone."

Benjamin talking to her mother. She'd be grounded for life. "Naw, man, that's okay."

"Don't be chickenshit. I swear to God her mom'll be clueless."

"Naw. Thanks, anyway."

Benjamin stood impatiently. "What the hell's the matter with you? I'm tellin' you her mom'll never figure it out. Trust me."

Bethy. He did want to talk to her. And the whole grounded thing was a bummer. "I swear to God," he said, "you'd better not screw this up." He reached for the phone, closed his palm around it. "I'll dial," he said. He waited until he heard a ring, then two, and handed it back to Benjamin fast. He could feel his heart beating. It was in his throat right under his Adam's apple.

"Last name?" Benjamin whispered urgently.

"Smithson," Andrew whispered back.

"Smithson?"

"Yeah."

"Is she a PTSO sort of mom?"

"What?"

"You know, PTSO, Girl Scout, cookie baker, all that." He was talking faster but he was still whispering.

"Oh, yeah, yeah, that'd be her."

Benjamin's mouth broke into a broad smile. "Hello? Mrs. Smithson? Hi. My name is William Pettagrew. I think you probably remember meeting me at school a while back? No? Well, I was with my mom and dad and my teacher introduced us? Yes. Yes, ma'am. It's been a while. Well, I'm in Bethy's math class and I lost my homework assignment and I looked on line because sometimes assignments are posted there but today they're not. Could I speak to her please?" Andrew watched him roll his eyes and smile cleverly. "Grounded? Oh, yes, ma'am. We won't talk long. I promise. Yes, ma'am." He gave a thumbs up. Andrew couldn't believe it. This Benjamin guy was crazy good. He reached for the phone but it jerked backward. "Thank you, Mrs. Smithson. I look forward to seeing you again too. Okay. Thank you. Hi, Bethy, this is William from math class. You know, William, William Pettagrew. Well, a lot of people don't remember me. I sit in the back corner." He paused. "Okay," he said conspiratorially. "Here's Andrew. You're supposed to give me a math assignment. Be careful what you say and you can't talk long." He handed the phone to Andrew.

"Bethy?" said Andrew.

"Yes! Yes, now I remember you. Sorry. There're just a lot of kids in that class."

Her voice soothed him, excited him. "They found Joey. He was with his girlfriend."

"Yes! I heard," she said. "No, ah, problem. Let me get my assignment sheet."

"I was gonna call you tonight but I'm grounded too."

"I'm glad you called, William. Just a second. Um, let's see. You need to read chapter 12 and do all the odd problems at the end of the chapter."

"I miss you."

"Yeah, I know what you mean. Me too, for real."

"Sorry I got you grounded."

"No problem at all, William." She giggled.

"Joey'll be back tomorrow. And I'll be outta here soon. I'm gonna live with Thomas."

"Really? That's excellent! Those, ah, problems are hard to do."

"Do you miss me?"

"So much! I know, she does give so much homework."

He wanted to say it but not in front of Benjamin. Love. He loved her.

"See you in class, William," she said. "Um, I guess I'd better go."

He didn't want her hanging up so quick. "Yeah, me too," he said. "I'll call soon."

"Please do that," she said. "Goodbye." He stood listening to the click and the dial tone.

Benjamin reached for his phone but Andrew swung his right hand high and fiddled with the buttons. No way could Benjamin have the phone until he'd erased the number. "I owe you one," he said pressing Delete. "You'd make a badass actor, dude."

"Not me," said Benjamin. "I'm business all the way. I like the feel of the green stuff."

"Yeah, well. You know what you're doing'll get you put away."

Benjamin put his hands on his hips, turned his head and spit off to his right. "What the hell you talking about?"

"Receiving stolen merchandise for one."

"What merchandise?" he asked as he turned and walked toward the inlet. "I've never seen nothin'. You haven't either if you know what's good for you. That guy Tony, he doesn't screw around. He has more guns stashed than a pawn shop, if you get my meaning."

Andrew knew he was right. Snitching on Tony was asking for a drive by. But for some crazy reason it bugged him Benjamin was in so deep. "How do you know this guy Tony anyway?"

"Why?" Benjamin's feet splashed water up onto the ragged cuffs of his jeans as he crossed. Hand me downs, probably from the Metamorphosis clothing closet.

Andrew stopped at the water's edge and rolled up his pants. The water looked deeper and there were more rocks on the bottom. "Didn't we cross down there?" he asked. "Where it's shallower?"

"Don't be a girl."

Andrew stepped into the water. It seeped, cooler than before, into his tennis shoes. They were already stained green gray from algae and lake muck. "I just wondered where you guys met."

Benjamin grabbed hold of a vine and pulled himself out of the water. "When I was little I stayed with my aunt. He lives with his grandmother. We rode the bus together. I'd get him stuff and he'd give me cigarettes."

"That vine back there, the one you grabbed, that hairy one," said Andrew.

"Yeah?"

"It's poison ivy, dude."

Benjamin shrugged. "Whatever." But he wiped his hands back and forth on the sides of his jeans.

"How old were you?"

"What are you? Writing a novel?"

"No," said Andrew. "Just curious." Benjamin was slick. Probably doing stuff since he was four or five.

"Eight, nine maybe." He climbed the hill on all fours.

Andrew copied him. Dirt under his fingernails. Little pebbles avalanching toward the water. Grit in his mouth somehow. His feet slipped. It was a tough climb. The stuff in his pockets felt bulky and annoying. Sweat dripped into his eyes. "Shit," he said.

Benjamin stopped when he reached the top and looked down at him. "When we get back, let me do all the talking, dude, and you be sure to stick to my story. And hurry your ass up." Without waiting, he turned and loped toward the cottage.

Andrew broke into a slow trot to keep up. He didn't like it. There were thorny brambles everywhere, snagging his jeans, his socks, his shirt, climbing all through the trees. One scraped his cheek. He rubbed the back of his hand against his face and looked for blood. Just a little. His sweat made it burn. "Slow down."

"Can't. It's been almost forty five minutes. At an hour they call Tuscaloosa PD and our social workers, too."

Andrew's stomach churned. "The police? You didn't tell me about the cops."

"Don't sweat it," said Benjamin. "We'll get back in time. Just shut up and run."

56

"He tells me he isn't interested in leaving here," said Reverend Jeremiah Lincoln. "In fact, he gets quite defensive whenever I bring up the topic of foster care. I'm wondering, what's your take on his reaction?"

Dr. Luke scanned the edge of the woods. It had been almost an hour. It was time for Benjamin to make his appearance. Benji always cut it to forty five, fifty minutes, tops. And then there was Andrew. Why was Andrew following Benjamin's lead? He didn't seem like a follower. But this was the second time they'd taken off together. Smoking, maybe. Or drugs, or drinking, or sex. Adolescents were wild cards. Nothing could be ruled out. "I think Benjamin's frightened of change and confused by feelings about his parents," Luke answered still scanning the wood's perimeter. "And he's comfortable. He doesn't have to form any primary bonds here, not like he would living with a family."

"So what are you saying?" asked Jerry Lincoln. "The Alldridges would be a good two parent home for him. They're very child focused and he'd get a lot of attention and time. He'd probably go a lot of places he may not see otherwise. They travel frequently."

Dr. Luke squinted into the undergrowth. Still no sign of them. He glanced at his watch. "I wonder where they are," he said, more to himself than to the Reverend. A fleeting image of Benji and Andrew standing beside a road, thumbs out, brought a frown to Luke's face, but he couldn't take it seriously. Some kids did thumb their ways across the country, but not Benji. And not Andrew now that Joey was coming home. "The way Benji's been running recently," Luke said, "I'm not sure he's a candidate to move anywhere. His impulse control problems seem to be worsening. And we learned today he's in contact with a serious delinquent."

"Are you sure it's a problem with impulse?" asked Reverend Lincoln. "Maybe he plans his little escapes. Maybe he's up to something."

"That's actually looking probable," Luke said. "I just wish we could figure out where he's going all the time."

"Maybe your new boy Andrew will tell you," suggested the Reverend.

"I doubt it," said Luke. "He's pretty closed mouth. Good kid, but holds it all in."

"I think you've answered my questions about Benjamin," Jerry Lincoln said. "Can't have him running off from the Alldridges every day." He glanced at his watch. "They've been gone close to an hour. I was hoping to minister to Andrew today but if they don't get back soon, he'll have to wait until my next trip out."

Ten minutes. Then he'd have to call the police and the boys' legal guardians. Benjamin knew that. "I have a feeling they'll come popping through those woods any time now."

Jerry Lincoln opened his mouth as though he were going to say something unpleasant. Like, if Benjamin's runs were that predictable maybe his treatment wasn't addressing the problem. Luke could feel it. It was in the square posture of the Reverend's shoulders, the blue vein pulsing across his forehead. Instead, the Reverend's shoulders slumped. He turned his attention to the woods. "How's Andrew settling in?" he asked. "How's he coping with his mother's death?"

Luke was glad to leave the subject of Benjamin. "I don't think he's really dealt with it yet," he said. "The murder, her promiscuity, it's a lot for him to sort out. There's lots bubbling around inside him."

"Is he in the clear?" asked Jerry Lincoln. "I mean, clear of the murder?"

"Actually, no. I personally don't think he's guilty but there're still enough red flags to make him a suspect. And if it turns out his brother's the murderer, Andrew's going to have a really tough time of it."

"Do you think he'll want to talk?"

Luke smiled. "He doesn't strike me as a highly religious adolescent," he answered. "But these kids surprise me all the time. It'll be interesting to see what he might say to you. Sometimes they open up more to you than to us." It was true. Even though Luke hated to admit it and didn't understand it, there were times the kids talked more freely to Jerry Lincoln. He tried not to let his ego get in the way of that. Just as long as they talked, he told himself. Still, it bugged him.

Reverend Lincoln nodded to the left toward a stand of wild plum bushes. "Right on time," he said, "just as you predicted."

Luke felt the muscles in his shoulders loosen. "With six minutes or so to spare," he said. Benjamin'd cut it too close this time.

"I was wondering," said Reverend Lincoln. "Do you think it might help Andrew if I told him his mother came to my church years ago when Joey was a baby? Perhaps he'd have some questions . . ."

Luke watched Benjamin turn toward Andrew like he was telling him something important. Telling him what to say, no doubt. "I don't see how it could hurt, Jerry, just don't go into the promiscuity angle. Why don't you mention it and see where he goes with it?" Luke's phone barked.

"I meant to ask you," said Jerry Lincoln. "Where the hell'd you find that Doberman ring tone?"

"Downloaded it," said Luke putting the phone to his ear. "Bramson. Hi, Lydia. The suitcases? Sure. How about ten minutes? Maybe less." He pocketed his phone. "Sorry," he said. "That was about the suitcases your church donated last month. We're distributing them in the Monarch cottages today." Suitcases. What a difference in the kids' lives. Not having to carry their worldly possessions from place to place in green and black garbage bags.

Reverend Lincoln's mouth broadened into a wide smile. Like a giant bullfrog. "Our congregation is delighted to be of help. But back to Benjamin for a minute. So we're agreed? I'll table his placement in our program for the time being?"

"Right," said Luke. "I'll run it by his treatment team but I think they'll concur." He watched the two boys approach. Andrew lagged behind. He looked apprehensive. Benjamin was striding forward swinging his arms, that crooked little grin on his lips. Benji already knew they'd be grounded and he hated being stuck in his room. Maybe his medications needed adjusting. He'd grown several inches recently. Maybe just a little increase to help curb his impulsivity. He'd consult with Lydia. "Okay," he said as the boys made their final approach. "Let's see how Benji tries to squirm his way out of this one."

* * *

They paused to catch their breath when the cottage came into view. No one was outside except Dr. Luke and some tall stocky man with huge ears Andrew didn't know. The men were standing in front of the Luna cottage.

"Crap," said Benjamin.

"What?"

"It's that asshole Lincoln. He's trying to put me in a foster home."

"That's bad?"

"You try living with strangers," said Benjamin. "No way I'm leaving here."

"Can they make you?"

Benjamin cleared his throat and hocked a big loogie. "Not really," he said flashing a wise-ass smile. "I'll act up so much nobody'll take me."

Andrew took a step backward. Dr. Luke was staring at him. His face grew hotter and he wiped the sweat off his forehead with his arm. Benjamin wiped his cheeks and forehead with his palms.

"The oil, dude," Andrew said.

"What oil?" asked Benjamin.

"From the poison ivy. Keep your hands off your face."

"Damn! You are a girl."

"And you're a crazy sonofabitch."

"He's really not a bad dude, that Lincoln guy," Benjamin said. "He buys us kids stuff out of the machines and sometimes he lets us call friends from his phone. I'll go with him today. I could use a drink and some chips. Stay out of my room a little longer. Being grounded's a bitch." He stepped forward, heading straight for the two men. Andrew hesitated. When he tried to swallow his throat was dry. It felt like the hangy-down thing in the back was stuck to his tonsils.

"Come on," hissed Benjamin. "Hurry up. And keep your mouth shut."

"So," said Dr. Luke as the two boys approached. Benjamin cool, not looking at all intimidated, the right side of his lip curled ever so subtly. Andrew nervous, maybe almost embarrassed. And both of them filthy and scratched and wet. "I'm glad your watch keeps accurate time, Benjamin," he said sarcastically, glancing at his own. "You're only four minutes under the wire."

Benjamin smiled. Mischief glistened through his eyes, traveled across his mouth, down into the hand sitting squarely, self confidently on his hip. Luke felt himself being drawn in. Benji had a way of doing that, no matter how angry people got with him. "Okay, Benjamin, where'd you guys go?"

"To see the blue bomber," answered Benjamin sweetly. He was pouring it on heavy.

Andrew's head jerked around. It was an automatic response and he knew immediately he'd screwed up. Dr. Luke was watching him, he hadn't missed the movement. The other man didn't appear to be paying attention at all. Andrew jerked his head from left to right several more times and put his hand up to rub the back of his neck. "Crick," he said. But he knew it was a pathetic cover.

Dr. Luke didn't look convinced. He turned his attention back to Benjamin. "The blue bomber?"

"Yeah," said Benjamin enthusiastically. "It was a bet. I told Andrew we had a bird down at the lake as big as an ostrich. He said no way." Benjamin nodded toward Andrew for confirmation. Andrew stopped rubbing his neck and nodded back. "Anyway all us kids call it the blue bomber 'cause of the way it lands. But Ms. Moffiti looked it up on the computer and she says it's a great blue heron."

"You know it's against the rules to get near the water without staff," said Dr. Luke.

Benjamin lowered his head. "Yes, sir," he said. "But we weren't anywhere near the water, were we, Andrew? We watched him from the woods."

Andrew didn't answer. He felt Dr. Luke's attention shift to their tennis shoes. Andrew's were greenish brown with lake muck. Broken stems and vines stuck out from them like quills.

"What have we said about telling the truth, Benjamin?" Dr. Luke asked but he didn't wait for an answer. "And Andrew." Andrew heard disappointment in his voice. "I guess you like it here and want to stay longer than you originally planned."

The jewelry bulged in his pockets. It felt heavy. His skin itched. He still had dirt in his mouth. And he'd bummed up his tennis shoes. "No," he said. "No, sir."

"Well," said Dr. Luke, "Can you understand how your behavior indicates you're in no hurry to leave? Think about that the next time you decide to take off running."

Dr. Luke's eye contact was firm. It was the same way Thomas looked at him and Joey when he was establishing the rules. Except Dr. Luke's eyes were the bluest he'd ever seen. Andrew looked away. "Yes, sir."

"Okay," said Dr. Luke. "I'll talk with each of you alone about this later. But for now you're both on level zero for a week."

"A week! A whole week!" whined Benjamin. "It was just a bird, Dr. Luke."

"And a runaway," answered Dr. Bramson.

57

"So I still don't have a clue where they're going on these little jaunts of theirs," Luke said to Lydia Hutchinson as he pushed the hand truck up the sidewalk toward the classroom observation room. "But I feel certain Benjamin's up to something. He's the ring leader of all the Luna cottage's runs, I'm sure of it."

"Did you check their pockets?" asked Dr. Lydia.

Luke paused momentarily. "Damn," he said. "How did I miss that?"

Dr. Lydia smiled. "It's called being human."

He pushed the hand truck forward again. His hands absorbed the metal bar's vibrations as the cart moved along. It was a large hand truck with a flat bed that would accommodate eight or maybe even ten stacked suitcases at a time. "I've checked Benji's pockets several times before, though," he said. "Except when we catch him with phones I never come up with anything."

Dr. Lydia smiled again. "He's a loveable rascal, that Benjamin," she said. "But he'll be a handful in a foster home I'm afraid."

"Actually," said Luke, "I was just talking to Jerry Lincoln about that. I want to take it before the treatment team but I'm thinking it's too early for Benjamin to leave us." They had reached the main building. Luke waited while Dr. Lydia slid her key into the door's lock. He pushed the hand truck into the small, dark room. "Actually Benjamin himself is saying he doesn't want to go."

Dr. Lydia followed him inside. The metal door slammed behind them. Luke waited for his eyes to adjust to the low light.

"Then he's probably not ready," she said.

"Next time we're in the office and I can grab his chart, I want to talk with you about his medications too," said Luke. "I'm wondering if his growing spurt might necessitate an adjustment to his meds."

Dr. Lydia moved toward the suitcases against the back wall. She pulled one off the top of the pile and carried it to the hand truck. "Sounds like a reasonable avenue to pursue," she said laying the suitcase on its side.

"Let me do that, Lydia," he said moving toward the suitcases. Her hair brushed his arm. It was still wet from the pool and she was wearing flip flops and a turquoise pullover made of terry cloth and the whole observation room smelled like chlorine. He breathed deeply. He loved the smell. Summer time, curly cue slides, lifeguards' whistles and Marco Polo. He'd always been great at Marco Polo.

"We'll both do it," she said grabbing another.

"I was just thanking Reverend Lincoln for his church's donation," he said. There were enough suitcases for both the girls' and boys' Monarch cottages. The Monarchs were younger than his Lunas.

"I don't guess you and Addie have had time to discuss my proposal about your eventual directorship at Metamorphosis," she said as she pulled another suitcase onto the cart.

"Actually, no," he said pushing the stack of suitcases forward to allow for another row. "Not yet. Addie's so busy working the Beaty murder case. I hardly see her these days. And honestly, as flattering as it is to think about, it'll probably take us some length of time to come to a decision."

She stood up straight, her hands rubbing the arch of her back. "Of course it will," she said. "I'd be worried if it didn't. Take as long as you need." She chuckled. "Just ignore my impatient questions." She reached for another suitcase. "How many do you think we can stack on here at a time?" she asked.

He suspected the cart's vibrations might jiggle them all off already. Unless they held them steady with their hands. "Maybe four more, tops," he said.

"Good," she said. "Just one trip after this one and I'm ready to get back to the pool."

*   *   *

At first he wasn't going to go. But what Benjamin said made sense. Time out of his room during grounding. A free soda and some barbeque chips. He decided even before they reached the machines he wouldn't buy jalapeno flavored ones. He missed Bethy too much already.

"Andrew, I'm Reverend Jeremiah Lincoln," the man had said. The man had a blue vein that ran sideways up and across his forehead and disappeared into his hairline. Like a blue river. The Amazon maybe.

"I dropped by hoping we might chat a while." Who the hell chatted? Chatting was lame. But it was as simple as that and there he was, walking with Reverend Lincoln up the hill and into the main building toward the snack machines. As simple as that plus the look of astonishment on Birthday Benjamin's face that the minister hadn't come to see him. Benjamin's face all screwed up in surprise made it worth going with the man. But as Andrew waited in silence, listening to the whir of the machine after he pushed D10, watching the bag of chips move toward him through the glass then wriggle free of the metal coil and fall, he wasn't sure about it at all. He didn't like talking to strangers. And the guy was a minister. That alone was freaky.

"All set?" asked Reverend Lincoln, eyeing the drink and the bag of chips. "I'm a sour cream and onion man myself."

Andrew didn't reply. Five minutes tops. He'd make up some excuse to go back down to the cabin.

"What're we gonna talk about anyway?" he asked. The question was stupid. It just came out that way and he wished he hadn't asked. He knew the answer anyway. Death. Murder. Grief. Loss. God. Church. No way were they going to chat.

Reverend Lincoln smiled in a laid back, kind sort of way. "That's up to you," he said. "I just wanted to put a face to your name. I was on your admissions committee so I already feel like I know you in some ways. And a group of us ministers take turns coming out to Metamorphosis to make sure the needs of the residents are being met."

"You mean praying, church stuff."

The man chuckled. "Ministers do talk about other things, you know. But some residents enjoy talking about their lives and God and some ask us to pray with them, for their families and such."

"Not me," said Andrew as the two walked up the dusky hallway. Ms. Moffiti's classroom door was open. The room was empty and dark.

"No problem," said Reverend Lincoln casually. "Looks like the classroom's free," he said. "Why don't we chat in there?"

He could smell something on the minister's skin. Aftershave, maybe. Some sort of musky spice smell. It reminded Andrew of Thomas. He and Joey always teased Thomas about smelling like an old fashioned fart but Thomas said it didn't matter what they thought because it was Holly's favorite scent on a man. That was enough for him he said.

"My dad wears aftershave too," Andrew said.

Reverend Lincoln cocked his head curiously. "I thought . . . I must not be remembering right . . ."

"What?"

"I was thinking your records indicated that you don't know your father's identity."

Andrew had stopped just inside the doorway. He wasn't going further until Reverend Lincoln turned on the lights. "You've read my records?" he asked. His stomach tensed and that weird lumpy thing rose up in his throat. He wondered what his records said about him.

"Oh," said Reverend Lincoln. "I'm sorry to have sprung that on you like that. It's standard procedure on the admissions committee to read the records of new admissions. But my memory's obviously wrong." His hand paused on the light switches before he flipped them. "Shall I close the door?"

Andrew stepped into the room trying to sound nonchalant, swallowing hard to clear the lumpy thing. "Naw," he said. "No one else's around."

"So you were saying your dad wears aftershave."

Andrew leaned his backside against Ms. Moffiti's desk. He watched Reverend Lincoln pull up a chair and then another. He stayed put. The jewelry in his jeans pockets felt lumpy against his thighs. He wanted to get back to the cottage where he could stash the stuff he'd picked up with Benjamin. "I was talking about Thomas," he said. "My brother's dad. I'm moving in with him and his family as soon as I get out of here. Next week. Maybe sooner."

"Really?" asked Reverend Lincoln.

Andrew didn't answer. It was time to go back to the cottage. He'd say he had a stomachache. If the man read his records for real he knew his stomach always acted up. Reverend Lincoln sat quietly looking at him. Like he was waiting for Andrew to bring up something they could talk about. The same way Dr. Luke did. He popped the top of his drink and beige-ish fizz foamed and puddled on top of the can. "I have a stomachache," he said.

Reverend Lincoln leaned back in his chair and crossed his arms across his chest. "Yes," he said. "I remember reading that your stomach acts up a lot. Nerves, right?"

It sounded wimpy. Maybe Benjamin was right. Maybe he was a wuss. He shrugged. Back to silence. He looked in the two way mirror. All he could see was his own reflection and the minister's. It was weird how the little room where he and Benjamin stood watching Ms. Moffiti was invisible from this side of the mirrors. The son of a bitch was probably in there right now. Watching and laughing at him. "What happens if you run again after you're already grounded for running?" he asked.

Reverend Lincoln uncrossed his arms and leaned forward. "Why would you do that?" he asked. "Didn't you hear what Dr. Bramson said about your behavior affecting the length of stay here?"

"Oh, I didn't mean me," Andrew said quickly. "I just wondered, that's all."

"That's sort of a strange thing to wonder if he's not going to run," whispered Lydia to Luke from inside the observation room. The two had stopped piling suitcases and were standing near the mirrors. They were basically trapped. Opening the outside door would shine light through the mirrors.

"Agreed," Luke said in a soft gravelly voice. "I don't quite have a grip on what's happening inside that rapscallion brain of his." He used the word because it was one of Lydia's favorites. He didn't even have to look her way to know she was smiling.

"You'll figure it out," she whispered. In truth they didn't have to whisper and they both knew it. The room was sound proofed.

"Well," said Reverend Lincoln. "I don't know for certain what would happen, Andrew, but I'm guessing the grounding might be longer and maybe more severe."

"Good enough answer," whispered Dr. Lydia.

"Did you hear that Joey's been located?" Luke asked.

"Really? Excellent! Where was he?"

"He apparently went up to Amherst to be with his girlfriend," whispered Luke. "I'm still concerned about how this is going to pan out. Andrew'd go to the gallows for Joey, I'm sure of it."

"Well," said Reverend Lincoln. "How are you liking this place?"

Andrew shrugged. The man really did chat. He sighed. "I shouldn't be here. Everyone knows it. It was my mom's lame idea and now she's . . . Anyway, I don't need to stay here anymore. Thomas wanted me to live with them even before I came here but Mom said no. She's, she was, jealous of Holly."

"Who's Holly?" Casual and laid back, just like Dr. Luke.

Andrew swallowed. It was like a trick the way they got him to talk. "Thomas' wife," he said.

"Do you like her?"

Andrew jiggled his right leg. Boring, stupid, none of the guy's business. "She's okay."

"Do they have children?"

His leg jiggled harder. He took another gulp from the can. "I really do have a stomachache," he said.

"Is this hard to talk about?" asked Reverend Lincoln.

Pissed off. He was getting pissed off now. Chatting was a pain in the ass. He'd kill Benjamin when he got back to the cottage.

"Looks like it is," whispered Luke.

"Maybe," whispered Lydia. "Or maybe he's just private."

"That he is for sure," said Luke.

"No," said Andrew. "Why would it be hard to talk about? They have three little kids and Joey, of course, and now, me."

Reverend Lincoln smiled a relaxed friendly smile and leaned further forward. "You're not going to believe this, but I actually know your brother Joey. Well," he continued like he was measuring his words, "maybe that's a bit of an exaggeration. I should say I *knew* Joey when he was a little tyke. Three, four years old. Cute little fellow. I understand he's studying veterinary science at Auburn. Well, even then he loved animals. I remember when he brought a whole fistful of roly polys into church." Reverend Lincoln closed his eyes halfway and chuckled. "We found them later crawling all over the floor underneath the pews."

Andrew had never heard that story. The slug story, yes. His mother told the slug story all the time. But not the roly polys. "He was at your church?"

"Oh," said Reverend Lincoln. "I thought maybe you knew. Your mother came to my church before you were born. When she was pregnant with you she had horrible morning sickness, as I recall. Morning, noon, and sometimes early afternoon sickness." He chuckled again. "That made it kind of hard for her to attend church regularly."

Andrew's face felt hot. He glanced toward the mirrors. His cheeks were too red. He'd never heard about her morning sickness.

"Anyway, she stopped coming to church and I guess after you were born she was just too busy to come back, with two little ones at home, and if I remember correctly she was working on her graduate degree in education and teaching school, too."

Andrew opened his bag of chips and held them out toward Reverend Lincoln.

"Thanks," the man said as he removed several. "One thing I can tell you, Andrew, is that your mother was a very hard worker back then. She believed in the value of a good education." He put the chips in his mouth. Andrew heard them crunch. The blue vein on the man's face pulsed as he chewed. "What about you? What are your interests?"

Andrew thought about climbing up in the big magnolia tree and the Union soldiers swarming underneath him and Joey, and he thought about saying he really liked history but instead he shrugged.

"Well, you're still young. It'll come to you," said Reverend Lincoln kindly.

"Did my mom really come to your church a lot before I came along?" asked Andrew.

"Faithfully."

"He's sure got his interest," whispered Luke.

"Yes," whispered Lydia.

It was weird to think of his mother in church. She'd dropped him and Joey off at the Unitarian church a few times when they were younger but they'd never gone to church as a family and they'd never said grace or prayed or really even talked about God. He thought about the locket. Maybe Red went to church with her. Maybe Reverend Lincoln would recognize him. His breath fluttered in his throat. "Um," he said. "Ah . . ."

"Yes?"

His heels pushed into the floor and his chair scooted backward. The chair's legs squeaked across the linoleum. "Um, nothing," Andrew said. "I forgot what I was gonna say."

"I bet he was going to ask about his father," whispered Luke. "About Red."

There was an inviting, concerned look on Reverend Lincoln's face. "It's okay to ask, Andrew, no matter what it is."

Andrew cleared his throat. His heart was beating against his Adam's apple again and he felt sick to his stomach for real. What if it did turn out to be Old Iguana Man? He glanced at the mirrors again. His jaw looked tight, his neck defined. "Um, I was just wondering if she was ever with anybody at church back then."

"She was with Joey," said Reverend Lincoln.

"No, I mean, like dating somebody, something like that."

Reverend Lincoln squinted as though he were peering back through the years. "Yes," he said eventually. "Several men came with her at different times. She was, um, very popular."

"That's a sanitized way to put it," whispered Luke.

"But Andrew," continued Reverend Lincoln, "it's been a very long time."

Andrew rubbed his hand across the outside of his right pocket. The jewelry was lumpy and he knew the locket would be at the bottom. "I have a photo," he said. "Maybe you'd recognize the guy." He stretched his leg out and dug deep. The rings, the bracelets, the watches, came out in a tangled fistful. He put them down on Ms. Moffiti's desk. He dug deeper then frowned. Arching his back, he fished into the second pocket.

"Were those pieces in the admissions meeting with him?" whispered Lydia, moving closer to the mirror to get a better look.

"No," whispered Luke. The extra jewelry wasn't a good sign.

"Look," said Lydia. "There's the locket."

Andrew was holding it by the silver chain. Tattered tissue paper lay beneath it on Ms. Moffiti's desk. Luke could see the boy's fingers shaking. Shaking enough to cause the locket to sway. "I've got a photo," Andrew said again. "Maybe you knew the guy."

Reverend Lincoln reached forward to take the locket. He looked extraordinarily serious. "Where'd you get these things?" he asked sternly. His eyes traveled from the locket to the lump of jewelry on the desk and back to the locket. "Were they your mother's?"

"Dr. Luke knows I have them," said Andrew quickly.

"Some of them," Luke whispered.

"I think the man's name is Red," Andrew said. "It's probably his nickname. Or maybe it's not him at all. But I have a bracelet with the name Red on it and I have a class ring, too."

Reverend Lincoln was holding the locket's silver chain, pulling it toward him.

"No," said Andrew. "I'll hold it." His thumb and forefinger were wrapped around the chain.

Reverend Lincoln pulled the locket closer to his face and Andrew moved with the jewelry. "I want to hold it," Andrew said.

The minister's face moved even closer to the photo. He studied it for what seemed to be a very long time.

"And the bracelet's engraved to my mother, something about always loving her, and it's signed Red. Did you ever see them together? Did he ever come to your church?"

Later Luke would tell Addie that he was in the middle of an eye blink when Reverend Lincoln jumped to his feet and snapped his closed fist backward in an attempt to wrestle the locket from Andrew. Andrew grabbed hold of the locket itself. He jumped up, too.

"Give it to me," Reverend Lincoln demanded. "You stole it."

"Dr. Luke knows I have it."

Reverend Lincoln tugged harder. With his free hand he swung forward and grabbed Andrew around the chest.

"What the hell?" yelled Andrew. "Get off me!"

"I'm going in," whispered Luke.

Lydia caught him by the arm. "Wait. We'll stop it if it gets too heated. But I have a feeling . . ."

"We can't let . . ." said Luke.

"We won't," Dr. Hutchinson assured him.

Reverend Lincoln moved his right foot closer to Ms. Moffiti's desk. He grabbed toward the pile of jewelry. "I'm confiscating it all," he said. "Turning it in."

Andrew pounded the man's hand with a fist as it moved toward the pile. The jewelry and Ms. Moffiti's paper clips in a clear plastic tray bounced.

"You SOB," bellowed Reverend Lincoln. "You'll pay for that. Just wait to see what they'll do to you for attacking a minister."

Andrew stood frozen, one hand wrapped firmly around the locket, the other hovering above the jewelry on the table.

"Give me the locket," Reverend Lincoln said firmly, calmly. "Let it go. Now."

Andrew's eyes widened. "Oh, my God!" he exclaimed. "Oh, my God! It's you! You're Red!"

Reverend Lincoln let go of the chain and lunged toward his throat. "Give it to me," he yelled. "Give it to me you bastard."

Andrew ducked sideways. The man was slow. "*Your* bastard," he retorted. He backed away, shoving the locket deep into his pocket.

Reverend Lincoln barreled toward him again. Andrew picked up a chair and held it over his head.

"You're even more pig-headed than your mother," said Reverend Lincoln.

The chair, a yellow plastic molded one with aluminum arms and yellow plastic armrests waved menacingly in the air. "*You* killed her," said Andrew. "It was you. She was going to tell me and you killed her."

"Give me the damn locket," said Reverend Lincoln.

"You *killed* her," Andrew said again.

"I want that picture," said Reverend Lincoln.

"Oh, my God," said Andrew. "You really did kill her." The chair wobbled above his head.

"Priscilla always said you were perceptive," said Reverend Lincoln. "And smart. You're a hell of a lot faster than that lady cop in charge of the investigation."

Andrew moved the chair further back, higher, over his head.

"I can't believe it!" whispered Luke. He felt Lydia's fingers resting heavily on his forearm.

Reverend Lincoln's shoulders relaxed. He leaned against the edge of the desk. He picked up the bracelets and rings and watches and let them fall through his fingers. They clinked back onto the desk. There was a weird kind of smirky smile on his face. There was a puffy knot in his forehead vein. It was bulging, pulsing, tumbling sort of like level five rapids. It was hard for Andrew to pay attention. To keep his eyes off it. "We're not leaving this room until I get the photo," Reverend Lincoln said. "Just a dad and his son spending a quality afternoon together I'd say. Sad thing is, Andrew, no one will ever believe you. Say whatever you want. Kids make up lies out here all the time. They say all kinds of things about the adults. False allegations they're called. Murder? Ministers don't murder. Take a guess, who will they believe?"

"Okay," whispered Dr. Hutchinson rapping on the mirror with her knuckles. "That's it. We've got more than enough."

Luke opened the observation room door. The muted afternoon sun threw a triangle of light onto the floor and the wall. "I'm going into the classroom to get Andrew," he said, squeezing by the dolly full of suitcases. He pulled his phone out of his pocket. "I think Addie's in an interview," he said. "She may not answer."

Dr. Hutchinson had her phone up to her ear. "I've got 911 already."

58

Mrs. Rebeka Arrington's face reddened immediately upon opening her front door. Addie figured out the doorbell wasn't working after several tries before R.J. knocked on the door with his fist. It was a door that had seen better days, pocked with spots where its wood had rotted and splintered, and where brown paint, chipped and curling like sun baked mud, exposed wood grayed with time and weather.

"He's not been out in two days," said Rebeka. "Got stung by yellow jackets, a whole swarm of them, that's what he said they were. He had some kind of reaction, antifialactick, or something like that, the doctor called it. Could have died the doctor said. If there's been trouble, he's been here."

Addie studied the woman's face, cured into leather by the Alabama sun and by cigarettes that hung one after another out of the side of her mouth. She liked Rebeka. She seemed a good-hearted woman who cared for an invalid lady by day and sat with hospital patients most nights to earn enough to make ends meet for her and her grandson. Addie had been coming to the house long enough to know that at times ends didn't meet at all. Both of Tony's parents, Rebeka's daughter and her son-in-law, had been in and out of prison for manufacturing crystal meth and for possessing of all kinds of recreational drugs since Tony was about five.

Anaphylactic shock from yellow jackets. It was an interesting coincidence. "May we speak to him please?" Addie asked.

Rebeka's shoulders slumped in submission. She opened the door wider and stepped aside. She was wearing a cotton print robe that had little Dalmatians running all over it, right side up, upside down, sideways going up and down her arms, and brown slipper socks. Her hair was parted crooked and pulled haphazardly back with bobby pins. "He's not in trouble, is he, Miss Addie?"

"I hope not but he might be," said Addie. "Where is he?"

Rebeka's shoulders slumped further and her neck and head followed. "I don't know about that boy," she mumbled more to herself than to anyone else. "Poisoned in the mind by his parents, I tell you. I do

392

everything I can to do right by him, but he don't appreciate it. He says he does but he sure don't act like it."

"He's lucky to have you," said Addie placing her hand briefly on the woman's shoulder and on at least five Dalmatians as she passed. She moved down the hall toward Tony's room. "You remember R.J., don't you, Rebeka?"

"Sure do. You were here just last week, weren't you? I remember your checked glasses. Not a lot of men wear fancy glasses." She stubbed out her cigarette on a dirty plate in the kitchen as they passed. Addie saw lumps of green on the plate. Collards, maybe, or turnips.

R.J. laughed. "So you like my houndstooth spectacles?"

"Looks like that checked hat that dead football coach, that fella Bryant, out at the University used to wear," she said. "Seems like everywhere you look nowadays there's black and white checks."

The hallway was dark and smelled like mildew. There was a bare light bulb hanging from the hall ceiling and it wasn't on. Addie remembered from a previous nighttime visit that the fixture didn't work. She knocked on Tony's bedroom door. "Okay," she said to Rebeka. She opened the door without waiting for an invitation. "We'll need to talk to him alone."

"Figured so," said Rebeka. "I'll be in the kitchen washing up."

Tony was in bed under a sheet that had several cigarette burn holes in it. From the disoriented stare he gave them as they entered, Addie guessed he'd been asleep. There was a half-eaten cracker and the dregs of a beer sitting on a beat up bedside table.

"I'll pretend I don't see that bottle," said Addie turning on her digital recorder.

"It's not mine," said Tony. "A friend stopped by. He's legal."

"Right," said R.J.

"What the hell are you doing here anyway?" Tony asked leaning up on his elbows. "I haven't even been in the street. I've been stuck in this room for two fuckin' days."

He did look rough. His eyelids were swollen and his right cheek was redder, more pronounced, than the other. His chin was scarlet and puffy, and there were at least four red marks on his forehead. One eyebrow jutted out due to swelling. Addie could see he'd been stung on his left forearm too. "We've come to hear the yellow jacket story," she said.

"Damned bastards nearly killed me, that's the story," he said. "I couldn't even breathe. Throat closed up."

"Where were you? When you got stung, I mean."

He lay back against his pillows. Same eyes. She'd seen that look in his eyes ever since she'd first met him. Defiant, Luke would call it. "I don't remember," he said.

"Bull," said R.J.

Addie stared firmly into his defiance, no nonsense, unrelenting. She'd learned years earlier how to establish dominance. The whole Alpha wolf thing. Show no vulnerability. Show no fear. Keep up the pressure. Don't back down. Wear her Glock. "Have you ever known or heard of a woman named Dana Whitesmythe?" she asked.

Tony's puffy eyelids blinked, then closed. Addie hoped it was to escape her stare. "Whitesmythe?" he repeated. "No. Should I?" He rubbed his finger across his lip. "Damn things even stung me inside my mouth," he said.

"And you're saying you don't remember where it happened?" asked R.J. "Think a night in lock up might refresh your memory?"

"Man, that's so messed up," said Tony, reopening his eyes. He pulled his pillow up behind his back and leaned against it. "You're arresting me for getting stung by yellow jackets?"

"No," said Addie. "We'll take you in for questioning related to the death of Ms. Dana Whitesmythe."

"I don't think so," said Tony, staring back at her. "Strict bed rest. Doctor's orders. You can ask my Grams."

R.J. unhooked his handcuffs. "Looks like one of the cots down at the station has your name on it, Tony my friend."

"What the hell?"

"Tell us about the yellow jackets," said Addie.

Tony eyed the handcuffs.

"Odd coincidence that Ms. Whitesmythe's car was full of yellow jackets when she ran off the road and was killed, and here you are, face all swollen like a pomegranate, from guess what? Yellow jackets," said R.J. "That and the word that's out in the street. That you have a new business besides your theft ring."

Tony's jaw tightened. "I don't know what the hell you're talking about."

"Let me enlighten you then," said R.J. "Murder for hire. We've got information from multiple sources."

"Bull crap," said Tony. "That's just hype, man. To scare off some real bad ass dudes trying to set up here. West coast group. Make me look pansy ass."

Addie stepped forward. There'd been law enforcement workshops about some of the West coast gangs. He was right about looking like a pansy ass in comparison. "Look, Tony," she said. "If someone did hire you to put yellow jackets in Ms. Whitesmythe's car, they need to take the fall for murder, not you."

"Yeah? Well, I got into a nest of the damn things while I was raking a lawn for somebody. But what if it did happen the way you're saying, if someone did hire me, you're sayin' you'd deal?"

Addie took another step forward. She softened her voice. She saw his eyes flicker. "We need the name of the person whose lawn you raked," she said, "since it happened that way, just to back up your story. But if'd been different, if someone'd hired you to put yellow jackets in Ms. Whitesmythe's car, then, yes, we'd try to put together a deal. You'd get some time but we'd work with the DA, try to get it reduced from murder. Manslaughter maybe."

"What murder?" Tony scoffed. "Don't bullshit me."

"Yeah, well, it just so happens Ms. Dana Whitesmythe's dead," said R.J. "And there were yellow jackets in a drink bottle inside her car, and the bottle's been dusted for prints and sent off to the lab. It'll be a surprise to find your prints on the bottle if you were out raking someone's lawn all respectable like."

Tony sat up straighter. Addie could see his right thumb was swollen, too. His puffy lids blinked slowly. Brown eyes peering from behind puff. Calculating eyes. Devoid of emotion. A skill of the streets. Be unreadable. She glanced at R.J. Predator eyes. Hungry. Moving in for the kill. He was good. There were no prints. R.J. knew it. She knew it. They'd collected no helpful evidence at all. She watched the two try to read each other, each searching for cracks, vulnerability. An eerie, menacing quiet hung above Tony's bed. She could feel it in her gut. She knew R.J. could too. Tony was about to break.

"Fuck you," he said to R.J.

"That's the best you can do?" R.J. countered.

Tony looked toward Addie. "So why should I believe you? That you'll deal?"

Addie smiled. R.J. was bad cop. She got to play good cop. At least today. "Don't know," she said. "What you got?"

Tony's shoulder muscle twitched. He leaned against his pillow and shut his eyes. "He said it was a fucking joke. A prank is what he called it. On an old friend. Take the cap off the drink bottle and throw it in. A 1992 Chevy. Blue, beat up too. Try to hit under the passenger seat. The damn bottle was cold. It was in an ice chest. I said what kind of crazy ass person was he to keep bugs in an ice chest. He said some dumb ass thing like anything for a laugh." Tony's swollen eyelids fluttered, opened. He stared at the wall. "He'd drive me there, he said. The Chevy was in the DHR parking lot. We drove through and he said that one. The windows were down, he said. No breaking in. How the hell could I get the bottle under the seat throwing it through a window, I asked. Okay open the door he said, it's not damn rocket science. He'd drop me off down the street, he said, I could walk back to the lot, he'd meet me where he dropped me, take me back to the church and call my probation officer. Tell her I did a fine job raking the church yard."

"Yeah?" said R.J. "Who you talkin' about?"

"That guy at the church . . . Lincoln, that was his name. Like the president."

"You talkin' about *the* Reverend Lincoln?" asked R.J. "A minister?"

Tony blinked. Silence.

"Wasps get your hearing too?" asked R.J.

"Don't believe me," Tony said. "I don't give a shit."

"Yeah, right," said R.J. "So how much'd he pay you? Get you started in your murder-for-hire work?"

"Hey. I ain't murdered no one," yelled Tony. He jerked forward, swelled up his shoulders, his chest. "He said it was a prank. A joke, that's all."

"Yeah?" said R.J. taking a step forward, countering Tony's movement. "Tell that to Dana Whitesmythe."

Addie knew her breathing had quickened. She could hear it, fast and shallow. She stepped forward. "Tony, how long have you known Reverend Lincoln?"

His eyes still expressionless. But they were shifting around now, moving from object to object. "Met him that day. The day I got stung. The bastards got all worked up in the bottle while I was walking to the lot. Came at me when I took off the cap. The doctor said I almost died. Had to get four shots."

"How'd you meet him?" asked Addie. "Reverend Lincoln?"

"Ms. Myloh. My P.O. She told me to work for him. Part of my program. Call her, she'll tell you."

"And so you got there and he asked you to play the prank on his friend?" asked Addie.

"Yeah," said Tony. "I get there and he starts asking me crazy ass questions about if I was saved and what I'd done to get into trouble and if I went to church."

R.J. shook his head. "This is bullshit," he said. "Save it for the jury."

"Yeah?" said Tony swinging his legs off the bed. Addie let her hand fall toward her holster. R.J. moved toward him swiftly. "Back off, asshole," Tony said. "I'm gettin' something out of my drawer."

R.J. took another step but stopped when Addie's finger lightly grazed his arm. "You don't call me asshole," said R.J. "I'll tell you right now that won't fly."

Tony leaned across the space between the bed and his dresser and opened the top drawer. He winced with the sideways movement. It was a cheap dresser, thrift store type. Banged up. Handle missing off the lower drawer. Four or five different colors of chipped paint. Addie rested her hand on the butt of her gun. Alert. Ready.

"I've got proof," Tony said. He pulled a digital recorder out from underneath a pair of underwear. Addie saw that the underwear was pulled away from the elastic waistband at least a third of the way around.

She reached out with her left hand toward the recorder. It was silver, about the size of a small remote control, but thinner. A nicer model than her own. "What's this?" she asked.

"Proof," said Tony. "Like I said. I ain't stupid. You record your business, I record mine. Only my people don't know they're goin' on record."

"Let's see," said Addie.

Tony pulled his hand back and sheltered the recorder with his other palm. He pressed an arrowed button, then the button at the top. Crinkling static. Addie looked at R.J. Her partner was still poised to pounce. "So get the bottle in the car. Under the seat on the passenger side is best. We'll drive by once to make sure you get the right car. Don't want to prank the wrong person." Chuckle. "And remember, take the cap off before you throw it in. And when we get back I'll call your P.O. and tell her you worked like hell raking." Silence. Crinkly static. "I don't know, man. I never liked them things. They hurt like hell when they sting." It was Tony's voice, no doubt. A man's laugh. "You a weenie, or what? Anyway, they're cold. You can let 'em walk all over you when they're cold like this and they won't sting anything." Another pause. "What kind of crazy ass person keeps these SOB's in an ice chest?" So Tony was telling the truth. Another laugh. "My buddy'll laugh like hell," the voice said. "Just make sure nobody sees you and if they do, act like it's your car." Static. "Then what?" Tony's voice again. Pause. "I'll, ah, I'll meet you down the street and bring you back here. And that's it. Like I said. I'll call your P.O. and let her know you put in a full afternoon of work."

Addie looked at Tony. He returned her stare with smug satisfaction. For what he had the DA would deal. They both knew it. Static. A man's cough. "I'll, ah, I'll even sweeten the pot with a C note." Breathing. Tony's voice. "Two fifty. I'm takin' a chance, ya' know. Those damn things sting." Longer pause. Static. "Anyway it's a crazy ass prank if you ask me." Silence. "Two fifty if it's smooth," said the man. Pause. "And it never happened." Pause. "My congregation would never understand the joke." Pause. "So what I'm saying is that the prank never happened. If I get word anywhere, anytime that you've talked, I'll take you down for felony theft and it'll be bye-bye Tony." Static. Tony's voice. "What the hell you talkin' about?" Muffled movement. "Those brass crosses in the chapel can disappear mighty fast if you get what I'm saying. Disappeared about the same time you were here working. I'm telling you, just take care of the joke and keep your mouth shut."

Tony put his index finger on the side of the recorder and pushed the button. He smirked at R.J. before he turned toward Addie.

Reverend Jerry Lincoln. It was unthinkable. Unbelievable. Luke would be in shock. She tried to process it, think it through, figure motive. She'd been around long enough to know there were skeletons in the most unlikely closets. It was no prank, no joke, she was certain of that. Larry Ryan'd said Ms. Whitesmythe was terrified of stinging insects. Jerry Lincoln must have known that. But why? What was the connection? "So you record all your conversations?" she asked Tony.

Tony's swollen eyes narrowed until they were practically closed. "I recorded this one," he said. Addie smiled. They both knew any others on the recorder would incriminate him.

She pulled an evidence bag out of her purse. "I need it," she said. He held back. "What's it get me?"

"Get you?" asked R.J. "It means you're one lucky SOB. Some smart lawyer'll convince the grand jury you really did think it was a prank. You won't go down for accessory to murder."

"A smart SOB," countered Tony. "Luck don't record business deals."

Addie reached back into her purse and pulled out her bag of Animal Crackers. "For starters, it'll get you a snack," she said tossing the bag toward him. It was still about half full.

Tony let it fall beside his knee cap. He laughed. "I ain't no baby," he said.

"I'm hooked on them myself," she said, making strong eye contact, being careful not to blink. She held out the evidence bag and Tony let the recorder fall in. "I'll do what I can," she said. "We'll be in touch."

"You're not near as damn smart as you think you are," R.J. said to Tony. "If you *are* smart you'll stay off the streets. We're watchin' you, my man, twenty-four, seven." Addie looked at her colleague. He was staring a hole right through Tony. R.J. played a great bad cop. Much better than she.

She stepped out of the room into the hall. Mrs. Arrington was sweeping the kitchen with what looked like a new broom. A dust tuft and a green leaf and a confetti sized piece of paper whirled slightly when the broom stopped mid-sweep. The plates were resting vertically on a drain board. "He in trouble?" she asked tentatively.

"Probably, Rebeka," said Addie. "But not as much as before we talked to him. I'll let you know as soon as we get it all sorted out."

Mrs. Arrington went back to her sweeping. "I do my best by him," she said, again more to herself than to anyone else. "But youngsters today, they don't think they got to go by the rules. No sir. They just stay on the streets and smoke grass and wear their pants down around their butt cracks. And get them damn tattoos. Bye, Miss Addie," she said without looking up. "Bye young man."

* * *

Addie leaned against her car trunk and stared at everything and nothing down the street.

"So Reverend Lincoln needed to get rid of Ms. Whitesmythe or at least was harassing her," said R.J. He sucked in air, a slow monotone whistle. "Unreal. Absolutely unbelievable."

"I bet she cleaned his church," said Addie. "That's the most logical connection." She opened her car door. "It's time to bring Reverend Lincoln in for questioning," she said. "And let's get a DNA sample from him. Ask the lab to check it for paternity of Ms. Whitesmythe's fetus."

R.J. nodded. "My thoughts exactly," he said. "I'm on my way to pick him up. I'll radio it in."

"Thanks." She slid into the driver's seat and pulled her phone from her purse. Luke had called four times. Unusual. She pressed direct dial.

"Addie!"

"Everything okay? I had my phone off. We just finished with Tony. It was a shocker interview."

"It's been shocking here, too," Luke said.

"Go ahead," she said.

"No, you first."

"R.J.'s on his way to pick up Reverend Lincoln. We're bringing him in for questioning in the death of Ms. Whitesmythe. The evidence against him is pretty compelling."

Silence. Addie knew Luke was trying to process it. Jerry Lincoln ministered to the kids at Metamorphosis, he helped place them in foster homes, his congregation donated a lot.

"Fascinating," Luke finally replied. "Actually, the police have already picked him up, Addie. They arrested him here. Andrew nabbed him. Got him to admit to Dr. Beaty's murder. Seems like Reverend Lincoln's a very busy man."

"You're kidding!" said Addie. It was just a saying. She knew he wasn't.

"Yeah, he admitted to being Andrew's birth father. Can you believe that? It was all about Dr. Beaty revealing his identity. The risk of losing his reputation, all he'd worked for. That was his justification. Andrew unwittingly laid a trap and Jerry stepped right in."

"No way." Addie's brain grid locked. Facts, fragments of evidence, interviews, motives. "It's so hard to believe," she said.

"I know," said Luke. "I'm trying to wrap my brain around it, too. Never any same-old, same-old for us, is there?"

"You're right about that." He heard her turn on her squawk box. Static. Curt, mumbled interchanges. Code talk. "Well," she said. "I guess I'm headed toward the station. See how it all shakes out. I may be late."

Luke chuckled. A naughty little chuckle. "I'll wait up."

"Hmmm. I'll hold you to that."

He laughed again. "You'll hold me to what?" He imagined her lips curling into a subtle smile.

"Behave, Dr. Luke Bramson," she said. "See ya' tonight."

The phone went dead. Luke pushed his chair away from the desk and leaned back until the seat tilted like he was taking off in a jet. He liked tilting backward, reaching the balancing point, rightly or wrongly sensing that if he leaned any further the chair would topple over. Adrenaline rush. Not quite the same as bungee jumping or white water rafting, but a buzz in any case. He punched Shelby's number into the phone and waited. It rang four times and he prepared to leave a message.

"Hello?"

"Shelby. Hi."

"Mommy, look, Mommy," he heard Molly say in the background.

"That's looks nice, Molly. Now sit down and color the doggie. Let Mommy talk on the phone. It's Dr. Luke."

"Can I talk to Dr. Luke too, Mommy?"

"Maybe in a minute, honey. Color the doggie. Here's a brown crayon."

"I want purple."

"Okay, here's the purple. Let Mommy talk now." There was a pause. "Sorry," she said.

He smiled. "No, I'm sorry to interrupt your at home time. But I knew you'd want to hear the news. Jerry Lincoln's been taken in for questioning for the deaths of both Dr. Beaty and Ms. Dana Whitesmythe. He physically attacked Andrew today while Lydia and I were observing. From what he said, he's Andrew's father."

"No way!" exclaimed Shelby. She paused. "Oh my gosh! It gives me the creeps thinking about the way he looked at me the other day."

"Yep," said Luke. "Your instincts were right-on, Shel. Looks like it was all about not wanting Dr. Beaty to expose him."

"Mommy!"

"Just a minute, honey. But, how does Ms. Whitesmythe fit into it all?"

"Don't know for sure yet."

"That's so pretty! Are you going to color his ear? Well, how's Andrew handling the shock?"

"So far, so good," said Luke. "But I doubt it's sunk in. Mr. Chalot's here with him now so I may not really get a chance to talk to him 'til tomorrow. I'll stick around a while though and see if I'm needed."

"Want me to come help?"

"No. You stay home with that smart little girl of yours and color. Just wanted you to hear the latest."

"Is it okay for her to say hi?"

"I'd be hurt if she didn't."

"Molly, Dr. Luke wants to talk to you."

There were muffled sounds of phone transfer. "Hi, Dr. Luke."

"Hi, Molly."

"Mommy and I are having broccoli trees and potato mountains for dinner."

He laughed. "Sounds delicious." Shelby told him once how she made vegetable landscapes on their plates. "Eat a broccoli tree for me, okay?"

"Okay, bye."

"Bye, Molly." He smiled as he hung up. One day before long he hoped he and Addie would have three little broccoli tree eaters of their own. Or at least one. He couldn't wait.

*   *   *

The Bramsons' lights were blazing, beacons guiding her, welcoming her, in an otherwise dark sea of houses. She'd dropped back by the office. Big mistake. When she looked at her watch after filing her reports it was almost one in the morning. She didn't feel tired even so. The adrenaline was still pumping and the coffee R.J. made in the precinct kitchen hadn't hurt either. She turned her key in the lock. Miss Agatha Kitty greeted her with a soft meow and an endearing gurgly noise. She reached down and scooped up the cat and held it against her chest, letting their noses touch.

"Hi Agatha," she whispered. Agatha's purr vibrated through her chest like a woofer speaker. There was nothing quite like the purring of a cat. "We nabbed a big one today, Miss Agatha. He's claiming he's innocent but we know better, don't we, girl?" She moved into the den, draped

Agatha across her shoulder and shuffled through the mail on the coffee table. Power bill, lower than normal. Cruise the Caribbean flier. One day they'd do it. A reminder for Agatha's yearly shots. No sound from Luke. The night light was on. A bedroom lamp threw soft light into the hall.

"Let's go to bed," she whispered to Agatha. Agatha purred louder. "I missed you, too," said Addie.

He'd left the bedside lamp on for her. The book he was reading was perched like a tent across his nose. She put Agatha on the foot of the bed, carefully removed the book, turned off the lamp and slipped out of her clothes. She snuggled against him, skin on skin. He rolled toward her and laid an arm across her stomach. Dark. Comfortable and quiet. The only sound, rhythmic purring coming from somewhere down near her toes.

59

He was handcuffed to his father's hairy wrist. The cuff was on his right arm and it cut into his skin and pressed hard against his bones. Jeremiah Lincoln, the Reverend with the pulsing blue vein, kept jerking on his arm trying to throw him into a fire. It was a huge blaze and its heat licked his face like the University's homecoming bonfire did every year when he was a kid. Andrew didn't even believe in a fiery inferno or Satan. But there was Lucifer, looming forward in the jail cell, black hollow eyes and bony, hungry fingers grasping into the space that separated them. His dad was wearing a black minister's robe and the hem was already smoldering. Andrew wiped the sweat from his face and braced his body against his father's weight. The handcuff jerked again and the metal sliced further through his skin. Scalding hot metal. Flames licking the soles of his shoes. "Stop!" he yelled. Blood spurted from his wrist. He was going to bleed to death, live out his days in hell. Or did a person live out his days in hell? He felt dizzy. Weak. "Take him," said the Reverend Jeremiah Lincoln. "Take my son."

"Andrew? . . . Andrew?" The voice came out of nowhere. A man's voice. Gentle but intrinsically strong.

Andrew swallowed, looked around, blinked and leaned back slowly in Dr. Luke's recliner. He cleared his throat. His heart was doing double time and his stomach was queasy again. He'd stuck his finger down his throat five or six times last night to get relief. None had come. Rico heard him throwing up and noted it on the night records and the nurse gave him something to calm his stomach this morning. Nerves, she'd said. Nerves or maybe the stomach flu. There was a lot of it going around campus. "I'm sorry," he said. "I didn't sleep much last night."

"I'm sure not," said Dr. Luke. "We were talking and then you got real quiet and just nodded off. I had paperwork to do anyway so I let you nap. But then you yelled 'stop'." There was concern in Dr. Luke's eyes.

"I keep having this nightmare."

"Can you talk about it?"

He shrugged. "Sounds lame," he said. "It's no big deal."

404

Silence. That odd comfortable silence. He knew Dr. Luke was waiting, inviting him to talk.

"I just don't get it," Andrew said finally.

"What?"

"How can a minister be a murderer? Somebody he'd loved, that makes it even weirder. I just don't get it."

"Yeah," said Dr. Luke. "It's hard to understand how he ever got to that place. With your mom and with Ms. Whitesmythe, too."

"She was gonna tell me who he was. That's why he killed her."

Dr. Luke nodded slowly. "Yes. She'd made that decision. She told us that." He paused and Andrew heard him sigh. It was a long, sad sigh like he was trying to sponge up all the bad energy in the room.

"She kept his identity from you all those years as a way of protecting you, your feelings I mean, at least that's the way she explained it to us. But she'd had enough."

Tears, unexpected. Andrew jumped up and walked to the window. The leaves and grass and sky all fuzzed together. He wiped his cheek with his sleeve. In the nightmare, he'd heard her calling him. She was coming to get him. She'd kick his dad's ass.

"Healthy men cry when life sucks," said Dr. Luke.

Andrew didn't answer. He blinked hard several times. Tears spilled onto his face. The outside blurred even more. "This blows your gray line to hell," he said. "There was no good in my dad, no matter how many people he supposedly helped. It was all bullshit."

"I can understand why you feel that way," said Dr. Luke.

"I just don't get how a minister can turn evil." It was safe to turn around again. He returned to the recliner.

"Maybe one day it'll all be clearer. Or maybe you'll never know."

Andrew's knee jiggled. "Before all this happened Joey showed me where he'd cut on himself," he said. "Freaked me. But last night I wanted to cut myself. Get his evil blood out of me."

"Are you still thinking like that?"

Andrew thought carefully. He didn't want to lie. "My wrist was spurting blood in my nightmare. But I won't," he said. "It's fucking crazy to think like that. I know it wouldn't help. Anyway, I told myself I'm the same person I was before. Nothing's different about me. My blood's the same as it's always been. It's just his crazy ass I want to get rid of."

Dr. Luke leaned forward with a smile. "That's good healthy thinking," he said. "Are you able to promise me you'll seek the help of responsible adults, tell them what's happening with you before you hurt yourself in any way if you get to feeling like that again?"

Andrew stared into the man's eyes. Strong and as stupid as it sounded, safe. "Yeah," he said. "I can promise that. But it's all cool. I'm not gonna do anything mental." He curled his lips in and pressed down with his teeth. He wished he could talk about sometimes making himself sick. It was embarrassing the way he did that. He had a feeling Dr. Luke would know what to do. That he wouldn't think he was psycho. He coughed. No way would he talk about it. "I don't get why his name was Red," he said. "Even in the old picture he didn't have red hair. Only thing red about him were his ears and his nose when he was coming after me in the classroom."

"That's another question you might never get answered," Dr. Luke said. "There'll probably be lots of others." He cleared his throat. "Maybe you could write down questions as they come to you and one day send them to him wherever he's serving time. Or maybe you'll decide against asking him anything. Either way, you don't have to decide that today."

Andrew stuck his index finger and thumb halfway down into his pocket until they found a sheet of notebook paper. It was folded into a tiny rectangle. He pulled it out. Rico'd let him get up in the middle of the night to write down some of his thoughts. "I did write this last night," he said handing it to Dr. Luke. He felt kind of shy and embarrassed and sort of like a nerd while he watched Dr. Luke unfold it carefully, study it and smile.

"Interesting work," said Dr. Luke, still reading it. It was a graduated gray line. White on one side and black on the other. *Wanted to tell me who my dad was. Learning real important to her. Had a good job and gave us stuff we needed. Let Joey keep Winx. Put up with my bullshit. Let Thomas be like my dad. Was fun sometimes when we were little. Had too many boyfriends. Boyfriends were more important than us. Was a slut. Sex with Dr. Greene hurt Joey bad. Her perfume stank. Her damn fingernails. Toenails too. Gave D-Tail away. Cheered loud with her dumb ass clock. Sang too loud with the radio and CD's. Her voice sucked.* The phrases were placed on the continuum, both positive and negative.

Dr. Luke smiled quizzically. "Cheered with her clock?"

"Yeah," said Andrew. "She had this dumb ass clock. Alabama football, of course. It has this plastic football player that comes to life and runs with a plastic football and it does the yellowhammer cheer. I think it plays the fight song sometimes, too. I smashed the first one but she got another one from a boyfriend and I was gonna smash it before I ran but I didn't." He stopped and swallowed. "And now," he continued more softly. He didn't understand it at all. "And now, I want to get it and put it in my room." He laughed awkwardly. "It's messed up crazy."

Dr. Luke smiled ever so slightly. "No, that doesn't sound messed up crazy at all. It sounds normal and healthy to me." Silence. The silence seemed to go on forever.

"She'll be cremated," Andrew said to fill up the silence. "I'm gonna burn this and scatter it with her. And I'm getting D-Tail back. Thomas said I can keep him in my room in the winter and we'll build an outside cage for summer." It was a great idea. Cleaning up the aquarium all the time was a bummer.

"Excellent," said Dr. Luke. "And this stuff you wrote's important. How'd you feel about doing it?"

Andrew shrugged. He didn't want to say it but Dr. Luke's approval felt good. It didn't make sense. "Good, I guess."

"Yeah," said Dr. Luke. "You know, I don't think we've grown up until we've learned to see our parents as plain old humans with strengths and needs and complicated lives of their own. Some folks might disagree with me but it's worth thinking about anyway."

Andrew wondered about Dr. Luke's parents. Maybe his mother acted crazy around men, too. "Were your parents complicated?" he asked.

Dr. Luke smiled again. He didn't want to say that there was a professional boundary between them and that he rarely shared information about his personal life with his clients. He thought about Addie's onion analogy. "One thing I've learned as I've grown older, Andrew," he said, "is that all people are sort of like onions. We've all got layers and layers of experiences and feelings and beliefs and accurate memories and inaccurate memories and accurate perceptions and misperceptions and all of it gets pretty complicated. I think that's life."

Andrew's pulse got faster. He didn't understand why it did that. There was something he wanted to say but he wasn't sure. It was too important to get messed up. He coughed. "I have something I need to tell you but I'm not sure . . . Everything I say here's confidential, right?"

Dr. Luke's body leaned forward attentively. "Yes," he said. "Unless it's something about abuse or has to do with immediate serious harm or threat of harm to you or someone else."

Andrew paused. He could feel Dr. Luke's eyes watching him. Waiting. "You can't let on that I told you," he said. "You have to act like you figured it out for yourself."

Dr. Luke's eyebrows moved downward toward his nose. One hair on his left eyebrow was too long and stuck out in the wrong direction. He wondered if Dr. Luke knew that. "I'll try," said Dr. Luke. "But I can't promise 'til I know what you're talking about."

He hesitated. He looked back at Dr. Luke's eyebrow hair. "Um," he said. "Are you sure nobody can hear us?"

Dr. Luke reached across his desk past the magnet men and turned on a radio. "The room is soundproofed," he said. "But let's add some satellite radio in any case."

A high pitched voice cut into the room. Andrew bolted upright in the recliner. "Oh my God," he said. "That's the song!" The cotton of his pajamas, night air sweltering and laden with familiar scents of unnamed blossoms, the car's upholstery sticky against his skin, the singing of crickets and cicadas and frogs, Joey beside him sometimes asleep, his mother always singing along to the same song on the car's CD. High pitched and loud and in some weird language and always off key.

"The Habanera from Carmen?" asked Dr. Luke. "What song?"

He wanted to stuff his fingers in his ears. "The song she always sang when she woke us up at night to go for rides."

Dr. Luke cocked his head the same way Winx did sometimes when he heard a noise and was trying to figure it out. "Interesting," he said. "But maybe it makes sense in a way. It goes sort of like this." He squinted into space. "L'amour est enfant de Bohème, il n'a jamais, jamais connu de loi. It loosely means love is a gypsy's child, it has never known the law."

Andrew shook his head. "Never mind. It's okay. Can you turn it off?"

Dr. Luke moved his hand back to the radio. "Sure." Silence.

He took a deep breath. His pulse was beating fast again. He thought about Dr. Luke's words. Love, a gypsy's child that didn't know the law. It didn't feel that way with Bethy.

"Do you need to take a few minutes?"

Andrew leaned back in the recliner. "No." He refocused his attention, pulse still fast, stomach tightening. He wished again he could tell Dr. Luke about his stomach, the way it felt sick, the way stuff globbed up against his Adam's apple. "I need to tell you . . . I'm no snitch but some kid, ah, some kid has a key to Ms. Moffiti's observation room and she changes her clothes in the classroom after school before she goes jogging and the boys, um, some of the boys I mean, they pay this kid to watch her . . ."

Luke tried to block the visual. Her hot body. Kids in the observation room watching her. It was Benjamin, he was sure of it. But what the hell would possess Ms. Moffiti to change clothes in her classroom? She knew all professional staff had keys. It was poor judgment and that disturbed him. He'd tell Lydia about it in the morning. "So you and somebody else saw Ms. Moffiti changing?" he asked.

It was too embarrassing. Andrew ignored the question.

"How much did you pay this kid to do that?"

"No way," he said. "I'm no pervert. I sure as hell don't want to see any teacher in her underwear. He took me there."

"So you didn't pay him?"

"No. No, sir." The sir was dweeby. He wished he hadn't said it.

"How much does he charge the others?"

Andrew shrugged. "He said a dollar."

It had to be Benji. But where was he stashing the cash?

"And at night some of them are sneaking out the bathroom window and meeting some Luna girls."

Dr. Luke's expression grew even more serious. Sex. Where the hell was staff? Sleeping? There'd have to be an investigation. God, he hoped no one was pregnant. They'd have to figure out who all was involved. Take them for VD screens. "How do you know this?"

"They invited me. I don't know who all went. I didn't go."

"And this happened more than once?"

Andrew shook his head, raised one shoulder. "Maybe. They talk like they do it a lot."

"Can you remember who was on staff the night they asked you?"

Andrew curled his lips inward, gnawed at them. "No. Not really. I didn't know the dudes."

Dr. Luke cleared his throat. "The things you're telling me are very serious, Andrew. I'll try to figure out a way to discover them on my own. But if I can't, we'll have to take action anyway."

Andrew knew that. Somehow he liked the crazy bastard Benjamin. He didn't want to screw up the guy's life. He paused, teetering. He liked Dr. Luke, too. He didn't want Benjamin to know he was a snitch. He sure as hell didn't want Tony to ever figure it out. "There's, um, one more thing . . ." His voice sounded gravelly and small and distant. He hardly recognized it as his own. "There's, ah, a tree, a sycamore, you know the ones with white trunks, with lots of big holes in it about half way up. Seven. Seven holes. Down by the lake. Um, near a boat landing. And it's full of stuff a guy named Tony's stashing there. He's got help from the inside."

"The inside?"

"Yeah," Andrew said. "From here."

"Stuff?"

Andrew looked down at his tennis shoes. They were still stained gray green from lake mud. "Yeah, you know, DVDs, jewelry, phones, video games, that kinda stuff. But Tony doesn't play. He'd waste me if he knew . . ."

Dr. Luke didn't say anything. His eyeballs looked big and frozen in place. The eyebrow hair was still sticking out the wrong way. The silence, the look on Dr. Luke's face, made Andrew nervous. Tony scared him shitless. He wished he'd kept his mouth shut.

"Benjamin," Dr. Luke finally said. "We knew he was up to something. We just hadn't figured it out."

"I didn't say it was him."

"And you? Is that where you got the new jewelry, the stuff that wasn't there when you checked in?"

Andrew moved his hands toward his jeans pockets protectively. "It's my Mom's stuff," he said. "I swear it's all hers. I had to get it back."

"How'd Tony get it in the first place?"

A wad of phlegm gooey around his Adam's apple. He guessed it was phlegm. He looked back at his shoes. "I stole it," he mumbled. "Sold it to him."

So Addie was right. Tony and the green haired kid in the park. Andrew after all. Complicated lives. He felt old. Bone tired. Weary. At times like this he always wished he'd studied botany. Or engineering.

Or French. He wasn't even good at French. Barely passed French II. But he thought Benji was doing better. The whole treatment team did. He thought they were running an efficient treatment center. And all the while there were layers of deviant behaviors, layers upon layers, the secret lives of the residents. "I wonder," he said, and at first Andrew thought he was talking only to himself. "Could you find the tree, Andrew? The one with all the stuff?"

He didn't want to. "I can maybe tell you how we got there. I don't know. I'll think about it." Tony. Tony had eyes everywhere.

Dr. Luke reached out and touched Andrew's shoulder. "Thanks," he said. "Thanks, Andrew."

The hand sat on his shoulder for only a second or two. But somehow it calmed him. Weird how it reassured him.

"I know it took lots of guts to tell me all this," said Dr. Luke. "Guts and maturity." First thing tomorrow he, Dr. Lydia, and Shelby would put their heads together, establish a plan of action.

* * *

There was a guitar and harp duet playing on the Bose when he entered the house. It was late and he was tired and Andrew's reports about what was going on underneath their noses at Metamorphosis trumped even the bizarre news about the Reverend Jeremiah Lincoln.

"Addie!" No answer. The house smelled like garlic and olive oil. Spaghetti maybe. He was hungry. "Addie?" He moved toward the music. She was wearing his red corduroy shirt like a dress. It was an old shirt, ridges worn flat on the fabric until it was rag soft, and sleeves cut and rolled up to her elbows. She was facing away from him, her right hand up in the air, fingers softly spread and poised off to the right. Her left foot was out in front and her gaze was fixed on her left hand which was positioned in the air directly above her foot. Her left fingers were cupped softly. Crane Spreads its Wings. She moved her right foot toward her left gracefully, slowly letting her right hand fall, circle around. He joined her as she began Wave Hands in the Clouds. They moved with slow, fluid motion, deliberate and controlled. He closed his eyes and concentrated on his breathing. In through his nose. Out through his mouth. His tongue almost touching the roof of his mouth near his front teeth. Rooster Stance. Grasp the Bird's Tail. Snake Creeps Down. Even with his eyes closed he could intuit her motion beside him. See the Moon. He felt the craziness and tension of his day begin to melt. Collecting chi, positive energy of the universe, pulling it back toward himself, and Addie, toward herself. Warding off negative energies, pushing them off. God knows they were surrounded by enough negative energies each day to last a lifetime. But positive energies, too. Unsung heroes everywhere, quietly going about their lives.

He watched Addie sit cross-legged on a floor cushion when they finished the T'ai Chi form. He sat across from her and closed his eyes. The beach. Bright sun toasting his skin. The sound of breakers. Water swirling around his ankles. His toes sinking in the surf. The sound of gulls. Sandpipers on little stilt legs. Pelicans flying. Blue sky. Blue water. Cool wet sand. Powdery warm sand. A sandcastle. Broken shells. The smell of salt in the air. The taste of salt on his lips. Addie in her green bathing suit. Addie in his old corduroy shirt sitting across from him. He smiled and opened his eyes. "Have I ever told you how much my worn out shirt turns me on?"

She opened her eyes slightly. "Ummm," she said. "I don't remember. Maybe you should tell me again."

He stood, stooped and kissed the top of her head as he passed by. "I'll finish dinner. Spaghetti?"

"No, pizza," she said uncrossing her legs and following him into the kitchen. She'd made pesto two days earlier, basil, garlic, olive oil and pine nuts zapped in a blender and smeared like a sauce on store bought dough. He added left over chicken, mushrooms, onions, banana peppers and feta. She grabbed a handful of animals from her Volkswagon cookie jar and popped a hippopotamus and a rhino in her mouth at the same time. "Want one?" she asked.

"No thanks," said Luke. "Pizza'll be done in a few minutes."

"Well," she said as he put it in the oven. "Jerry's not talking but we've got enough to charge him with both murders. The scene you and Lydia witnessed with Andrew and the recording Tony made are both pretty damning, but we'll probably need more to convince a jury. I just don't see him confessing unless his lawyer convinces him to plead down. He knows most juries will give a Baptist minister the benefit of the doubt. He's as much as said that already."

"Probably true," said Luke. "But there might be other women he's victimized out there. I didn't mention it earlier but Shelby told me she got really bad vibes from him on a chance meeting during lunch hour recently."

"Really?"

"Yeah. It was all pretty sketchy but she felt like he was coming on to her."

"Well, R.J.'s working to secure his phone records, and his home and work computers have already been seized. Larry Ryan tells me Ms. Whitesmythe cleaned that Baptist church for years. Bet you anything she was carrying Jerry Lincoln's child and that's why she died. We'll see what the DNA says. I have this crazy idea all of Larry's children might be Jerry Lincoln's. Supposedly they all have the same birth dad."

Luke stared at her, two glasses of ice poised in the air. He moved toward the faucet. "If that turns out to be true," he said, "Andrew'll have a lot of half-siblings."

"Yeah," said Shelby. "All of Larry's kids and Mrs. Lincoln's children as well."

"And of course his half-brother, Joey."

Addie put her hands over her head and stretched to each side. "A minister preying on vulnerable women," she said. "No pun intended. It's nothing to joke about." She placed the sole of her right foot against her left inner thigh, hands together at her heart then rising into the air toward the ceiling. Yoga tree stance. Great for the abdominals. Great for balance. She still had cookies in her right fist. She popped three in her mouth without even looking at them then raised her hand again.

Her legs were bare under his corduroy shirt. He knew she was wearing bikini underwear and no bra. It was an enticing thought even though he was too tired and too hungry to do anything about it. She cocked her head to the right. "Do you see Shelby as vulnerable?" she asked.

"Perhaps," he said. "In her own way she might be." He thought about Molly's father, Steve. A mental splinter Shelby carried around daily. He opened the oven, heat meeting his face, and slid the pizza off the rack onto a wooden cutting board with the help of a spatula. "Ummm," he said. "I'm starving." He rolled the pizza cutter across its diameter.

"I'm just glad it wasn't Larry Ryan," Addie said. "And that it wasn't Andrew."

"Or his brother, Joey. I think even Andrew suspected his brother." He turned the cutting board and guided the metal cutter across the pizza again, then diagonally twice more. He pulled two plates out of the cabinet, two forks out of the drawer and the salad out of the refrigerator. "Incidentally, I learned something of interest about your friend Tony today but if you can, hold off on it for a day or two. 'Till I figure out how to discover the loot myself."

She put her foot back on the floor and lowered both arms. "Loot?"

"Apparently. Andrew told me in confidence that a guy named Tony, and I'm one hundred percent sure it's your Tony, has been stashing stuff in a sycamore tree on Metamorphosis property. Apparently he has inside help from one or more of our kids. I'll meet with Lydia and Shelby about how to best handle it tomorrow morning. Even then it might take a while to locate it."

Addie put her hands on her hips. "Ha!" she said. "R.J.'s looked everywhere for his stash. Wonder how he's getting it there."

"I should know soon," said Luke. "I'm guessing he sends middle schoolers, you know, the wanna-be's, over with it at night. But somebody'd have to drive them. Doubt it's him."

"Drive them to the tree?"

"Oh, it's apparently near the boat landing." He handed her a plate. He wanted to tell her how disappointed he was feeling, how lousy his day became, but he didn't want to spoil the moment. There was time later. "Ma-dame," he said, bending deeply at the waist, right arm bent at the elbow. "Dinner is served and work is officially over. Let's both take a break until morning."

She stood on her tiptoes and kissed his chin. "Sounds like a plan."

His right hand cupped her left buttock and she laughed softly. They'd have something better than animal cookies for dessert, he felt certain.

60

The five of them were sitting comfortably around Dr. Lydia Hutchinson's office. She'd prepared peppermint tea and some sort of lemon cake for the occasion.

"I feel so sorry for her," said Shelby. "I mean, being a minister's wife has to already be hard, everyone watching you all the time to make sure you're a Godly woman, and then to have a husband who turns out to be a sham."

"Of course the Reverend's still denying it all," said Addie, "but the evidence is certainly building against him. Both his phone and computer records indicate he and Dr. Beaty were in contact on the day of her murder and he was planning to meet her that night. And I don't think it's any coincidence the bomb threats to DHR coincide exactly with the days Ms. Whitesmythe was scheduled to see you, Zenah. Both his personal phone and his office phone were used to call DHR around the times those threats came in."

Miss Elenrude's eyebrows rose toward her blond spiked hair. Her eyebrows were still dark brown.

"Why would he do that?" Shelby asked.

"I'm sure to intimidate Dana," said Miss Elenrude. "Keep her away from me and DHR. She told me her lover was blaming her for getting pregnant again. He probably feared she'd spill the beans, give away his identity, the same as Dr. Beaty, really. But to be honest she'd have never told a soul. She was oddly protective of him. Secretive. And she didn't even seem particularly alarmed by his threats. Laughed them off to tell you the truth."

"I can sort of understand that," said Addie. "Would you expect a minister to murder you?"

"You've got a point," said Miss Elenrude.

"Assume nothing," said Dr. Lydia Hutchinson. Luke smiled.

"I bet he called DHR from here when he excused himself from the records meeting," Luke said. "If I remember correctly, DHR did get a call about then and I never did hear his phone ring. Not even vibrate."

"I can't stop thinking about Mrs. Lincoln and her children," said Shelby. "Their whole world's ripped to shreds."

"It is sad," said Addie. "And three other women have already come forward to report relationships with him. All three were church members who sought his help when they felt like their lives were falling apart. I'm sure there'll be more. Larry Ryan says he feels certain all his children will turn out to be fathered by him. DNA testing should confirm it. Dana would've been an easy target."

Shelby shuddered intentionally and ran her hands up and down her arms. "It gives me the willies just thinking about it all," she said.

"R.J.'s looking into cold cases, too," said Addie. "We feel pretty sure we have a serial philanderer and murderer on our hands."

"He's out on bond, right?" asked Miss Elenrude.

"Yep," said Addie. "Mrs. Lincoln bailed him out as soon as she could."

"I can't stand to see a woman get shafted like that," said Shelby kicking her crossed leg up into the air, swinging it erratically. "And even worse, his children."

Addie noted the eye contact between Luke and Shelby. There was something not being said. An intimacy. A shared confidence. Or something. "We'll know more when we get the DNA results back," she said. "And the lab is doing some elaborate testing on the yellow jacket bottle. Even though there were no apparent fingerprints on it, we hope the label picked up some microscopic fibers from the church. We have our fingers crossed."

"Seems like you've got him nailed with the evidence you've already got," Miss Elenrude said.

Addie sighed. "I think we'll get the grand jury indictment. But we'll need more before his trial. You know yourself, Zenah, you never can tell about a jury. But we *have* had a little bit of a break. Someone called Crimestoppers and reported seeing the Reverend walking up Dearing, not far from the Beaty's home, sometime around 6:30 on the night she was killed. That's a start, anyway."

Dr. Lydia glanced at her watch and shifted her weight to stand. She put her left hand on the desk to ease herself up. "I hate to abandon our party," she said, "but I've got a meeting with the ministerial association. They wanted to meet to reassure us their other members are solid citizens, safe to be around our children." She looked at Luke and smiled.

"I told them a meeting wasn't necessary, of course. We all know there're bad eggs in every profession and Reverend Lincoln's problems don't impact on the good works of the others. Not even on the good works of his congregation, for that matter. But there are some legitimate questions to answer. Like how to discuss Reverend Lincoln's situation with our residents and their legal guardians."

Luke and Shelby exchanged glances.

"We'll have to come up with a strategy for that pretty quick," Luke said. "It's already in the press."

"I'll pick the ministers' brains and get back to you right after the meeting. Good work cracking the cases, Addie. You all feel free to use my office as long as you wish."

Addie smiled. For all practical purposes the cases had cracked themselves.

"If you don't mind me changing the subject," said Miss Elenrude, "what are we doing with my two boys? Is Andrew still leaving today with Mr. Chalot?"

Luke glanced at his watch and nodded. "Yep. Thomas and Holly Chalot will get here right after work today, around five thirty or six. Joey's back and Andrew's jumping out of his skin to get out of here. I'm offering him outpatient counseling though, and I hope he'll think about it. He's got some things going on in his life that worry me. But in a lot of ways he's got a pretty steady head on his shoulders. For a teenager especially."

Miss Elenrude frowned. "Wish that were contagious," she said. "What on Earth are we going to do with my wild child Benjamin?"

Luke glanced at his watch. Ten minutes. "Well, we'd better start by dipping him in a vat of something to get rid of the poison ivy he's found somewhere," he said. "He's itching from head to toe and his face looks like a raw steak. Beyond that, I think the jury's still out, Zenah. A lot depends on what all we uncover during the next couple of days."

Addie stood. She had an appointment with Dr. Harry Greene and if there were time she hoped to catch up with Bob Tulane before the day's end. She'd swing by Victor Abernathy's classroom tomorrow. Reverend Lincoln's arrest made the front page of the *Tuscaloosa News* and aired on the local television station, WVUA, so she was certain his arrest was already no surprise to them. But she liked to personally meet with people she'd previously identified as suspects. It seemed the decent thing to do. "I need to go," she said.

"Shelby," said Luke, "do you have time to fill Zenah in on what we know about our residents' night-time carousing so far?" He stood beside his wife. "As you know I actually have an impromptu meeting of sorts with Benji in just a few minutes."

"Happy to," said Shelby.

"Thanks. Addie, I'll walk you out."

"What we've done, Zenah, is meet individually with all our Lunas, asking general questions about how things are going at the Center, and steering some of the questions toward any knowledge of rule breaking. Benjamin's been implicated, I'm afraid, in . . ." He closed the door on the rest of Shelby's explanation. It was bound to happen in virtually any residential facility no matter how careful and vigilant staff was. But it was always distressing. They'd contacted all the legal guardians to let them know their children might be at risk for recent sexual contact. Medical exams for all implicated children were already scheduled. An internal investigation of staff supervision and policies was underway and DHR was already investigating the individual reports.

"Let's eat out tonight," Luke suggested. "Maybe get a river front table? Watch the tugs and barges?"

The back of her hand brushed his. Smooth, cool skin.

She smiled to herself. Maybe one or two barges with a tug. Maybe one fishing boat. Maybe a kayak or canoe or two before dark, and if they were extraordinarily lucky, a beaver. The river around Tuscaloosa was pretty quiet at night. "Seven thirty?" she asked.

"Perfect." He lowered his voice even though he saw no one else in the hall. "So when are R.J. and the others picking up the stash in the tree?"

"Sometime this afternoon," Addie replied. "They may have already gotten it. Hired some tree professional to climb up to get it." She laughed. "I considered calling Bob Tulane but under the circumstances . . . Anyway, R.J.'ll be confronting Tony down at headquarters once it's all squared away today. Tony won't be a happy camper, I'm sure of that. But given his bigger problems I expect he'll cooperate."

"I bet you're right," said Luke. He wondered how deeply Benjamin would be implicated. He didn't want him implicated at all but there it was. Benji'd fooled them all. And all the time it looked like he was behaving so much better. There was still the question of whether other Luna residents were involved too. He did a quick sweep of the hallway with his eyes before he leaned over and kissed the top of her head. "Isn't it ironic," he said rather robustly, "that you and I, being the nature lovers we are, would decide this very morning to take a relaxing pre-work walk through the woods here at Metamorphosis and that we'd stumble upon, of all things, contraband? Imagine, a corner of a DVD sticking right out of a hole way up in a sycamore tree! What a coincidence, especially you being a detective and me being the therapist for a lot of the boys who might be involved."

Addie bumped against him playfully. "Today's our lucky day I reckon." She unzipped her purse and grabbed the little plastic bag. "I'm starving," she said, "and it's four more hours until dinner."

"Me too. Despite Lydia's delicious lemon cake." He held out his hand and she poured. His nose wrinkled. His eyebrows moved closer together. "Ha!" he said popping a handful of little oat O's into his mouth. "Fooled me!"

"I need to make a run to the store to get some more little critters," she said. She put a handful of cereal in her mouth and crunched. She studied his forehead. "Did you know you have an errant eyebrow hair?"

"A what?" he asked. "Never mind. Tell me later. I'd better go. I can't afford to be late to this meeting. See you at dinner. And don't let me forget. When I grow up I want to be a hot air balloon pilot or a river barge operator or a game warden in Alaska. Not a residential treatment center director."

She laughed. He laughed. And they both knew they still had some serious considering ahead.

*   *   *

Luke used his key to open the metal door. He slid quickly into the darkness. There was a chair near the wall and he picked it up and moved it even further back. He sat down and closed his eyes. The silence was calming. It was squirrelly little Ernie who clued Luke in during the Luna investigations. Honest Ernie, as earnest to help as his name implied despite his own set of complicated behaviors. Ernie'd spilled the beans on it all. He was always awake when the kids sneaked out, he said. Benjamin was always one of them. The main one, he said. No, staff wasn't sleeping, they were in the laundry room folding clothes. Well, the last time anyway. One time it was when a staff went to the bathroom. Once staff was cleaning up in the kitchen. Sometimes it was just one or two boys. That was when they were going to the tree. No, he didn't know exactly where it was, but it had stolen stuff in it. That's how Benjamin got his phones. If you paid him a dollar he'd let you make a call when staff wasn't looking. And he charged a dollar to see Ms. Moffiti change clothes, too. No, he'd never gone to see it himself but he'd thought about it. In fact, Benjamin was planning an excursion today. Yes, excursion was a big word, but that's what Benjamin called it. One or two boys had already paid. Joseph and Traverias, he thought.

Luke heard voices outside the door. He stood and pressed the wall with his back and scooted toward the door. He knew he'd only have a few seconds and he'd probably only catch Benjamin.

"Shhh!" rasped Benjamin. "Shhh! She'll hear us. Hurry your asses up! When I open the door, get in fast."

Luke heard the key turn in the lock. There was a burst of light and Benjamin led the way in. Luke stepped forward to block him, separating him from the other three boys. Unreal. Squirrelly Ernie was one of them. Ernie and Joseph and Traverias. "Well, hello, boys," Dr. Luke said, flipping the light switch. The other three pushed against the door and ran like their pants were on fire. "You boys have two minutes to get yourselves back down to the cottage," he called after them.

"Joseph! Traverias! Ernie! The three of you, get back to the cottage now. Where'd Benjamin go?"

It was Rico. Dr. Luke imagined him running up the hill in hot pursuit.

"Dr. Luke got Benjamin," he heard Earnest Ernie yell.

Benjamin tried to push his way past but Dr. Luke stood solid. He pulled his chair up against the door, blocking the exit, and sat with deliberate calm. "So, Benji," he said. "Let's start today's meeting by your handing over the key."

61

The sun was setting and the van smelled like cheese curls and Thomas' aftershave and sprigs of fresh rosemary hanging from the rear view mirror, tied by their stems with a narrow blue cord. Holly Chalot grew the herb in pots on her back porch and cut it fresh for the van every week. Andrew breathed deeply through his nose. It smelled oddly good. Bethy smelled good too, like lemon soap, and her hand was warm. When she moved her interlocking fingers against his, he was acutely aware of their movements. He was sitting in the middle of the bench seat, knees jutting against the back pockets of the seats in front. Something pointed and hard was digging into one knee and he reached forward with his free hand and dug down into the mesh and pulled out a plastic dump truck. He and Bethy looked at each other in the dusky light and smiled as he rolled it across his thigh and parked it. He'd asked Thomas to bring Bethy with them when they came to Metamorphosis to pick him up but he wasn't sure her mother would allow it. He wasn't even sure Thomas would agree.

Joey let his window down and Andrew breathed deeply again, letting the April evening fill his lungs. Spring was their mother's second favorite time of year. Of course, football season was her favorite. The night was almost perfect, Thomas and Holly sitting in the front seat, the van's radio playing jazz that the announcer said was by some guy named Thelonius Monk. Andrew thought it'd be a bitch to go through life with a name like Thelonius but the music was cheerful and catchy, and even Joey's left hand was tapping in rhythm against the van's arm rest. His other arm was curled snugly around the dog's sausage body. Winx wriggled and put his head out the window, back arched like a rainbow, long skinny tongue flapping sideways out of his mouth. His tags jingled. Little globs of dog slobber flew against Joey's shirt and Bethy watched it and laughed.

"Sterling does the same thing to me," she said. "But since she's so big I get a lot wetter."

Joey's smile seemed forced, distracted.

Thomas and Holly brought Bethy and Joey and Winx but hired a sitter for their younger children. This was Andrew's night, Thomas explained to Dr. Luke. A new life chapter, and he and Holly wanted to make the memories of moving into their home as positive as possible for him. Thomas had always been intuitive and wise. Somehow he knew the night would be perfect if everything were just like it was, Andrew in the van with the people he loved and with Holly whom he liked, moving into the Chalot's home to finish growing up, if only their mother still lived in their house on Dearing Place. Andrew didn't think he'd even care if she were with some guy as long as it wasn't the Reverend Jeremiah Lincoln or Dr. Harry Greene. He wouldn't even really care about Dr. Greene except it would upset Joey. It was unsettling and annoying, the haunting emptiness he felt and her being gone and knowing his birth father's identity and knowing what the man had done.

"So, was it as bad as you expected, Andy?" Joey ran his hand along Winx's back as he asked.

"What?"

Thomas turned on the headlights. He brightened the dashboard's lights, too. The street lights were already on.

"Staying there. At Metamorphosis."

Andrew felt Bethy run her thumb up and down against his. His pulse quickened. He moved his finger reciprocally. It was hard to concentrate. "Not really," he said. "I mean, I wouldn't want to live there but it was kind of funny, for real. Especially this crazy guy named Benjamin." Benjamin actually choked up when staff let him out of room restriction long enough to say goodbye. Freaked him out. No guy had ever cried about him leaving anywhere before. Andrew told him to stop, and that he was a dumb ass for grabbing onto that hairy poison ivy vine and that he looked gross with his face swelled up like a catcher's mitt, raised scratch marks crisscrossing angrily. And Benjamin said Andrew was a sonofabitch for getting out of Metamorphosis so quick before they had time to have fun together. And Andrew gave him his best University of Alabama tee-shirt and his phone number and told him they'd keep in touch. The tee-shirt was from his mother but there were at least five more in his dresser at home and he figured if she were still alive she'd want Benjamin to have it anyway.

"Everybody seemed real nice," said Holly. "Especially that fellow, Dr. Luke, did you call him? And the lady who runs the place Dr. Lydia, and the woman you called Ms. Shelby."

"Dr. Luke's dope," agreed Andrew. It was a new word for him even though it'd been around school for years and around the country even longer.

"I don't like that," said Thomas. "Try another adjective, Andrew."

"Yes, sir."

Bethy squeezed his hand. Out of the corner of his eye he saw her grinning. In truth, he didn't want his relationship with Dr. Luke to end when it was time to leave. It was like the man understood stuff and made it easier for him to figure stuff out and didn't judge him for hating his mother and loving his mother and being glad she was gone and being afraid she was gone and being lonely without her. When Dr. Luke asked him in front of Thomas if he might want to keep coming to therapy once a week for an hour just to talk and think about things that might be bothering him, Andrew shrugged and said he'd think about it. But before he left he told Thomas and Dr. Luke yes. So it was agreed and Andrew felt glad he'd still get to see the guy who was there when he found out about his biological father, and about the secret of his grandfather and his mother, and who'd be going to court along with Dr. Lydia to testify about what they heard and saw. It was kind of funny they were spying on him from the same place he and Benjamin saw their teacher in her underwear. And her name, Mo-titti. Andrew laughed, halfway giggled actually, then quickly coughed to cover the odd sound. Benjamin was crazy as hell.

"What's funny?" Joey asked.

"Nothing," he said but he kept smiling anyway. "I just feel good." No one said anything and the quietness made him feel sort of like an asshole because he was laughing and saying he felt good even though his mother's funeral was tomorrow and they were going to take her ashes in the cardboard box she'd come in from Atlanta and walk her around the statues of the football coaches who'd won national championships at the Walk of Champions before they scattered her in the Black Warrior. Andrew wanted to scatter her on the football field but Thomas said University officials almost certainly wouldn't allow that, but wouldn't it be a good idea if the University had a columbarium in one of the ends of the stadium where fans like his mom could forever cheer the Tide on to victory. Joey'd scowled just at the mention of their mother and Andrew wondered if his brother knew the story about their grandfather and why their mother was so messed up around men. There were lots of girls at

Metamorphosis like that. But not that girl Esmeralda whose dad kept poisonous snakes in their house and who'd wanted him to sneak out that night with the others. Benjamin'd said she'd kick a guy's ass for trying stuff with her. She was all right.

"Joey," said Holly, turning in her bucket seat so she could see at least a corner of him. "Do you know yet when you're going back to Auburn?"

"You're going back?" asked Andrew. The hole that was already in the pit of his stomach expanded sharply. "I thought you'd wait til next term, I mean."

Joey rubbed Winx's neck and looked out the window. They were on University Boulevard heading toward the mall to grab a bite to eat before taking Bethy home. Her mother had given her a nine o'clock curfew.

"I'll probably go back tomorrow after the funeral," said his brother. "I might not stay for the family get-together afterward so I can get back before too late. I've got meetings with my professors and the head of the department day after tomorrow to see if I can salvage the semester. I'm hoping they'll understand. Let me make up the work."

There were tight lines on Joey's face. Andrew hoped his brother would go see Asa even before he saw his professors. He wondered if Joey'd care if it turned out he wasn't Andrew's only brother. Dr. Luke and Thomas said it might end up Andrew had so many half-brothers and half-sisters that it'd take him a while to really get to know them all. It all depended on the DNA. There might be Mr. Ryan's adopted children and the minister's children with his wife and other kids nobody even knew about yet. "He was just like my mom," Andrew said when they told him. "A horndog." Neither of them'd answered. Andrew guessed they didn't know what to say. But all those kids. Plus the Chalot's children who'd be like sisters too. He didn't know how he felt about it. Joey was the only brother he'd ever needed.

"Plan to stay for a brief while after the funeral, Son, you know, come back to the house and let folks extend their sympathy to you and Andrew," said Thomas.

Joey sighed and shifted his right leg, accidentally kicking Andrew in the side of his shin, jolting the dump truck onto the car's floor and upsetting Winx who tried to jump out of Joey's lap. Joey grabbed the dog by his back and held him in place. He rolled his window back up. "I don't want to stay long," he said. "I need to be rested before the meetings, Dad. If I can finish out the semester maybe I can still do some sort of vet assistantship this summer."

"And we want that for you, Son," said Thomas. "But not at the expense of a proper goodbye for your mother."

The tight lines were back, jaw chiseled in place. It scared Andrew.

"Is there somewhere else in T-town you can work this summer?" he asked, and he could tell his voice was soft and gentle, sort of like Dr. Luke's.

Joey turned sideways and stared like he was thinking about something before raising his hand to the ceiling, switching on the light. He stretched his leg sideways and lifted his butt, still holding Winx tightly against him, and dug into his jeans pocket. He handed a piece of folded paper to Andrew. Andrew thought about the jewelry in his pockets that was gone. Loaned to the police, put in evidence bags, to be used in court against his father. His birth father. Thomas was his real father. A tall skinny cop thanked him for the jewelry and a lady cop swabbed the inside of his mouth with a cotton stick. DNA they'd explained and he said okay. There was still the remote chance, and he was investing all hope in it, that Reverend Lincoln's DNA and his own would not match.

Andrew wanted to unfold Joey's paper without letting go of Bethy's hand, but she wiggled her fingers away before he could shake the paper open. Black silhouettes of dogs and cats and horses and birds in the paper's margins. Dr. Harry Greene's name and address on the top. It was addressed to Mr. Joey Chalot at Thomas' and Holly's address. Andrew chuckled softly. It was weird to call Joey a mister. *Dear Mr. Chalot, The summer position previously extended to you was based on your personal and academic accomplishments and your career potential. Nothing has changed in that regard. Please contact me prior to May 15*th *if you are still interested in working in my clinic. I hope you will also accept my deepest sympathy regarding the loss of your mother. Sincerely, Harry Z. Greene, DVM.* The signature was full of loops and swirling lines. The ink was a rich black. It looked like one of the names in his history book. Like from the Declaration of Independence or something. "Great!" he said. "Are you gonna do it?"

Joey was staring out the window like he was avoiding eye contact. "I don't know," he mumbled. "Lesa wants me to."

"Good advice," he said. He felt calmer. Reassured. Joey'd be home for the summer after all. He folded the letter along the creases and pushed it toward his brother's hand. He reached up and turned out the van light. Dark again. He reached carefully toward Bethy's knee and put his hand over hers. Her palm turned upward and she slid her fingers back between his.

They were coming up on the old Moon Winx. There were broken dead vines twisted in and out of the rusty fence, the chain link bent in places and pulled away from its metal posts in others. The vines resembled dark threads in the evening light. Threads of his life. Of Joey's. Of their mother's. Late night drives when the air hung heavy with honeysuckle. Afternoon drives, their windshield yellow with pine pollen. Wistfulness in their mother's voice and that song about the gypsy's child. About never knowing the law.

"This is where we got Winx," he said to Bethy. "Right here. Late one night in the parking lot. Mom'd wake us up sometimes, take us for drives. She almost always turned around in this parking lot. And one night, there was Winx. Remember that, Joey?"

Joey's hand stroked his dog's back. "Yeah. I do." His voice sounded a little more relaxed. A little happier. "She almost didn't let us get him."

He laughed. "You didn't give her a choice, bro'. You jumped out of the car before she could even think."

Joey laughed too. "Yeah," he said. "I did, didn't I?"

"And then he whined and whined every night in that cardboard box until we'd sneak him up into your bed, remember?"

"Yeah. Yeah, I do." He was running his hand the length of Winx's back. "And that damn moon always winking."

"No cursing," said Thomas.

"Sorry," said Joey.

Andrew studied the moon's smiling face as they passed. He loved the sign. "Mom used to say it was winking at all the secrets it kept, remember?"

Joey didn't answer and Andrew wondered. Was he missing her, too, those sticky nights when the crickets chirped and the peeper frogs made funny noises from the grass at the road's edge, and when the smiling crescent moon through their sleepy child-eyes was magical, and did wink of secrets held close and sacred? It was true. They believed it. Their mother told them so. It might have saddened him to think longer but

426

just at that moment, while Joey was still looking out the side window and Winx had settled down in the darkness to sleep on his brother's lap and Thomas and Holly were quiet and holding hands in the front of the van, Bethy lifted their interlocked hands to her mouth and kissed the back of his knuckles with only a breath of her lips. He turned to look at her face but he was too late. She was already nestling her head softly down against his shoulder. He could smell the citrus in her hair and feel the tickle of it on his chin and he closed his eyes. The van was quiet. Peaceful. He felt like he could fall asleep. Instead he thought of the guitar song he was writing about how wonderful she was and about her amazing gray eyes. And he knew even before it was finished that he'd probably never get up the nerve to let her hear it.

"Hope everybody's worked up an appetite," Thomas said. Andrew opened his eyes to catch Thomas glancing at them in the rear view mirror. The little sprigs of rosemary were darkened forms and they danced along beneath Thomas' mirrored eyes that Andrew knew were taking in the view of Bethy snuggled up tight against him. His dad's eyes sparkled with reflected light from the car driving behind them, shadows and lighter shadows weaving in and out across all their faces, a gentle strobe playing on Thomas' upturned lips. As the van turned into the mall parking lot Andrew allowed his body to flow with the movement even closer to Bethy. And when he looked back toward the mirror he couldn't be sure but he thought he was sure that he saw Thomas wink.

Author's Note

On the 27th of April, 2011, sixty-two confirmed tornadoes descended upon Alabama. The scope of damage to the city of Tuscaloosa made international news and brought volunteers and material aid from around the nation and the world. Faith based groups provided the backbone for these efforts.

Much of Tuscaloosa's Alberta City area was reduced to rubble, the EF-4 twister gouging a continuous path a mile and a half to two miles wide. The Moon Winx Lodge was equally hard hit. When electricity was restored to that part of the City, however, there it was. A yellow crescent moon with red smiling lips and a blue blinking eye winked hope through very dark nights to all who passed.

In January of 2012, the Crimson Tide football team won their fourteenth national championship against the LSU Tigers in New Orleans. Coach Nick Saban and his University of Alabama football players, forefront in volunteerism throughout the recovery process, publicly dedicated their championship win to all who were impacted on that fateful April day.

CPSIA information can be obtained at www.ICGtesting.com
Printed in the USA
LVOW081723210613

339728LV00003B/402/P